THE BOVINE CONNECTION

A NOVEL

KIMBERLY THOMAS

Kimberly Thomas

This book is a work of fiction. While, as in all fiction, the literary perceptions and insights are based on experiences, all names, characters, places, and incidents either are products of the author's imagination or are used fictitiously.

Copyright © 2014 by Kimberly Thomas
All rights reserved.
ISBN-13: 978-1503102170
ISBN-10: 1503102173

Cover design by Patrick Blaine

The Bovine Connection

For my mother...

Kimberly Thomas

> *"Can you bind the beautiful Pleiades?*
> *Can you loose the cords of Orion?"*
> *Job 38:31*

Prologue

Somewhere within her mind were the dark spaces holding the suppressed memories her subconscious was not yet ready to reveal. Angelica lay uncomfortably in a dimly lit room with her eyes tightly shut on a tan leather sofa. This was her fourth visit, and Angelica was certain this time he would be able to help her. The memories were painful and deeply hidden. Her mind was a locked vault and she had forgotten the combination. If only she could remember and purge the darkness out of her. She would be healed. She would feel whole. But the shadow memories had faded over time and would break the surface only on occasion, and then retreat in a mist of confusion.

"You must concentrate on clearing your mind," he said softly. "Go deeper inside where your true self resides. You are not relaxed, Angelica! You must relax!" He spoke low and firmly sending a chill up her spine.

"Dr. White, I am trying," she nearly yelled. "I do everything you ask of me! I'm tired today! I just don't think I can." Angelica released her breath in frustration. Suddenly she heard the chair squeak as he lifted from it.

"What is he doing?" she wondered. Angelica cupped her hands together across her belly as if they were a shield for protection.

"I would like to help you relax," Dr. White whispered.

Angelica wasn't sure she was comfortable with him so close. She took a deep breath. The air felt thick. She had a restricted space. Angelica opened her eyes as he approached her. *"How did he get from the chair to the sofa so quickly?"* she wondered. He was now in her guarded space, and she felt uneasy.

"Close your eyes," he said softly as he placed his hand over her palm. She was reluctant, blinking a few times before finally relenting and doing as he said.

"Now you are letting go... relax and listen to only my voice. I am going to count from ten to one, and when I get to one you will be so relaxed, so relaxed that you will only want to do as I say."

Angelica squirmed on the sofa. "Do as he says? What is he going to ask me to do? *Why did I even come here?"* she wondered. His words raced through her mind. Her hands started to tremble. She clutched them tighter.

He glared at her face as her eyes were squeezed tightly shut. She was so delicate and fragile, so innocent, he thought.

"Ten... nine."

The smell of the old musky building was distracting her, she couldn't relax. It smelled faintly of mildew, and soot from the old fireplace. But no fire burned that day. The heavy drapery kept the light out. Large Persian rugs covered the worn wooden floor.

The Bovine Connection

"Six... five."

Angelica wanted to trust him, but knew very little about him, in fact, nothing at all. Although he spoke a great deal, the conversations never revealed personal details about him. He had a way of using words, almost playing with them. He was older and distinguished, father-like. When she found him on the internet and called, he said he was confident he could help her. She had to trust him, and Angelica never trusted anyone.

"One... you are now in a deep relaxed state. So deeply relaxed that you will do exactly as I say. Take a deep breath and then release it. Good, and another, good... you are so very relaxed now," he said softly. So relaxed that you are focused on your breath... In and out. Good. Now, I want you to focus on releasing the tension in your neck, in your chest, in your arms, your abdomen, down to your thighs, down to you calves, and to your feet. Feel now as all tension has now been released, and you are so very relaxed.

Now, I would like you to focus on a time in your life when you were truly happy. I want you to pull that image in and hold it. Can you do that?"

"Yes, I have it," she smiled and whispered softly.

"Good... what do you see?"

"I see my grandmother's house. I am playing in the tall grass, looking up at the house."

"Go on..."

"I see my grandmother walking along the old porch. She is smiling and holding fresh cut flowers. She is humming. I think it is a hymn," Angelica smiled.

"How do you feel?"

"I feel happy," she spoke softly in a little girl's voice."

"Good... Now I want you to take a deep breath... and hold it... Now release. Take another deep breath... and hold it... and now release... Feeling so very relaxed... I want you to focus on a time when you were not so happy, in fact when you felt the most afraid. Remember, you are safe in this room with me. Do you understand that this is just a memory?"

"Okay, I understand," Angelica said as she released an anxious breath.

"It is okay to re-enter this memory. Are you ready?"

"Yes," she said softly.

"Good... go there now."

Angelica was still for a moment and then suddenly she squeezed her closed eyes tight, causing her forehead to wrinkle. Her breathing sped up and became heavy, almost panting. Angelica started to shake her head slowly from side to side against the sofa pillow.

"Where are you?"

"I am at my grandmother's house," she spoke nervously, and as a little girl.

"What do you see?"

"No, I can't."

"You must," he said sternly. "We must go further."

Angelica shook her head rapidly. "It's dark. I am outside of the house."

"Are you alone?"

"Yes, I think so. I don't see anyone else."

"Go on."

The Bovine Connection

"I'm walking in the pasture, but they are gone. I do not see them tonight."

"Who is gone?"

"The cattle! No! No! I'm afraid," she cried out.

"What is it? What do you see?"

"I see them!" Angelica's voice trembled. "I see them," she repeated in a whisper.

"Who do you see?" Dr. White asked curiously.

"They are standing around it. Oh," she gasped, "Now they are looking at me. Their eyes are so large and dark. I am afraid." Angelica's voice shook. Suddenly she screamed, frightening Dr. White, causing him to go rigid.

"No! Please don't take me! No! Please!" she screamed.

"Angelica..." he spoke quickly. "I am going to count to five, and when I am finished you will be out of trance and safe here in this room with me. One, two, three, four, five! Angelica, open your eyes!"

Angelica's jaw was trembling as the tears streamed down her cheeks. She lay on the sofa staring blankly at the dingy, water-stained ceiling. The doctor stood up from his chair beside the sofa and moved toward her. He placed his hand back over her palm causing her to flinch and pull it away.

His face was soft and his tone gentle. "You are making such progress," he said. "It will take some time but I believe I can help you. You were able to move beyond the house this time. You did very well."

Angelica turned and looked into his sincere, dark blue eyes. She believed him. "Thank you," she said, as her wet eyes probed his face. "I'm sorry I could not do what you asked."

Dr. White wanted to help her. He gazed at her frightened pale face and light blue eyes. He knew he needed to be careful not to push her too hard, too quickly. Dr. White also knew he could become lost in her. She was as fascinating as she was beautiful. The doctor quickly turned his head and shook off the provocative thought.

Angelica sat up and adjusted her blouse, straightened her skirt, and then attempted to smooth the wrinkles out. "When should I come back to see you?"

Dr. White walked over to his desk. "In two weeks unless you would like to start coming once a week."

Angelica glanced down and then back up to meet his eyes. "No, two weeks." The emotional toll of the sessions had started to drain her. She felt as if she were unravelling.

"Okay then, I will see you the Thursday after next. Is the same time--eight o'clock in the morning--still good for you?" he asked.

Angelica stood up and walked over to get her purse on the wooden coat rack. "Yes, that works fine."

"Perfect." He smiled as he peered up from his schedule book. He stood dumbstruck at the sight of her soft, innocent posture. Then he straightened his glasses and cleared his throat.

"Yes, Thursday... we will continue to make progress. I will walk you out."

Angelica was petite and appeared more fragile after the session. She moved in almost a floating fashion across the room. He noticed a light reflection as it bounced off a diamond pendant around her neck.

Dr. White opened the door and stepped aside so Angelica could pass through. He pulled the door closed and locked it before starting down the creaky staircase of the old building. Angelica followed quietly beside him, looking down at her feet with each step.

"I do feel better," she said as she glanced back up and met his eyes. He nodded and quickly turned his attention to the door. As he pushed the old, heavy wooden door open, the rays of sunlight lit the lobby.

"Well hello!" a woman's voice appeared suddenly.

"Hello Sarah, dear," Dr. White replied.

Sarah looked oddly at Angelica. Her eyes shifted and moved down to Angelica's expensive nude heels and gradually to her slightly unbuttoned blouse. Sarah's mouth cracked open, hesitating before she spoke. Her cheeks pink, from the heat, against her olive skin.

"This is my wife, Sarah?" Dr. White stated in a warm tone. Sarah looked at Angelica and smiled. Angelica sensed Sarah's smile was not sincere.

Sarah tilted her head to the side. "Aren't you just lovely, like a delicate flower," she said in a patronizing tone and smiled.

Dr. White shifted timidly and stepped away from Angelica, closer to Sarah. "We just finished up... Perhaps we should be going or we'll be late." Dr. White took Sarah's hand and tugged gently for her to follow his lead. Sarah remained still; she did not budge as she continued to observe Angelica.

"Yes, I must get to work," Angelica said as she glanced away feeling uncomfortable.

Sarah softly pulled her hand from Arie's grip. Angelica didn't notice. She was looking downward. Her shoulders were slouched; she was distracted, still recalling the traumatic details from the session.

Angelica glanced back up blankly. "Thank you, Dr. White. I will see you again on Thursday. Nice to meet you, Sarah."

Dr. White nodded his head and maintained a straight lip. "Yes, see you Thursday, Ms. Bradley."

Sarah watched as Angelica rushed across the street. "Well, she's quite lovely, wouldn't you say, Arie?" Sarah observed Arie's face.

"She's a troubled young lady, Sarah." Arie knew Sarah had a tendency to be jealous, and after the run-in, he had been hoping to avoid, he knew Sarah would inquire about Angelica the entire day.

Chapter One

Another unusually hot summer day in Washington, D.C. was beginning to take its toll. The thick heat was like a cosmic equalizer. Senators grabbed at their collars and loosened their ties while sweat soaked t-shirts stuck to the bodies of young men who expressed their artistic ability in the form of graffiti.

At the headquarters of the *Liberator Magazine*, it was no different. The heat of the day was symbolic of the truth. The magazine's universal mantra was that the truth would always come out exposing itself to the light of day, if given the opportunity. Much like the constant fusion of the sun, it would painfully enlighten all that were in its presence... whether they liked it or not.

Her head pounded from the lack of sleep from the night before and the intense hypnosis session that morning with her psychiatrist, Dr. Arie White.

She sat at her desk, staring into the distance, unconsciously twirling a strand of her hair with one hand while her index finger of the other glided softly up and down a clear glass mug of coffee, once hot then turned cold.

Her uniform for the day consisted of a short cream tweed skirt, black silk blouse with the first two buttons undone, exposing perfect alabaster skin against her light blonde shoulder length hair that framed her light blue almond shaped eyes and high cheekbones. She wore red lip color and nude peep-toe heels. It was a devilish combination underpinned with the looks of an angel.

Office attire had obviously changed since the days of the turbulent 1950's, in the aftermath of World War II, an era where woman would be considered scandalous for wearing anything other than scarce nylon stockings and knee-length skirts. Not only had journalism's dress code changed, so had its culture, and women now dominated the field.

The décor at the *Liberator's Magazine* headquarters was modern and minimalist: dark brown glazed concrete floors and white painted brick walls that stood strong and confident between the panes of glass.

Amongst the mixtures of dark and light furniture, art throughout the building was comprised of vibrant abstracts with hues of blue, grey, and brown. The new building proved *"The Liberator Magazine"* was ready for the leap into the new millennium. It was a true sign of the times.

Unlike the journalists, writers, proofreaders, editors, and other employees of the *Liberator*, as the CEO and Founder, Angelica was one of the few with a large corner office with walls constructed of mostly windows. She sat in a white leather chair at a shiny, sleek white desk with square chrome legs, preoccupied with an unshakable eerie feeling from the dream she had the night before.

"Angelica?" a voice erupted and then echoed through the air causing her to jerk. "Everything all right?"

Angelica dropped her finger from the mug and with a distant stare, looked up to see her colleague Andrew standing in the open doorway. He had knocked on the door and stuck his head inside.

"I'm sorry, what did you say?" Angelica appeared puzzled.

"You look a million miles away... I asked if everything was all right. I called your name several times. Did you not hear me?" Andrew leaned his shoulder against the door frame.

"Oh...," Angelica said as she snapped out of her deep thought and life emerged back into her eyes. "Yes, I'm fine."

Andrew turned to look behind him as voices approached in the hall. They both stayed silent until the voices were gone.

"You seem distracted... Fun girls night?" he whispered and smiled sheepishly.

Angelica rolled her eyes and smirked playfully. "Seriously?" she asked. He immediately discerned that Angelica wasn't her usual buoyant self.

"Andrew, I have tons of work to do," she said, trying not to look him directly in the eyes. "Can we chat later?" Angelica tried to focus on her laptop.

After a moment, Angelica raised her eyebrows and smiled as she realized he was still in the doorway waiting for her to turn back around, his expression neutral.

Andrew was polished from his groomed thick, copper tinted straight brown hair to the Berluti shoes. He was tall and lean. His eyes intense, light brown. He had a way of narrowing them and looking seductively at Angelica just to watch her reaction. A technique he had mastered. The playful eye contact and sneaky glances at each other around the office kept their secret romance exciting, she thought.

Only Angelica's closest friend, Gail, knew she was sleeping with Andrew. Since Angelica was his boss, it was a well-guarded secret. Angelica often regretted becoming involved with him. She knew it could end disastrous. But he was impeccable in bed – always leaving her exhausted and longing for more. She suspected the other woman in her office would agree, although she could never inquire.

Angelica fought back feelings for Andrew and kept herself emotionally distant. She was afraid of her own vulnerability, and she knew very well that fear caused her to sabotage most of her past relationships.

Andrew noticed the vacant look in her eyes as she glanced in his direction. "Angelica, are you sure you're…"

Angelica peered at Andrew and interrupted him. "I saw my doctor this morning. Now I'm behind on work," she murmured petulantly.

Andrew looked down at the floor and then slowly and seductively back up, fixing her with an intense stare, his lips puckered into a pout. "Okay, but I missed you last night. I was disappointed you canceled. You know how much I enjoy our time together. The other night will be ingrained in my memory forever," he said, his eyes deep and soulful.

Angelica's face softened, she smiled and tilted her head, unable to resist his overtures. "I enjoyed it, too," she whispered. "Now I have to get some work done," Angelica announced as she grinned, knowing it would be hard to redirect her thoughts.

Andrew shook his head and smiled in a way that made her body feel warm. "Okay, I'll talk to you later sexy," he whispered before turning and walking away. Angelica smiled inwardly as she turned her attention back on work and continued typing. And suddenly her cell phone rang. "Hello, Angelica Bradley," she answered business-like.

"Angelica, hi! How are you?"

"Hello Gail... I'm okay, a little tired today."

"Are you coming into the office?"

"I'm here now," Angelica said as she sat up in her chair, fidgeted with her wavy blonde hair, tucking it behind her ears.

"Oh, I didn't see you in there." Gail sounded surprised.

Angelica turned her chair and looked out the large window. "I just got into the office a short while ago. Saw my doctor this morning." Angelica moved her head in a circular motion to loosen the stiffness as she firmly rubbed the back of her neck.

"Are you still having those dreams?" Gail asked sincerely.

"Yes, and they are getting worse," Angelica said in a deep breath.

"I'm sorry... I hate to hear that. Well, wanted to run something by you. Carl has come across an interesting story. Just recently there was a cattle mutilation over in Montana. Apparently, he's been following the incidents over there."

Angelica interrupted Gail, "I'm sorry... did you just say 'cattle mutilation'?"

"Yes, I know... but hear me out... Carl is calling it 'The Bovine Mutilations: Mystery on the Cattle Ranch'. We should keep the title, it's good... That is, if you are okay with us covering the story. It happened next to an Air Force base. I'm sure you've heard the outlandish theories around these mutilations. I think it'll be a fascinating story for the magazine."

After a long moment of silence, Gail sounded frustrated. "Are you still there?"

Angelica sensed Gail's impatience. "Yes, I just..."

"Oh, thought I lost you," Gail interrupted.

"Can you email the file to me?" Angelica murmured.

"Yes, I'll send it over now..."

"Okay." Angelica leaned back in her chair and glanced over at the last story she covered while at the *Washington Post* a few years prior, involving the Republican Senator Jay Hollins. Angelica kept the file as a reminder of the price she'd paid covering such a high-profile story. She reached over and removed the newspaper clipping from the paperclip on the front of the file. Senator Hollins was a seedy, yeasty man, and Angelica was out to prove it from the moment she received the call from her anonymous source. After she was able to verify the story with another source, it went to print.

Angelica placed the newspaper clipping on her desk and turned her attention back to her laptop. She then opened the email on the cattle mutilation and read through the documents.

There was a knock at her door. Angelica looked up to see Gail standing there.

"I emailed you the file. Here's more," Gail stepped over and placed a file on Angelica's desk. "What's that?" Gail asked inquisitively as she pointed to the clipping.

"The Hollins story," Angelica said flatly.

"Oh yes, the Senator who had a preference for seventeen-year-old Asian call girls. He was quite kinky," Gail snickered. "According to the photographs you obtained from your source, it appeared he enjoyed black leather attire and spankings more than his usual business casual." Gail laughed. "I'm sorry but they were amusing." Angelica smiled and nodded, however she still looked weary. She swallowed hard, her throat felt dry.

Gail continued... "That seems like a lifetime ago... If I remember correctly, shortly after your article hit the newsstands, Hollins was found guilty of the sex scandal and sentenced to serve time for statutory rape. His wife retreated back to Tennessee, didn't she? Poor thing."

"Yes, and the Republican Party certainly didn't need a Senator like Hollins to taint their 'God and apple pie' image... That story cost me a lot," Angelica frowned.

"Yes, but you gained a lot as well. The *Liberator* may not have ever happened if... well, you know," Gail noticed Angelica bite down on her bottom lip as she continued to stare at the file.

Angelica reflected on the backlash that followed. Angelica didn't earn herself any new friends in D.C., thanks to her relentless pursuit to expose Senator Hollins. She was fired and snubbed in many circles around D.C. No one would hire her. It was a low point in her life that almost destroyed her.

A year after losing her job at the *Washington Post*, Angelica founded the *Liberator Magazine* and brought Gail and Carl, the *Post's* best two editors with her.

Playing in the world of politics, and in the capital of the U.S., was a challenge and she had the battle scars to prove it, she thought. Angelica had worked hard to be taken seriously as a journalist, although it took her longer to earn respect than she had hoped. She was grateful she had made it as a successful and well-respected journalist, and founder of the *Liberator Magazine* at the age of thirty-two, and all done while keeping her skirt on. Of course, jealousy was fierce amongst her colleagues. She had heard the rumors while at the *Post* that she had won it on her back.

Angelica turned and looked at the file Gail had placed on her desk. "Wow, that's thick! Carl's been working hard on this," she appeared surprised as she lifted it and looked up at Gail.

"Sweetie, I've been meaning to talk to you. Lately, you seem distracted and kind of down." Gail sat in the white leather chair in front of Angelica's desk. "You really just aren't yourself." Her voice was soft and concerned.

"Yes," Angelica said as she dropped her shoulders and put the file down. "I'm not sleeping well, and I saw my doctor again this morning. The sessions are just so draining." Angelica shook her head and glanced down. "Those damn dreams…" Angelica looked back up and forced an awkward smile. "I'm fine, really, I am."

Gail nodded and narrowed her eyes, "Yeah… So, did the session go well?" Gail frowned sympathetically.

Angelica turned to her laptop and clicked open the "the bovine mutilation" file folder again. "Yes, it went well," she murmured as she turned her attention to the documents. "So, it's happened just recently over in Montana, huh?" Angelica took a deep breath as she continued to read the document. "Gail… I think I'm going to cover this one."

"You are?" Gail sounded shocked. "Seriously? Why?" Gail stared in disbelief.

Angelica leaned back softly in her chair and glanced back over at the newspaper clipping from the "Hollins" file. She pursed her lips. "Tell Carl I'll take it from here. Judging by the size of this file, I'm sure he'd rather I cover it than a less experienced journalist. Don't ya think?" Angelica said sarcastically, as she swept aside one loose strand of hair and smiled.

Gail's eyes widened, "Yes, of course… I think he'll be quite pleased after the initial shock wears off." Gail looked at Angelica speculatively. "Are you sure you really want to take this on? You already have so much on your plate running the magazine. And Angelica, this really isn't your type of story." Gail said flatly.

Angelica dropped her shoulders and ran her fingers through her hair, pushing it away from her face. "Yes, I'm sure... I want to get back out there. Get out from behind this desk. I'd like to leave tomorrow."

"Tomorrow? Okay." Gail stiffened, her face blank.

"I need to get out of D.C. It'll be good for me." Angelica picked up the file and thumbed through the reports made by ranchers, the local veterinarian, police officers, and UFO investigators.

Angelica began to assimilate her thoughts as Gail reached over and picked up one of the documents.

At the bottom of the pile, Angelica noticed the words "Cattle Mutilation"... also known as "Bovine Excision" scribbled in red ink and in Carl's handwriting across the top. Angelica looked soberly at Gail. "So tell me what you think about the mutilations."

Gail lowered the document she was holding and peered up at Angelica... "Well, I'm not sure what to think. It is a very strange phenomenon. Apparently the killing and mutilation of the cattle are caused by unusual or nefarious means, from what I've read." Gail tapped the file folder with an index finger. "It's the surgical natural by which the animals are mutilated that has people baffled. All the blood is drained and organs are removed. Then you have the fact that the reproductive systems are precisely removed. Quite disturbing. Oh, and the anal area is cored out."

Angelica's eyes were wide. "Cored out?!" Her expression shifted to disgust.

The Bovine Connection

Gail swallowed hard, nodded and continued. "Anyway, the animals appear to have been dumped, and there are never any tracks or markings around the carcass, even when found in mud. Very odd. Carl was saying that the surgical instrument used on the animals appeared to be some sort of laser cauterizing device. It's all in the file."

Angelica lifted up a black and white sheet of paper with a photo on it of a dead cow. "Appears someone is removing the skin and flesh from the cow's skull as well. Ew, look!" Angelica flipped the sheet of paper around.

Gail appeared disgusted. "Yes, and doing it with perfect precision," she said. "That is why people find it hard to believe a predator such as the coyote could be responsible for the kills being reported like in this Montana case."

Angelica put the sheet of paper down. "This is very fascinating. I have a lot of work to do before my flight."

"Okay." Gail stood up... "I'll tell Carl."

Chapter Two

Angelica turned off the light and closed her office door. As she turned, she caught sight of Andrew walking toward her. She was exhausted and had hoped to sneak out of the building unnoticed.

"Do you want to grab dinner tonight at the Bistro?" Andrew whispered.

He then stepped in closer and narrowed his eyes as he observed Angelica, recalling her unusual mood earlier.

"I can't tonight, I have to work," Angelica said softly as she lowered her satchel to the floor and pulled her hair back into a ponytail. "Sorry I was edgy earlier... I've been having bad dreams lately... I didn't get much sleep, and then the therapy session with my doctor this morning. Anyway, I need to pack for my flight to Montana tomorrow."

Andrew frowned, curious and maybe a little miffed... "What's in Montana?"

"A cattle mutilation..." Angelica began, and then fell silent.

"What... You gotta be kidding? Why are you covering it?" he asked, tilting his head and staring directly into her tired eyes.

Angelica looked away from Andrew with a curious, yet reflective expression as she pursed her lips. "Don't know," she mumbled. Angelica looked back at Andrew.

The Bovine Connection

"It'll do me some good to get away. Do you mind if we catch up later?" Angelica smiled sincerely, and then walked away briskly leaving Andrew still standing there confused.

Chapter Three

After an exhausting commute home, Angelica pulled her 528i white BMW up alongside the curb and parked. The old historic streetlights were flickering against the twilight sky, emitting a soft golden glow. She walked up the moss-covered brick steps surrounded by flawlessly hedged boxwood shrubs and unlocked and opened the front door, heavily painted black from a century of redo's.

Her modernly renovated two story colonial townhome in the quiet Waterfront neighborhood of D.C. was close to the Capitol and the Smithsonian.

Angelica walked into the dark den and dropped her satchel at the desk. She gradually made her way through the kitchen, lit up by the streetlight from outside, to the butler pantry to pour a Macallan 18 year old single malt Scotch. She didn't see any reason behind diluting a perfectly good Scotch with water.

The ice cracked as she dropped one cube into the golden liquid to let it breathe. After learning from the talkative man at the liquor store that the whiskey was aged in old sherry barrels, it immediately became her nightly sleep aid.

Angelica walked over and turned on the light in the kitchen. The walls were painted Sage Blue... a soft, modern color she had seen at the Restoration Hardware store. The kitchen was bare, free of clutter, with only a Keurig coffee maker, a set of knives in a wooden block and a large bamboo cutting board.

The white granite with specks of grey and brown countertops was pared stylishly with white cabinets standing out against the dark walnut stained hardwood floor. It was simplistic and elegant, the way Angelica liked things.

Continuing her nightly routine, Angelica opened the stainless steel refrigerator. With carrot juice, imported cheese, olives, Pinot Grigio and a takeout container being the only options, she opted for the two-day-old take-out container of Greek pasta salad.

After opening and smelling it, she took the risk. Grabbing a fork along with her Scotch, she pushed the refrigerator door shut with her elbow while turning and walking back into the den, kicking her nude heels off behind her.

At her turn-of-the-century St. James style black desk, she turned on the clear glass lamp and took a bite of her cold dinner, dripping oil down her chin. Angelica quickly wiped below her bottom lip with the side of her palm. She then picked up the glass of single malt and took a sip, feeling the liquid run down her throat and warm her chest. Angelica pulled her ponytail loose, letting her hair fall around her face.

She had an unsettling feeling she was being watched. Noting the silence in the house, she glanced around to look into the dark spaces barely illuminated by the glow of the kitchen light. Angelica took a deep breath and turned back around.

Feeling exhausted, she wanted to go on to bed, but she leaned over and rustled through the papers trying to locate her laptop from her satchel. The squeak of her chair resonated through the silence as she rose back up and placed it on her desk. Angelica Google searched the words, "Elberton, Montana."

Several sites appeared of cattle ranches for sale and rustic lodges for weekend getaways. At the top of the screen was a strip of photos: one of a town square right out of the Old West. Other photos were of a whitewater river running along pine woodlands, and scenic scenes of endless flat land against the snow-tipped Rocky Mountains.

After opening a few websites, she realized Elberton was an old mining town with a rich history. She learned that Montana had attracted a heavy tide of emigration in the late 1800's after the discovery of gold and silver.

Angelica relaxed into her chair and sipped her Scotch as her mood lifted, researching the history of Elberton. The thought of getting out of the city she had become enclosed in was starting to sound more and more appealing.

After looking through several lodge websites and-- not to her surprise-- she decided on the most expensive: Elk Lodge right outside of town along the Elk River. The lodge was situated at the portion of the river that turned into a creek, with knee-deep water, clear and swift. Well-known for its fly-fishing, it appeared to Angelica that there wasn't a more perfect place to stay in or around Elberton, to suit her taste.

The Bovine Connection

Looking through the website photos, Angelica began to envision herself there, relaxing in the mornings on her room's balcony and admiring the exquisite pine-covered Rocky Mountains off in the distance.

After booking her room online, she wandered back into the kitchen and poured another Scotch. Her eyes were heavy. Angelica yawned as she turned out the light in the butler pantry and grabbed her glass.

Returning to her desk, she typed in the search engine "cattle mutilation reports in Elberton, Montana."

Feeling a sharp pinch in the arch of her foot, she leaned down to work out a cramp beginning to form and causing her foot to curl up. As she continued to massage at the cramp, she came across an article concerning the military and UFO sightings. Angelica quickly pulled her hand up, lifted her glass, and took another sip as she leaned in curiously.

Monday, April 19, 2013; Matthew Tillman from the Elberton Tribune Reports, Military Connection to Strange Lights in Sky over Animal Mutilation Sites. "Although the government officials at the Newton Air Force Base have declined to comment, many witnesses have come forward with their stories. The same strange lights have been spotted over Newton Air Force Base near Elberton, Montana as seen in areas of animal mutilations on local ranches. According to UFO investigator, Paul Colbeck, the lights also appeared near the Newton Air Force Base on the very night the Keller ranch mutilation occurred. 'I believe the military is involved and working with these other worldly visitors.' Colbeck says."

"Interesting," Angelica thought aloud.

At the beginning of any investigation, Angelica always kept an open mind no matter what information she gathered. This was one of the traits that made her an accomplished investigative journalist. However, this article stretched her discipline. She contemplated whether there could be any validity to the researchers' claims. Could it be possible that UFOs were behind these events? She quickly caught herself and laughed... It is entertaining and would make for a great story. But just not possible... There has to be another explanation, she thought. Barely able to keep her eyes open, she realized the Scotch had started to kick in.

Angelica leaned down and grabbed the file from her satchel. After opening it, she noticed a report from University of Colorado Head of Veterinary Bio-Medical Sciences, Dr. Walter Goolrick. She rested back in her chair and with the Scotch still in her palm she read...

"In the case of March 6, 2013 in Elberton, Montana, I do not believe scavengers or predators to be the cause of death due to the nature of the incisions and extraction of internal organs. There had been removal of extensive tissue along the head, neck, abdomen, and anus. There had also been extraction of ocular tissue from the eyes and careful removal of tissue from the ears. The tongue and several muscles were extracted. The types of cuts on the carcass were surgical in nature, and the incisions were done with precision. The lack of bleeding suggests the possible use of an instrument

producing acute heat, thus cauterizing almost immediately the edge of the wounds. It is my opinion that these types of wounds are quite uncommon and not of natural causes."

The doctor made it sound as if the culprit had a high level of intelligence and technology to go along with it. "Who the hell would show up on a cattle ranch in the middle of nowhere and mutilate a cow?" Angelica murmured and shook her head in disbelief. "Perhaps a sick individual with a medical background and supplies from a hardware store," she concluded.

Her mind drifted back to her college days. Her favorite dissertation was on the legendary "Jack the Ripper" cases in London. Her mind went back to the gruesome pictures she uncovered while researching the case.

"Surgical ... intelligent ... calculated ... still unsolved," she reflected. She had remained fascinated with the old news reports of the Ripper cases while interning at the *Post*. However, in this case, these were defenseless animals roaming lonely pastures, not women walking the seedy backstreets of London. She paused and considered it entirely likely that the Ripper viewed his prostitute victims in much the same way. Angelica locked that thought away in the back of her mind. A line of reasoning that could be useful later on, she concluded.

Angelica sat the glass of Scotch on her desk and wrote down a few notes. The way she always got to the truth was much like a doctor determining a diagnosis. First, rule out the obvious, then work your way from there. If it's not a run-of-the-mill disease, you dig deeper. She scribbled down her theories... natural predators, scavengers, devil worshippers, disputes between ranchers, hoaxes. Angelica then picked up her cell phone. Perplexed by the eyewitness statement given by the rancher, Jack Keller, she had read earlier at her office and Dr. Walter Goolrick's report, she called Gail.

"Gail, it's Angelica. I've been reading through the file, and the report from the Bio-Med doctor at the University of Colorado is very intriguing."

"Yes." Gail sounded half asleep. "Carl had those sent over yesterday. You'll want to check with the local authorities for more statements once you get there. I'm sure you noticed before this recent mutilation, there was a mutilation reported in Elberton back in March of this year, and another one reported in 2000. It's apparently a hot spot."

"Yes, that is interesting," Angelica murmured and then yawned. "I should get some rest. I'll catch up with you tomorrow sometime." Angelica said as she stood up from her chair.

"Go get some beauty rest. You looked exhausted today... No offense."

"Yes, you've already said," Angelica mumbled sarcastically.

"Goodnight, sweet girl," Gail whispered and hung up.

The sleep disruptions were wearing on her, mentally and physically. She yawned once more and turned off the desk lamp, and with just a little left of

The Bovine Connection

her Scotch in hand, she headed off to bed wondering what the hell to pack for a trip out West.

Chapter Four

Without warning, Angelica was jolted awake by what sounded like a door slamming shut. The room was dark. She noticed the time on the clock was three thirty-three in the morning.

Her heart pounded in her chest as she pulled her covers up to her neck and anxiously watched her bedroom door. Angelica was sure the sound came from inside her townhouse. She expected the sound of footsteps outside her room. The walls felt closer, the ceiling, lower. As a single woman in a dangerous city, unusual sounds in the night had a tendency to take on a life of their own. Lying in her bed, frozen with fear, she waited anxiously. The footsteps never came.

Chapter Five

Angelica woke feeling unusually euphoric about the trip to Montana. She decided to consider it a much needed escape from the city, and hoped the change in scenery would alter the sleep disturbances. Her curiosity with the story was driving her, and she wasn't entirely sure why.

Angelica routinely looked at her iPhone calendar. It was Wednesday, June twenty-third, three days after the last mutilation in Elberton. She had to admit this was completely different from her usual stories of politics. After reading through the file the night before, she was eager to find out what was going on in Montana.

Angelica looked outside and noticed the yellow cab waiting. She put her coffee cup down, grabbed her bags, opened the solid black front door of her townhouse, and motioned for the cab driver to come over and retrieve her luggage from the porch.

Once in the cab, the driver asked, "Where to?"

"Washington National, please," Angelica announced as she adjusted in her seat.

Angelica looked out the window and noticed an attractive couple in their mid-thirties in the car next to her. Angelica watched as the man stroked the side of the woman's head. They appeared to be in love.

Angelica leaned her head back against the seat and closed her eyes. She saw an image of herself in love.

His soft touch of affection as he put his arms around her and pulled her to his chest. Then the image of the faceless man disappeared. Realizing it was a foolish fantasy, she pushed the thought away, feeling a chill of loneliness.

At the airport, she immediately felt the excitement of the fast-paced atmosphere as people rushed to their gates. A man in a dark suit pressed by her, almost bumping into her and knocked over her satchel. Maintaining her poise, she grabbed her bags and continued on to check in.

The man at the counter asked Angelica for her boarding pass and ID. She pulled them out of her diminutive black Chanel purse and handed it to him. He stepped around to take her luggage. "Are you checking these bags?"

"No, I'll carry them on," Angelica said as she pulled her satchel and suitcase close to her.

"Where you headed?" he asked.

"Yellowstone Regional," Angelica replied, meekly.

"Really... Yellowstone Regional?" he asked with a playful grin as he looked around the counter once more and down at her light pink high heels.

"Yes," Angelica responded softly as she observed him; it was apparent he was amused. She glanced down at her high heels. She obliviously did not fit the profile of a nature loving, wilderness type, she thought.

Angelica finished checking in and went briskly through security. She was an old hat at it, although it felt as if it had been too long since she traveled.

The Bovine Connection

Angelica thought about her last trip as she passed by the familiar gift shops and the restaurant where she and Andrew had sat, sipping champagne while waiting for their flight. She recalled how she and Andrew had managed to sneak off for a long weekend to Turks and Caicos. Andrew was an exciting travel companion – athletic and up for anything. She reflected on the passion between them, but then remembered on the flight home feeling as if something were still missing. She frowned at the memory and hurried past toward her terminal.

Angelica made it down the busy terminal and found a small store next to her gate for a coffee, and the latest issue of her magazine, the *Liberator*. As she entered the store she noticed a man in khakis and a dark blue dress shirt with a bottled water securely stuck between his arm and chest, grabbing one of the *Liberator Magazines* from the newsstand. She wondered how many passengers from around the world were reading her stories that morning as she pushed through to the counter to check out.

Angelica stepped out of the store and found her gate, noting the long line of passengers preparing to board the same flight; she dropped her shoulders, releasing a breath of irritation.

On the plane, Angelica was relieved to see it wasn't completely full by the time she boarded.

After finding her seat, she lifted her satchel and suitcase into the overhead compartment, accidently bumping into a woman with short jet-black hair trying to pass by. The woman wore an outdated purple blazer with a black leather collar and heavy gold jewelry. Angelica looked around to apologize, but the woman disregarded her and shouted hastily in Italian, "Stronza!" Angelica gave her a confused look and rolled her eyes, then she rubbed her throbbing skull while wondering what the lady had said. Her tone didn't sound complimentary. Angelica glanced down and shrugged her shoulders at a young lady staring and sitting in the aisle seat across from her.

"I think she called you a jerk," the young lady whispered sympathetically. Angelica gave her a wry smile before sitting down in her seat.

Not thinking, she lifted the lid and raised the coffee cup to her mouth, burning the tip of her tongue. The morning wasn't getting off to good start, she thought. She put the cup between her knees and wiped her bottom lip with the back of her palm. She couldn't believe she had done it again, forgetting to blow before sipping it slowly. She touched the tip of her tongue to her lip to test the numbness, and then looked around to see if anyone was observing her. Angelica noticed a young man wearing oversized headphones staring at her while bobbing his head. She gave him a quick smile and turned back around. Angelica shifted to get comfortable in her seat and then opened the latest issue of her magazine.

She found one of her articles. A self-proclaimed perfectionist, she felt there was always a story she could have written better or more she could have added. Already printed and out on the newsstand by the time she'd second-guessed herself, she had to let it go and be content with her work.

Her mind drifted back to Elberton. She went through, one by one, the salient points of the articles and documents she had read on the cattle mutilations. She felt that familiar tingling sensation of excitement on the back of her neck and shoulders as she did when she started a new story. However, something deep in her subconscious seemed to be trying to break through, giving her a slight unsettling feeling.

Chapter Six

After a brief layover in Salt Lake City, the plane made a rather bumpy landing at the modest Yellowstone Regional Airport in Cody, Wyoming.

Angelica pushed her feet forward in an effort to counterbalance the quick deceleration on what was obviously a short runway.

It was quite a contrast from D.C. and she immediately felt pleased as she looked out the terminal windows at the vast openness of rolling mounds in the distance.

The airport was painted shades of gold and pale yellow and displayed large scenic photos of Yellowstone National Park's mountains and wildlife. Her surroundings were fresh, giving her the impression the airport was newly constructed.

Washington, D.C., although rich in history, was covered with algae and moss and usually had a musky scent. The streets and buildings of D.C. bore evidence of a significant history long gone. And while charming, she longed for something new and fresh.

Angelica made her way to the rental car company inside the airport. After a few minutes in line, she was at the counter.

"Hello... Angelica Bradley... I have a reservation."

The female clerk looked up from the computer screen. "Yes, let's see... yes, I have you right here. Will you be needing a navigational system?"

Angelica rubbed at her temple as she thought for a moment. Her headache had lessened while she slept on the flight and had become barely noticeable. "How far is it to Elberton, Montana from here?"

"Oh, it'll take you a good forty-five minutes," the clerk said. "I suggest a navigational system. They are always good to have."

"Okay," Angelica agreed. She didn't like the idea of getting lost--especially in the wilderness--so she took the lady's advice and finished signing the forms.

In the rental car lot, Angelica found her economy silver Nissan Altima. She entered the Elk Lodge address into the navigation system, and then turned on the radio.

Flipping through the stations, she was struck by an evangelical preacher giving a sermon, so she turned the volume up and listened curiously. His voice was high-pitched as he shouted... "Then I saw another angel flying directly overhead, with an eternal gospel to proclaim to those who dwell on earth, to every nation and tribe and language and people. Revelation 14:6." Angelica let his voice drift away as she thought back on her childhood in Asheville, North Carolina. The little white church tucked away in between the Blue Ridge Mountains. She always dreaded the Sunday morning services while visiting her grandmother. Angelica remembered the haunting hymns filling the air, the smell of moth balls, and being terrified of the preacher as he shouted, yelled and stomped down the aisle while giving his well-rehearsed sermon to the congregation.

Angelica recalled as a child, tucking her head into her grandmother's arm, watching with one wide eye as the congregation stood and moaned with their hands raised and swaying in the air. Women or men would shake back and forth, as if they were having convulsions when the preacher lay his hand on their head and yelled, "Devil be gone!" Angelica shivered and quickly turned off the radio. She shifted her thoughts to the cattle mutilations. She was eager to get to Elberton and get started on the story.

While finishing the last few minutes of the drive, she tried to ignore the slight smell of sweat and tobacco in the rental car, making her sick to her stomach and her headache worsen. Angelica cracked the window and let the warm summer air blow her hair away from her shoulders.

She took in the mountain views starting to emerge. She then slowly moved her range of sight to the tall evergreens becoming abundant as they expanded out and around her. "Such an amazing place," she said softly.

Chapter Seven

Right on the edge of town sat an old gas station. Angelica pulled the rental car into the empty lot. She got out of the car and surveyed her surroundings, glancing up to see the deep blue sky with only a few enormous white cotton ball clouds. She shut the car door, walked over and stepped onto the old wooden porch of the country store. Angelica lifted her arm to smell her shirt sleeve. She frowned. The smell in the rental car was in her clothing.

Angelica didn't see anyone as she stepped through the glass door. She gazed around, searching for the cooler containing the Red Bulls. Locating it, she walked to the back corner of the store, opened the cooler and took one out.

On her way to the register, Angelica grabbed a small box of Aspirin. She stood at the counter quietly for a moment, looking around, but the place appeared empty. After a few moments of anxiously waiting, she yelled out, "Hello!"

Hearing her yell, an older man appeared from an office in the back. "Yes, I'm here! It's just me, and sometimes I don't hear people come in. It's usually kind of quiet," he said as he hurried to the counter. His clothes were worn and dirty with oil stains.

"Oh, well, here," she said, her tone disparaging. Angelica sat the Aspirin box and Red Bull down on the counter as her subconscious sneered back at her for her unintentional tone. She was tired from traveling and her head still had a dull ache that was trying to emerge into something bigger.

While the man rang up the Red Bull and Aspirin, Angelica glanced around the old country store. She noticed different framed photos hanging on the walls of the old man in fishing gear holding up a large trout.

Angelica looked back to the gray-haired man with a thick, unruly white beard. He had his glasses balanced on the tip of his nose. He raised his head to take a closer look at Angelica, appearing distracted by her clothing.

Angelica noted his eyes moving down to her heels. "Do you know where I can find a liquor store?" she asked politely to cut through the uncomfortable tension in the air.

"Sure do! Just continue down this road here...," The man pointed outside the window. "Once you're in Elberton, you'll find it just past the town square on the left," he responded moving his glasses back up over his nose as he politely looked down at the cash register.

"What brings you to Elberton, young lady?" He looked back up and then down at Angelica's pink heels and up to her skirt, continuing to her blouse that revealed the top curve of her cleavage. The outfit represented her usual attire, so she was familiar with the man's not-so-subtle expression. Tired from the long day and not interested in small talk, she replied with a forced smile...

"Sightseeing," Angelica winced inwardly at her little lie.

The man tilted his head, and looked suspiciously at Angelica. He lowered his eyebrows curiously and looked back at the cash register, surprised by her response. "Sightseeing? Okay... well let's get you outta here so you can get started. Would you like your receipt?"

"Yes, thank you," Angelica smiled.

"So where are you staying?"

"Elk Lodge."

"Oh, fancy place."

"Yes, quite fancy," she murmured as she glanced around the store.

"Are you traveling alone?" he asked, concerned.

Figuring it impossible to dodge his questions, she reluctantly responded... "Yes. Look, I apologize, I shouldn't have said sightseeing. I'm doing a story on the cattle mutilations," Angelica observed his expression closely.

"Really?" he appeared curious.

"Yes, ranchers are finding mutilated cattle on their property. People are even saying something about UFOs. I know crazy... right?" Angelica laughed sarcastically.

"Yes, I know all about it," the man rubbed at his shaggy beard while peering at her.

Angelica stood up straighter. "Really, what do you know?" Angelica had now leaned in closer, fully attentive.

"About ten or so years ago there was a cow cut up on a ranch here in Elberton, you know." The look on his face grew serious. "I remember hearing folks talk about it. It was a big deal. Folks around here couldn't wrap their minds around the thought of someone cutting up a rancher's livestock. You know, they take that personally." The old store clerk plucked at his beard a little. He continued, "The cattle are the rancher's livelihood. We ... well, most of us thought it was some animal, maybe a coyote, but when we read the details of the mutilation in the paper... let's just say, a lot of people got nervous and started carrying their guns out in the open... It was like being back in the Old West," he said as he chuckled. "They had to call a town meeting before people started shooting somebody by accident just for showing up, you know, on their property. It was a pretty big deal. It had kind of a ripple effect into surrounding towns."

Angelica was trying to ignore the throb in her temple.

"You know, all that died down eventually, and then back in March... there was another one, and now... another dead cow. Now, as you can imagine, people are afraid again."

Angelica held eye contact with the talkative cashier. She thought the story was certainly interesting so far. "I can't fathom," she murmured as she reached over and grabbed the box of Aspirin, opened it, and took two out.

"Well a gentleman came in a little while back, you know. I overheard him talking back there on his cell phone about it. He told the person on the other end that he was convinced it was going to be like the ones

The Bovine Connection

in Kansas. And he said something about it happening by the Air Force base."

"Really?" ... Angelica raised her hand to cover her mouth as she cleared her throat. Her throat felt dry. The man pushed her Red Bull on the counter closer to her.

"Thank you," Angelica said, before clearing her throat again and opening the can of Red Bull. "Please continue... Did he say anything else about the Air Force base?" Angelica put the pills in her mouth, tasting the bitterness, and took a sip before washing it down.

"Yes, I believe he said something about it being odd that another one had occurred near another military base," he answered confidently.

"Interesting," Angelica examined the man's face curiously. "What else?" Angelica had started tapping her finger lightly on the counter.

"He said he was meeting with the police in Elberton. He was going to examine the carcass, you know, the dead cow," his eyes widened as he raised his hand and cupped his chin, reflecting back.

"And..." Angelica nodded with straight lips.

"You know, he said something about there being no blood, or something like that. He didn't say a whole lot else. Hey, you know, there's a reporter in Elberton that's been doing the stories on the mutilations for a while now. You might want to talk to him." The man shook his head and looked sharply at Angelica. "You can imagine what the locals were saying after reading the one about the UFOs being involved," he said as he chuckled while enthusiastically continuing to shake his head.

"What did he say in the paper?" Angelica unconsciously twirled at a strain of her hair, eagerly anticipating his response.

"He was talking about some sort of UFO being reportedly seen on one of the nights of the killing... strange lights shining down and spot-lighting cattle." He laughed and shook his head. "Yep, UFOs... can you imagine that?"

Angelica observed the man for a moment, "Well, I don't believe in UFOs. There clearly has to be another explanation," she said, straight-faced. Deciding that once in her room, her first call would be to that conspiracy-peddling journalist. "Do you happen to remember his name?"

"Which one?" the man asked.

"The reporter," Angelica responded softly as she started to search her purse for a piece of paper and pen.

"Matthew Tillman. Nice guy. He's the only reporter writing about the mutilations, so he's fairly well-known around these parts."

"That's great!" Angelica looked up and closed her purse, after recognizing the name. He was the reporter that she stumbled across during her Google search. She had the very copies of his articles in her satchel.

"Thank you!" Angelica grabbed her Red Bull and Aspirin from the counter and turned toward the glass door.

"Good luck, young lady!" The pleasant old-timer waved goodbye, then rubbed at his beard as he watched Angelica leave the store.

Chapter Eight

After what felt like an endless day of traveling, she was ready to get to the lodge. In the rental car, Angelica followed the directions given by the female voice on her navigation system.

"Turn left onto Long Hollow Road..." After a brief pause, the woman's voice said, "Right onto Elk Creek Road; you will arrive at your destination in zero point one miles." Angelica thought about the jokes the men in her office made about the female navigation voice and rolled her eyes.

Driving along the charming road up the hill to the lodge, winding between tall evergreens, she suddenly saw the slopes of the rust-colored roof of Elk Lodge. Her reaction was immediate. It took her breath. The lodge was illuminated with lights in the darkness. The scenic mountain drive led her up the ridge and right into the grand entrance of The Elk Lodge, tucked away in the wilderness slopes of Montana – like a perfectly well-kept secret.

Angelica rolled down her window, took a deep breath of pine-scented fresh air, and thought about how lucky she was to have such an amazing career that allowed her to travel to places most people would only dream of.

Angelica was ready for the change in pace. She was still feeling the lingering burned-out effects of covering the same type of stories back in D.C., where she had spent most of her career knee-deep in political dirt. A story of mystery and intrigue in Montana may have been exactly what she needed.

Angelica pulled up to the valet under the large log canopy, an elegant area lit by large black iron and glowing gas lanterns. The walls were a mixture of stone and smoothly carved jumbo logs. Looking through the lobby doors, her eyes were drawn to the fireplace of smooth grey stones, stretching from the floor to ceiling with a massive white bull elk mounted above it.

Angelica smiled coyly, glancing around. "Exactly what I needed," she thought as she dropped her shoulders and released a deep breath, feeling suddenly relaxed.

As she checked in, she noticed people passing by dressed in their evening wear. A few couples sat in front of the fireplace sipping cocktails while listening to a man in a tuxedo playing jazz standards on a black grand piano. Immediately taken with the lodge's combination of warm, rustic elegance and a hint of modern sophistication, she was ready to relax in a hot bath with a drink.

In her room, her headache had eased but she felt exhausted. She put her bags down and glanced around. The room was exquisite, and it should be, considering how much it cost per night, she thought. She walked through, admiring the black granite countertop in the bathroom and elegant amenities. It was well worth the price.

The lodge was known to be a hotspot for high rollers since there was a private jet airport offering air charters nearby.

As she strolled around, admiring the room, she thought about her last trip home. The lodge reminded her of the Biltmore Hotel in her hometown, where she stayed last year for her cousin's wedding. It had been a while since she had spoken to her mother, still living in Asheville. She debated whether to call her and say hello. Angelica remembered the headache she had fought all that day. The Aspirin seemed to be working, except for the tension she felt in the back of her neck. She didn't want to risk a reemergence, so she decided to wait and call her mother in the morning.

Angelica stepped over and turned on the lamp on the bedside table. Patting the bed, she noticed it even had the same overstuffed goose down comfortable bedding as the Biltmore, which she was eager to try out.

Angelica walked over and opened the door to the balcony. The night air had turned cool. A soft breeze lifted her hair from her shoulders, and she heard music from the bar below. Angelica leaned over the balcony and saw couples dancing on a small square parquet dance floor situated under streamers of soft glowing balls of light. A woman sang Billie Holiday's version of "I'll Never Be the Same." The nostalgic sound was at once comforting and haunting to Angelica. She recalled a wedding reception she attended while still in college at Georgetown University. After the celebration had died down, she and her date snuck away from the party to a secluded area near the Potomac River. The same song had played in the distance under streamers of lights. She recalled tasting the sweetness of blackberries on his full, soft lips... Lips she told him even angels were jealous of.

Angelica squeezed the rustic railing as the memory faded, and looked out into the darkness to notice the lights from the lodge shining down on the white bubbles foaming around the rocks in the fast moving Elk Creek.

She stood and listened to the music from below, feeling the breeze as it gently blew through her hair. A strange new thought and sensation came over her. The constriction in her chest had released and she realized she felt relaxed and peaceful, nothing else mattered. She closed her eyes and swayed to the music, inhaling the scent of fresh pine, but was quickly jolted back to the pressures and responsibilities of the day when the music abruptly stopped.

Feeling a sharp pain, Angelica placed her hand over her belly, realizing she was hungry. She hadn't eaten anything since breakfast so she walked inside, and closed the patio door.

Angelica went over to the bedside table and dialed room service, ordering the house specialty. She finished her order with a glass of a moderately priced Pinot Noir, and a glass of single malt Scotch to help her sleep.

Chapter Nine

Possessed by a strange and uncomfortable numbness, Angelica awoke – paralyzed. She immediately realized she wasn't dreaming. Angelica's mind raced as her eyes rapidly surveyed her surroundings.

Angelica remembered she was in a hotel room in Montana and not at her townhouse in D.C. ... and as crazy as it seemed, she heard it again! Was it a helicopter? "It must be," she thought. She quickly concluded the sound was unfamiliar. Angelica tried to lift her arms to cover her ears with her hands but they wouldn't budge. She resigned herself to the irrational emotion that she was dying. The noise was everywhere. Angelica couldn't concentrate. Her heart was racing at an extraordinarily fast pace. She gasped for air and without any apparent reason the noise stopped. She felt as if every cell had been hit by an electrical charge and then the numbness slowly retreated.

Shivering, she took a deep breath and gently glided her hands across her face and mouth. Wet with sweat and disoriented, she lifted the moist sheets from her body and then rose from the bed. Steady on her feet, she walked past the mirror and caught a glimpse of her pale nude body in the moonlight.

Angelica turned on the bathroom faucet and splashed her face with cold water, observing each drop of water as it ran down her face. Staring at her ashen reflection, she noticed her eyes were red and puffy. She glanced down and saw a drop of fresh blood in the sink. Angelica gasped as she looked back up at her face in the mirror and saw the blood running from her nose. She leaned in and took a closer look and then rubbed her index finger along her nose, smearing the blood across her cheek.

Her mind swam. She grabbed a hand towel and turned on the sink. Angelica held the towel under the water and dampened it, and then wiped the blood from her face. Questions assaulted her. Why was her nose bleeding? The odd sound had originated from outside of her window. Had anyone else heard it?

If she could track down anyone else who had noticed the noise, she'd know she wasn't going crazy. She'd check with the front desk in the morning, she decided. "Someone had to have heard it," she thought aloud.

Walking away from the sink, she grabbed a large white bath towel and wrapped it around her body, twisting it tightly above her breast and then she turned off the bathroom light.

Angelica went over to the desk, turned on the lamp and then opened her laptop. She entered, "Waking up to strange humming or whooshing sound in the middle of the night" into her browser search bar. The nightly occurrences had started abruptly and were happening too frequently. If it wasn't a helicopter, there had to be a medical explanation, she thought.

Links with information on UFOs and abductions appeared on the screen. "Are you kidding?" Angelica blurted and laughed uneasily at the synchronicity as she got up to retrieve the glass of Scotch left over from dinner.

Waking up in the middle of the night to strange sounds was taking its toll. Angelica leaned back and opened the first link: "Reported Alien Stories ... the following stories are reported by people who claim to have been abducted by ETs."

"What the hell am I doing?" She laughed.

Angelica stood up from her chair and looked around her hotel room. She quickly closed the site, turned off the lights, and decided to go back to sleep.

Collapsing onto the bed, she turned to her side. After fluffing her pillow, she noticed the soft silver glow of moonlight shining through the French doors leading to the balcony.

The cool beauty of the night gripped her, the emptiness of her bed and her heart, the trauma of waking up... it all seemed to collapse upon her, a crushing weight of loneliness. Tears began to softly well up in her eyes, and she drifted back to sleep.

Chapter Ten

The alarm on the bedside table was going off at eight o'clock in the morning. Angelica turned over and pressed the button at the top of the alarm clock and then lifted the covers, slowly getting up from the bed. She realized she had left the curtains open from the night before. The room was bright and warm from the sunlight.

She found her bag and pulled out a pair of grey and white striped boxers and a white tank top. She slipped the tank top over her head as she went into the bathroom and noticed the spots of dried blood on the countertop. Angelica gasped. "It wasn't a dream," she said as she pulled her hair back into a ponytail.

Angelica stepped out of the bathroom and remembered she wanted to meet with the Elberton reporter, so she went over to the desk and entered into Google "Matthew Tillman with the Elberton Tribune."

Once she found him, she took her cell phone out of her purse and called the number from Elberton Tribune's website directory. A man answered, "Hello, Matthew Tillman, Elberton Tribune."

"Hello Matthew, my name is Angelica Bradley with the *Liberator Magazine*. I'm in town from D.C. doing a story on the cattle mutilation at the Keller Ranch."

"Yes, wow, okay, Angelica... how can I help you?" he replied, completely surprised.

"I'd like to meet with you. I have a lot of ground to cover in a short period of time, and I would like to start with someone who's been covering the story. Are you available to meet today?"

"Yes, would you like to come by my office? Are you close to the town square? Where are you staying?"

"I'm at the Elk Lodge."

"You're close. I could be there in a couple hours, say ten o'clock."

"Perfect, I need to spend some time on my computer this morning," Angelica said relieved and surprised by his flexibility on short notice.

"I'll meet you in the restaurant there at ten."

"Thank you, Matthew. I'll see you then."

Chapter Eleven

Angelica could hear the sounds of the restaurant to her left as she stepped out of the elevator and into the lobby. She wondered if Matthew was already seated. She needed to stop by the front desk. She couldn't stop thinking about last night. Angelica anxiously walked over to the counter. "Excuse me. Hi… I have a question for you." Angelica forced a smile.

The middle-aged brunette woman at the front desk smiled politely. "Yes, how may I help you?"

"Well," Angelica paused for a moment, "Well, I was just curious. Do helicopters fly over the lodge at night?"

"No ma'am, that wouldn't be permitted," the woman responded quickly. Her eyes turned mindful as she tilted her head and lowered her eyebrows.

"Did any of the other guests complain of hearing a loud noise last night around three thirty in the morning?" Angelica's eyes probed the lady's face.

"No, I don't believe so. If you'll wait here for a moment, I'll go ask my manager."

"Oh no, that won't be necessary, thank you." Angelica stepped away but had a second thought, then quickly turned back around. "Wait, yes, I would like to speak to your manager."

The woman tilted her head again. "Okay, just a moment," she replied, before she turned and walked through the door behind the counter, and returned immediately with a heavyset middle-aged man.

"How can I help you?" he asked, his voice robust, as he smiled politely.

"I was wondering. Well, I heard a loud noise in the middle of the night last night and... well, did any of the other guests complain of a noise around three in the morning?" Angelica asked anxiously as she glanced over to see a couple checking in, staring at her oddly. She pursed her lips, suddenly uncomfortable asking about the noise.

"No, ma'am, no one has complained of a noise." He appeared concerned.

"I see. Thank you," Angelica turned and slowly walked away. Looking down at the rustic red and tan southwestern style Persian rug as she moved across it, she paused briefly and shook her head, "Just doesn't make sense... It was so loud," she mumbled.

Chapter Twelve

The restaurant was noisy as Angelica walked in and glanced around for Matthew, becoming distracted for a moment by the view of the mountains through the large windows on the other side of the room.

Angelica saw a man who appeared to be in his mid-thirties, light brown hair, wearing a tan cowboy hat, sitting alone in the corner close to the fireplace; so she took a chance and walked over to him. "Are you Matthew Tillman?"

"Yes. You must be Angelica," he smiled, his eyes widened. He looked both startled and pleased.

Angelica heard the subtle crack in his voice. Matthew fidgeted in his seat. His face still appeared surprised. Angelica could see Matthew had become slightly nervous. She knew too well the signs of a man taken aback by her.

Angelica made an effort to relax him with a joke. "So, do all Montana journalists wear cowboy hats?" she asked politely and smiled.

Matthew chuckled, "I believe they probably do ma'am." He lowered his eyes appearing bashful. "I helped a friend on his ranch this morning. I wear one on occasion." He took off his hat and revealed a crease in his hair. Then he stood up from his chair so she could take a seat across from him.

Matthew put his hat back on and adjusted it self-consciously. Angelica turned to notice the server standing beside her.

"I'll have coffee and a bowl of fruit, thank you."

The server smiled, nodded, and then looked at Matthew... "Anything for you?"

"Steak and eggs over easy," he announced and then peered at Angelica.

Angelica smiled in the same innocent way she always did, before leaning down to retrieve her digital recorder, note pad and pen from her satchel.

"Angelica, I have to admit, you're not what I expected. I mean..." Matthew hesitated after hearing Angelica let out a breath of frustration while raising back up and turning on the recorder.

Immediately, he realized he had just created an awkward moment. "So, where would you like to start?" he asked, swiftly.

Angelica appeared irritated after closing her satchel and placing her pad and pen on the table. He had been doing so well, she thought. Angelica stared at him and sized him up for a moment, trying to ignore the lack of couth. "Let's start with you and what you think is causing the mutilations," she said in a business-like tone.

"Okay, well, I think there is something very extraordinary going on, and it's far more bizarre than the general public realizes." His tone was flat.

"What are you saying, Matthew?" Angelica lowered her chin and smirked, remembering what the man at the gas station had said on her way to Elberton.

"Is it the government or something even more nefarious?" she asked sarcastically, widening her light blue eyes curiously.

"That's an interesting question, Angelica," Matthew's smile turned to a smirk. "That's a subject most people won't touch and you just opened that can of worms right up." Matthew let out a nervous laugh.

"You're one of those tough journalists," he said. He leaned back and stretched one of his arms around the back of his chair. "I bet you're a real go-getter over in D.C."

Angelica looked unmoved by his comments as her eyes penetrated his.

Matthew smiled, amused. He realized he could enjoy getting a rise out of her. "Well, to answer your question... yes, but it's complicated."

"What do you mean by complicated?" Angelica asked. "Who's doing the mutilations? Is the government somehow involved in this? It seems very coincidental that all of these mutilations happen close to military bases. Are they doing some sort of experiment?"

Matthew put both of his elbows on the table. "I don't believe so, no." Lowering his voice, he added, "But I believe they could be in contact with who is."

"Okay, Matthew, I don't speak in code." Angelica bristled. "Are you saying that you believe other entities beyond the government are responsible, and the government is aware of it? You're kidding, right?"

Matthew dropped his arms and leaned forward just as the server was placing their food on the table. He had finally had enough of the browbeating. "Angelica, this is going to be a game changer for you. Just be sure you're ready for the truth because once you go down this rabbit-hole, your life will never be the same. And there is no turning back."

Matthew took a bite of his steak, holding eye contact. Angelica, intrigued, took a sip of her coffee and a bite of her fruit. "Okay, give me what you have."

"Well, back in 2000 was the first time it happened here in Elberton that we know of. It was Hugh Anderson's ranch. He called the local police department and reported finding his second year heifer dead, "all sliced up." Those were his words exactly.

I did the story on the mutilation and although I didn't know it at the time, it would later be considered a "Classic Signature." That's what they call the mutilations with all the classic tell-tale signs. You know... in a remote area, reproductive organs removed... the removal of the tongue, an eye, an ear, drained of all blood with no blood on or around the carcass, no visible tracks or prints on the ground, no evidence of a struggle... rectal area bored out, jawbone exposed. You get the picture," Matthew took a deep breath.

Angelica shook her head and raised her hand. "Whoa, whoa... slow down!"

Angelica put her pen down. "Really? So, that's what happens in a mutilation case? So you're saying they're pretty much all the same?"

"Every once in a while they may have a few differences, but most of the things I described are usually prevalent and consistent. That's how you know the difference from a scavenger and a "Classic Signature."

Angelica picked her pen back up. "Fascinating."

Matthew smiled his boyish smile before turning serious. "Some will still try to say it was some sort of animal, like, coyote, even after they've seen evidence suggesting otherwise... and there is hard evidence suggesting otherwise." Matthew shook his head as he looked down. He cut a piece of steak and ran it through the undercooked yolk of his eggs.

"What you find," he told her, "is that most people don't want to believe anything outside of their comfort zone."

"Yes, I know... cognitive dissonance is the psychological term. We all have it," Angelica responded smugly.

Matthew appeared frustrated. He considered himself an expert on the cattle mutilation phenomena. "I have dealt with plenty of opposition," he said defensively.

Angelica noticed he was watching her closely. "So, what makes you think it's not a satanic group or some bored kids looking to create a sensation? Clearly, predators make the most logical sense of all the explanations."

"Angelica, I would rather believe any of those theories, but I've been investigating this subject for ten years, and I've come to the conclusion that there's something much more sinister going on, and it ain't no human or animal doing it," he said in an authentic western drawl as he lifted his hand and rubbed across the rim of his hat.

Angelica casually turned around to see if anyone was eavesdropping on the conversation. "Well, that leaves us with Bigfoot, ET's or whoever killed Jimmy Hoffa," she said laughing freely, but Matthew wasn't amused.

He leaned back and bowed up his chest by raising both arms over the back of his chair. His lips parted into a sneaky grin and then he smirked.

Angelica noticed the shift in Matthew's body language and decided to ease up on him. "I apologize. It all just sounds so bizarre to me."

Matthew nodded with straight lips and continued... "After the incident in 2000, I couldn't get it out of my mind. I saw the carcass with my own eyes and spoke to the local veterinarian on the scene. That animal had been diced up, and those cuts were too precise. I mean, you should have seen it. The anal area was cored clear out, no tears, no blood. The head was stripped of all skin and tissue clear down to the skull," Matthew glanced around the room and then leaned in closer.

"I went back to the scene repeatedly, obsessed, trying to find an explanation. I just couldn't make sense of it. I couldn't rationalize why someone would do it. Not to mention, who would do something so disgusting? The area was so remote. Nothing fit." Matthew's voice cracked, he was clearly emotional over the incident.

"The case stayed with me and then in town one day I met this lady. I overheard someone say, 'There's the town crazy! She claims she knows who is cutting up them cattle.' As they laughed, I looked around to see who they were referring to, and that's when I first met Ellen McKinney. She didn't look all that crazy to me... more like a sweet older lady. However, that's not the point, I heard them say 'cut up cattle' and 'she knows' in the same sentence and that's what got my attention. I went over and cut up with her, and we became friends instantly." Matthew smiled, clearly amused with himself.

Angelica nodded, unmoved, considering she thought Matthew rather unsophisticated but friendly.

Matthew noticed Angelica's flat expression and shifted in his seat. "Anyway, she's a real sweet lady and I have come to believe most of what she says. Oh and get this... her husband is an aeronautical engineer retired from Newton Air Force Base."

"He is? But you just said 'most of what she says'... About what, Matthew? What are we really talking about here?"

Matthew leaned in over his empty plate of dried smeared egg yolks. "I know all this sounds ridiculous, but stay with me here. I've personally gathered soft tissue and sent it off to a pathologist. I've worked with the UFO investigative group RUFA. I've interviewed and worked alongside scientists, veterinarians and the police. Even read the reports from the FBI, by the way... a load of crap. They don't want the truth out... a policy of denial, you'll soon discover. Oh and not to mention, I've had my life threatened - strange calls telling me to walk away from the story if I knew what was good for me."

Angelica wondered if he was telling the truth. "Your life has been threatened?" she asked, in disbelief.

"Yes," Matthew nodded with a straight face.

"Angelica, I want you to meet with Ellen McKinney and her husband, Blake. I'll call and set up a meeting."

"Great, yes, I'm looking forward to meeting the town crazy", she glanced up from her pad with a Cheshire cat smile. "What were some of the things she shared with you?"

"Now keep an open mind... She believes extraterrestrials are responsible for the mutilations. And the government knows about it."

Angelica laughed aloud. "An alien agenda... Are you hearing yourself, Matthew?"

"Angelica, in the beginning, I was just like you. I would have laughed until I cried if early on someone would have said something like that to me."

The noise in the restaurant was dying down.

"All right," Angelica said, "tell me about Jack Keller. What do you think of him and his eye-witness accounts of the mutilations?"

"As you know, journalists have it hard," Matthew stated matter-of-factly. Angelica bit down on her lip and nodded.

"Unfortunately," Matthew continued, "we are living in a world where people are afraid of ridicule and condemnation from others. A lot of our reporting is off the record. Stories get squashed if they're too provocative. Hell, I'm not telling you anything you don't already know." Matthew shifted in his seat.

"Well, anyway… when you get permission to go on the record, you're left with very little information to piece together. In addition, as you know, subjects of this nature, well… you have less on the record that you can officially report and that just doesn't cut it when it comes to factual and unbiased journalism."

Angelica nodded and checked her recorder. It was still capturing Matthew's candid speech.

"Jack didn't want to go on the record," Matthew told her. "And I know Jack well. Jack is the kind of guy that states the facts, a no-fluff type of guy, and he said some real interesting things about the nights of the incidents." Matthew grinned, a glint of pride in his eye. "Anyway, these guys are hardworking, no-nonsense cowboys, and Jack especially. This guy has nothing to gain by killing one of his own cattle. What would his reason be? Not publicity, trust me." Matthew shook his head. "It's time people know the truth. My question is… are you going to have the courage to write the truth in the end?" Matthew raised his eyebrows. Angelica nervously shifted in her seat. Something about the way Matthew said the word "courage" unnerved her.

"What did he say?" Angelica glanced up while continuing to take shorthand notes on her pad.

Matthew turned and saw the server standing there.

"Can I get you anything else?"

Matthew looked into his cup and then back to the server... "No, thank you. I believe I'm finished. We'll go ahead and get the check."

The woman walked off as Angelica glanced down at her watch. "I have to say, Matthew, this conversation is... well, I'm just going to shoot straight with you. This all sounds a bit farfetched to me." Angelica said as she pushed her plate forward. She turned off the recorder and looked around for the server.

Matthew noticed Angelica was in deep thought so he nudged the table causing her to flinch. "Would you like to go to the Keller Ranch and have a look at the carcass?"

Angelica was suddenly back in the moment. She turned around to face Matthew. "Carcass?"

Matthew pushed his chair back and got up from the table as he watched Angelica gather her things. She was rather petite and a bit fragile behind that tough persona, he thought. "Why don't you just ride with me to the ranch? I can bring you back later."

"Perfect," she responded enthusiastically. "Yes, that would be great."

"Okay, let's head on over there. I'll call Jack."

Chapter Thirteen

The Western sun shone radiantly over the mountain scenery as they pulled out of the lodge parking lot and headed down the hill, past the tall evergreens.

Angelica noticed the rushing river's white-capped rapids breaking on the rocks. Down further was a calm area of the river, called Elk Creek, where she could barely make out figures standing in knee-deep water fly-fishing as sparkles of sunlight glistened off the surface. The sun reflected off the lines as they stretched their arms back to cast into the river. Relaxed, she had forgotten the story's disturbing details and was fully present in the peaceful moment.

Angelica's heart suddenly fluttered and her stomach sank as she heard Matthew utter the word "carcass," causing her to quickly snap back to reality. Matthew was speaking with Jack Keller on his cell phone, and she was just catching the tail end of their conversation.

"Thank you, Jack, see you soon." Matthew put the phone back in his pocket and looked at Angelica. "He said he'd speak with you. He'll be around the ranch throughout the day so we can head on over." Matthew grinned. "Along with the Hoffa conspiracy theorist," he whispered.

"Perfect," Angelica smiled and looked back out the window.

Matthew glanced over at Angelica, "So, you married... got a family back home in D.C.?"

Surprised by the question, Angelica slowly turned her head toward Matthew. "No. Are you?"

"Nope, I was once. She met a guy. It was bad timing for me." Matthew shrugged his shoulders. Angelica looked over at Matthew and smiled sincerely. The sun was shining through his window, illuminating a soft glow around his light brown cowboy hat.

"Every cowboy has a story." Matthew shook his head while still looking out the front windshield. Angelica gave an impressed nod while silently observing him.

"The only thing that really hurts a cowboy is getting his heart broken," he said. "Of course there was that time I fell off that horse in the middle of a briar patch--ouch!" Matthew laughed.

Angelica was amused. Matthew had a quirky sense of humor, she thought. Still smiling she shook her head. "I'm sorry about your wife. Are you really a cowboy, Matthew?" It was an idea she found hard to believe, even with the cowboy hat.

Matthew laughed, "Nah... Not my cup of tea!" Angelica smiled wryly as she turned to look back out the window.

Matthew realized Angelica could use some quiet time to enjoy the view after the long conversation in the restaurant. "Beautiful, isn't it? Just relax and take it all in while you have a chance."

Angelica's eyes were sincere as she looked over at Matthew with a kind smile and nodded.

Chapter Fourteen

Angelica had dozed off while enjoying the scenery.

"There it is!" Matthew announced. Angelica jerked her head at the sound of Matthew's voice.

It was just as she had envisioned when she read the eyewitness statement from the police report: a typical Midwest ranch with lush meadows, hay bottoms, and rolling hills.

They drove through the private entrance and past rustic posts and rail fencing. Angelica felt anxious. She saw the cedar-sided house with a cedar shake roof, extending out to cover the front porch that stretched along the length of the front of the house. The porch was bare except for two rocking chairs and a sleeping German Shepard.

Angelica envisioned a man and woman sitting there at night looking up at the stars. It reminded her of her childhood visits to her grandmother's house in the Blue Ridge Mountains outside of Asheville, North Carolina.

She and her grandmother would lean back in the porch swing after dinner and gaze up at the stars. Angelica would compare the night's sky to her grandmother's black and white speckled casserole baking pot. Her grandmother would rub her head and hum quietly over the orchestra of crickets in the distance as Angelica would think about how small she felt under the stars. A curious young girl, she wondered where it all began. What was behind the speckled blackness? Where did it finally end? The list of questions would go on until she would finally pull herself back, knowing she had gone as far as her young mind would comfortably allow. Her childlike wonder was fascinated with the black space behind the stars, and the idea that there could be life out in the vast darkness... somewhere... on another planet, maybe just like earth, inhabited by curious minds similar to hers.

The car bounced as it drove over a large dip, snapping her out of the memory. Gravel crunched under the tires. She didn't see anyone around as they continued down the bumpy road, past the house and horse barn.

Matthew turned to Angelica, "Good people, Keller and his wife. I hope you'll get to meet her. They don't have any children. Heard from folks around town that she's not able to conceive. Sad situation--seems she's become more reclusive after each miscarriage. The doctor had told Jack and Elizabeth her uterus was too full of adhesions. Odd scar tissue had formed that must have been from some past infection and she'd never have children. At least that's what I overheard. Small town, ya know."

Angelica lowered her eyes, "So sad."

"Yes, it is. Apparently, Elizabeth had changed after the news, becoming delicate from the grief, and Jack had become more protective of her. Like I told you, Jack's a good man and you'll find him to be sincere,"

Matthew cocked his head and looked Angelica straight in the eye then swung his head back around. Angelica caught Matthew's point. He had figured her out fairly quickly, she thought. She'd tame her personality and be careful not to offend the Kellers.

Angelica noticed a group clustered in the pasture. She looked over at Matthew. "Are they the men from the UFO group?"

"Not sure, but I suspect they could be." Matthew pulled up beside the other cars parked in front of the fence.

Angelica organized her things and grabbed her recorder, pad, and pen from her satchel. "So, do you think the carcass will be in decent condition," she asked, "with the weather being so warm?" Angelica wiped the sweat from above her lip. It had only taken a few seconds for the air in the car to warm up after Matthew turned the engine off. "I could only imagine with the sun beating down on it all day... I'm sure it smells pretty bad."

"One would think it'd be in awful shape. We'll see here in a minute," Matthew leaned over, grabbed a tissue out of the glove compartment, and handed it to Angelica. "This is all I have, just in case."

Angelica took the tissue and put it in her pocket. They both opened their doors at the same time and got out. Angelica walked alongside Matthew as they approached the group of men standing in the dry dirt. She felt prepared as she pulled her satchel strap up over her shoulder.

Following Matthew, she walked over towards the men. Matthew shouted, "Look who it is! Well there's Paul Colbeck! How are you, man?" Matthew patted him on the shoulder. "I wasn't sure if you'd still be here."

"Yes, we'll be here all week doing research," Paul said.

"Getting anywhere?" Matthew glanced over at the other men and smiled, then back to Paul.

"Yeah, saw some lights in the sky last night, and followed them until they disappeared right as they approached the Newton Base. They were just as Jack had described. We were sitting in the truck bed doing some sky watching and after a few non-eventful hours, they showed up to say hello," Paul chuckled. "Two bright lights appeared and grew larger as they approached us. Once they were about a hundred yards from our truck, they froze for a few minutes, and then they danced around each other. I don't know of any man-made craft able to maneuver like that. When they started moving away we followed them and ended up a couple hundred yards from the base. We got it all on video. We'll take it back and analyze it." Paul bowed up with confidence.

Matthew looked at Angelica, then back to Paul, "Danced around each other, huh. Did you see a craft?"

"Not last night," Paul said as he smiled at Angelica while stepping toward her and extending his hand. "Hi, I'm Paul Colbeck."

"Sorry, how rude of me. This is Angelica Bradley with the *Liberator Magazine*. She's here to do a story on the mutilations," Matthew said.

"Fantastic to meet you, Angelica!"

"Nice to meet you as well," Angelica said as she released their handshake.

"What do you think so far?" Paul asked, completely straight-faced.

"I have to be honest with you Paul, I'm not much of a conspiracy theorist. I don't buy into the ET stuff." Angelica raised her eyebrows and shrugged her shoulders.

Paul laughed spontaneously. "It's nice to meet you all the same." He then looked at Matthew and winked.

Matthew looked down and shook his head. He couldn't help but get a kick out of Angelica's straightforwardness. "Let's step over here so you can see your first 'classic signature case.'"

Matthew walked away from Paul, and Angelica followed. They walked quietly for about seventy yards. "There she is." Matthew pointed down to the carcass. Angelica's eyes grew wide as she looked down to see the poor creature. She wasn't sure what the carcass was going to look like, but she had to admit it was nothing like she could have imagined.

The cow was on its back, its legs straight up in the air. Rigor mortis had set in, but surprisingly there was very little odor. The tissue on one side of the head and neck had been removed down to the skull with no blood splatter visible. As she leaned down over the carcass and took a closer look, she saw one of the eyes was missing along with one ear. "Why would they remove one eye and one ear?" she asked.

Matthew was beside her, but didn't respond to her question since he knew it wasn't directed at him. She was just trying to make sense of the situation as everyone does when they see a mutilated animal for the first time.

"It's hard to fathom that someone could be so cruel to an innocent creature," Angelica thought aloud. They both stood there for a moment and didn't say a word.

Matthew pulled a pencil from his pocket and stepped around to the other side of the carcass. "Take a look here at these two holes," he said as he used the pencil to point to what appeared to be gunshot wounds. Matthew put the pencil inside one of the holes and lifted it at the edge so it stretched enough for her to see the size. "See how precise it is?"

"Looks like a gunshot wound to me," Angelica announced.

Matthew paused and then nodded, "Well, it isn't. Does it look like a coyote bite?" Matthew asked sarcastically. "This is a 'classic signature' wound and after evaluation it was determined that it wasn't caused by a gun shot. They never are. As a matter of fact, the heart and other organs were removed and somehow sucked through these two small circular incisions, so we speculate. Makes you wonder, whatever did this wasn't all that concerned with the condition of the organs. Think about it. Look at the size of these holes. Can you imagine getting a five to six pound heart through this? Look at the condition of them? Exact, clean, no tearing and no blood, which suggests the use of a laser-like instrument. And according to a scientist friend of mine, this was done with surgical precision and done quickly."

Angelica's eyes were wide and her muscles tense. She was at a loss for the right words. "Oh," she mumbled after being a little mortified to realize her mouth was gasping. "But... wait, how do you know the organs were removed?"

"I was here when Dr. Goolrick and our local veterinarian did their examination."

Angelica took her cell phone from her pocket and took a few pictures of the carcass while walking around it.

Matthew stepped over and touched Angelica's shoulder. "Now Angelica, here is the really interesting part. Take a look..." Matthew leaned down onto one knee and pointed to the rectal area of the carcass. "This is very common to see with female cattle mutilations. It's not unusual to not only see anal coring but the teats, vagina and uterus extracted as well."

Angelica stepped closer to Matthew and leaned down to see a hole—twelve inches in depth—where the flesh had been removed from the anus. Angelica fought disgust. She looked back at Matthew in anguish. "Matthew, who would do such a thing? This is far beyond what I expected. When I read about it, my mind didn't quite register the scope of gruesomeness."

"Yep, I agree." Matthew wiped the sweat from his forehead with the rolled-up sleeves of his shirt.

"Okay Angelica, I want you to think about this... What's most compelling with the female cattle mutilations is, along with the digestive tract tissue being removed from the anal area, this case is a carbon copy of the surgical technique we've seen in so many so-called UFO-related animal mutilation cases. Are we supposed to believe someone outside of an expert surgeon would be capable of such a precise and difficult procedure? Even medical professionals are baffled."

Angelica looked at Matthew, "I don't know what to say. Matthew, why would someone be so interested in cattle? The government sure wouldn't need to mutilate rancher's cattle. They could do that on Plum Island or a myriad of other undisclosed locations. These are questions that need to be answered." Angelica shook her head, perplexed.

"It is definitely not a scavenger event, based upon my eyewitness account here today. That narrows it down to a hoax, or some other human deviousness. If we rule those out, then it really starts to get interesting," Angelica murmured.

Matthew stepped away from the carcass as he listened intently to Angelica and put his hands on his hips. "I think it is very important now for you to meet my friend, Dr. Walter Goolrick. I know he'll meet with you, but you'll have to go to Denver, I suspect. After getting to know you, he'll see you're not a typical journalist."

Angelica looked curiously at Matthew, "What do you mean by that?"

"Angelica, I don't believe in accidents. I think there's a reason you're here covering this mutilation. I can tell you're not going to make quick assumptions and you're not going to give up until you uncover the truth behind what's happening to these poor animals."

Angelica walked back around to the head of the carcass and bent down, then looked back up at Matthew and said, "Poor creature. Regardless of whether they're human or non-human... you're right, I want to know who did this and why."

The heat was starting to weigh down on them and Angelica was growing weary. Her blouse had moistened from sweat and was sticking to her back. She was pulling her blouse away from her wet skin as she heard a male voice in the distance.

"Hey there!" Jack Keller was approaching with a slight limp.

"Hey there!" he said again while waving as he walked toward them.

Angelica looked at Matthew, "That's Keller, isn't it?"

"Yep, that's him," confirming her suspicion. Jack stopped briefly to say something to Paul. Angelica noticed as the men laughed. Jack then continued toward Angelica and Matthew.

His suntanned skin caused him to appear older than his actual age of forty-five. He was a pleasant looking man with reddish-blonde hair and light brown eyes. He wore a dark tan cowboy hat and wranglers. Right down to his cowboy boots, he fit the part of a Montana rancher.

He extended his hand toward Matthew, "Good to see you, buddy! You can't stay away!" he chuckled and then looked at Angelica still smiling, "You must be the reporter from Washington!"

Matthew looked at Angelica with a sly grin. "Yep, this is Angelica Bradley from Washington, D.C. She's here to uncover the truth," Matthew said sarcastically.

Irritated, Angelica quickly looked at Matthew and then to Jack. "Well, you could say, I'm here to write about the incident, and hopefully uncover the truth whatever that ends up to be."

Jack looked at Matthew and then back to Angelica and frowned. "Pretty awful sight... That's one of my second-year heifers. I was pretty disappointed to see they got one of my heifers." Jack looked inquisitively over at Angelica trying to read her body language.

Angelica looked up at Jack and smiled while she reached into her bag and tried to retrieve her digital recorder, "Do you mind if I record our conversation? It would be for my notes. I would only publish what you agreed to release. You just say what's off the record. And I don't mind giving you an alias to protect you and your family."

Jack looked down at his boots as he slid them across the dry dirt, leaving a long imprint. Angelica looked intensely at Jack and patiently awaited his response.

"Look, Mr. Keller, I understand your situation, and I understand how difficult it must be to experience something so unusual. But it's in all of our best interest to find out what is happening to these animals and why it's happening."

Jack nodded at Angelica and then looked at Matthew, "I like her. Yes, thank you for your sincerity. I trust you'll keep your word. And call me Jack."

"Thank you!" Angelica turned on the recorder. "Let's start with the first mutilation on your ranch. In the police report, you stated that you were still in your car after returning home that evening when you noticed a bright light in the sky moving toward your pasture. Then you stated there appeared to be a spotlight shining down on your cattle, and after a few minutes, it disappeared. Is that correct?"

"Yes, that's correct. Actually, I heard an odd sound before I saw the light. My window was down... I was enjoying the evening air. The sound seemed to get louder as the light approached." Jack wiped the sweat from the back of his neck and continued... "At first, I thought it was some sort of military craft. I had never heard a sound like that before though, kind of a pulsating, humming sound. Almost like a sheet of metal being shaken back and forth, but it would have had to be a large sheet of metal to make a sound like that. I don't know how else to describe it, really. Other than it was loud... I'll say that!" Jack shook his head.

Angelica again felt that tingling sensation emanating from the back of her neck and down to her shoulders. "Humming?" she mumbled. Observing Jack's expression, Angelica realized Jack was also clearly uneasy talking about the incident. It was obvious he was still trying to make sense of it.

"Jack, you said a pulsating, humming type of sound?" *Was it the same sound she had heard in the middle of the night?* she wondered. A strange coincidence, she thought. She could feel the rapidness of her heart rate as it increased causing her to feel slightly faint. "Did you mention the sound to the police?"

Jack shook his head. "No."

"And you said 'pulsating,' correct?" Angelica rubbed at the side of her cheek with her pen grasped tightly in her palm.

"Yes, I said 'pulsating.'"

Angelica nodded, "Okay."

Angelica stepped in slightly closer, careful not to invade his personal space, a pet peeve of her own. "Could it also be described as a whooshing type sound?"

"Yes, most certainly. You know, come to think about it... I can't remember if I mentioned it or not. Heard it both nights."

Angelica tilted her head and looked at Matthew with a curious expression, "So you heard the sound again on the night of the second mutilation?"

"Yep, sure did. At first, I thought it was a helicopter, and then I realized it was the same sound I heard on the night of the first one..."

Angelica interrupted Jack, "That's right... I remember reading in the police report that at first you thought you heard a helicopter. And you are sure it was not a helicopter, is that correct?"

"Certain of it!" Jack raised his shoulders in confidence.

"Okay, anything else happen that first night?"

"Well, after the light moved around for a few minutes, it stopped, and after a second or two, disappeared. It wasn't until the next morning out on the ranch that I discovered one of my cattle all sliced up. I couldn't believe what I was seeing. As I was walking up, my first thought was that it had been attacked by a coyote. We have problems with coyote around here on occasion. But… upon closer inspection, I noticed there was no blood anywhere. Then I saw the cuts… the clean, precise cuts. Nothing like you'd see if a coyote got ahold of one of your cattle. It was strange so I grabbed a stick and poked around and noticed an eye was missing and an ear was gone. You'd think well, that would be normal in an attack by a coyote, but it looked as if someone had taken scissors to the ear and cut it clean off. I didn't feel right about it. And then it hit me… Whatever it was that caused the light and sound from the night before had something to do with it, so I jumped in my truck and drove back to the house to phone the Sheriff."

"What do you think it was?" Angelica asked cautiously.

Clearly made uncomfortable by the question, Jack answered with a slight hesitation. "I believe it was a UFO, Ms. Bradley. I know that sounds crazy, but I've tried to rationalize this over and over and I know what I saw, what I heard, and what my gut is telling me." His tone was flat. He stared Matthew straight in the eyes.

Watching his mouth as he finished his sentence… "Very interesting," Angelica said, careful not to sound condescending. "When you say UFO, do you mean to say, an alien craft?"

"Look Angelica, I know it's hard to believe, but…"

Matthew interrupted him, "Jack, it takes a lot of courage to tell your story, thank you."

"Yes, thank you, Jack!" Angelica said smiling warmly. Jack looked at both of them and tilted his head down, looking at the ground for a moment, then looking back up… "I don't understand why I had to be the unfortunate person to experience something like this, but it's changed my life and my faith to some degree. Angelica, I hope you can find some answers in your investigation. I'd like to know why they're cutting up our cattle."

Angelica could sense the emotion in Jack's voice. It struck her that Jack had said "faith". She drifted off for a moment, reflecting on her childhood thoughts of the possibility of other species existing out in the universe. With the innocence of a child, she wondered if there were other life forms out there, and if there were, were they created by the same God. Angelica caught herself drifting further from the present moment with Jack and Matthew. She stopped and refocused her attention.

"When I read the police report on the second incident, you reported the same occurrences on the night of the first incident. Was there anything different that happened that you may not have mentioned to the police?"

"Yes… there was…" Jack looked around nervously and then back to Angelica. His eyes appeared worried.

"I was standing on the front porch watching the light and when it stopped over the pasture and just stayed there... Well..." Jack looked visibly uncomfortable. "After a minute, I saw..." Suddenly Jack stopped in mid-sentence and looked out into the distance between Matthew and Angelica.

Angelica looked at Jack and said, "Yes, and?"

Matthew turned his head to see Jack's wife Elizabeth walking toward them.

"I'd rather Elizabeth not know everything. She's a fragile woman and she's been through a lot. I don't think it would do her any good to know the details."

Angelica looked at Elizabeth as she approached, "I understand".

Elizabeth was moving quickly toward them. Angelica noticed the golden highlights in Elizabeth's short dark blonde hair.

"Hi honey, this is Angelica Bradley with the *Liberator Magazine*, and you know Matthew."

"Yes," Elizabeth nodded at Matthew with a kind smile and then turned to Angelica, "Hello, I'm Elizabeth Keller, nice to meet you."

Angelica extended her hand to Elizabeth slowly, as if she were a porcelain doll, mindful of her fragility. "Hello Elizabeth, so nice to meet you," Angelica spoke softly and smiled.

A slight build, and cachectic blue veins protruding from her emaciated looking tan arms, the frail Elizabeth looked over at the carcass, "Gruesome isn't it? How long have you guys been out in this heat? Why don't you come inside into the air conditioning for some iced tea?"

"That would be nice, thank you," Angelica gleamed and looked over to Matthew, "How about some tea?" Angelica's blouse was moist and still clung to her back.

Matthew smiled at Elizabeth and spoke to her as if he were speaking to a toddler. "That sounds wonderful. We'll meet you back at the house after we say goodbye to Paul and the guys."

Angelica and Matthew walked away from Jack and Elizabeth toward the RUFA crew.

"Hey Paul, we're heading out. Are you guys gonna be around town any while you're here?"

"Yes, we usually show up at the billiards hall around dinner time. Why don't you come out and have a beer with us?"

"Sounds good, maybe tomorrow night I'll stop by. I'll touch base with you tomorrow," Matthew said as they continued past the group.

"Great, looking forward to it... Oh, and it's nice to meet you, Angelica."

Angelica was distracted, watching as Jack helped Elizabeth into his truck.

"And good luck with your story. I look forward to reading it," Paul shouted.

Angelica quickly turned around, "Thanks. It was nice to meet you, as well." Angelica smiled warmly.

Chapter Fifteen

Before Angelica could knock, Elizabeth showed up at the screened door. "Come on in."

Angelica felt at ease immediately with Elizabeth. A salt of the earth type of woman... kind but by appearance, feeble. Elizabeth seemed to be very open and accepting. As they stepped in, Angelica noticed Elizabeth already had two glasses of iced tea starting to sweat, sitting on the coffee table.

"Have a seat and relax, the tea is real sweet. Hope you like it that way," she said with a southern drawl.

"Are you originally from Montana?" Angelica asked as she took a seat on the sofa.

"No, I'm from Macon, Georgia."

"Really, what brought you to Montana?" Angelica leaned back curiously.

"Love," Elizabeth gleamed.

Intrigued, Angelica examined Elizabeth closely. Matthew immediately felt an inquisition about to unfold so he attempted to change the subject. "This is real good tea, Elizabeth," he announced.

Elizabeth looked over at Matthew, "Well, thank you. So, Angelica, what is your interest in the cattle mutilations here in Elberton?" Matthew watched as Elizabeth examined Angelica. He thought she was probably fascinated with Angelica's big city appearance.

"Angelica, your name is truly fitting. You have the face of an angel. Where do you live?"

"Thank you, Elizabeth, you're very kind... I live in Washington, D.C." Angelica looked at Jack as he squinted to suggest that Angelica not answer all of Elizabeth's questions. She raised her brows and peered back at Elizabeth.

"*The Liberator Magazine* is interested in what may be causing these mutilations," Angelica continued. "I'm an investigative journalist. I was with *The Washington Post* before I decided to start my own magazine."

Matthew eyes grew wide; he appeared impressed.

Elizabeth appeared surprised. "Wow, impressive, you look so young." Then Elizabeth turned serious. "Well, the first one happened about eleven or twelve years ago -- shocked us all. Poor Hugh Anderson, he really had a hard time after it happened on his ranch. It was the first incident here in Elberton. The town folk were suspicious of Hugh after that, or at least I think he felt they were. They were good people, the Andersons." Her voice was gentle.

Elizabeth continued. "Hugh's wife was a beauty... long black hair, dark skin and hazel eyes that would stop you dead in your tracks. The men in her family were coal miners. Their family settled here from Italy. It was real sad when she passed. Tragic... her death... She died suddenly." Elizabeth frowned.

"Hugh was never the same," she told them. "After her passing, I'd see him in town. He looked so sad and lost. He was pitiful. I think they were deeply in love. Oh and Michael, their son, broke my heart to see him lose his mother at such a young age, and he looked so much like her. Must have made it harder on Hugh... seeing such a strong resemblance of his wife every day."

Angelica leaned towards Matthew and whispered, "Can you set up an interview at the Anderson ranch?" Then she quickly turned back to Elizabeth. "I can't imagine... how sad."

Matthew got up from the sofa across from Elizabeth in her old rocking chair. "Yes, as a matter of fact, I'll call now and see if we can stop by there on our way back to the lodge." Matthew walked out the screen door, accidently letting it slam shut behind him startling Elizabeth and Angelica, causing them to flinch.

Angelica looked at Jack. He was leaning against the opening between the dining room and living room. "Was there anything unusual you remember? Or anything that stood out with the incidents on your ranch?" Angelica was peering at Jack, choosing her words carefully, mindful of Elizabeth.

"Well, let's see... It was a cold day. The air was sharp and frigid since winter had set in. I awoke earlier than usual. I remember lying in bed, staring out the window. I couldn't sleep so I decided to get on up. As I looked around for my overalls I sensed an eerie feeling in the air." Jack was reflectively peering off into the distance as he spoke.

Angelica was struck by Jack's detailed recollection as he recreated the scene in his mind. This story reminded her of why she loved being back in the field.

"I went downstairs to the kitchen where I found Elizabeth cooking. She's always up at dawn cooking my favorite breakfast – fried eggs, country ham, and biscuits with a warm fire burning in the fireplace." Jack glanced over and smiled at Elizabeth.

"After breakfast, I usually relax in the rocking chair in front of the fire, finish my coffee, and talk to Elizabeth about the chores to be done that day, and then we listen to the preacher on the radio. I'm not much of a religious man. I believe... but, well Elizabeth over here is a God-fearing, good woman." He looked over at Elizabeth and nodded. "She loves to talk in bed each night about the sermon from that morning and I enjoy listening." Jack walked over and sat in the other rocking chair.

"Anyway," he went on, "I had grown weary of the preacher shouting through the radio that morning, and knew I'd get the full version of it in bed that night, so I went on out to the ranch." He chuckled and winked at Matthew. Matthew smiled warmly at Elizabeth.

"Jackson!" Elizabeth interrupted playfully... she knew he was teasing her about the preacher. Jack looked over at Elizabeth and winked and she smiled in approval. Angelica thought they were a sweet couple, but she knew Jack was obviously trying to take his time to communicate the details about the mutilations without revealing too much to Elizabeth. Maybe even trying to throw Elizabeth off track, she thought. Angelica was sharp and understood his motive, but was frustrated nonetheless. She was fidgeting and nodding her head.

Jack leaned forward and placed a hand on each knee, "I stepped out onto the front porch and looked around for the herd, but they were nowhere in sight. It was a strange occurrence given the time of day, you know. The cattle were usually down around the feeder panels. As I looked around, something didn't quite feel right. I glanced around the ranch and realized the dogs were missing. Those dogs never left the perimeter of the house unless they were with me, or Elizabeth. Knowing the dogs liked to nap on the hay in the barn, I decided to look there first. When I went into the barn, the horses were grunting and snorting... They were pacing in circles around their stalls, acting wild. I realized something was wrong, and after searching the property, I noticed down by the reservoir one of the dogs."

Angelica, Matthew, and Elizabeth all sat and listened with rapt attention.

Jack tensed a little, just recalling the incident. "Once I got down there," he said, "I saw the other dog looking at the opening underneath the old outhouse so I bent down and looked in – and there was Rosie, one of our German Shepherds. She was trembling. The light was shining on her little blue eyes so I knew she was looking right at me but she wouldn't come to me. Something was clearly wrong with her so I reached my hand in to comfort her. 'Come on out girl', I said... 'It's okay.' Hell, she growled at me as if she were going to bite me. I couldn't believe it. This dog sat in my lap every night." Jack shook his head and looked at Elizabeth.

"Injured dogs have been known to bite their owners," Elizabeth said, as she glanced over and squinted in confidence at Angelica.

"Then I heard a voice coming from behind me," Jack continued, "so I turned around. It was my brother walking from the house. I yelled out to him that something was wrong with Rosie so he rushed down to help. After my brother lifted the corner of the outhouse, I reached in and pulled her out. She was shaking pretty bad. I examined her carefully, but she didn't appear hurt. She sure was scared; the way she was shaking... like she had seen a ghost! That dog's never been the same. Well..." Jack hesitated. His hands were gripped tightly together on his thighs. "When I looked away from that dog, I caught sight of a bright light in the sky. At first I thought it was a star but as I watched it, I noticed it was moving oddly, dancing around and flashing on and off. I didn't say anything to my brother. I watched it come close enough to realize it was no plane or helicopter. It was a moving ball of light." Jack stopped and slung his head downward. He had said more than he had intended to in front of Elizabeth. Elizabeth's eyes were grave as she sat and stared at him.

"Interesting," Angelica said anxiously, shifting in her seat.

"After it disappeared, I looked out at the pasture wondering what the hell was going on. Something didn't feel right and the night before with the..." Jack paused and then continued, "Well, anyway, it was very odd."

Angelica looked at Elizabeth who was staring at Jack strangely with her jaw dropped. When Elizabeth noticed Angelica was looking at her, she quickly rose from the sofa and smiled, "Would anyone like some more tea?"

Angelica realized she wasn't going to get a lot of facts about the mutilation from Jack as long as Elizabeth was around, so she stood up and said politely, "It was so nice to meet you. Thank you for having me in your home and for the iced tea. We should probably get going."

Elizabeth smiled and nodded, "Oh yes. We didn't mean to keep you so long." She smiled.

Angelica opened the screen door and turned back around before stepping out of the door, "Thank you again." Matthew had stepped off the porch and took his cell phone from his pocket.

Matthew glanced over at Angelica while talking on his cell phone outside. His second attempt to reach the Keller ranch was a success. "All right... well, looks like we may be heading your way now. Is that all right with you? ... Okay, great, see you soon." Matthew put his cell phone back into his pocket. "We can head on over to the Anderson ranch."

Angelica smiled at Matthew, "Perfect."

As they walked toward the car, Elizabeth hollered out to Angelica from the porch, "You don't believe ETs did it, do ya?!"

Angelica stopped and turned to look at Elizabeth, "No, I don't!" she stated confidently. Elizabeth raised her hand to wave bye and smiled. Matthew had already started the car. Angelica looked at Jack as she leaned down and got in the car. Jack's eyes said enough as they met hers. "These people are clearly scared," she thought.

Chapter Sixteen

Angelica glanced up. The beauty struck her instantly. Her eyes widened as they pulled onto the dirt drive leading to the large, rustic log home. Angelica looked over at Matthew, "It's beautiful!" she mused.

The Anderson home sat grandly nestled against tall pine trees with snow tipped mountains in the distance behind it.

Constructed with the same oversized logs as Elk Lodge. With many different angels to the roof, the cozy structure was an architectural wonder. A covered porch with four Adirondack rocking chairs, it was almost as exquisite as the Elk Lodge, she thought. The porch was supported by dark cherry stained logs stretched twenty feet high. Large windows were strategically positioned to take in the panoramic view of the property. The landscaping was perfectly groomed, resort-like. It made Angelica wonder if the same architect was used for both.

Next to the red-tin-roof barn, she could see the silhouette of a man standing beside a horse.

Un-groomed dark hair fell out around the edge of his black cowboy hat as he unsaddled a black horse. He was tall, well-built. Angelica looked over at Matthew, "Is that Michael?" she asked, shocked.

Matthew laughed. "Yes ma'am, that's him," Matthew shook his head.

Matthew was instantly taken with Angelica that morning in the restaurant, and he had started playing around with the idea they might become closer. However, at that moment in the car he understood they'd probably never be anything more than friends.

Michael turned around... a surprised, yet interesting grin lit up his face exposing perfect teeth, causing Angelica to turn to Matthew and smile, unaware of how obvious her reaction was.

Matthew rolled down the window as they pulled in and yelled, "How about it, Cowboy?" Michael laughed.

Matthew stopped the car and got out. Angelica grabbed her satchel from the floorboard. Hesitating for a moment, she put it back, flipped down the visor and took a quick look at herself in the mirror. She opened her mouth to check her teeth and quickly ran her fingers through her hair and fluffed it. Angelica grabbed her satchel, opened the door, and stepped out feeling a subtle nervousness.

Matthew and Michael were already talking as she walked toward them.

Michael glanced in her direction while speaking to Matthew. His expression changed – suddenly he appeared curious.

Angelica extended her hand and said, "Hello." Her tone soft and her posture unusually submissive.

Michael smiled, "Hello." His hazel eyes appeared light blue-green with specks of yellow between his thick black lashes.

Matthew was amused as he observed them silently hold eye contact for what felt like a long moment. He was well aware of Michael's effect on woman, however he had never seen that particular expression on Michael's face, and with a low chuckle and quick shake of his head he said, "Michael, this is Angelica Bradley with the *Liberator Magazine*."

Michael reached his tan, broad hand out slowly and placed it into Angelica's small hand, already extended.

Michael grinned once again exposing his perfect smile. "Hello, Angelica Bradley with the *Liberator Magazine*. Nice to meet you. So, you're doing a story on the cattle mutilations?" Michael asked as he kept his eyes locked on hers, taken with her beauty.

"Yes, I'd like to speak with you about the cattle mutilation on your ranch in 2000, if you don't mind," she said softly as she glanced away shyly making eye contact with Matthew and then back to Michael.

Michael broke eye contact, looked at Matthew and then back to Angelica... he was no longer smiling. Angelica's face felt red. She was startled by his reaction.

"I'll tell you what my father told me. I wasn't living here at the time it happened."

Matthew spoke quickly before Michael could finish his sentence... "Hugh was Michael's father and sadly passed away several years ago.

"Oh, I'm sorry for your loss," Angelica said sincerely.

"Michael came home to take over the ranch. He was off traveling the world like a big shot."

Michael interrupted Matthew, "Would you like to go in the house where it's more comfortable? I'll start coffee."

"Yes, thank you, coffee sounds nice," Angelica answered politely in a girlish way. Confused by her completely new persona, Matthew amused, looked over at Angelica suspiciously.

Michael patted his horse on the back and then walked toward the house. Matthew led the way as they stepped up onto the high vaulted porch and into the silent house. Michael's house was well kept. A large grey cobblestone fireplace took the show and above it hung mounted antlers. Angelica was convinced that it was the same team that assembled the Elk Lodge. The décor was rustic western, yet stylish. Original art and photography from different regions of the world hung on the walls.

There were spectacular views of the ranch from each window.

Angelica took in a breath and whispered, "Wow." Looking up she noticed wood beams held together by big black iron bolts, and noticed a loft with a view through the tall a-frame windows along the front of the house. She wondered if the loft was Michael's bedroom. Looking back down, she saw the men were in the kitchen talking. Michael was starting a pot of coffee while Matthew was pulling a chair out from the table.

Angelica walked into the kitchen. "You have a beautiful home. It looks like new construction."

"Yes, I had the house renovated a few years ago. We practically tore the old house down, but kept most of the original hardwood floors. I put in the grey slate countertops and the stainless steel. Knocked out all the walls to open it up... Got rid of the second floor and created a loft. Big project," Michael said as he turned around to take the cream from the refrigerator.

"Michael's a city cowboy," Matthew said, smiling mischievously at Michael. Angelica noticed Michael giving Matthew a mocking look while narrowing his eyes.

"That's an oxymoron!" Angelica said as she laughed. "Well, he certainly has good taste," she whispered softly as she glanced back around.

Angelica pulled the chair out and sat down at the table beside Matthew, "I guess we should get started," Matthew suggested.

"Oh, yes... you're right!" Angelica pulled out her pad and pen and didn't hesitate, "What can you tell me about the cattle mutilation?" Angelica asked in true journalist's tone. Angelica leaned over and grabbed her digital recorder from her satchel.

Michael looked at Matthew and raised his brow causing his forehead to wrinkle, "I'd rather you not record the conversation, Ms. Bradley."

Angelica rose and softly pushed her hair back away from her neck, "Oh, okay," her voice dropped. She laid it down on the table, "I understand."

Michael sat down at the table, "Like I said, all I can tell you is what my father shared with me before his death. He was very ill toward the end. I was traveling back here to the ranch as often as I could to be with him. We'd do a lot of fly fishing and cooking, you know... just talking and spending time together, that's when he shared bits and pieces with me." Michael gazed at Angelica. For a moment, his eyes appeared vacant.

"My father was a good man." Michael said with a reflective expression, but Angelica noticed a deep sadness in his eyes. She felt that pull and turn in her chest as she sat there for a minute and observed his face.

Matthew looked gently at Michael, "Tell Angelica what your father shared with you."

Michael looked down, "One evening we were in the kitchen sitting down for dinner and he said, 'Michael, I need to share something with you about the night of that cattle incident.' I said 'okay, what is it, Dad?' He looked serious. He was usually smiling or laughing and cutting up, so I knew by the tone of his voice that this was important."

"He was an honest man," Michael continued, "hell, I don't think my dad ever told a lie in his life." Michael looked up as Matthew turned away, trying to hide sympathy.

Angelica looked at Michael and smiled sincerely, then lowered her eyes with an expression of concern, "What did he tell you about the incident?" she asked softly.

"He said he saw some strange things and he had never told a soul. He said no one would have believed him anyhow. They would have had him locked up in one of those loony hospitals. I told him I'd believe him no matter how crazy it sounded. He went on to say that he was shutting up the barn for the evening a little after six and noticed a light in the sky off in the distance. He said the light got larger as it moved closer to the ranch. He didn't think too much about it and just figured it was a helicopter or aircraft from the Newton Base. However, it was making a strange buzzing sound, unlike a typical plane, so he stood there for a minute and watched it. All of a sudden, he said he saw a flash of light and then felt dizzy."

Angelica's jaw dropped, "That's interesting."

"Then he woke up on the ground by the barn. He said he was confused and disoriented. He got up, dusted himself off and went into the house, and when he got inside the time on the old grandfather clock was eight-thirty."

"Dad was a punctual guy," Michael continued, "and went by a schedule. He always closed the barn up and was in the house around six-thirty every evening. He would clean up and prepare his dinner by seven or seven-thirty. He said he couldn't figure out where the time had gone. He was baffled, couldn't figure it out... waking up on the ground after seeing the flash of light. He said 'It really bothered me, son, I couldn't shake the feeling something had happened to me during the time I was unconscious. He didn't believe he'd had a stroke. I asked him if he was sure. He said other than being confused and a bit disoriented, he 'felt fine.'"

Angelica looked up from the pad and raised her pen in the air as she spoke. "So, he passed out by the barn after seeing a strange light in the sky?"

Michael met her eyes. "Yes! He also noticed a puncture wound about the size of a pea on his lower abdomen and there was dried blood around one of his nostrils. He said the hair around the wound was gone. He was shocked, as you can imagine. He said he knew for certain it wasn't there before he went unconscious, and he would have felt it if it had happened while working on the ranch that day."

"What did he think caused it?" Angelica asked while examining Michael's face.

"He didn't know."

"Couldn't he have landed on something when he fell... maybe on some sort of farming equipment?" she asked.

Michael thought for a minute, "Maybe, however he said the wound had completely..." Michael hesitated and glanced nervously toward Matthew. "He said the wound was gone the next morning."

"Really?" Angelica blurted out unable to hide her shock.

Matthew looked over at the coffee pot and noticed it was full. Careful not to interrupt the conversation, he quietly got up and opened the cabinet doors and searched for the cups. "Sorry to interrupt, but everyone wants coffee, right?"

Both Angelica and Michael said, "Yes, thank you," but never looked his way.

"No cream please, just black," Angelica announced.

Angelica noticed behind Michael, through the large pane-less window in the living room, brown pine swirled in the wind. "It's very peaceful here."

"Yes, it's comfortable," Michael replied softly.

Angelica glanced around as she thought for a moment... "Yes, it is." Angelica moved in her seat to fully face Michael. "What happened next?"

"Well, he said after he showered and dressed the wound, he ate his dinner and went to bed. After a few days, he had forgotten about it. Then about a week later, he was sitting in the chair on the front porch reading and he heard the strange noise again. When he looked up, he saw the light in sky.

This time it was already pretty close, right out over the pasture. He sat there and watched it. He said it was spotlighting his cattle." Michael scratched his head and looked nervous. "He said it stayed in one spot for a second or two and then he said he saw one of his cattle get sucked up into the beam of light. Sucked right up into the beam of light... can you believe that?" Michael planted his palm on the table firmly and laughed nervously.

"Wait a minute!" Angelica almost stood up in disbelief, "Did he say 'sucked up?' He said he saw one of his cattle sucked into the beam of light?"

"Yes, he did," Michael said defensively as he sat up straight -- ready for her to challenge him. Angelica observed Michael's body language and looked down at her pad, before looking back up inquisitively.

Michael was uncomfortable. He shifted in his seat and anxiously rubbed his palms together, clenching them tightly. "I know how this sounds, but my father would never lie. He just wasn't that type of man." Michael shook his head. "I don't know what to think." He released a deep breath.

Angelica bit down on her bottom lip. "Was he taking any medication during this time? You said he was sick."

Michael quickly responded. "He was sick when we talked about it in 2006, but back in 2000, he was healthy as an ox. When he first told me in 2006, he hadn't begun the treatment for his cancer and was still pretty together. It wasn't until they started giving him the chemo toward the end that things started to change for him. He got really sick." Michael glanced into the kitchen at Matthew before turning back and making eye contact with Angelica.

"I'm sorry for your loss... You lost your mother as well, right?" Angelica hesitated. "I didn't mean to be rude... Elizabeth Keller mentioned it... Must have been tough to lose both parents."

"Yes, it was. Thank you." Michael smiled sincerely.

Angelica quickly changed the subject, "So Matthew, did you know about this? About the floating cow?"

Matthew nodded his head. "Yes."

Michael spoke before Matthew could finish his sentence. "Yes, I told Matthew one night over a few beers, in confidence. We were talking about Jack Keller and I needed to get it out. I hadn't told anyone about what my father had said up until that point.

Look, I'm still not sure how I feel about telling you this information." Michael was antsy, "I don't want my father's name, or mine, for that matter, in your magazine. And frankly, I think the only reason I'm sitting here telling you now is because of Matthew."

Angelica leaned back in her chair. "I see."

"I hope you will treat my family and the others in this town with respect, and I trust you will do a good job reporting the story, in a discreet manner."

Angelica sensed Michael's father had told him more. "Yes, you have my word. What else did you father tell you?" Angelica leaned forward intently.

"He said there are things going on just too shocking to comprehend."

"What things going on, Michael? Are you saying you and your father believe it was something beyond this world?"

"Yes, I think I do, and after talking to Jack today, don't you, as well?"

Angelica appeared puzzled. She shot a curious look at Matthew. "Well, it was an interesting conversation, but..."

Michael looked at Matthew before interrupting Angelica. "Jack didn't tell her?"

"No, Elizabeth walked up." Matthew answered.

Angelica looked anxious. "Tell me what?"

Matthew took a deep breath. "The same thing happened on his ranch the night of the second incident. Jack was about to tell you before he saw Elizabeth walking up. You see now why he didn't want her to hear the conversation. She's a very religious woman and it could shake her faith." Matthew shook his head. Michael appeared concerned.

Angelica's mouth fell open slightly, "Oh! So what you are trying to tell me is that he saw one of *his* cattle sucked up into a beam of light, as well?" Angelica shook her head briskly and rolled her eyes.

"Yes," Matthew answered. "He didn't tell the police. He's only told me, as far as I know."

Angelica's face went flat. "Okay, go on…"

Michael looked at Matthew approvingly, "Go on—tell her the rest."

Matthew walked over and sat back down at the table. "Angelica, he said his cow was lifted into that white beam of light, almost as if it were sucked up by a vacuum… He ran down toward the pasture and stood there looking up. He said he heard a loud humming noise and he yelled, 'What do you want?' That's when the light went out and then came back on. He said he kept yelling, 'Leave my cattle alone! What the hell do you want? Who are you?' He said he could hear it but he couldn't see it - the light was too bright. Then the light went out and it was gone, it just vanished. When I interviewed him, I shared some of Michael's father's experiences, and since he trusts me… Well, he said it scared the hell of out him so he went in the house, found an old bottle of whiskey, and got wasted, and he hadn't had a drop of alcohol in ten years before that night. He said Elizabeth had to help him up the stairs and get him into bed. The next morning, he lay in bed worrying if he was going to find one of his cattle dead, and what he would say to Elizabeth," Matthew paused.

Angelica looked lost as she surveyed Matthew's face. "Go on," she mumbled.

"When he finally got up the courage to go check… well, he found it, and that morning he knew for sure he was dealing with something very scary and unexplained."

"Okay", Angelica interjected… "But could it possibly be something that is obvious? There is an Air Force base around here, right?"

"Yes, however I don't believe it's military. Now, that's not to say that they aren't involved in some way. It's hard to believe that this could be happening right under their noses without their knowledge," Matthew said, confidently.

Matthew took a breath and got up from the table, "More coffee anyone?" Angelica looked at Michael, but didn't speak, still trying to take it all in.

Michael sat silently observing Angelica. "How long are you in Elberton?" Michael asked.

Angelica glanced back at Michael. His eyes were intense with desire. She did a double-take, completely caught off guard. She felt an odd sensation in her stomach. It took a moment to find her voice, and finally answered, "I don't know? As long as I need to be, I suppose."

Matthew now standing beside the table put his coffee cup down firmly to break Michael and Angelica's penetrating eye contact. "I should probably get Angelica back to the lodge. It's been a long day, and I'm sure she's starting to get tired."

"Yes, thank you. It has been a long and unusual day." Angelica placed her pad and pen in her satchel. "Thank you for agreeing to the interview, and for the coffee." Angelica took one last sip of her coffee and put the cup down on the table. She looked down and thought for a moment, and then back at Michael. "Do you mind speaking with me again before I leave town?" she asked. "I'd like to hear more in regards to your father's experiences?"

Michael nodded, "Sure... But I believe I've told you just about everything I know. Let's see, tomorrow I'm tied up all day but the following day would work. I'll be finished up around two o'clock in the afternoon, so could you be here around two-thirty?"

"Two-thirty is perfect." Angelica turned and started slowly toward the front door, admiring the art in the living room as she walked away.

At the door, Angelica stopped and looked back at Michael. "Bye," she said girlishly as she raised her hand, and then turned and stepped out.

Michael looked at Matthew and smiled. Matthew tilted his head, and laughed before whispering, "Oh man, I see where this is going. You'd have to be blind not to notice what was going on between the two of you." Michael patted Matthew on the back as they walked to the door.

Already outside and almost to the car, Angelica's subconscious scolded her. "You're working a story, stop flirting," she thought aloud. Suddenly she noticed Matthew on his way back to the car.

Matthew opened the door and sat down while smiling at Angelica suspiciously. "You got him in your head, I can see it in your eyes," his voice hypnotic.

Angelica didn't respond as she thought about Matthew's words. She turned quickly and nervously to look out of the passenger window, catching a glimpse of Michael as he walked back into the house.

As she and Matthew drove down the driveway, Angelica said, while unable to make eye contact with Matthew... "Michael is interesting, isn't he?" She bit down on her index fingernail. "Not your typical cowboy... well, you know what I mean... He's cultured." She peered reflectively out of the windshield in front of her.

Matthew glanced over and smiled as he whispered, "Interesting, huh?"

They turned off the dirt drive back onto the main road, as she mumbled to herself... "Very interesting."

Chapter Seventeen

She breathed appreciatively. "Thank you for today," she said softly. Matthew turned and smiled at Angelica.

The evening sky was partly cloudy. It had become cobalt blue. Rays of red and pink casted down between the clouds onto the lodge, creating a warm glow. "Just lovely here, don't you think?" she announced as they pulled back up to the lodge.

"Yes, beautiful place," Matthew answered. "So, I'll work on lining up the interview for tomorrow with Ellen McKinney. What time works for you?"

"Anytime is fine with me. I'm feeling jetlagged, so I'll probably wait to work on my laptop until in the morning. So ten?" Angelica grabbed her satchel and got out of the car.

"I'll be here in the morning, say, around eleven o'clock to pick you up. That way you're not rushed. We can grab coffee or lunch with the Sheriff at the diner in town. I'll work it out and let you know in the morning."

"That sounds great, thanks Matthew." Angelica started to shut the car door and then stopped. She leaned down. "Really, thank you for all your help, I'm sure you're busy. I do appreciate it."

Matthew grinned, "No problem, I'm enjoying it, actually... gets a little boring around here at times."

Angelica narrowed her eyes and smiled, "Sounds like things have been anything but boring around here."

Chapter Eighteen

Angelica's eyes shot open. She felt panicked as she surveyed the room. She turned and looked at the clock to notice it was three thirty-three in the morning. She slowly lowered her chin and saw the goose down comforter on the floor beside the bed.

Angelica was burning up and drenched in sweat so she quickly peeled the sheets away from her wet body, while at the same time, she noticed a humming sound faintly descending, and then gone. Her nightmare had left her disoriented and immediately depressed. There was an odd heaviness in her uterus. It was that same familiar feeling after a vaginal examination from her doctor.

Angelica rubbed her belly while she got out of the bed, feeling increasingly worried, and found her suitcase. She pulled out an oversize Red Sox t-shirt she had confiscated from an old boyfriend. More comfortable in her own sleepwear, she went into the bathroom.

Angelica noticed the heaviness in her uterus again while she sat on the toilet. She couldn't ignore the strange and subtle feeling of pressure in her pelvic area. She ran her hand through her hair trying to re-orient her mind. Angelica turned out the light, walked over to the French door leading to the balcony and just stood there in a daze staring at the half moon shining down and reflecting off the Elk Creek stream.

The Bovine Connection

A peaceful feeling began to slowly emerge from her core as she realized she was exhausted. She pulled the heavy curtains shut, and walked over to the bedside table to make sure the alarm was set. She lifted the goose down comforter back onto the bed, and pulled the covers up to her neck, curled around the bedding and fell back sleep.

Angelica awoke to the alarm still buzzing at eight thirty-three. She had set it for eight thirty so she had some time before meeting Matthew out front. Forgetting her macabre dream, she jumped out of the bed and picked up the phone, ordering her usual coffee and bowl of fruit. Angelica walked over and opened the curtains to let in the sunlight.

She slowly turned around and looked for the hotel robe, and noticed it was hanging on the closet door. She stepped quickly across the floor and slipped it on over her Red Sox t-shirt.

She opened the French doors to the balcony where there were two rustic lounge chairs, crafted from cedar. She tilted her head back and took a deep breath. She then closed her eyes, and listened to the rumbling of the river rapids. Angelica's thoughts drifted to the day before on Michael's ranch.

His eyes penetrating, his unruly silky black hair, his smile - he was perfection, she thought. He looked like a man from a vintage romance novel when she first noticed him standing by his horse. Angelica let out a sigh and bit down on her lower lip.

Angelica quickly caught herself and decided to let the fantasy go, and with a pouty puff of air she sank deeper into the chair.

After a day filled with dead cattle and handsome men... she was anxious to see where the story was headed next. Angelica couldn't help but laugh as she recalled some of the details from the interviews the day before. It all sounded so crazy. *"Were these people all nut jobs?"* she wondered.

After a moment, Angelica stood up and went inside. She pulled her pad of notes from her satchel and opened her laptop.

There was a knock at the door. Startled, she rushed through the room and opened the door. The server came in.

"Where would you like your tray?"

"On the desk is fine, thank you."

"Lovely day isn't it?"

Angelica didn't answer, she had glanced back over to the desk, distracted by the notes she was deciphering from the Michael Anderson interview. However, the server didn't appear to take it personally.

"Enjoy your stay", he said as he shut the door behind him. Angelica still distracted, poured her coffee and laughed. "Why am I thinking about that cowboy Michael Anderson when there appears to be a lot more interesting men roaming around here in Elberton? ... Little green ones..."

Chapter Nineteen

Angelica hovered in the valet area for a moment watching the guests as they loaded luggage into their rental cars, until she noticed Matthew sitting in his car reading a newspaper.

Angelica walked up to Matthew's window and knocked, causing him to jump in surprise, crumpling the page of the newspaper as he lowered it to see what the noise was.

"You startled me!" He laughed.

Angelica smiled smugly. "Good Morning."

Matthew leaned over and moved the rest of the newspaper out of the passenger seat by placing it in the backseat.

Angelica put her satchel on the floorboard and got in.

"Good Morning, lovely lady! How did you sleep?"

"Same as usual, thank you. Were you waiting long?" Angelica smiled sincerely.

"No, just a few minutes."

"Good! So, what's on the agenda for today?"

Matthew started the engine and pulled out of the valet area. "We are meeting Sheriff Taylor at the town diner, and then we'll head over to Ellen McKinney's place."

"Perfect!" Angelica leaned back, shifted in her seat, and looked out the window as they drove off.

Coming off the mountain and onto the main road, Angelica glanced over to notice Matthew was fidgeting.

"So how'd you like Michael? Great guy, huh?" Matthew asked. Matthew was curious. He wanted to observe Angelica's reaction as he teased her about Michael.

Angelica looked back out her window. "He was nice," she said, trying to cover up any indication that she might be interested in him.

"Nice?" Matthew laughed sarcastically. "Hum, he was nice?" Matthew laughed again with less sarcasm. "Sure looked like you two had a connection."

"Really, it did?" Angelica swung her head around and looked at Matthew surprised, and then slowly turned back around to look out the window.

"Interesting," she said softly.

Matthew shook his head. "Nice... Interesting... You're interesting." He chuckled. Angelica flashed him a quick smile.

"Okay, so changing the subject... What are you thinking about all this UFO stuff so far?" Matthew asked in western slang.

Angelica pursed her lips and narrowed her eyes. She needed time to think. "I don't know, Matthew. Michael was convincing... He appeared to be telling the truth yesterday. He seemed very sincere." Angelica frowned and pursed her lips. "And Jack Keller was obviously trying to hide something from Elizabeth... and then there was the carcass. There just has to be a more believable explanation."

Matthew nodded. "Yeah, it will get stranger after you meet with Ellen McKinney, for sure."

Angelica looked at Matthew. "So what keeps you in this small town? Oh, by the way, do you mind stopping by the liquor store later? I need something for the room."

Matthew nodded. "Sure don't... can't blame you."

Angelica inserted... "Trouble sleeping, you know."

"To answer your question... it is a small town, and not a lot to do, but it's home."

Angelica looked over at Matthew, observing his side profile. An average build, he was geeky, but handsome, she thought. He had an all-American look.

"So, why aren't you a cowboy?" Angelica giggled sarcastically.

Matthew turned and looked at Angelica, caught off guard by the question. "Thought we covered the cowboy thing." He laughed.

"Well, my father was a rancher. His ancestry went all the way back to when his family first settled in Montana, about the time the cattle industry first started here." His voice was deep as he shot a glance at Angelica.

There was something in Matthew's tone when he spoke about his father, almost bitter, she thought. Angelica was curious. She analyzed him closely as he continued to speak about his past.

"The rancher lifestyle has been in our family for generations. It just wasn't for me," he said dryly as he glanced back over at Angelica. "I had my head in books, an inconvenient hobby for someone growing up in

Elberton, Montana." He shook his head as he reflected back on his childhood.

"I wanted to write, dreamed of writing since the day I discovered my passion for it. I didn't get along with my father. He was a hard man." Matthew's tone became even more bitter

Angelica frowned. "Oh."

"He didn't like my interest in the page, thought I was an embarrassment. He was disappointed." Matthew's eyes grew grave.

Angelica looked down… "How difficult."

Matthew looked over at Angelica clearly moved by her sympathy. "Anyway, how'd I get started on this conversation?" He laughed, "Oh, I forgot, I'm with an investigative journalist."

Angelica looked sincerely into his eyes. Matthew did a double take and then looked ahead at the road.

"You don't have to talk about it. I find you fascinating--that's all."

Matthew nodded and smiled. "I'm fascinating--that's good to know. Thank you for saying that. Well, when I was growing up, I'd hear my father in his bedroom, right beside mine, loudly stumbling around as he did each morning, bumping into furniture all pissed off from the hangover he had brought upon himself from the night before. I wasn't much of a morning person myself, so I tried to stay out of his way. Not to mention, I definitely wasn't eager to be up at dawn to shovel horse shit." Matthew looked irritated. "My father would push my door wide open and with red, bloodshot eyes, and a rage in his voice, he'd say …

'Ranchers don't have the luxury of sleeping in, boy. You better get used to the dawn.' Those are my childhood memories." He laughed sarcastically.

Angelica wrinkled her forehead. She felt sorry for him. "Was it all bad?" she asked softly.

"Not really, I had my grandparents, you know, my mother's folks. They encouraged me to continue with my writing. Grandfather told me, 'You don't have to feel guilty for not following in your father's footsteps. The rancher's way of living is not for everyone.' He'd say, 'Stay true to yourself and follow your own path.' So, I did. I was the first male on my father's side to go to college. Besides, my older brother has always been my father's favorite. Anyhow, I'm happy." Matthew peered over at Angelica suspiciously. "How'd you get all that out of me?" He chuckled.

"Have you ever thought about leaving Elberton?" Angelica tilted her head inquisitively.

"You know, Angelica, some of us have no desire to live a fast-paced lifestyle, and look around you at this view." Matthew took his hand off the steering wheel and waved it around. "So many people come here to escape and take their vacation. Hell, I get to see this every day."

Angelica looked out of the window at the mountains in the distance and exhaled. "That's great, Matthew." Angelica's index finger glided softly along the top of her lip. "I do grow weary of D.C. from time to time. I could definitely come back here... to get away."

Matthew smiled, "I hope you will... come back."

Chapter Twenty

Matthew pulled up to the curb just outside the old-fashioned diner on the corner of the town square. "Well, here we are!"

Angelica got out and looked up at the diner's old sign. Matthew had grown up in Elberton so she imagined he had spent a lot of time at what appeared to be the only hangout that didn't serve liquor within a twenty miles radius. She thought about him as a young man, sipping milkshakes, loaded with whipped cream and a signature cherry on top while reading the Alfred Hitchcock book series, "The Three Investigators." She had read it herself when she was young, and wondered if Matthew had too.

Angelica kept pace behind him as they entered into the loud room. She heard the old tin bell chime against the glass door as it shut behind her.

She noticed a blonde woman in her early thirties staring at her. Angelica felt uncomfortable. As Angelica passed by her, the lady glanced away with a crooked smile.

Angelica was clearly an outsider in a small town. She noticed several people with the same piercing stare, as she walked by.

There was a time when Angelica would have been offended. These people had no clue what she had gone through, even being spit on while trying to question an indicted Councilman while he was making his way into the courthouse. She knew it was par for the course, so she took it for what it was... humanity at its finest. She clutched her purse tightly and continued behind Matthew.

Matthew caught the awkward stares and low whispers so he casually turned around to Angelica. "Don't let it bother you, just smile and nod. They've had their share of big city folks that come over from Elk Lodge."

An older lady with tanned, leather skin walked up. "Hello, Matthew! Who you got here?"

"Hi Bev, this is Angelica Bradley with the *Liberator Magazine*. She's in town from D.C., doing a story."

Bev appeared friendly, but uninterested. "Well, that's just nice... what will y'all be having today?"

Matthew rubbed his hand together like a boy and with his boyish smile he stated, "How about a slice of that chess pie, and some coffee." Matthew responded a little too excited, Angelica thought, as she laughed inwardly.

Bev looked to Angelica. "And you, honey?"

"I'll have the same, thank you."

They sat down in the booth. Angelica glanced around the diner to see if the patrons were still staring at her. There were a few quick glances her way, but everyone appeared to be pretending to mind their own business.

The bell on the door chimed again, and in walked Sheriff Taylor, all neat and groomed in his brown official uniform. He took his hat off as he came in and rubbed his hand across the top of his forehead to smooth the black hair back into place, at the same time wiping away the shine of sweat.

He was a thin man and in his late fifties. He appeared to be a happy, confident man. As he crossed the room toward Angelica and Matthew, he stopped and talked with the town folk along the way.

Angelica found the Sheriff amusing to watch. He was a politically savvy showman. He would gently pat a person on the shoulder, then roll his head back and let out an obnoxious chuckle, giving the impression he was genuinely interested in the conversation.

It was obvious he was well-liked and respected by the people in the town. He finally made his way over to the booth. He wiped his palm across his forehead to smooth his hair once again while he placed his sheriff's hat on the hook fixed to the side of the booth.

Sheriff Taylor's voice was assertive. "Hello, Matthew!"

Matthew got up from the booth. "Hello, Sheriff. This is Angelica Bradley with the *Liberator Magazine*."

Angelica rose up from the table and extended her hand. "Nice to meet you, Sheriff!"

"Call me Bob," he said with what appeared to be a fake smile as they all sat down.

Angelica turned to smirk discreetly. Sheriff Bob Taylor... this would make a great Twilight Zone episode, she thought.

"So you're here to investigate the cattle mutilations?" Sheriff Taylor stated, direct and to the point.

"Yes, I came in from D.C. two days ago. This is not typically my type of story. I'm more of a political investigative journalist," Angelica stated with an arrogant air as she sat her coffee cup down.

Sheriff Taylor held eye contact as he tried to size her up, as people usually did with Angelica.

"So what's your take on the mutilations, Bob?" Angelica reached down and grabbed her recorder from her satchel.

"Hold up young lady, I need to get me a piece of that famous chess pie and cool off with some cold sweet tea. It's a hot one out there," he smiled and looked at Bev while she placed Matthew's and Angelica's pie down in front of them.

"Oh yes, sorry." Angelica nodded blankly.

"So… you want my opinion. Well, I don't believe little grey men are doing it, like Matthew over here, if that's what you're asking," the sheriff said, as he nudged Matthew with his elbow and chuckled. Matthew rolled his eyes.

"Honestly, Ms. Bradley, I'm not sure what to make of all this mutilated cow stuff. I've been investigating the incidents since the first one back in 2000 at the Anderson ranch. I thought it was probably from coyote. Then, after examining the carcass and speaking with the local vet, I thought maybe it was a revenge killing."

Bev walked up and placed the sheriff's pie and tea down in front of him.

"I suspected a dispute may have taken place between Hugh Anderson and somebody, but couldn't find any evidence to suggest that was the case. And frankly, Hugh wasn't the sort of guy to cause anyone hard feelings." The sheriff looked at Angelica as he cut a bite-sized piece of pie. "Love the chess pie here!"

Sheriff Taylor, holding his fork like a shovel, cut off another rather large piece of pie and took another bite, and with his mouth full, went on to say... "Then we started looking at the possibility that we had some sort of sicko on our hands."

Angelica couldn't help but notice the pie moving around in his mouth as he spoke. Trying to focus on what he was saying instead of his lack of manners, she nodded her head and maintained eye contact.

"After all the leads ran dry," the sheriff said, "we put the file away and as time passed, we moved on."

Angelica took a bite of her pie. "Delicious," she thought. She hadn't had chess pie since she was a young girl in Asheville.

"That was, of course, until the second mutilation that occurred on the Keller ranch," the sheriff told her. "When I got the call, I thought 'here we go again.' That's when we were put in contact with Dr. Walter Goolrick, the Chief Veterinarian of Sciences over at the University of Colorado. Dr. Kenneth Tidwell, we call him KT, who is our local veterinarian, recommended him. KT was just as perplexed as we were."

Angelica heard the door chime again. She glanced around to notice a young man and woman walk into the diner. Her attention had wandered. Sheriff Taylor cleared his throat causing Angelica to turn back around and see he had paused waiting for her attention. Angelica was fully alert. "Yes, go on," she said.

"Dr. Goolrick concluded that the wounds were surgical," the sheriff said, "due to the 'incisions and extraction of internal organs,' were his words. The incisions were too precise, he said. Someone took great care and probably speed while cutting up that animal. That was, as you can imagine, quite disturbing news. We realized we were dealing with a sicko who had some smarts."

"Interesting!" Angelica exclaimed. "Yes, I read his report, as well. Did you follow any leads in pursuit of this sicko?" After asking the question, Angelica glanced over at Matthew. Matthew raised his eyebrows and tightened his lips. Angelica looked back at the sheriff.

"We've pursued every possible lead and they all lead nowhere," the sheriff told her. "Here in this small town, we may appear dumb, but we're not. I was born at night, just not last night, Ms. Bradley."

Angelica looked intensely at the sheriff wondering if, and how she had offended him... "So you don't believe any of the other theories out there?"

"Ms. Bradley, are you asking if I believe in ETs?" Sheriff Taylor put his fork down on the side of his plate, turned and looked around the room before looking back at Angelica. "No, and don't get that crap started again in this town!"

Matthew and Angelica were equally surprised, and Angelica was offended. She squinted suspiciously and although she was struggling to believe the ET theory, she challenged the sheriff. "Really, you haven't entertained any thought that there might be something truly unusual going on around here?"

Sherriff Taylor rolled his eyes and dramatically shook his head.

Angelica didn't believe the sheriff. She saw the look in his eyes and she knew his type. She dealt with those assholes every day in D.C. She knew that even if an alien beamed down right in front of him, he'd later deny it ever happened for the sake of his sanity. Remembering that neither Hugh Anderson nor Jack Keller told the sheriff everything they had witnessed on the nights of the mutilations, she dropped it.

Angelica turned off the recorder. "Would it be all right if I come by the station and take a look at the files?"

"That'll be fine," he stated confidently. "I'll have them ready for you. Just ask for Sergeant Hamilton and he'll show you to them. However, your editor has already been sent copies of everything we have so it may be wasted time."

"Oh," Angelica said softly. "Well, thank you."

Matthew shifted in his seat and put his hands on the table. "Well, thank you, Sheriff, for meeting with us," Matthew grabbed the check and they got up from the booth.

"You'll let me know what you uncover before you leave," he said directly to Angelica with a stern look in his eyes. The sheriff announced throughout the diner for everyone to hear, "The pie was delicious, as usual… Outstanding!"

Bev, who was walking to the cash register to meet him said, "Glad you liked it, Sheriff."

Sheriff Taylor turned and looked back at Angelica. "Hope you're enjoying your stay at the Elk Lodge... Impressive place!"

Angelica smiled and agreed, then glanced around to see Michael standing outside on the curve helping an attractive brunette woman into the passenger side of his black Escalade. Her heart fluttered. The woman was stunning. Angelica suspected she was his girlfriend.

As she and Matthew walked out of the diner, Michael and the woman drove off. Suddenly self-conscious, she changed her expression in case Matthew noticed. "Ellen McKinney, huh... This should be interesting."

"Yes, this will be an interview worth remembering." Matthew laughed.

Chapter Twenty-One

It was very quiet in the car. Angelica was thinking about Michael and the beautiful woman. *Why couldn't she stop thinking about Michael?* she wondered.

"Do you mind if I stop by my house and grab something?" Matthew asked.

"As long as you stop at that liquor store first." Angelica pointed to an old western style building with cherry stained cedar shingles and a front porch held up by two large posts.

Matthew pulled into the front parking spot. After a few minutes, Angelica came out and got back into the car. "Friendly fella in there! Thanks... my nightly sedative," she said, as she held up the brown paper bag. Matthew noticed the box of Macallen 12.

"And it's cheaper. The hotel's probably real expensive," Matthew said, as he smiled boyishly.

Driving through town, she tried to imagine what it would be like living in Elberton. *What the heck is there to do around here*, she wondered, *except eat chess pie, look at the scenery and gossip?*

Back in D.C., Angelica went to the gym every day after work, or on occasion she'd skip her workout to go to the popular bar around the corner to meet Andrew or her girlfriends for drinks. She looked out the window at the dime store shops with outdated window dressings, along the main avenue as they passed by. "So, do you guys have a Starbucks?"

Playfully ignoring her question, Matthew looked at Angelica and smiled. After a few blocks he announced, "Here we are. Would you like to come in for a minute?"

Angelica opened the car door, and stepped out onto the loose pea gravel driveway in between a strip of grass. As she turned around she saw an old Victorian white house with a small white picket fence encircling it.

"It's lovely. Yes, this is how I pictured you," she smiled confidently. "Is it haunted?" she asked, straight-faced.

"Haunted?" Matthew laughed. "Not every old Victorian house is haunted. You watch too many movies!"

Angelica looked up at the windows above the front porch overhang as they walked up the steps. The white paint was cracked, chipped, and had turned grey. It looked as if it hadn't been painted since it was originally built. However, it would be charming once redone, she thought.

Matthew opened the front door, never bothering to pull out a key.

"Do you just leave your front door unlocked? Aren't you afraid someone will come in and rob you?" Angelica couldn't imagine leaving her doors unlocked in D.C. The idea unnerved her to even consider.

"No one's gonna rob anybody in this town! You're in Mayberry, Angelica! We even have a Sheriff Taylor!"

Matthew proceeded through the old glass pane door and into a grand foyer. Grand in its day, now it was just an old house with character. The living room was to the left. Next to the winding craftsman's style staircase and to the right was Matthew's study.

The round table in the foyer was cluttered with newspapers, unopened mail, tattered half packs of breath mints and loose change Matthew obviously emptied from his pockets each evening.

She walked over to the table and examined the contents curiously. She was nosy. "So, is it just you here?" she asked as she moved toward the staircase and ran her hand along the dark wood railing, as she admired the craftsmanship.

"Yes, just me and Lady, my cat... She's not loyal though. She cheats on me with the neighbors."

Angelica stepped toward the living room and noticed a beautiful art deco antique lamp. The furniture was worn and from the 1920's and 30's era, some of it older. "You have some amazing antiques!" she yelled out into the house.

"This was my grandparent's house. Most of the stuff you see was theirs," Matthew yelled back.

Angelica wandered through the living room and picked up old family photos still in their original frames. As she moved through the room, she rubbed her fingers gently over the pieces as she passed by them, before she stopped at a black and white photo of an attractive young couple wearing 1930's period clothing. She was strangely drawn to it, so she gingerly picked it up. Angelica realized the couple in the photo must have been Matthew's grandparents when they were probably newlyweds.

"Got it, you ready?" Matthew walked into the living room with a book in his hand to find Angelica holding the picture frame of his grandparents. "They were amazing, a true love story. You ready?"

"Yes," Angelica whispered as she gently put the frame down.

For a moment, Angelica could almost hear the laughter and voices of Matthew's grandparents in her mind. The distant echoes of a house once filled with love and affection. She visualized the man of the house arriving early on a Friday afternoon, carrying a bouquet of roses, and for a split second she thought she could smell their fragrant aroma. Their home was still majestic in its own way, and she imagined at some point in time it was very much alive. Now, in its dilapidated beauty, it just seemed dejected, barren, and stoically resigned to its current fate. In the deep recesses of her heart that she kept carefully locked away... Angelica felt an unearthly connection to the bricks and mortar of its uncontrollable destiny.

Chapter Twenty-Two

Right outside of town, and five miles from Matthew's house, sat Ellen McKinney's outdated ranch home, a box of rust-colored red brick. Looking around, Angelica felt depressed. The scenic mountains were in the distance, but Ellen's house sat in a valley where there were only a few old rundown houses scattered throughout. "How could anyone live this way? So lonely and depressing," she said aloud while running her hand along the side of her head. Matthew glanced over with tight lips and nodded in agreement.

As the car pulled into the driveway, several large mutts ran over to greet them. Angelica was hesitant to get out, but she noticed Matthew wasn't frightened of the dogs, so she opened the door and stepped out, cautiously.

One of the larger black dogs jumped up on her. Matthew shouted, "Down, get down, Bear!"

Angelica looked distraught. She softly pushed the dog back and raised her hand to smell the stench left behind. "Wonderful," she thought as she rubbed her hand across her pant leg hoping to wipe the foul odor away.

A woman's voice suddenly appeared, "Scat, y'all! Scat now!" Ellen McKinney was leaning out of her front door yelling at the raggedy dogs. "Sorry about that! They get excited when people show up to the house. They're harmless! Come on in!" Ellen let the metal screen door swing shut behind her as Angelica and Matthew continued to walk down the sidewalk to the house.

Angelica had tried to get a good look at Ellen before the door shut, but all she could make out was short wavy auburn hair with heavy streaks of silver.

Ellen had already sat back down on her plaid brown and burgundy sofa with her attention turned to the television as they entered the house.

"Don't you love this show?" Ellen pointed to an outspoken personality on the television, who Angelica recognized immediately, known for arguing with her guests.

"Ellen, this is Angelica Bradley with the *Liberator Magazine*."

"I know. You told me over the phone." Ellen turned to Angelica, "And here you are, young lady." Ellen picked up the remote and turned off the television. Angelica observed Ellen curiously.

"My dear, have a seat. Would you like some tea or water?"

"No, thank you," Angelica said, as she sat down on the other end of the sofa, as far from Ellen as she could possibly get. She didn't know why, but Ellen unnerved her.

Matthew placed the borrowed book down on the coffee table and took a seat in the worn brown recliner closest to Angelica and then glanced around the room, before turning to Angelica with an odd smile. Angelica swallowed hard.

"They watch us!" Ellen pointed to the ceiling. Angelica looked at Ellen, flabbergasted.

"*They* watch us?" Angelica repeated with an emphasis on "they," while looking curiously up at the ceiling.

"Yes, Angelica, the non-humans," Ellen said, as if it didn't sound ridiculous. Angelica took a deep breath. She felt uncomfortable. She dramatically shot a wide-eyed look over at Matthew and then toward the door to suggest they make a run for it. Matthew smiled at her, and then turned his attention to Ellen in anticipation of what she was going to say next.

Angelica dropped her shoulders, leaned back and listened.

"They are inter-dimensional beings."

"What are inter-dimensional beings?" Angelica interrupted through a breath, indicating her frustration.

"I'm sorry... this is all very new to you. Okay, just give me some time to explain before you cut me off," Ellen said, as she laughed, playfully.

Angelica tilted her head and frowned.

"Inter-dimensional beings would be travelers from another space-time continuum. There are different groups. This particular group I'm referring to, well, they're more like our angels or guardians, as they like to be considered." Ellen smiled smugly.

"Seriously?" Angelica said, while positioning her elbow on her knee to cup her chin into her hand, staring in disbelief.

"They are... well, from another star system." Noting Angelica's expression, Ellen explained further and more patiently, almost as if Angelica were a small child. "I know this is all very confusing, but just stay with me and I'll explain." Ellen smiled but her tone was condescending.

"Wait a minute... What?" Angelica stood up as she looked over at Matthew. "Are you serious? You believe this. This is wasting time, Matthew." Angelica glanced over at Ellen. "My apologies, Mrs. McKinney, I didn't mean to sound rude, however..."

Matthew appeared uncomfortable, obviously concerned Angelica had offended Ellen. "Yes, please sit down, Angelica."

"You need to keep an open mind." Ellen spoke softly as she looked intensely with her dark grey eyes at Angelica's pale blues.

"Okay, go on!" she blurted as she sat back down and smoothed out her pant legs with her palms. "So, what does this have to do with the mutilations, Mrs. McKinney?"

Almost like a reflex reaction, Ellen immediately looked at Matthew and then back to Angelica. Ellen appeared annoyed. "We'll get to that soon enough. First, hang on. There is someone you need to meet." Ellen stood up and walked down the hall into a room. Angelica could hear Ellen speaking with someone. The mumbling got louder until Angelica could hear each word clearly.

"I told you I wasn't going out there! I'm not getting involved!" a male voice erupted forcefully.

"Oh yes you are! Why else would they have told you she was coming...? 'Expect a woman with light hair from a big city with small buildings.' That's what they said and she's in the living room. Therefore, I think they want you out there! Now get your ass in the den!"

Angelica felt like jumping up and running for the door. She looked over at Matthew and asked sternly, "What is going on?"

Matthew was still leaning in the direction of the voices, not looking at Angelica but towards the hall, answered, "It's Blake, her husband. I hope he'll come out."

Angelica frowned. "Why?"

The door opened and Ellen made her way back to the living room with her husband reluctantly marching behind. "Angelica, this is my husband, Blake. He retired from the Newton Air Force Base last year. He said he wanted to stay away from all this ET stuff, but I think it is important that he share some things with you." Ellen looked over at Blake as he rolled his eyes. He was agitated and looked a mess.

A tall, rounded man with a white butch haircut, he had a scowl on his face and Angelica imagined that was probably the way he always looked. In blue jeans and a white-collared, button-down shirt with a pen clipped in the front pocket, he stood there like a punished schoolboy, unwilling to speak.

"Go on, Blake. Tell her!" Ellen scolded.

Blake let a loud puff of air, physically and not so subtly alluding to his solemn irritation. "Ms. Bradley, I recently retired from Newton Air Force Base and let me just cut to the chase... They know exactly what's going on. I worked alongside these things on a top secret project at Newton's underground base. However, first you should know..." Blake sat down on the worn sofa, on the other side of his wife, positioning himself to face Angelica. Blake was restless--as if he didn't know what to say next.

It made Angelica so uncomfortable she felt she was coming out of her skin. Angelica let out a deep breath and listened as her head began to tingle.

"You're getting caught in a very large web of deception," Blake said. "You need to be careful. You are already being monitored by a myriad of entities. One in particular I'm talking about is a secret group, a private, rogue military group with no one at the top of their totem pole. Catch my drift?"

Angelica pressed her lips together causing them to turn from pink to white. "Rogue military group, huh... well, that's interesting, because I've heard mention of such a group and it was proven to be a crazy theory created by some internet conspiracy nut!" she said sarcastically. Angelica held eye contact with Blake.

Blake's jaw tightened at the insinuation.

Angelica had come across an article online when she was researching the humming sound while at the lodge. "The secret military group that you mentioned," she told him, "was debunked by an ex-military insider."

"This agency is not a hoax, Angelica, quite the contrary!" Blake snarled.

"How do you know this? What exactly is going on, Blake?" Angelica's eyes grew wide as she looked him square in the face, trying not to show a slight bit of intimidation.

"Look, I'm not going into all that other than to say... smoke and mirrors!" Blake looked over at Ellen... "Smoke and mirrors! The government has a policy of dis-information. Always keep that in the back of your mind, Ms. Bradley."

Angelica looked suspiciously at Blake. "Really?" she said with a slight hint of sarcasm.

Blake observed Angelica with a doubtful expression, questioning whether to continue, giving Angelica the impression that Blake thought she was in over her head. Blake glanced at Ellen and caught her facial expression indicating she was getting irritated, so he carefully continued. "Look, there are a myriad of things going on from beamed energy propulsion to anti-gravity technology. "I'm sure you've heard of solar thermal propulsion, which makes use of an available power source from the Sun. Much like solar panel energy, crafts powered by the sun eliminate the need for alternate sources, like carrying a heavy generator. A solar thermal craft has only the need to carry the means of capturing solar energy." Angelica raised her brows curiously.

"However, there are more advanced technologies, such as zero point field and beamed energy propulsion... Let's just say there are folks out there that are teaching us concepts that would have taken us a lot longer to discover--if at all. We're talking about propulsion energy systems that would replace oil, gas, coal, and even nuclear power. There is so much to be learned from them. I only hope it will be used for good, not for reprehensible means." Blake glanced over at Matthew. "You know, Oppenheimer, the inventor of the atomic bomb said, 'I have become death. The destroyer of worlds.'"

Matthew nodded, "Yes, I've heard the quote… more than few times," he mumbled.

Angelica shifted in her seat and listened carefully. He had her full attention but she still wasn't sure where he was going with it.

"While working on these projects," Blake said, "I met and worked alongside other scientists and from them I learned of the hybrids. It was never explained precisely, but I gathered this… A new human DNA has been created by some benevolent highly evolved race and it's unique, I'll say that. Apparently, people with this advanced DNA are evolving at an exponential rate, have very strong immune systems, and I'll just say other special gifts, so I've heard." Blake cleared his throat and looked at Ellen.

Ellen looked at Angelica and spoke softly. "And, they appear to be unaffected by radiation, right Blake?"

Blake nodded and quickly continued. "Essentially, they are changing rapidly. Silly term, but what the hell, I'll say it… They are becoming exponentially stronger – super-humans. From what I understand, they can't get sick and are immune to human diseases." Blake continued where Ellen had left off.

Angelica blurted out, "becoming stronger and immune to diseases?"

Ellen interrupted Blake as he started to speak. "For whatever reason, this DNA strand has been dormant and now it's being activated. And as this new DNA strand evolves, the new species step out of polarity and no longer judge. They begin to understand everything is interconnected in all ways. You can't hide anything from them, they are a remarkable phenomenon. They can see the future," Ellen looked sincerely into Angelica's eyes. "It is said that they will lead the way."

Angelica took a breath. "Let's just say hypothetically that all of this seemingly irrational discussion is true. What does this really mean?" Angelica asked.

"To move into a state where you are immune to disease is extraordinary. In a world where viruses and bacteria are growing stronger, their kind will survive and maybe over time the new and higher level race will be resistant to all diseases," Ellen responded enthusiastically.

Blake nodded as he spoke. "Ellen is correct."

"But how would it be possible?" Angelica squinted, trying to process it all. She still couldn't wrap her head around what Ellen and Blake were saying--the idea of a super-human sounded ridiculous, she thought.

Angelica looked at Blake blankly as she thought for a moment. "How would that be possible?

"I imagine through nighty visitations, and procedures on their crafts," he said, straight-faced.

"We are talking about highly evolved beings here, Ms. Bradley."

Matthew observed Angelica grappling with all of this from a state of perplexity.

Ellen leaned closer to Angelica. "They don't just walk in on you in the middle of the night and say, 'Hi, I'm an alien, and you're coming with me!' Well, they might, but that's probably rare." Ellen giggled.

Angelica sat there for a moment bewildered, wide-eyed, and trying to contemplate the provocative conversation. "Blake said procedures."

"Well, with this particular kind, yes. However, the others do it differently. They steal your eggs, and create the life form in their lab."

Angelica planted her feet defiantly. "So you are talking about two different races that are creating hybrids?" Angelica peered over at Matthew. He was nodding his head. She thought it sounded entirely too far-fetched, and yet Matthew seemed to endorse the idea.

Ellen looked over at Blake and nodded to proceed. Blake started patiently. "The benevolent race looks very similar to humans, but is much taller and more muscular... kind of angelic. Most people have reported seeing the ones with light skin, light eyes, and light hair. However, they are not limited to those features. One of my former colleagues said he had seen an Asian-looking one with light blonde hair while working at the underground base. Supposedly they have been around a long time. This is the group creating a new race of super-hybrids here on Earth."

Blake rubbed his fingers across his lips. "Why? We do not really know. There are a lot of theories out there."

"Are these human-like beings working with our government?" Angelica asked, as nonchalantly as she possibly could.

"I do not know why they were at Newton," Blake frowned. "This other race appears androgynous and supposedly originated from a star system near the Orion Constellation. I question whether they are the future version of us coming back for some reason. Who knows? Maybe they know our future and are harvesting the human genetics. Anyway, these things are also creating the hybrids, however for a completely different reason, it's speculated, and they are taking the human-hybrid females eggs, like a fox in the night. In other words, the child is never born on Earth."

Angelica gasped. "They steal a woman's eggs? They steal her baby!" Blake and Ellen nodded. Matthew didn't say anything, but he appeared to believe the McKinney's.

"Wait, I'm confused. You said there was a group creating hybrids here on Earth, right?" Angelica spoke quickly.

Blake nodded. "Yes."

"Okay, now you say another group is creating hybrids with the eggs of the human-hybrid female that was created on Earth by the benevolent race. Is that correct? I'm sorry but this is confusing." Angelica glanced at Matthew and shook her head.

"Allegedly, yes," Blake answered. " They are using the super-human hybrid DNA, combining it with their own. I've heard it's considered genetically superior to most of the intelligent life forms that exist out there."

Angelica looked over at Matthew again in disbelief, and then to Ellen before holding eye contact with Blake. She was feeling abnormally submissive. "Go on, please... I'm fascinated." Angelica leaned in closer and rubbed her temple.

"The non-Earth inhabitant hybrids supposedly look more like the grey ones than human. Like the ones you see on the television." Blake sat up.

Ellen interjected, "Yes, as you've seen on TV and in the movies, the grey ones have large black eyes."

Angelica thought back on her hypnosis session, and the beings with large black eyes she visualized in her mind at her grandmother's farm. She swallowed hard, her face ashened.

Ellen put her hand to her mouth and thought for a moment. "Now, it gets a little confusing, so just digest what you can, honey. There are inter-dimensional beings that can move between time and space and operate on different levels. These beings can move between dimensions and appear paranormal to us such as shadows, dreams, disembodied voices, etc. You get the picture." Ellen shifted around, causing the sofa to squeak, startling Angelica.

"But we won't go into all that," Blake's voice deeply erupted. "You look confused enough." Blake chuckled.

"Blake!" Ellen scolded, as she reached over and squeezed his arm.

Angelica—suddenly conscious of her expression—shifted and sat up with a poker face. "All right, but there's one thing I'm struggling with, outside of the idea of these hybrids, of course, which is the craziest thing I have ever heard..." Angelica laughed nervously.

"Let's get back to the focus of my investigation. We seem to have gone off track a little bit. Who's doing the cattle mutilations? And why would beings travel billions of miles to our planet to cut up our cattle?" Angelica scratched at her cheek, and then grasped a few strands of her hair and started twisting it in a circular motion. Catching herself in the act, she let go of her hair and put her hand back in her lap.

Blake didn't hesitate, "That is a good question. I'm not entirely sure, but there is definitely a connection. While at the base, it was an area of experimentation that was very secretive. My theory revolves around something within the cattle DNA that is similar to human DNA and maybe they use it when creating the hybrids.

Angelica glanced over at Matthew and observed him nodding in agreement.

"As you investigate this, you'll hear the grey ones are mutilating the cattle, and then you'll hear it's the supposed benevolent ones. You'll even hear on occasion that they're collaborating. I don't want to speculate any further. One thing is for certain... It is significant. I hope you get to the bottom of it and find some answers," Blake said coarsely.

"I overheard a scientist at the base say the grey race had to leave their planet because it had become depleted of its resources, and they've colonized on an earth-like planet four hundred light years away from earth. He said we've located the earth-like planet with the Hubble telescope and its orbiting in the habitable zone of Lyra, with a similar star to our sun. They call it a 'Goldylocks Zone' because it is just right for organic life. It apparently has a surface temperature in the comfortable seventies. They're calling it the "Spring Planet," since it's comparable to a spring day on earth. When I heard that, I thought, 'Hell... that sounds like heaven – a perfect utopia... When do I leave?'" Blake chuckled.

Angelica looked over at Matthew. "I don't know what to say... wow, okay." She took a deep breath and shook her head.

"Supposedly, there are beings that don't believe the human race is capable of evolving because of its current genetic structure. Too many mutations have been created through pollution, genetically modified food, and vaccines. They don't believe enough humans will shift to a higher consciousness, and thus create a new paradigm as they had hoped. So they are now being very selective.

"To them, we are lost, too far gone to save ourselves. However, the benevolent ones do believe in the human race and they have created, through hybridization, their way-showers. These hybrids are an important part of the future of the human evolution. They're born with a very special purpose."

Angelica leaned back further into the sofa and thought for a moment. "This sounds like some bizarre science fiction movie." She nervously scratched her neck. After she lowered her hand, her neck revealed red splotches. Matthew noticed Angelica had started to break out in a rash.

Angelica dropped her shoulders and looked blankly at Ellen, and then Blake. Was Ellen even credible? And Blake, just because he worked for Newton... didn't mean squat. It was just too unbelievable, she thought.

Angelica looked at Matthew and opened her mouth to speak, but nothing came out. She then turned back to Ellen. "Forgive me, but I'm at a loss for words," Angelica whispered.

Ellen smiled sympathetically at Angelica. "It's understandable."

Angelica looked over at Matthew. She was afraid to ask any more questions for fear it was just going to get weirder. Suddenly, her filter vanished and she realized she was speaking her thoughts out loud. "This is too much! There are hybrids... come on. Seriously?" Angelica challenged, shaking her head.

Ellen got up from her corner position on the couch next to Blake and sat next to Angelica, causing the interruption she had planned. Angelica looked at Matthew and shrugged her shoulders, mouthing the words, "What is she doing?"

Matthew shrugged his shoulders and mouthed the words, "I don't know."

Ellen was in Angelica's space. Angelica leaned back into the armrest. Ellen lowered her head and then looked back up. Angelica noticed little sparks of light no further than a few feet from above Ellen's head.

There were several flashes, similar to fireflies, as if they just entered the room. She looked over at Matthew who was watching Ellen intensely. It didn't appear that Matthew had noticed them; he was looking downward. Maybe she was starting to faint.

Ellen patted Angelica's hand and smiled as Angelica just sat there with her jaw clinched, facing Ellen. Matthew decided to intervene. He stood up from the recliner and said, "Well, we should be going."

Ellen appeared genuinely concerned. "Oh? Well, all right. But she doesn't look well. Maybe she should sip some water before she leaves."

"No, thank you, I'm fine. I just need some air." Angelica managed a smile as she spoke through clenched teeth. The only thoughts in her mind were the traumatic images from her last session with her doctor. Did she really witness the terrible scene as a child? Her mind flooded as she felt disoriented.

Ellen stood up and gave Angelica some room to get up from the sofa and apologetically stepped back. Angelica stood up, leaned over to grab her satchel, and then followed Matthew to the front door. Before she stepped over the threshold, she looked back at Ellen and Blake. "Thank you. I must confess... this was not at all what I had expected."

Ellen walked over and took Angelica's hand placing it gently between hers. "Angelica, I know you are leaving here today questioning what you've heard. You may convince yourself it's not true, but you'll come around soon enough. If you need anything, please do not be afraid to reach out to us. We will help you in any way we can. Good luck my dear and be safe."

Angelica smiled at Ellen as she gently slid her hand away and turned toward the door.

Before she was outside, Blake spoke in a hardy tone. "Angelica, keep a healthy guarded suspicion! It's very hard to tell who the good guys and bad guys are, and it will get even more convoluted and complicated the deeper you go into your investigation. Use your intuition and watch your six!"

"I will. Thank you," Angelica appeared dazed. Angelica sensed the hidden pieces to her past were now falling into place. The thought gripped her.

Matthew stepped off the porch and turned back to Ellen, still standing in the doorway. "Thank you, Ellen. I'll see you soon."

Ellen raised her hand and gave him a slight wave. "Yes, Matthew, see you soon," Ellen turned around and went back inside, letting the metal glass door shut behind her.

As Matthew backed out of the driveway, he caught a glimpse of Angelica. She was staring warily out of the passenger window. "Are you all right?"

His words took a moment to register. Angelica looked over at Matthew. "Yes... interesting afternoon. The McKinney's are out there. Aliens... Hybrids... wow! This is all so crazy!" Angelica drew a sharp breath.

Matthew bellowed a laugh. "Hey, I was going to meet the guys for a beer after I dropped you at the lodge, why don't you come along. It will help you unwind -- change of pace."

"Okay, why not," she said, barely making eye contact with Matthew before she turned back around to look out the window toward the old house.

Ellen pulled back the dated curtains and watched as they drove away. Blake stepped up and peered motionless behind her.

"Why didn't you tell her? You should have told her everything," Ellen said in a whisper while watching Matthew's car drive away. Blake moved in closer and carefully squinted over Ellen's shoulder as if he were looking through the scope of a sniper rifle. "Don't worry. She'll find out soon enough."

Chapter Twenty-Three

Angelica turned to see the sunlight fade into the darkness as the door to bar glided softly shut behind them.

The RUFA crew was playing pool. Angelica noticed Matthew's face had lit up. He looked different, younger in the dim light, as she imagined he had looked in his college days meeting up with his frat brothers. Matthew waved his hand and shouted across the loud pool hall, and then peered back at Angelica. "Look, the guys are already here!" Angelica smiled, amused at Matthew.

The pool hall smelled heavy of tobacco smoke. The only lighting came from red and white stained glass pool table lamps and the rather dull neon signs on the walls. It appeared to be a happening place though, probably for the simple fact that it was the only bar with pool tables in Elberton, she thought.

"Hey there, man!" Paul said, turning around to face Matthew just after knocking a ball in the hole. The other men heard Paul and sauntered towards them as Matthew and Angelica approached the table.

The sound of pool ball strikes was piercing and all around her. She started to feel it was a mistake to accept Matthew's offer to grab a beer. Her nerves were on edge. She realized she would have been more comfortable unwinding back at the lodge, soaking in a hot bubble bath, sipping Scotch, and listening to her favorite iTunes playlist.

Angelica felt a sharp tap on the back of her shoulder, her heartbeat spiked. She turned around to a conspicuously intoxicated man in a cowboy hat smiling devilishly at her. Angelica flushed scarlet.

"Would you like a drink, pretty lady?" The man slurred as he swayed ominously toward her. By his appearance, he looked as if needed a shower. Angelica noticed oil stains around his fingernails and in the creases on his hand as he clutched a beer bottle in front of his chest.

"Oh great, can this get any worse," she wondered. Angelica stepped back and smiled out of uneasiness rather than politeness. "No, thank you!" she responded harshly as she squirmed at the thought.

Matthew turned around and caught a glimpse of the cowboy swaying back and forth, staring Angelica up and down with a look of desperation on his scruffy face.

Angelica was leaning back. Her eyes bored into the man. Matthew laughed and nudged Paul. "Look at Hal! We better save her. Or maybe save him... she has that look." Both Matthew and Paul laughed simultaneously. "Hey Hal, leave the lady alone! Isn't Kelly gonna be looking for you soon? If she comes in here and sees you talking to this pretty young lady, she'll have your ass!"

Hal shot a look over at Matthew, and then his head started wobbling back and forth. He raised his fat dirty index finger and pointed at Matthew as he slightly lost his balance. "Yep, you're right... Kelly." He looked back at Angelica... "Kelly's my crazy wife," laughing, he then turned and swayed off.

Angelica looked at her small team of body guards, "Thank you!"

Paul stepped over to Angelica. "You're a long way from D.C.," he announced with a wry smile. "It's quite a bit different here in Montana, not the same sophistication."

"Yes, it's quite different from D.C., but similar in ways you might not imagine." Angelica shot an irritated look back over at the drunken cowboy stumbling his way back to the pool tables. "It's beautiful though and the scenery is amazing." Angelica relaxed her shoulders.

Paul put his pool stick down and one of the other guys grabbed it. "How long are you here?"

Angelica remembered her meeting with Michael Anderson the next day. "I guess I'll be leaving in a day or so. I haven't booked my return flight yet. I need to interview Dr. Walter Goolrick, so I'll hopefully be heading to Colorado next." Angelica thought a moment. "I'll head back to D.C. after I meet with Goolrick. I should be back in my office Tuesday at the latest," she said with blank eyes appearing to be working the details out in her head.

"Anyway..." she snapped back and refocused on Paul. "I'd like to ask you some questions as well, since we're here. Would you mind speaking casually over a beer?"

"Of course not, I was wondering when you were going ask." Paul appeared polite and easy going.

"Great, let's grab that table," Angelica pointed to the booth beside the guy's pool table.

Matthew walked over and set down two shots of tequila on the table. "Thought you two would like a shot," he said. She picked up the glass, licked the salt off the rim, and tilted her head back drinking it in one swift gulp. Then she picked up the lime wedge and sucked it, making a sour face.

"Wow, it's been awhile since I've done that. Thank you."

Paul laughed while shaking his head. "You did it like an old pro."

Angelica turned and looked around at the bar patrons and then back to Paul, "I'd better not have any more of those, I tend to..." Before she could finish her sentence, Paul was already calling over to the bartender for two more. "Well okay." She nodded in approval and smiled nervously.

"It will relax you." Paul smiled and winked. "You seem a little tense."

"Well, I'm more of a wine girl... and Scotch on occasion, but okay."

Angelica grabbed her digital recorder, turned it on, and sat it on the table in front of them. "I'm not sure if the background noise will interfere, hope not." She pushed it to the middle of the table between them. All right Paul, What's up with the mutilations?"

Paul, taken aback, "Boy, you get right to it – direct and to-the-point, I like that! Well, no one seems to know for sure." He smiled with kind eyes as he leaned back into the booth.

"I think it could have something to do with genetics. I've learned cattle blood ..."

Angelica interrupted Paul. "My apologies... I did not mean to interrupt you. Did you also speak with Dr. Walter Goolrick, the veterinarian scientist the police called in?"

"Yes," Paul said. "He talked about how bovine hemoglobin closely matches human blood. However, you know, the police didn't call the doctor. He called them... for whatever it's worth. Not sure why it was turned around like that... anyway, he told them he had been independently investigating cattle mutilations for some time and thought he could assist them with the case."

Angelica looked intrigued. She envisioned the stiff carcass with all four legs in the air at the Keller ranch.

Paul took a sip of his beer and shifted in his seat. "Back to my conversation with Dr. Goolrick--He said cattle DNA could be used to fill in the gaps of the genetic sequence codes that do not have enough DNA on the human strand." Paul paused at the sound of laughter erupting from Matthew and the guys over at the pool table. "Matthew is a funny guy. Bet he has you laughing a lot," Paul mused.

Angelica thought for a moment. "Yes, he has a great sense of humor. Go on about Dr. Goolrick." Angelica leaned in closer.

"Well, that would suggest they are doing something with human DNA," Paul told her, "like possibly highly evolved hybridization."

Angelica laughed impulsively. "Here we go again with this outlandish theory. Let me guess. They're creating hybrids by combining extraterrestrial DNA with human DNA... oh, and just for good measure, filling in the gaps with cattle DNA. And the military is monitoring it, right?" Angelica dropped her hand down on the table, leaned back in the booth, looked around the room and then back curiously at Paul.

"Wow, you seem to be a step ahead of me for some reason," Paul said. "Yes, I do believe that's true, and I'm obviously not the only one that believes this theory. Continue with your research, Angelica," Paul said sharply, while trying to stay polite. "You'll probably come across the theory that not only is the cattle DNA assisting in the experimentations, the cattle DNA is used to feed the ETs."

"What?" Angelica thought aloud.

"By the way," Paul added, "humans have been genetically altering DNA in seeds and animals for years to feed themselves," he finished sarcastically and then smiled warmly.

Angelica buried her face down into her hands for a moment and then looked back up. "Okay, let's talk about the mutilated cattle on the ranch. You don't believe someone or something else could have done it?" Angelica examined his face while biting down on her lower lip.

"Angelica, think about it... let's say the military is killing these cattle... they'd have to drop down and harness these animals. That is a lot of weight for a military helicopter to lift and transport without being seen." A startling thought hit Paul. "Well, I'm sure it's possible, but hard to hide. There's absolutely no evidence at the scene to suggest it, such as boot prints, tracks and so on. I just don't believe that's the case. With that being said... the area under the animal always appears depressed, as if the animal was dropped on the site from the sky. The fractures to the animal's bones are consistent with a dumping injury. Furthermore, there are usually reports of a small black military helicopter showing up after strange lights have been seen in the sky. Whether they are trying to cover up the activity by deflecting the focus away from the sightings, we don't know... all speculation right now. I personally believe they're monitoring them, you know, keeping an eye on the ETs."

Angelica's eyes narrowed as she took a sip of the beer Matthew had quietly snuck in front of her.

"I'm sure Matthew mentioned the high levels of radioactivity around the carcass," Paul said.

"No, I don't believe he did," she replied wryly and shrugged.

"Well, anyhow, you wouldn't think radiation would be present with a military helicopter," Paul told her. "And one researcher found reports of animals coated with an ultraviolet substance after lights were seen in the sky... and some of those coated were later found mutilated."

"No, Matthew did not give me that much detail," Angelica murmured.

"I'm sure Matthew's probably covered as much ground as he could with you so far," Paul said. He glanced briefly toward Matthew and then added: "He's been researching this for over a decade. For example, in ninety percent of the cases, the cattle are between the age of four and five years old."

Angelica thought for a moment. "Perhaps that's a coincidence?"

"Yes... maybe," Paul said, as he nodded.

Without even thinking, Angelica had reached down and taken her second tequila shot causing her to squint and shiver. "Whoa!"

Loosened up just a little by the booze, Angelica did her best to summarize her understanding. "So, the cow is sucked up by a light into an alien craft... organs are removed, blood is drained. Why?" Angelica tilted her head.

Paul looked curiously at Angelica. "I've sat in heated conversations on numerous occasions and asked the very same question... opinions differ. Some say they are replacing the human race due to how we treat the planet. Others say they plan to inhabit our planet, alongside humans with their DNA."

Angelica thought for a moment. "What about other races. Are there others out there?" Angelica paused... "Say a benevolent race? Does this ring a bell?" Angelica shifted -- conscious of how uncomfortable it felt to utter those words.

Paul smiled. "You're doing your research. Yes, there are supposedly many races, interesting you are bringing up a race allegedly considered to be helping us. The race we investigators refer to as 'The Benevolent,' are said to resemble humans. A lot of people have reportedly come in contact with these beings."

"The way it's been described to me is this..." Paul continued. "They are what biblical accounts and religious beliefs throughout the centuries refer to as Angels, and technically, they would be right. Now think about this: How would someone from early biblical times describe an encounter with one? The Old Testament defines Angels as superior beings created by God, living in another realm, which is described generically as Heaven. For instance the Bible talks about Angels appearing to adults as strong and powerful beings, startling those they visit."

Angelica raised her elbows to the table and rested her chin in her dainty fingers. "So it seems reasonable to conclude that you are making some sort or comparison here... Okay, please continue," she whispered and narrowed her eyes. She had started slurring her words.

"Angelic beings," Paul reflected, "supposedly have been around since the beginning of mankind and you will find them referenced in all religions around the world. In fact, if you looked through the Bible, you would find countless examples of extraterrestrial encounters."

Angelica did her best to go on listening without bias.

"Angels," Paul told her, "are always appearing during a major event and every time they are described almost to the tee like 'The Benevolent.' I'm not saying they are what we consider to be angels; it's just interesting to note similarities. Now don't forget, Angelica, even though you may not be in the South, you are surrounded by a bunch of God-fearing people. I did grow up in the South. I was born and raised in Huntsville, Alabama. I guess you could say the love of science and space is in my blood and that tends to change your beliefs somewhat."

Angelica nodded in understanding.

"Anyway, being from the South," Paul explained, "if there is one thing I know a little bit about, it's the King James Bible. Now I am going way out on a limb here, but once again, let's think about this semantically. Mary had Jesus by 'Immaculate Conception.' In other words, she was impregnated by God, a superior, all-knowing entity from Heaven. This miraculous event occurred during the night and while Mary was sleeping. And get this... an Angel appeared in the middle of the night to Joseph, Mary's husband, to tell him of the event. Nice that the Angel took the time, and if it was a 'Benevolent,' it must have been very convincing because if I were Joseph I don't know that I would have taken it that well... Strange coincidence, huh?" Paul shook his head, smiling inwardly as he took a sip of his beer.

Angelica's lips went straight as she held his gaze. She was quiet. She looked unimpressed, but she was considering Paul's hypothesis.

"So one could say, technically, she was the first historically documented human to be impregnated by a non-human or alien..." Paul paused for effect. "...if you believe the story. The definition of an alien in its purest form is someone 'not from around here.' God would qualify, wouldn't He?"

Angelica nodded. "Wow, but..."

Paul interrupted her. "Now, I'm not saying I believe or don't believe in what I have been taught my entire life, and I am certainly not trying to shake anyone's religious faith, but start looking at the historical records of ancient civilizations. You will find clues everywhere, but you will have to understand that they were writing the accounts the only way they knew how to at the time with their limited knowledge."

Angelica nodded trying to stay focused, but she was feeling her buzz. The third tequila shot was now sitting on the table in front of her.

"You better lower your voice while saying stuff like that. You just said God was an alien." Angelica looked around the pool hall and then back toward Paul, catching a glimpse of the shot glass on the table. "Hey, where did that come from?" she said, surprised.

Angelica picked up the shot, swung her head back, and then slammed the glass down on the table. "Oops! I didn't mean to put it down that hard," she announced as she picked up the lime wedge and waved her pinkie finger at Paul before sucking the juice from it.

"Well Paul, I may be drinking but that was fascinating and made some sense, however... Well, as much sense as any other conversation I've had today," she mumbled. "Of course, I am a bit of an agnostic... I need to continue to investigate this interesting, and might I add-- controversial-- line of thinking." Angelica's words slurred.

"Hey, these benevolent beings... if they exist, where are they, and why don't we hear more about them – Why are they so elusive?" Angelica smirked. "There's a question for ya."

Angelica laughed as she pushed the empty glass away... "I better not have any more of these! So, are they involved with creating hybrids?"

Paul thought for a moment. "I believe they are. Apparently, but it's all speculation. I'll just share what I've heard from other investigators. 'The Benevolent' created a group of hybrids on earth, and no one I've spoken to seems to have a clue why. I heard someone say that 'The Benevolent' do not support the grey race's agenda, but will not interfere due to higher universal laws that we don't understand. I don't know for certain, but I often wonder if these hybrids have something to do with moving the world to a new and better horizon. Maybe it's wishful thinking, but isn't that the whole symbolism around Man's obsession with a God-like being from Heaven watching over us and affecting our destiny? Of course, we have to be good little boys and girls to make it to this utopia we call Heaven, right?" Paul lifted his beer and took a sip. "All sounds crazy, huh?"

Angelica turned around for Matthew. He was putting his beer down to make a pool shot. Matthew glanced over at Angelica and caught her looking at him. She smiled and waved. He looked suspiciously at her and waved back.

Angelica's vision blurred, fully aware of her buzz again, she became slightly dizzy. She turned back to Paul and with wide eyes said "Whoa! Don't let me drink anymore – from what I recall of Tequila, I could get a little wild."

Paul grinned. "I'm sure no one would mind if you got wild. Look around you," Paul chuckled.

Angelica refrained from rolling her eyes at Paul's statement. Angelica seemed weary as she looked down at her recorder to make sure the light was still on. She lifted her hand and pushed her hair back from her face, swaying from the alcohol. "Thank goodness it's on because I may not remember a word of this crazy conversation." They both laughed. Paul smirked before taking a sip of his beer, observing her body language. The thought hadn't occurred to him that she shouldn't have any more alcohol.

Angelica leaned in closer, lowered her voice, and whispered, "Shew! How many shots have I had?"

Paul chuckled. "I believe you've had three. Well, see that gentleman right there?" Paul politely waved to a man at the bar looking their way, smiling deviously. "He's sending them over to us."

When Angelica made eye contact, the man smiled seductively. Angelica turned back around to Paul. "All rightly... I better not have anymore – seriously!" Angelica sat up straight and shivered.

"I have to say, this story will go down as one of my most bizarre." Angelica looked down at her lap, shook her head then looked innocently back up at Paul. "God knows..." Angelica searched for the right words. "Boy, you guys have vivid imaginations."

"Well, that is funny, look at you! This is an interesting side of you, Angelica Bradley... I like it. How's that tequila working for ya?"

Angelica turned and looked up to see Matthew standing beside the booth with a pool stick in his hand.

Sneering, she answered, "I'm doing just fine, thank you very much, Matthew. I have a slight buzz, but nothing I can't handle. And how are you and the guys over there?" Angelica lifted her hand while holding a Corona Light and pointed her pinky finger at the pool table, then clumsily leaned into the back cushion of the booth.

Paul smiled at Matthew and shook his head.

Matthew peered down at Angelica, "You should eat something!"

"But I'm not hungry!" Angelica's light blue eyes looked sleepy.

Matthew pursed his lips and glanced at Paul, "She hasn't eaten all day."

Angelica turned and looked inquisitively at the man at the bar, and then swung her head around and frowned, "There are some strange characters around here. Hell, this town is strange... Bunch of crazies!" Angelica lowered her head and giggled. "I feel like I'm in 'The Twilight Zone,'" she mumbled.

Matthew glanced around the pool hall and then looked back at Angelica. "Can you play pool?"

"Well, I've played before. I can't say I'm very good," Angelica said as she laughed and turned to Paul. "When I was in college." Angelica was slurring her words.

"Come on, play me a game," Matthew said. Angelica reached down and turned off her recorder and put it in her purse before getting up from the booth.

Matthew lined up the balls and re-chalked his stick. Angelica looked around for a pool stick and started off to find one. Luke, one of the RUFA guys stepped in front of her and handed Angelica his.

"Here, it's a good one and it's already chalked." Luke extended it out for Angelica to take it.

Angelica smiled and said "thank you," then turned and swayed back to the table.

Luke looked at the other guys, pushed his chest out and smirked devilishly in an attempt to be funny, they all laughed. Luke was skinny, in his early-twenties with dirty blonde hair, a small face, small eyes and thin lips.

Matthew made the first shot and broke the balls. A solid-colored red ball went in. He continued to knock them in a few more times before finally missing. Angelica was up. The men were standing around one of the tall tables watching. Angelica was stunning. Her blonde hair fell down around her shoulders and up against her pale, flaw-less skin as she leaned over the pool table, exposing her cleavage.

The tequila had relaxed her into the sexier side of her personality, where she could freely feel her power as a woman and relax into it. She hit a striped ball and it shot across the table right into a corner pocket. She jumped in excitement and clapped her hands. "Look, I hit it in!"

The men laughed. "You're hilarious!" Matthew whispered and shook his head. "Let's see if you can do it again," he shouted over the music.

Angelica walked around the table as if she were an old pro and sized up a few possible shots, then settled on an easy one. She hit another striped ball into the pocket and jumped in excitement again. "Yay, I forgot how fun this is!" She smiled at Matthew.

"Hey, you want to do another shot of Tequila?" She looked over at Paul standing by the other men who were too shy to speak to her.

Paul threw his hands up. "Sure, why not. How about you Matthew, you want another, as well?"

"No, I better not. I need to make sure this party animal gets back to the lodge safely."

"Party animal?" Angelica narrowed her eyes flirtatiously, glancing up at Matthew while leaning over to make a shot. Matthew felt an odd sensation in that moment; he was starting to fall for Angelica. He thought she was beautiful, interesting and smart. He was pretty sure that the only thing he'd ever be to her was a friend. It was a common, reoccurring theme with him and beautiful women, he had concluded. Matthew leaned the pool stick against the bar stool.

Angelica barely grazed the corner of the eight ball. "Oh, I thought I had that one," she announced, as she swung around to see Paul approaching with two shots, rimmed in salt and lime wedges.

"Here you go, lovely lady!" Angelica took the tequila, licked the salt from the rim of the glass, and shot it. Then she sucked the lime and made a pucker face.

"Shew, that was strong," she shivered, and then she finished licking the salt from the rim. "You guys ever get out dancing?" Angelica started to sway to the music coming through the speakers. "What is this country song? I like it!" She started to sing the lyrics… "Maybe next time he'll think before he cheats…"

Matthew interrupted, leaned over, and whispered to Angelica. "Okay, we better be getting you back to the lodge before you do something you'll regret in the morning." The RUFA guys all started laughing.

"Wait who sings this?" Angelica looked inquisitive and pointed to the speaker hanging from the corner of the room, continuing to sway and sing along. "I took a Louisville slugger to both headlights…" She dramatically shot her arm up in the air with her index finger extended, and twisted her upper body.

A male voice shouted out the country singers name and another male voice shouted… "Hey, leave the lady alone! Can't you see she's having a good time?"

Everyone looked around to see a well-built, handsome cowboy in tight wranglers, a black tee shirt, and a black cowboy hat standing with a group of cowboys at the table beside them.

"No, it's past this cowgirl's bedtime, we best be going," Matthew declared firmly.

Matthew walked over with Angelica's purse under his arm and took the pool stick from her hand, and placed it on the table. He put Angelica arm inside his allowing her to lean into him as they walked toward the door. Angelica turned back around, pulling Matthew with her, and yelled back to Paul and the guys. "Goodnight!" ... while making eye contact with the good looking cowboy as she turned back around. "Wow, he was cute! Where did he come from?"

The guys yelled back "Goodnight, Angelica!"

Matthew looked down at Angelica's droopy eye lids. "You'll thank me tomorrow."

Matthew got Angelica in the passenger seat and shut the door. Angelica slid her hand down to find the handle and lowered her seat, pulling at it too hard. The passenger seat dropped, causing her to bounce and giggle. Matthew looked over and smirked as he shut his door. "You okay over there cowgirl?"

"Just fine, thank you. Your seat must be broken – you should get that fixed."

Matthew laughed and shook his head while he watched her shuffle around trying to get comfortable.

"Interesting day, huh," he said, inwardly laughing.

"Yes, very."

"So you got a boyfriend back in D.C.? You said you weren't married, so I..."

Angelica interrupted him, "No time for men. I'm too busy for nonsense. Thought we covered this already. It's chilly in here – do you have heat?" Angelica wrapped her arms around her body and shivered.

"I see – a little high-strung- are we?" Matthew asked, as he prepared himself for her response.

Angelica shot a look at Matthew. "I am well aware of your perception of me, and you may view me differently than I view myself; however, while I appreciate your effort to lift my layers, some people don't want their layers lifted. Ha! That sounds like a tongue twister. I couldn't say that if I was really drunk," Angelica announced, slurring her words before she leaned her head back and closed her eyes. Matthew cut a sharp glace at her just before he backed out of the parking lot.

Matthew cocked his head toward Angelica amused and somewhat glad she had fallen asleep. "You are a high-strung woman," he murmured.

Chapter Twenty-Four

Angelica screamed as she abruptly felt the weight of her body. She was shaking. As she looked down she noticed she was naked and lying on a cold metal table under a bright light. She quickly raised her hands to shield her eyes from the light. Feeling a strange sensation in her belly, and then pain, a sharp stabbing pain, she placed both hands over her stomach and started to rub as she moaned out.

She looked up into the room and saw it coming towards her. Angelica gasped. She began to tremble uncontrollably. "What are you?" She screamed. The light was too bright... the details were too hard to make out. Suddenly, her body was frozen stiff and she was only able to move her head. "What do you want with me? Please, please, someone help me!" The tears were running down her cheeks and she could feel their warmth as they ran into her ears. She rapidly turned her head side to side, trying to find someone to help her. She screamed out, "Someone please help me!" She tried to move but couldn't. "Let me go, please!" Angelica continued to probe the room for an exit or someone to help her. She looked back and the figure was standing over her. When she saw his translucent skin, she screamed uncontrollably. "Please, what do you want?" Angelica whispered through her trembling lips. The being touched her neck and she felt a sensation of heat run down and along her collarbone, as it tilted its head and peered at her with large dark, vacant eyes, presenting no emotion.

Angelica was moist with sweat and shivering uncontrollably. "Please let me go!" She pleaded... but she could see it was unmoved by her. It peered at her, tilting its head, as if it were studying her. Its long fingers moved down her chest, between her breasts and along her breastbone to her belly, then stopped. As she looked down trembling, she noticed it only had four fingers as they extended out across her belly.

The being tilted its head back toward Angelica and then, suddenly, images started to race through her mind... Images of a baby, then a young boy, the same boy growing older... Image after image like an ancient eight millimeter film projected on a wrinkled cotton sheet hanging from a wall. Static... vague... yet familiar. Angelica shook her head. The being was somehow putting images into her mind.

Angelica looked around the room again, looking for anyone to help her. She could make out several of them moving from the shadows but they appeared not to notice her. Angelica caught sight of what looked like test tubes filled with a viscous green solution containing human fetuses. She let out a blood curdling scream. She was incapacitated. She looked towards her feet and saw another pale, grey being approaching her. It was holding something shiny in its horrific long, skinny fingers. She thought it was a scalpel, but she couldn't fully make it out. "No, please don't!" She begged and pleaded while squinting, trying to get a better look. "Please don't hurt me!" Suddenly she saw a flash of light.

Chapter Twenty-Five

Angelica gasped for air as her eyes popped wide open, right out of a deep sleep. The room was dark. She didn't feel alone. "Who's there? Is someone in here?" She rose up and promptly hit the button on the lamp, slowly pulling the covers back, and looked around with grave eyes. She was disoriented and her hair a mess. Her heart was pounding hard in her chest. She got up from the bed and slowly walked toward the bathroom.

"Is someone in here?" There was no reply, so she continued to the door, reached her arm around the bathroom door, and cautiously turned on the light. The shower curtain was open. There was no one in the bathroom. She turned off the light and looked in the closet again as she passed by it, noticing only the metal luggage stand and her clothes neatly hung on wooden hangers.

Angelica glanced around and saw both doors were still locked. Her head was pounding so hard she felt as if it were vibrating. She was still intoxicated and she realized her balance was off. Mildly anxious, and wide awake, she realized she was hungry. She thought about calling room service, but noticed it was two thirty-three in the morning, so she went over and got back into bed.

After pulling the covers back up, she leaned over and turned the light switch off. Snuggling into the goose down and repositioning herself, she closed her eyes and drifted back off to sleep.

Angelica woke up after feeling as if she had another strange dream but she was not lucid enough to remember it. There was, however, a lingering sense that she had been violated. Angelica placed her hand on her pelvis as she looked over and noticed the message light was blinking on the room phone beside her. She turned on the lamp, picked up the receiver, and listened to the voicemail.

The message was from a male voice she did not recognize. "You may be in danger, Angelica. You need to meet me as soon as you get back to D.C. I will leave a note with instructions under the front door of your townhouse. And in the meantime, please be careful."

Angelica hung up the phone and looked at the clock. It was eleven thirty-three in the morning. She sat there for a moment trying to collect her thoughts. Her mind was still in a fog and she was having a hard time processing what she had just heard. She vaguely remembered Matthew's comment about his experience with threating phone calls. However, this wasn't a threat, it was a warning. She picked the phone back up and listened to the message again. This time she listened carefully to the voice inflection and tried to determine if she could recognize the voice. It was deep, authoritative, and confident. Her instincts told her that the person on the other line was sincere and it was not a prank. Without a doubt, she did not recognize the voice of the mysterious messenger. And he clearly didn't want to tell her who he was on a voice message.

Angelica looked around the room and saw sunlight shining through a crack in the heavy curtains. It looked like it was going to be another warm day in Elberton. Angelica suddenly remembered she was to meet with Michael Anderson on his ranch at two-thirty that afternoon. She quickly jumped up, rushed over to the mirror above the desk, and examined her complexion. Her face was red and dull after all the tequila. Surprisingly, there were no bags under her eyes, and although the corners were slightly dark, and her mascara was smudged down her cheeks, considering her night before at the billiards hall, she didn't look as bad as she felt.

Angelica started to get snapshots of the night before and suddenly remembered dancing and singing aloud to a country song in the bar. Immediately, she felt embarrassed and turned crimson, wanting to get back into bed and hide under the heavy duvet. She made the decision never to drink Tequila again.

Angelica glanced down and noticed she had her hand against her pelvic region, just below her belly button. She was applying pressure in the way she often did with menstrual cramps. Feeling a dull heaviness in her uterus, she shivered and thought back on the evening before. She remembered coming to her room alone after Matthew had dropped her off and breathed a quick sigh of relief.

What that must have looked like as she stumbled through the lobby... Oh God, she thought, as she raised both hands to her open mouth and blushed. She may have been intoxicated and made a fool of herself, but she was certain she went to bed alone.

Angelica slipped off her panties, dropping them at her feet, and walked into the bathroom. She turned on the bathtub faucet to let the water warm up.

Chapter Twenty-Six

The elevator opened to the front lobby. Angelica looked refreshed and beautiful after a long hot shower. She immediately noticed most of the attention in the lobby was on her. She felt a sudden nervousness in her stomach and ran her hands down her thighs concerned that she should have picked looser fitting pant. The black leggings and brown lace up ankle boots might have been too much for an interview with Michael Anderson, she thought.

She had matched it with a cream-colored knit blouse trimmed in sheer cream lace exposing the top portion of her back. Gail had convinced her to buy it while shopping at a boutique in Georgetown. Gail said it was youthful and slightly sexy.

Her wavy light blonde hair rested on her shoulders. She had added an extra dab of perfume. Angelica had prepared carefully, as she did when she was going on a date, battling with her subconscious each time it snarled at her. "It's a business meeting, Angelica!" But she ignored it.

Angelica made eye contact with each person as she passed by. She learned through her years of fighting to be a respected journalist that you must never appear insecure.

In D.C., it was a battle of the superior, like animals in the wild, she had concluded. Angelica wasn't the type of person interested in feeling superior to anyone. To her it was all a silly game.

At the hostess stand, Angelica raised her index finger, announcing gracefully, "Just one."

She was seated at a small table on the veranda. A petite white ceramic vase with a pink peony was placed squarely in the middle.

She took her laptop out of her satchel. She moved the silverware over and sat it in front of her on the white tablecloth. She then pulled out her cell phone to call Gail.

"Hi, how are you?"

"Hey you! I'm good. How's it going?" Gail asked.

"I'm still here, but planning to leave tomorrow. I'm actually working on my flight right now as we speak," she said, while logging in to the airline's website on her laptop, holding her cellphone between her shoulder and neck.

"How's the story coming along?"

"Well, as you know, it's unusual... I'm still tying it all together. There are some wild theories out there, Gail, and some are quite extraordinary, to say the least." Angelica went on, "Listen Gail, here's the deal... Some folks around here think it's a race of ETs or as some call them non-humans. It's crazy! And I..."

Gail cut her off. "Look, Angelica, you're a journalist. Write it all! Remember, you write from a neutral perspective. Plus, it will make a damn good story. Readers love crazy stuff like this!"

Angelica took a deep breath. "Okay, I have one more interview here in 'The Twilight Zone', and then I'm planning to fly to Colorado tomorrow for an interview. That's only if I can arrange the interview on such short notice.

"Go get 'em girl! Stay in touch!"

"Will do. Talk soon."

Angelica hung up and immediately called Matthew only to get his voicemail. "Hey Matthew, it's Angelica. I'm meeting with Michael Anderson today and then I'm flying out tomorrow morning. I wanted to thank you for all you've done to assist me with the story. Oh, and getting me home last night. I hope I didn't say or do anything too ridiculous." Angelica exhaled a loud breath as she rolled her eyes. "Anyway, let's stay in touch. Call me. Bye."

Angelica put her cell phone on the table and looked for Dr. Goolrick's number. She found it along with his address at the University. It was at the top of a report he had written for the Elberton police. She dialed his number and after a few rings a baritone, assertive voice sounded off on the other end of the line.

"Hello, Walter Goolrick speaking!"

"Hello, Dr. Goolrick, my name is Angelica Bradley with the *Liberator Magazine*. I'm in Elberton doing a story on the cattle mutilations. I've been working alongside Matthew Tillman. I read your report and have a few questions for you. Are you available for an interview tomorrow? I would fly to you, of course."

After a moment of silence, he responded. "Yes, I guess I could be available. I could meet you for dinner tomorrow evening. Where will you be staying?"

"I'll be staying at the Brown Palace Hotel."

"Beautiful place, I'll meet you in the hotel restaurant – say, six o'clock?"

"Perfect, look forward to meeting you, Dr. Goolrick." Angelica hung up the phone and looked out at the mountains as she relaxed back in her chair. "I almost hate to leave this place," she thought aloud.

"Yes, it is extraordinary! Hello, ma'am. Are you ready?"

Angelica quickly turned to see the server standing beside her. "Oh, yes. I'll have a glass of the Velante pinot grigio, a caprese salad and the straciatella soup, thank you."

The server smiled. "Excellent choice!" He took the napkin from the table, shook it out, and placed it on Angelica's lap. "Are you enjoying your stay at Elk Lodge?"

"Yes, very much," Angelica looked back to the mountains. "I'm going to miss this view."

The server looked out at the mountains. "Yes, they are stunning! You'll have to come back when the weather is cooler. It's very nice here that time of year, as well."

"I look forward to it," Angelica met the man's eyes and smiled before he turned and walked away.

Angelica slid her laptop closer to finish making her flight and hotel arrangements for Colorado. She was able to book a flight for departure at twelve-twenty in the afternoon, giving her plenty of time to get to the airport and be in Denver in time for dinner with Dr. Goolrick.

The Bovine Connection

She clicked on the "Elberton Cattle Mutilation" file in her documents and started typing her story. "Of all the places I find myself, Elberton, Montana is not one where I would have expected to end up; however, I have to say, it is quite an interesting place. Following in the footsteps of those who've walked this journey before me-- journalists, investigators, scientists and law enforcement-- I have pondered the very same questions in search of answers in the case surrounding the horrendous acts of mutilated cows. In the land of white elk and fly fishing, acreages give way to lush green wilderness, forest, streams and open spaces of prairie grass-- an elegant backdrop for a crime of this nature. A crime so unusual, law enforcement officials have called in help from the best scientists and experts to crack the case. However, what they've discovered has this quiet, Midwestern community afraid of the dark. The details of eye-witness accounts are stranger than fiction. From glowing balls of light and unfamiliar sounds coming from the sky, the story gets more extraordinary, taking us beyond the limits of the human experience and rational explanations. Are we seeing the evidence of life beyond our world? Following the path of a long, convoluted history of ET encounters and research, this strange phenomenon opens new doors into this controversial subject. A cattleman's nightmare, the grisly mutilations of livestock have plagued farmlands worldwide for decades and perhaps longer. Described generically as cattle mutilations, these bizarre deaths happen also to horses, goats and as reported in South

America, even humans, though the most common victims are cattle. Utters, ears and tongues among other organs are somehow surgically removed without a trace of blood at the scene. This story will explore through facts and eyewitness accounts, the prevailing theory that extraterrestrials may be responsible for these heinous acts. The delicate and precise manner in which these gruesome acts were committed poses the question – Who or what would be capable of performing such an operation in the dead hours of the night in the vast wildness? Does our government know who is responsible and most importantly – why? Ten years ago, this quiet, sleepy town experienced..."

"Miss... Excuse me, miss, your lunch," Angelica looked up.

"Oh, thank you. I'm sorry, let me move my laptop."

The server glided the fine white china down smoothly in front of Angelica. "Hard at work?" the server asked.

"Yes, working on a story."

He nodded. "Very nice... Enjoy your lunch."

Chapter Twenty-Seven

Angelica turned off the road onto the drive leading to the Anderson ranch. An old red diesel truck and a black Cadillac Escalade pickup were parked close to the barn. Angelica parked beside them. She looked in the rearview mirror and fluffed her hair before checking her face.

She stepped out of the car. As she shut the car door, she heard voices coming from the barn, believing it had to be Michael; she walked toward the barn, trying to make out what they were saying.

When she stepped inside, she saw Michael standing with his back turned speaking with a short, older man. The man suddenly noticed Angelica and stopped talking. Michael turned around and met Angelica's eyes. Her stomach sank as she returned his smile, and then Michael turned back around and told the man something Angelica couldn't hear.

Angelica stood there awkwardly. She wasn't sure if she should walk over to them or stay put. She anxiously straightened her blouse while looking around the barn. After a moment, they turned around and started toward her.

"Hi, I'm Sam."

"This is Sammy!" Michael smiled.

"Nice to meet you, Sammy, I'm Angelica Bradley."

"Very nice to meet you, ma'am." Sammy turned back to Michael. "I'll talk with you later."

He placed his hand on Angelica's shoulder patting her gently as he walked past her. Moved by the warm gesture, she turned and watched him walk toward his truck.

When she turned back, Michael was standing within a foot in front of her. "Well, hello, you are beautiful," he said. He was taller than she remembered.

Suddenly Angelica's confidence shifted and she felt a strange sensation - shyness - as she looked down before returning his gaze. "Hi! Thank you," she said. Her nerves were causing her to tremble slightly as she glanced back toward the trucks.

Angelica took a step back to create more space between them. "Who is Sam?"

"Sammy worked for my father," Michael told her. They were best friends. Once my father passed away and he realized I wasn't going anywhere, things just continued on. He takes care of the horses, cattle and the land. He doesn't say much... but he smiles a lot."

Angelica watched as Michael's lips opened.

"Sammy has a small cabin at the edge of the property that he and Dad built," Michael continued. "Dad deeded him the parcel his cabin sits on. I couldn't imagine selling the property... and poor Sammy would be lost without the ranch to care for. My father would have wanted it this way... this is his home."

Angelica was watching Michael's lips as he spoke. An odd thought popped into her mind. She wondered how they would feel against her lips.

"So how about I take you around and show you the property? I can show you where it happened."

Angelica snapped out of her infatuated gaze and looked around. For a brief moment she had forgotten why she was there.

"Oh yes, I would like to see the location."

"Let's get you a saddle." Michael walked over and grabbed a brown saddle and a halter from the shelf.

"I'll put you on Zane. He's gentle. Have you ridden a horse before?"

Angelica followed behind Michael and walked around Zane to size him up. "He's beautiful, and very big. Yes, I have, but it's been a while." She rubbed the top of Zane's nose. "Nice to meet you, Zane. I do hope you'll be a gentle horsy," she said softly.

Michael smiled and turned around to get the saddle for his black horse.

Angelica watched him walk off, admired his physique for a moment. Embarrassed, she quickly turned her attention to the barn.

Smiling, Michael looked over at Angelica inquisitively while walking over to saddle his horse.

"So, when are you going back to D.C.?"

"I'm flying to Denver tomorrow and then I'll head back."

"Oh... so soon?" Michael sounded surprised.

"Yes, I'll miss the mountains," she said softly, as she noted the smell of fresh hay mixed with manure.

"Let's get you up on that horse." Michael walked over and stood beside Zane. Angelica put one foot into the stirrup. Michael put his hands on Angelica's waist and swiftly lifted her up. Angelica blushed, startled by his forcefulness, but she kind of liked it at the same time.

Angelica adjusted herself comfortably on her saddle and watched as Michael got up onto his shiny black Stallion. The beautiful beast pulled his head back and let out a snort as Michael pulled on the bridle to lead them out of the barn. Angelica patted the side of Zane's neck as he followed closely behind.

Angelica squeezed Zane between her legs feeling slightly uneasy. Michael led them to a trail between the tall evergreens behind the barn. The sky matched Angelica's pale blue eyes. There were only a few clouds scattered about like cotton balls.

"What an amazing day!" Angelica mused, as she put her head back and admired the sky.

"Yes, a perfect day!" Michael looked back with a sneaky smile and then looked up to the sky to notice several hawks gliding above. They both watched as the hawks gracefully and effortlessly glided along the northerly wind.

The gentle swaying of Zane's hind quarters and the sound of the clump, clump of his hooves was putting Angelica in a blissful trance. She had loosened her grip on Zane and felt more relaxed. Angelica peered off into the distance, becoming mesmerized by a small cabin, but then forced herself to snap back into relative coherence. She needed to focus, she thought.

"Was Sammy around on the evening of the mutilation?" she asked Michael. "You said he lives on the property. Did he hear or see anything?"

Michael, still looking ahead while leading, answered, "No, he said he never saw or heard a thing. By the appearance of the cow, he agreed with my father that it wasn't a coyote or any other animal. He's seen a lot of coyote and bear attacks in his day. He never said much else about it. He's like that... stays to himself and doesn't have much of an opinion on things... easy going."

"I've heard some bizarre things in the last few days. Do you think it was ETs, Michael? I talked to Paul at the billiard hall last night and he seems to think so, and Matthew does too. Well, as a matter of fact, that seems to be the general consensus, except for your sheriff."

"Believe it or not, I lean toward the ET theory too, but who knows." Michael glanced back to observe Angelica's expression. She was completely unaware she was chewing on her bottom lip.

"My father seemed to believe it, and what he said he experienced on the craft"... Michael paused for a moment then stuttered, "...like I told you the other day." Michael shook his head.

Angelica turned towards him, trying to stay balanced on the saddle. "Did you mention this during our interview the other day? I don't recall you saying anything about him being on a craft." Angelica appeared confused.

"Maybe I didn't mention that part." Michael clearer his throat. "He said some strange things. He confided in me a lot before he passed away, almost like he needed to get it all out so he could move on."

"What were some of the things he told you?"

"Look Angelica, once he started taking the meds, I'm not certain he knew what he was saying anymore," Michael said.

"Like, the night he woke up on the ground in front of the barn. That was before the medication and chemo, right?" Angelica asked curiously.

Michael narrowed his eyes. "He did have high blood pressure. Maybe the wound was from landing on something and he didn't notice it until he took his shirt off to shower. I don't know, Angelica." Michael shook his head. "I questioned him a lot. He said he understood it was all hard to believe. Initially, he wasn't going to tell me. He said he wanted to put it away and forget about all of it. But over time the memories wouldn't go away. They were coming back like a speeding train."

"Okay... So he was recalling events from when he was supposedly unconscious? Events such as being on a craft?"

"Yes, but again, this was after the meds that he mentioned being on a craft," Michael said vaguely.

"What did he tell you?" Angelica was impatient and she knew he was holding something back. "Michael, what did he tell you?" She tilted her head to get a look at his face, but he wouldn't turn around.

"He said he saw them with his own eyes. He said he remembered being on a surgical table in one of their crafts. He also said right after the cattle incident he saw two of them standing beside his bed and he was frozen, unable to move or speak. He said he panicked and then heard in his head 'stay calm' before he saw a flash of light. He then woke up on a craft of some sort. He said there were other humans there in distress as well. He saw a young woman laid out on a surgical table beside him. He looked over and held eye contact with her. He said she was crying. He said he tried to comfort her. The fear in her eyes... it continued to plague him until his death." Michael dropped his head. "He spoke about her again the day he died. He had always wondered what had happened to her. Well, the next day of that particular incident he had strange cuts on his thigh and abdomen about an inch long." Michael shook his head.

"But Michael - isn't it possible he just dreamed the two aliens were in his room and about being on the craft?"

"Honestly, I don't know what to think," Michael blurted, appearing frustrated. "He was a very pragmatic, down-to-earth man. These so-called experiences had an effect on his spiritual beliefs."

Angelica nodded and softened her tone. "Did he describe them to you?"

"Yes, he said their skin was dull, translucent, and a light, pale grey. They had no hair... anywhere on their bodies and their eyes were large and dark. He said there was no soul behind those eyes."

Angelica swallowed hard and thought for a moment. "Okay, but Michael..."

"Shh!" Michael slowly put his hand up with his palm facing Angelica. "Shh," he urged again. "Look!" Michael pointed toward the tree line.

Angelica sat silently and looked in the direction Michael was pointing.

"What is it?" she whispered.

"It's a snowy owl," Michael whispered. "It's perched on the branch watching us. Strange to see it in these parts. Beautiful, isn't it?"

"Oh, there it is... Yes, it is!" Angelica agreed excitedly. They both became silent as they slowly passed the owl.

"He's still staring at us," Angelica whispered.

"Yes, probably hoping we'll just keep moving," Michael responded.

"Have you ever seen a white owl before?" Angelica was fascinated by the creature.

"Never... never a white one. You would never know it by looking at him, but he is a ruthless, meat eating predator. You don't want to be close to those talons when he is in a bad mood. Owls are nocturnal, so they do most of their hunting at night," Michael explained.

"Wow, this all sounds very familiar. Do you think these owls are related to our extraterrestrial friends?" Angelica asked sarcastically.

"Very funny, Angelica. I get the feeling you are not taking me very seriously," Michael said with a hint of disappointment.

Angelica pursed her lips. "I apologize." Her eyes were sincere and almost whitish-blue in the sunlight.

Michael nodded and grinned. "You are gorgeous." Surprised by Michael's comment, Angelica smiled and lowered her chin.

Once they were a good distance from the owl, Angelica raised her voice. "Back to the ETs your father saw."

Michael stopped his horse and looked back at Angelica. The way she said it, he realized how outlandish and unbelievable it sounded. He suddenly felt silly.

"I know how this sounds," he said dryly.

"How do you think it sounds?" Angelica peered inquisitively at Michael.

"Now you sound like a shrink rather than a reporter."

Angelica corrected him softly. "A journalist."

"I didn't mean to sound condescending, my apologies."

Michael nodded. "Anyway, he said, after one visit from them, he said his neck hurt for two days, and he had one of the worst headaches he had ever experienced. He said, "Son, I think they did something to my neck." Michael took a deep breath clearly wanting to change the subject.

"Wow, that is extraordinary, Michael." Angelica then looked off in the distance, remembering her dream.

Michael spoke gently. "Angelica, I don't want my father's name in your story."

Angelica looked Michael in the eyes. "You have my word. Honestly, I don't know how I'm going to write this story anyway," Angelica shook her head. "It all just sounds a bit too far-fetched. And perhaps, a little crazy!" Angelica half-laughed.

Kimberly Thomas

Rounding the trail, Zane stepped on a boulder and lost his balance, jerking Angelica forward. She flinched as she felt a rush of panic, just before Zane got his bearing back. "That was a close one!" She wiped off the sweat that had formed above her top lip.

"So what's your story, Angelica?"

"My story?" Angelica responded slightly taken aback by the question. "Why do you want to know my story?" She smiled and squinted suspiciously, as she met his eyes.

Michael didn't respond. He just stared back coolly, inquisitively looking at her.

"Well, let's see. I grew up in Asheville, North Carolina. I interned at *The Washington Post* while in college and eventually became a journalist there. Then started my own magazine. My story isn't all that interesting," Angelica said very matter-of-factly, hoping to shift the conversation back to an investigative interview.

"I mean... Do you have a boyfriend, husband... children?" Michael asked, as he looked forward while leading them along the trail.

Angelica put her head down, looking at her bare ring finger. "I've never been married and no children. I've had a few boyfriends." She laughed. "But they never last long. It's usually them or my career. I stay pretty busy. Anyway, ultimatums never work for me," she mumbled. "I'm happy, though--grateful, actually. I mean... a women in my profession and in D.C., one of the journalism meccas of the world. I guess a husband and kids will happen eventually." Angelica thought for a moment before looking up to Michael... "I hope it will... I'm still young." Angelica looked toward the mountains. "Who knows, maybe it won't, but I'd be okay with that, too, I think... if it didn't." She realized she was beginning to ramble.

Michael looked back at Angelica intently. Angelica took notice. "Why do you keep looking at me that way?" She laughed.

"You are an interesting woman, Angelica."

Angelica turned her gaze away from Michael. *"Why does he make me so nervous?"* she wondered. "I hope that's a compliment." She smiled but her face appeared worried.

"Oh... it's a compliment." Michael was captivated by her. He observed her nervous response. He wasn't going to let her off the hook easily.

"So what was life like for Angelica Bradley growing up in Asheville, North Carolina? You know, I traveled there once and took some photos of the beautiful Blue Ridge Mountains. You're familiar with them, I'm sure," he smiled sheepishly. "They called it the 'Paris of the South'... I stayed at the Grove, a beautiful resort and spa built in the early 1900s, if I remember correctly. I fell in love with Asheville. Always planned to go back and take some more photos. Do you ever go home to visit?"

"No, not often enough, I suppose. My mother comes to visit me in D.C. We're very close," Angelica let out a puff of air as a wave of nostalgia moved over her.

Michael looked back suspiciously. "That's great, so you're one of the lucky ones - to have had a good childhood. My mother's passing made my childhood difficult. I've sure missed having her around. I remember looking up at her face as she tucked me into bed at night. I remember how kind her heart was…" Michael's voice cracked suddenly. He cleared his throat. "My father said she was an amazing woman. Sadly, I have very few memories of her… I was young." Michael's eyes appeared deeply pitted with pain as he glanced away.

"I'm so sorry," Angelica's lips went straight and her eyes narrowed.

"Now I'm the one rambling. How did this all of a suddenly turn back to me, and my childhood? Forgive me. It's been a while since I've spoken of her."

Angelica was silent, hit with a feeling that she honestly couldn't remember having before. It was more than just empathy. A man had never exposed himself so openly to her. His pain was tangible, raw, she could feel it.

"I am so sorry you had to grow up without your mother. I can see how that affects you. I grew up without a father. My father walked out on us when I was a small child. My mother said they married too young, and he still had a lot of growing up to do… anyway… As our friend Matthew says… 'Everything happens for a reason and we're only human'… It's life. So I guess you could say that we had similar childhoods."

"We both grew up without a parent," Michael said softly, his words hovering in the air. Michael was struck by her childlike smile, forming the image of her as a young girl.

"Yes, and we grew up with pain." Angelica flushed at the unintentional comment. Michael analyzed Angelica's face.

"What sort of pain, Angelica?" Michael sounded concerned.

Angelica shook her head. "Oh, you know, typical childhood scars… Let's change the subject."

Michael continued to probe. "I'm a good listener." His eyes were kind and his lips were straight.

Angelica took a deep breath. "I haven't spoken about my childhood to anyone in years. It's just what it is, you know…"

"Know what?" Michael asked.

"He was an alcoholic… my step-father. Wow! I can't believe I just told you that! Let's get back on track with the incident on your ranch."

Michael could see Angelica was uncomfortable. "I'm glad you did. You know, Angelica, I believe our past molds us into who we are meant to be. Well, anyway, I'm glad you trusted me enough to share that part of your past."

Angelica thought for a moment. "You mean we are predestined to be who we are? We come in life with a plan?" She squinted at the thought.

"Yes, something like that. Who knows, maybe we have many lives and we choose particular ones before we are born."

"That sounds a bit crazy," Angelica said as she laughed. "So we go up to the counter and say, 'I'll have the number two with a diet coke and supersize it.'"

Michael had that expression in his eyes again, she noticed. Angelica turned her head nervously and looked over at the trees.

"There you go again, with that look," she said with a heavy breath and a knot in her stomach.

Michael appeared very confident with himself. "Angelica, I don't mean to pry. I'm just fascinated by you. You are pretty damn amazing."

Angelica slowly looked back at Michael to reveal her face had blushed from the inner dialogue going on in her head. "Thank you." Feeling uncomfortable, she shifted the conversation. "What a beautiful piece of property you have. It's spectacular!"

"Yes, it's a small piece of heaven… and I've been all around the world and seen some amazing places. See over there?" Michael pointed to a spot in the middle of the pasture as they came off the trail. That's where the heifer was found. Of course, it has been ten years so there's nothing to look at, but it gives you a general idea of the location."

"Oh!" Angelica took a deep breath.

"Sammy's little cabin is back over there to the left and the main house is over here to the right." Michael had his arm extended. "And see over there across from the house is the barn where my father was standing. So, although there is some distance between the site of the carcass and the barn, it's still close enough for my father to have seen what he claimed."

Angelica looked back and forth at both locations. "I agree." She nodded and continued to follow closely behind hoping Zane would get up beside Michael's horse.

"Well, I've told you all I know about it. What do you think? You've been here investigating and interviewing – so, have you come to any conclusions?

Angelica let out a girlish laugh, overly conscious of herself around Michael. "I don't know, Michael. I go back and forth. I still have so many questions. I believe each eye witness is telling the truth as best as they can recall, but I don't know... I need to interview some experts in the scientific community before I draw any conclusions. The mind can play tricks on itself. The problem with science, though, is that it's hard to cull out fact from theory. Einstein's brilliant discovery of relativity is still technically a theory. Think about that... In the end, our feeble human brains try to connect the dots to what are oftentimes impossible questions to answer. Einstein confessed that the more he learned, the more he discovered how little he really knew. Knowledge turns into humility, and I am feeling quite humble right now..."

Michael pursed his lips as his eyes lit up. "Feeble human brains, huh. You are a smart woman as well as a beautiful one. Now that's a combination that can sneak up on a guy if he's not careful! Come on, let me show you the view from the top of that ridge, and then we'll head back to the house so I can make you dinner."

Angelica laughed, but was a little stunned at his directness. She secretly liked it. When he turned to lead the way, she smiled. "Dinner... okay, that would be nice. Do you like to cook?"

Michael was still looking forward and now moving a little faster. "Yes, and I've been told I'm pretty good at it." He laughed confidently.

"Really... What's on the menu for this evening?" Angelica said sarcastically.

Fresh trout caught from the river early this morning! Oh and it will be paired with a nice Prosecco. You do like Prosecco, right?" Michael looked back at Angelica.

"Yes, I love Italian sparkling wine... but I obviously liked Tequila better..." she mumbled too quietly for Michael to hear.

"It's this way, follow me." Michael softly kicked his horse and shouted, "Let's go!" Michael's horse took off and was galloping fast.

Angelica kicked Zane softly and held on tight. "Let's go, Zane!" As she anticipated, Zane followed and sped up to a gallop, steadily behind Michael's horse.

The fresh air was moving through Angelica's hair, lifting it up. The wind brushed her face, and it felt exhilarating. She looked around, taking in the beautiful landscape of green wilderness bordering dark rocky mountains, and then up to the blue sky. All thoughts had left her. She had put her trust in Zane and Michael. She allowed the excitement to run through her... feeling more alive than she had in a long time.

As they continued, she saw Michael was heading toward another trail in the forest of pines. It appeared to lead up the mountain ridge. She held on tightly and followed behind toward the incline. Michael slowed down a bit and went right in. Michael picked up speed again as they started up the slope. The trail had become rocky and Angelica noticed the moss and ferns carpeting the spaces between the grey boulders. They continued to climb as Michael looked back at Angelica now and then. "You all right back there?"

"Yes!" she shouted.

Unexpectedly, the trail opened up and they were at the top where the view stretched for miles.

"Oh, wow!" Angelica blurted. "This is gorgeous! Do you come up here often?"

Michael looked out in the distance. "Not as much as I used to. I did quite a bit after my father died. See over there? That's Elberton. See the church steeple?"

Angelica looked where Michael was pointing but was distracted by another hawk gliding in the wind above. She remembered her childhood in Asheville and the hikes she would take with her grandmother. Her grandmother was half Cherokee Indian, and had always been more at home in nature. Although Angelica's cheekbones were high and her eyes deep and almond shaped, she had obviously pulled more genes from the Irish side of her family. Angelica had always considered her grandmother a peculiar woman and observed her closely. She recalled watching her grandmother's long grey-less dark hair hang loosely around her shoulders as she leaned over with moss in her hands so Angelica could run her fingers through it. Just like on this day, she looked up and saw a hawk circling the sky above them. She missed her grandmother. Reflecting on the memory, tears started to well up in her eyes. She turned her face toward the wind hoping it would dry her tears before they fell down her cheek.

"What do you like to do for fun back in D.C.?" Michael asked as he tilted his head and tried to look directly into her eyes.

Angelica gripped Zane tighter between her legs and nervously looked off into the distance. "Well, I ... Hey, I thought I was here to ask you the questions." Angelica laughed.

"You're here because you are supposed to be here with me." Michael grinned seductively.

"Oh, I see. I work a lot... not much time for fun."

"Tell me more about your work. How long did you say you've been a journalist?"

"Well, after my internship, I became a staff writer at *The Washington Post*. It was tough politically, at times. There is a lot of jealousy in corporate America. This is a much different way of life... much different." Angelica leaned down around Zane's neck and rubbed her hand through his mane to smooth it back down. She continued... "It's so peaceful here -- brings back a few old memories."

"Yes, but for me it's sometimes too quiet; it can get lonely here by yourself." Michael couldn't disguise the emotion behind his words. She could feel it in his tone.

"I've heard that before," she whispered, as she thought about Matthew. "I imagine it could be lonely at times. Do you have a girlfriend? I apologize, I'm being intrusive." She had already figured he wasn't married.

"No girlfriend and no, you are not being intrusive, Ms. Bradley." He smiled.

"Oh?" Angelica said curiously. "I saw you in front of the diner yesterday afternoon with a woman. I thought she may be..."

Michael interrupted her, "No, she was my best friend's wife. He was one tough soldier and the best friend I ever had. He passed away last year. I made a promise to him that if anything happened to him I would watch after her and his daughter. He was killed in battle."

"I'm so sorry," Angelica turned and looked back toward the steeple in Elberton. Michael appeared disheartened as he nodded.

Angelica noticed Michael had a sadness about him and it was drawing her in.

"His name was Scott. Anyway, why don't we head back toward the ranch?" Michael pulled the reins and led his horse back down the ridge. Angelica took one last look around and took a deep breath as she followed behind on Zane. They were quiet as they made their way down the rocky ridge. Michael looked back every so often to make sure Angelica was safely following behind. She looked into his eyes and smiled each time. She realized on the quiet journey back that she was falling fast for Michael, and she had a strong feeling that he was falling for her as well.

Chapter Twenty-Eight

The muscular figure crouched motionless in the camouflaged wooden platform. The old deer blind was in the perfect location and it was the perfect cover. If anyone spotted him, he was just another hunter waiting silently for his prey. The clear polycarbonate listening device was the size and shape of a large bowl and he was pointing it in the direction of Michael and Angelica on horseback below in the ravine.

He removed his earplugs and pulled out his cell phone. "This is location Alpha Two. I am confirming contact. Conversation does not warrant a move to code zero. They are heading back to the ranch. Alpha Three can pick up contact within twenty minutes."

As he hung up the cell phone, he gingerly stretched his legs. He had an awful cramp in his left calf muscle. He had been in the old deer blind and barely moving for several hours. At least their intelligence was accurate. "This cowboy was predictable. He did exactly what they thought he would do."

Chapter Twenty-Nine

Michael put his hands on Angelica's waist and slowly helped her down from Zane.

Since Sammy wasn't back from town, Michael tied up the horses alongside the barn, confident that Sammy would get them back into their stalls for the night.

Angelica stepped inside the barn and grabbed her small purse and satchel. As she stepped back out, she noticed the soft black waves around Michael's face moving in the breeze, as he pulled the saddles from the horses. He turned to look at Angelica and stopped for a moment, struck by the expression of desire on her face. She was unaware she was observing his every move. They both stood in front of the barn looking into each other's eyes. Both could feel it - the attraction was magnetic, and the earth stood still.

Michael extended his arm, opening his hand for Angelica to take it and walk alongside him.

Dusk had set in and the sky now had warm hues of orange muting the blue. The day spent with Michael horseback riding was unexpectedly perfect, she recollected. Angelica was feeling overwhelmed with emotions and consumed with desire. Her mind was flooded and her pulse raced. She glanced up at Michael. He smiled and gazed down at her with desire in his eyes. Angelica returned his gaze.

As they walked into the house, both were quiet. Michael walked over and lit the fire in the fireplace while Angelica walked around the room, running her hand softly over the pieces of art brought back from his travels.

Angelica picked up an old cracked dark-stained bowl and admired it. "Where is this from?" Angelica asked, looking over to Michael.

"That is an old Asian rice bowl."

Michael was walking into the kitchen. He pulled out a bottle of Prosecco from a rack in his refrigerator. "Would you like a glass of sparkling Italian white wine, beautiful?"

"Yes, thank you," Angelica replied, sweetly. "So where did you travel last?"

"Kitzbühel... a mountain village in Austria," Michael said with an air of sophistication.

"Really... What was it like?"

He answered her with a question. "Do you ski?"

Angelica put the rice bowl down and looked back at him. "Yes, some."

"Then you'd love it... best snow skiing. I can't imagine anyone not loving Kitzbühel; the medieval churches and traditional farmhouse style shops with long wooden balconies bordering snow-dusted sidewalks... it's heaven, but cold as hell." Michael laughed.

"Sounds lovely," Angelica said, as she turned and continued to glide through his living room, picking up and admiring each piece.

Michael walked over and handed her a glass filled with golden bubbles. She exhaled, holding his gaze. He observed her delicate frame as she stood childlike. She appeared fragile, yet he knew better. She was a gazelle with the strength of a lion, and the most beautiful woman he had ever seen, he thought.

"Thank you," she replied and looked into his intense hazel blue-green eyes.

"If you'd like to clean up before dinner, there is a bathroom in the guestroom down that hall to the left." Michael pointed past the kitchen, under the loft.

"Yes, that sounds like a great idea," Angelica sat her satchel down and with her small purse scrunched under her arm, walked over to the table and put her wine glass down. Michael reached into the refrigerator and pulled out a baking platter with a large rainbow trout topped with lemon slices. As Angelica walked into the guest room, he placed it into the oven.

The large rustic carved log furniture made the guest room appear cozy. Heavy earth tone quilts covered the bed. Michael obviously had great taste in décor or he had a fantastic decorator, she thought.

A picture of a stunning black-haired woman in her late twenties in a brushed metal frame stood out on the dresser. Angelica walked over and observed it. Due to the resemblance, she realized it was Michael's mother. Next to it was a photo of Michael, grinning, as he leaned against his tan horse, Zane. Michael looked handsome, she thought as she held the photo in her hand. His black hair, untamed. He wore green army pants and a dark t-shirt. The sky appeared stormy behind him, with heavy, dark grey clouds. She imagined how romantic it would have been to be with him on the ranch that day. Her heart beat rapidly in her chest.

She put the frame back on the dresser and went into the bathroom. She felt a rush of excitement as she shut the door and walked over to the sink to wash her hands. Looking into the mirror, expecting to need a major touch up, she was pleasantly surprised she still looked presentable. Her hair was wind-blown, but that could be easily fixed. Leaning in, she wiped the running liner from below her eyes. She opened her purse and pulled out her powder, patting her forehead and chin, and then she pulled out her chap stick and dabbed her peach-colored lips. She found a comb in the drawer, brushed and fluffed her hair. After straightening her loose blouse, she put everything back into her purse and looked inquisitively at herself in the mirror. Questions invaded her mind. "Staying for dinner... What are you doing, Angelica?"

She picked up her purse, rolled her eyes and dropped her shoulders. "Oh well... you only live once," she thought aloud as she turned off the light, walked out of the guest bedroom and down the hall to the kitchen where Michael was lifting a pot of herb rice from the stove.

The lit white candles in the living room created a soft glow as she approached. Angelica shivered, realizing Michael was setting the mood.

The aroma of herbs and fresh trout from the kitchen filled the air through the hall. Angelica realized she wasn't hungry. "Wow, it smells great in here," she announced. Michael turned around with a sneaky smile and suddenly his expression changed. Angelica's stomach fluttered and her face burned.

"You are beautiful." His eyes were serious and penetrating. Angelica's stomach fluttered again and she felt nervous.

He walked closer as she stood still, watching him in slow motion, and then he leaned around her and picked up her wine glass, and handed it to her while rubbing his fingers across hers. She looked down and then back up to his hypnotic hazel eyes, noticing the dark blue outline against the yellow and aqua green center. Her eyes widened as his lips moved toward her. She leaned in and their lips gently opened and touched. He leaned back and looked into her lost, soft blue eyes again.

"There's more to this cowboy than wrangling bulls," he whispered, reaching over and lifting her chin. Caught in the moment, she realized she was holding her breath, and suddenly and silently let it out.

Michael turned, walked back over and took the trout from the oven, leaving Angelica standing there speechless with her mouth slightly open. He picked up a book of matches and lit the candle on the table. Angelica, still at a loss for words... took a large sip of her Prosecco as she watched.

"I'm in trouble... I think he's had some practice at this," her subconscious sneered. *"Is this a mistake?"* she wondered.

Michael looked up at Angelica as she tried to push the thought away. "I hope you like it. It's been a while since I've cooked for anyone."

"I'm sure it will be delicious," Angelica replied, second-guessing her jaded thought. She pulled the chair out from the table and sat down. "Had you not planned on returning to Elberton?" she asked.

"No, after college I swore I'd never come back here to live. After my mother died and dad was alone, I watched how hard the rancher lifestyle was on him. I didn't want to be a rancher. I wanted to travel and see the world. And, I did… and after a while I realized I could have both. Elberton is my home, but I'm only here about forty percent of the time. Sammy manages things just fine without me."

Michael reached for his glass and took a sip before changing the subject, "You took my heart away in about two seconds," he said, as he shook his head and walked over to the stove, picked up a plate and scooped the herb rice onto it, then carefully lifted a section of the trout and neatly set it beside the rice. He grabbed a slice of fresh lemon and placed it on the trout, then walked back over and set the plate on the table. Angelica was still thinking about what he had just said as she sat down. It wasn't just what he had said; it was how he had said it. She felt the same way. But she felt they were moving rather quickly and it scared her. She rubbed at her temple. *He's going to be the death of me*, she thought.

"Do you have a headache?" Michael appeared concerned.

"No, oh no, I just... we should eat before it gets cold," Angelica said as she forced a smiled.

Michael brought his plate to the table and sat down in the chair across from her. He lifted his fork and took a bite and then a sip of Prosecco. His eyes were locked onto hers. "God, you're gorgeous! You just take my breath away!" He shook his head as he maintained eye contact.

Angelica let out a sigh, smiling bashfully. "You just come out and say whatever is in your head, don't you?" she said playfully as she laughed.

"Yes, I guess I do. I've always been that way; gets me in trouble sometimes."

She looked back down at her food as she moved her napkin around in her lap for a moment, and when she looked up Michael was getting up from the table and coming towards her. He pulled the chair out beside her and took her hand. She looked down at their hands touching. Her hand looked so small resting in his palm, she thought.

"Can you stay any longer, Angelica?"

Angelica softly pulled her hand from his and touched her fingertips to her lips cupping her hand around her chin. She glanced away and then back to Michael as her breathing increased and her heart raced. "No, I have to leave tomorrow. I have an interview in Denver and then I need to get back to D.C."

Michael broke eye contact and looked away. He appeared disappointed. "I'd like more time with you," he said as he rose up and took his plate to the sink while noticing she had barely eaten.

He opened the large stainless Viking refrigerator and retrieved the open Prosecco, and then walked over and poured more into her glass and then into his. He knew they were both too consumed with each other to eat. "How about we go in the living room and relax."

Angelica was disappointed, as well. *Why couldn't she have met him in D.C.?* she wondered. She followed Michael into the living room and sat down beside him on the floor in front of the fire. The fire crackled as the wind howled outside. A storm must be coming in, she thought. Michael leaned over and grabbed a poker to stroke the fire. Angelica watched as the sparks popped from the dancing flames. "Little warm out for a fire, he's good at this," she murmured, suddenly hoping he didn't hear her.

Michael reached over took a pillow from the sofa and gently wedged it behind Angelica's back and the sofa. Angelica leaned back and Michael leaned in closer. "I'm so glad you're here, Angelica." He put his fingers on her chin and tilted her head toward his as he leaned into her and kissed her soft swollen lips. Angelica began to tremble as she kissed back, connecting passionately with their mouths moving in perfect sync. The perfect kiss confirmed their unexplainable chemistry. After a few moments of kissing, she pulled slightly back, panting, she looked into his eyes. He was gazing deeply into hers, as if he were trying to see her soul. She looked sincerely back into his and they just lingered there without saying a word.

Suddenly the kitchen timer went off. Startled, she jerked back and looked toward the kitchen. Michael leaped up and went into the kitchen to turn it off. "Perfect timing!" he said sarcastically as he hit the button on the timer, laughing. "Hey, do you like Harry Connick, Jr.?" Michael walked over to the music player on the wall and pushed play.

"Yes, love him!" Angelica replied. The song, "Stardust" started to play. Angelica leaned back against the sofa and looked at the fire crackling in the large stone fireplace. Her heart was racing.

As the soulful melody began to play, Michael went into the kitchen to straighten up, placing the leftover trout in the refrigerator. Angelica wrapped her arms around her shoulders feeling a chill in the air as the haunting song flowed through the house.

Angelica looked over at Michael and unexpectedly felt sad. Harry Connick, Jr. songs usually did that to her, but it was the thought of leaving Michael that was causing it this time. How was she going to go back to her life after meeting him? She knew he would consume her thoughts. She feared the memories would drive her mad. Angelica realized she needed to prepare herself. Angelica observed Michael as he stood with his back turned at the sink. Her eyes drifted from his broad shoulders, down his back and settled on his rounded ass. Michael was muscular, and she thought he was sexy in jeans, and the white and blue plaid button up that had become slightly un-tucked. Angelica felt a rush of desire for him as she felt the warmth in her stomach move to her hips.

She wanted him to make love to her. She wanted him more than she had ever wanted any man before. She wanted to kiss his entire body, smell his skin, and their sweat to drench her body as their flesh touched. It felt strange to her, but she knew she was falling in love, and she had never fallen so quickly before. Her stomach was in knots. She quickly glanced away and took a sip of her Prosecco.

Michael turned from the sink. "Would you care for some more?" He lifted the bottle in the air and walked toward her. He was smiling mysteriously, and she smiled at him in a way she hadn't before. It was an invitation, and she knew he understood it. He sat the bottle of Prosecco on the coffee table and leaned down to his knees as he put his hands on her cheeks and raised her lips to his while looking into her worried eyes. She pressed hard against his mouth, her tongue glided around his.

Angelica's hands rose up to caress his lower back and then slid down along the back of his thigh, and then back up settling on the spot right in the lower curve of his back.

It felt as if their skin had merged. Their tongues circled passionately. Their faces were red as they turned warm from the heat and the pressure of their skin touching. They pressed harder into one another, slowly lying back on the floor, Michael above Angelica with his hands around her waist. He slowly lifted her knit top up over her head. She let out a sigh of pleasure and looked into his eyes, holding his passionate gaze for a moment, then she moved forcefully to his lips.

They kissed harder and deeper, losing the sense of their separateness. She felt as if they had become one.

Michael reached around and unsnapped Angelica's white lace bra, letting it fall open and away from her moist body. Michael leaned back and observed her face as he slid the straps slowly from her shoulders, and her nipples rose and hardened in the cool air as he pulled her bra away. Michael glanced down to her breast and his heart raced rapidly. She was stunning in the glow of the fire, he thought.

Angelica's hands slid down and unbuttoned his jeans and Michael slid them off.

He stared deeply into Angelica's eyes as he gently kissed her breast. She shivered although her body felt warm.

His hands glided down her smooth arms to her open palms. He squeezed her hands firmly before locking his fingers in between hers. Flooded with emotions, she felt completely vulnerable and submissive to him.

Angelica opened her legs and sighed in ecstasy as she felt the pressure of his tongue push down on her. Michael continued to gaze intensely into hers eyes as his tongue circled and licked aggressively, bringing her to the verge of climax. She was intoxicating, he thought, as he tasted her soft, wet flesh.

Overwhelmed by the pleasure, Angelica moaned loudly, feeling the exhilarating release as he brought her to climax.

Michael then raised up over her, moving steadily between her legs. Angelica caressed his hips and pulled him closer. She took a deep breath and moaned as he entered her. Michael pushed deep and slow causing Angelica to close her eyes and roll her head back.

Consumed with desire, he gazed with penetrating eyes at her soft face as she sighed with pleasure. He was addicted to her.

They made love as the fire burned beside them, becoming lost in the passionate connection of equals… inevitably and quickly devoured by it.

Chapter Thirty

Michael's arm was across her body as if he were trying to keep her safe. A storm had moved in. The wind howled steadily as they slept. The crackling fire had died down and had cast an orange glow over their nude bodies.

"Please stop touching me!" Angelica groaned and flung her hands into the air. "Stop! Why won't you stop? Can't you hear me?"

Suddenly Angelica heard a voice say, "Your pain is perceived." She screamed and her eyes popped open.

Michael jumped, startled awake. "Are you okay? What is it? What happened?"

Angelica was drenched in sweat. She stared at Michael with wide eyes. She was at a loss for words.

"Talk to me, baby," he touched her cheek softly.

"Yes... yes, sorry, it was a bad dream. I'm all right," she said, as she turned into him and rested her head on his shoulder and raised both of her hands, cupping them together under her chin as her knees rose up into fetal position beside him. She was like a little girl, he thought. He pulled her in closer to him as he rubbed her damp hair back into place while looking down at her. "Was it a really bad one?" he asked patiently, suspecting it was.

"Yes, I've been having quite a few lately. For several months, I've been having the same type of dream. Like your father had described, I wake up on a table during some type of operation with beings around me. The beings have these large dark eyes." A tear glided down her cheek and her voice shook. "Michael, I…"

Michael popped up quickly. "Angelica, why didn't you tell me earlier? Do you…?" Michael hesitated. "Do you think you may be experiencing the same thing or is this story just getting to you? Do you think…?"

Angelica interrupted him. "Oh God, yes, it's possible, Michael. I can't shake the feeling that I am," she finished in a whisper as she put her hand to her mouth and looked at Michael's face in the glow of the fire. His jaw dropped. He appeared stunned.

"Just now, I was dreaming that I was in a bright room, lying on a metal table, and my legs were spread apart. They were removing something from my uterus. I was screaming. One of them pulled out some type of silver wand, I saw a flash of light, and then I woke up." Michael looked intensely at Angelica.

"And I remember it said that my pain was perceived."

"Well, it was just a dream… you've been right here asleep beside me." He squeezed her tighter.

Angelica leaned in closer and shivered. "It felt so real, Michael."

"I'm worried about you, Angelica. I saw what my father went through." Michael lifted her chin and looked into her eyes. "I saw the look in his eyes as he spoke of his experiences and I see the same look in yours." Michael pulled Angelica closer. "I wish we had more time together. I want you to feel safe." His words lingered in her mind for a moment.

Angelica peered back into Michael's eyes and whispered softly, "I know."

Michael put his arms around her and squeezed her tight. "Promise me you will be safe."

Angelica suddenly recalled the voicemail from the strange man. Fearing it would worry Michael more, she decided not to tell him. "Yes, I promise, Mr. Anderson." She managed a saucy smile, as he leaned in and softly kissed her lips, and they leaned back in each other's arms onto the floor. She pulled back slowly and looked into his soulful eyes. Soaked with sweat, she felt cold and hot at the same time. He pulled her close, pressed harder into her and they kissed passionately.

Chapter Thirty-One

Angelica awoke to see Michael was gone. She looked around and saw he had folded her clothes neatly and placed them in the chair across from her. She slowly got up and started getting dressed. As she was putting her knit top back on, she saw Michael outside the window talking to Sammy on the front porch. She heard his voice get louder and then the door opened. "Well, good morning, beautiful, sexy, lady!" he announced cheerfully.

"Good morning, Michael," Angelica said as she shyly glanced down and then looked back up at him wondering how she'd ever find the strength to walk out the door. "What time is it?" Angelica asked as she looked around and noticed the clock on the microwave said seven twenty-two.

"Would you like some coffee?"

"Yes, that would be nice." Angelica grabbed her purse.

"Feel free to shower. There are fresh towels and a robe in my bathroom upstairs," Michael said, as he walked into the kitchen. Angelica went upstairs to the loft: Michael's room. There was a book and some clothes lying on the bed so she walked over, curious to see what he was reading. Several pages were folded and the book about Abraham Lincoln, titled "The Ancient One" was water-stained and worn. She reached down, picked up his t-shirt, and smelled it. It smelled of Michael and his cologne, she thought. She felt heat in her chest.

Walking around his room, she noticed a picture of his mother and father, and a few pictures of Michael during his travels. One, in particular, was Michael standing in front of the Sphinx and The Great Pyramid in Egypt. He was smiling and wearing the same white and blue plaid shirt from their day before. "He must love that shirt," she thought aloud. He had a unique smile-- wide and confident.

"If I just had one more day here with him... No, focus on the story," she quickly scolded herself.

After Angelica finished in the bathroom, she made her way back downstairs where Michael had prepared her an omelet. "Wow, thank you. That was very thoughtful."

Michael walked over and took Angelica's hands into his. He looked down at her palms, turning her hands over and rubbing the creases of her wrist. "See these lines? They were the first thing I noticed about you... Well maybe not the first." He smiled sheepishly. "But I don't know why, I couldn't stop looking at them," he whispered. He looked sincerely up at Angelica and then stepped away. "Here –- sit down and eat before you leave." He pulled out a chair from the table.

There was a strange uneasiness in the kitchen that morning. She was caught in the tug and pull of whether to stay or go.

"Okay." Angelica smiled as she sat down and started eating.

"When will I see you again?" Michael asked as he sat down beside her.

"As soon as you would like... Come to D.C.," she said, softly.

"Okay, when?" He smiled.

Angelica laughed, "Whenever you like... I'll be back there in a few days."

"All right... I have to be in New York later this week, so I'll stop off in D.C. on my way. Angelica, why hasn't some guy grabbed you up?"

"I don't know." She laughed. "Maybe it's because I love beginnings and endings. It's the middle that bores me." Angelica blushed. "I'm sorry - I heard that somewhere... love that line," Angelica said, playfully.

"You won't get bored with me, will you?" Michael asked. Angelica was taking a bite of her omelet.

"No way -- especially if you can cook like this!" She gleamed like a little girl.

Michael stood up to pour more coffee into his cup.

Angelica lowered her chin and wondered, "Is this really happening?" She glanced up and shook her head. "How did I end up in your kitchen on a ranch in Montana?" She smiled and exhaled a breath.

Michael grinned. "I'm glad you did."

Angelica rose up from the table. "I need to get back to the lodge and pack."

"Okay, I'll walk you out." Michael took Angelica's hand and walked beside her to her car, standing at the door. "Call me when you're in Denver."

Angelica smiled and then appeared sad as she shut the door and rolled down the window. "I will."

The Bovine Connection

They kept eye contact until Angelica turned the wheel and drove down the drive to the main road.

Chapter Thirty-Two

Just past the old gas station where she had stopped when she first arrived in Elberton, she picked up her cell phone and called her mother. "Hi Mom, sorry I haven't called."

"It's fine, Angelica, I know you're a busy woman."

Angelica heard the irritation in her mother's voice. "Yes, the magazine keeps me very busy. How are you?"

"I'm okay. How are you? Met a nice man to marry yet? You know, I'm not getting any younger. I'd sure like to have grandchildren before I die," her mother said in an extremely concerned voice.

"Mom, please, seriously?" Angelica released a breath of frustration and rolled her eyes. "Do we always have to have this conversation?"

When, Angelica wondered, would her mother stop asking her that question? Angelica wasn't sure she even wanted children.

"Angelica, having you was the best thing that's ever happened to me. I just want you to be happy. I worry about you all alone in D.C. And the drinking ... I noticed while I was visiting you, you were drinking at night. I'm not trying to lecture you, but drinking each night to sleep is a bad habit, and..."

Angelica interrupted her, "Mom, hey, I have a call coming in and I have to take it. Can I call you later?" she asked, feeling as if she were going to scream if she had to listen to one more lecture from her mother.

"Yes. All right, dear," her mother murmured.

"Okay, I'll call you later. I love you." Angelica said as she sighed and tossed her cell phone onto the passenger seat. "Geez!" she blurted.

After turning in her rental car, Angelica boarded the shuttle to the airport and placed her luggage on the metal rack. There were several people on the shuttle with her. Across from her, an older gray-haired couple; toward the front, an Asian couple in their early forties with a young boy; and tucked away in the back was a muscular man in his late thirties with dark brown hair, blue jeans, and a black baseball cap and black hoodie.

Angelica felt exhausted. She laid her head back and closed her eyes for a brief moment before the teenagers in their North Face clothing began rambling loudly about their trip through Yellowstone Park as they boarded the shuttle. Angelica planted her feet defiantly, opened her eyes and gazed around. She wanted to sleep.

The shuttle stopped at her terminal and Angelica grabbed her luggage and eagerly stepped off the bus. She passed through security, hurried to her gate and boarded the plane. Settled into her seat, her head began to bob downwards, and she quickly dozed off.

Chapter Thirty-Three

There was a hard jolt. The plane landed roughly on the tarmac. She began to regain her senses as the jovial flight attendant announced that the flight had arrived at the gate and everyone was free to use their cell phones. Angelica looked out the window and saw the dark grey clouds above the sparse golden prairie landscape surrounding the Denver Airport. She was surprised she had slept so hard and felt disoriented. The flight went quickly, she couldn't even remember taking off. She immediately thought about Michael and the little amount of sleep she had while they were together. She was missing him already, she realized. Angelica looked over and saw a man in a business suit sitting in the aisle seat beside her. He never looked her way.

Angelica leaned down and found her purse under the seat in front of her. She opened it and grabbed her mirror and small makeup bag. She pulled out her concealer and dabbed the dark circles under her eyes then ran lip balm across her lips while the other passengers unloaded their bags and exited the plane.

After almost everyone was off the plane, she stood up and lifted the overhead compartment to grab her bag. The only bag left was her black suitcase. Angelica felt an adrenaline rush of panic and started moving down the aisle, opening all the compartments that had remained shut. *Where was her tan satchel?* she wondered. She was absolutely certain she had placed it next to her suitcase. The flight attendant heard the commotion and looked out from the beverage area.

"Ma'am!"

Angelica didn't respond.

"Ma'am, is there a problem?"

Angelica yelled, "Yes, my bag is missing!"

"Okay, calm down Miss. I will help you look for it. What does it look like?"

Angelica was now looking in and under every seat on the plane. "I have to find my satchel!"

The flight attendant had now gathered the other attendants and they were each searching the entire plane. "I'm sorry, ma'am, someone must have grabbed your bag by mistake," the woman casually announced.

Angelica looked at her. "My laptop and my files… I can't believe this!" Angelica grabbed her purse and suitcase and ran off the plane, bumping into a slow-moving man as she passed by him. "I'm so sorry!" she blurted.

The attendant yelled, "Ma'am, ma'am!" Angelica didn't acknowledge her. The attendant looked at her colleague in the beverage area by the phone on the wall. "Call security!"

Angelica ran down the tunnel from the plane to the gate and slowed to a stop. There were so many people. She looked around, closely eyeing everyone's bags as they walked by. She was in a panic. Her heart was racing. She sprinted into the crowd, rushing in and out, pushing people and almost knocking them over with her suitcase. She grabbed at every tan-colored satchel or bag until a man snapped, "Hey, what the hell are you doing?" Angelica just looked at him and stopped in the middle of the crowd. She stood there frozen as everyone continued to push past her. She started shaking her head and her mouth was open in disbelief. She quickly turned to see two men in uniforms standing in front of her. "Miss, we need you to come with us."

Angelica gasped, "No, I have to find my satchel." She looked away toward to crowd of people moving past.

"Miss, you must calm down. Now come with us calmly or we will have to take you forcefully."

Angelica looked back around to the security officer and met his eyes. "Really, are you serious?"

"Yes, ma'am, I am. This way please." The officer turned and led the way. Angelica followed, as the other officer walked closely behind her.

They passed by a counter where a security officer was patting down a woman who looked like an average soccer mom; she appeared mortified. The officers then led Angelica through a door with bold letters that read, "Authorized Personal Only." Once inside they walked down a narrow hallway and entered into a bright room with a non-descript table and four chairs. "Have a seat." One of the officers said. Angelica let out a breath of frustration and sat down at the table. "Do you have your identification?" he said, as he extended his open palm. Angelica pulled her wallet from her purse and showed the officer her driver's license and then took out a business card and put it on the table. The officer laid her driver's license down and picked up her business card, "Ms. Angelica Bradley with the *Liberator Magazine*."

Angelica looked up at him with irritation. "Yes, that's me. Have I done something wrong, officer?" she asked with a taunt attitude. He looked at his partner and then back at Angelica.

"Couple things..." he said sharply. "First, if you continue with the attitude, we could just be here all day. I've had my lunch." The officer looked at his partner. "Have you had yours?" "Sure have," his partner responded.

Angelica looked sincerely at the officer. "I apologize... I've had very little sleep lately." Angelica felt tired. She'd just comply and hope to be on her way soon.

"Now, why are you running around this airport grabbing at other passengers' bags?" And what business do you have in Colorado?"

Angelica looked at him and let out another breath in frustration. "I'm here to interview a doctor at the University of Colorado - and someone has stolen my satchel! It was on the plane with me and then when I got up to get it from the overhead compartment it was gone. Look, someone has stolen it and there are very important and confidential documents in there." She thought for a moment. "And I can't even begin to tell you how important the files on my laptop are. So perhaps, you could just let me leave so I can go call my editor!" Angelica looked at him sternly but her heart was racing. She had never been in a small room with police before. She felt like a criminal.

"You're free to go." He raised his eyebrows, amused. "But you can't be causing a commotion like that in an airport! After 911, well, hell, I'm sure you know that being a reporter from D.C. and all," he said in a husky voice. "I'm going to let you go, but I want you to immediately leave the airport and be on your way. I'm sorry about your satchel. You can fill out some paperwork and give us a detailed description. I'll take charge of the search. If it turns up, where can you be reached?"

Angelica picked up the business card and handed it to the officer. "Here is my cell number. Do you have a pen? I'm staying at the Brown Palace Hotel. I'll write it on the card," she said, as she took his pen and wrote down the information. Angelica handed him the card.

As she was leaving the room, she glanced back to see the other officer who hadn't said but two words, giving her a flirtatious look. Angelica smirked at his audacity after the afternoon she'd endured.

Chapter Thirty-Four

In front of the airport, Angelica held her purse over her head as she stood in the rain in the cab line. After a few minutes, a cab pulled up to the curve and Angelica jumped in as the driver threw her suitcase into the trunk.

"The Brown Palace Hotel, please."

The cab driver looked around at Angelica while shutting the door. Her hair and clothes were wet from the rain. "Yes ma'am," he said without hesitation.

In the cab on the way to downtown Denver, Angelica took her cell phone out. "Hey, it's me."

Gail answered. "Hey you, how are ya?"

Angelica sank into her seat. "Terrible! I've lost my satchel with my files, laptop, the story... I'm freaking out!"

There was silence on the other end of the phone, and then Gail asked. "How?"

"It was on the plane with me and then when the flight landed, I woke up and waited for everyone to exit. When I went to get it out of the compartment, it was gone! I was exhausted. I slept the entire time so someone could have taken it at any time during the flight." The cab driver was looking up at Angelica in the mirror eavesdropping.

"Why would someone take your satchel - do you think it was taken because of the story? The weird phone call and all... what do you think?" Gail went silent.

Angelica looked out the window and bit down on her bottom lip. "It's odd... I don't know... I really just don't know. Look, I'm on my way to the hotel to meet with Dr. Goolrick. I'll see you in D.C. tomorrow."

"Okay, sweetie, bye," Gail managed to reply before Angelica hung up the phone. It had started raining harder on the way to the hotel. The drops of water were hitting her window and creating large splashes.

The cab driver looked up in the mirror. "It's really coming down now." Angelica met his eyes and nodded. She had been so tired from the lack of sleep that she hadn't paid much attention to anything since she had left the lodge. She laid her head back and watched the rain in the grey haze.

Chapter Thirty-Five

Her hair and clothes were almost dry as the cab pulled up to the valet in front of the Brown Palace Hotel. Angelica paid the driver and stepped out slowly. She grabbed her suitcase from the curb and pulled it behind her as she stepped through the front entrance of marble and stained glass. Angelica usually preferred more modern amenities, but she had a fondness for art deco architecture and was intrigued by the history of the Brown Palace Hotel. It reminded her of growing up around downtown Asheville. She had only lived a few blocks from the art deco, limestone, terra cotta trimmed buildings, where she spent a lot of time at the bookstore and pharmacy-deli.

Pulling her luggage through the lobby, she found the front desk and checked in. The ornate hotel was busy with guests.

Once she had her key, she hurried through the lobby, quickly passing the other guests and taking little notice of the golden marble walls, wrought iron railings, and ceiling of stained glass.

Angelica opened the door to her room and put purse on the dresser. Walking over to the bed, she stopped, looked around the room, and then collapsed onto the fluffy duvet comforter. She was still completely shaken from the ordeal at the airport, and exhausted from the sleepless night spent with Michael, but knew she needed to conjure up some energy for her interview with Dr. Goolrick.

As she thought about Michael, she considered calling him but decided not to. She needed to focus on work, and she knew he would be able to hear the stress in her voice. Angelica didn't want to tell him about her satchel, cautious not to worry him. She wasn't sure it was taken intentionally.

Angelica walked over to the phone and dialed room service. A woman answered warmly. "Welcome to the Brown Palace. What will it be this afternoon?"

"Hello, please send up a glass of a Macallen 12 neat... water... Oh, and ice, thank you," Angelica hung up the phone. She glanced down to notice an elegant dark mahogany bedside table. She reflected back on Paul Colbeck's comparison between ETs and angels, so she opened the drawer and pulled out the Gideon's Bible, randomly flipped through the first chapter, Genesis. Angelica stopped when she noticed 6:4 *"The Nephilim Giants were on the Earth in those days. And the Sons of God saw that the daughters of men were fair and they took wives unto themselves and bore children -- mighty men, of renown."*

Hearing something fall behind her, Angelica jerked and sharply closed the Bible. She looked around and noticed her suitcase had fallen over. She put the Bible back in the drawer. As she turned to walk into the bathroom and shower for dinner, she noticed sparks of light flickering in the air around the room.

Angelica rubbed her eyes, sat down on the bed and watched them flicker. She instinctually closed her eyes and then opened them, and the sparks were still there. She sat there curiously observing them for a moment before they suddenly disappeared. Angelica frowned. "Odd," she thought aloud.

After a hot and refreshing shower and pulling her hair back into an elegant side sweep twist, Angelica looked at the clock as she dabbed her neck with perfume and took sip of Scotch. It was five thirty-three. She realized she needed to get down to the restaurant to meet with Dr. Goolrick soon. She put the glass down on the desk and walked over to the mirror. She straightened her black silk blouse and black skirt, then retouched her lips with red color and slipped on her nude heels. She grabbed her small black Chanel purse, put it under her arm, and briskly left the room.

A nicely dressed couple smiled warmly at her as she stepped in the elevator. Angelica watched as the couple moved closer to each other. She discreetly observed their interaction as the man slid his hand down the woman's back and looked intensely into her eyes.

Angelica remembered the way Michael touched the small of her back when he moved beside her. She closed her eyes and let out a slow breath, noticing the smell of pleasing cologne lingering in the air. She felt relaxed, temporarily forgetting about her satchel and the time spent in the tiny, intimidating room with airport security. Angelica reluctantly shifted her focus from Michael to her interview with the Doctor.

Chapter Thirty-Six

The grand lobby of marble and ornate gold trim was all around her. Angelica looked up to see the beautiful stained glass ceiling and black wrought iron railing wrapped around each floor. She wasn't sure in which restaurant the doctor had intended for them to meet. While on the phone with him, she had forgotten there were several restaurants in the hotel so she took a guess and walked into the Ship Tavern first, and looked around.

There were only a few couples sitting at the bar, so she walked over to the Palace Arms Restaurant.

"Hello, has a gentleman come in alone tonight for dinner, maybe in the last twenty minutes or so?" Angelica glanced around.

The hostess thought for a moment. "No, I don't believe so."

"Thank you," Angelica turned and walked out.

Since it was still a few minutes until six, she decided to wait in the lobby. Angelica sat down in one of the chairs facing the front entrance and the direction of the restaurants. She folded her arms and looked up to admire the stained glass ceiling. After a moment, she noticed a gray-haired man with an American bomber style brown leather jacket and dark taupe slacks walk into the Palace Arms Restaurant, and then step back out into the lobby. He was looking around as if waiting to meet someone.

"That must be the doctor," she thought aloud. Angelica got up and walked over to him. "Hello... Dr. Goolrick?" she asked. The man looked around as he took his little oval-shaped reading glasses off and slid them in the inside pocket of his jacket.

"Yes, hello, Ms. Bradley, I went into the restaurant and the hostess said an attractive young lady had just come in and left. She was looking for a gentleman so I guessed that was you." His eyes were kind, she noticed.

"Yes, nice to meet you Dr. Goolrick," Angelica extended her hand and Dr. Goolrick shook it.

"Very nice to meet you, Ms. Bradley."

"So I see you prefer the Palace Arms? That sounds perfect," Angelica said, as they turned and walked toward the restaurant.

They sat in silence for a full minute at the table not sure where to start. Angelica looked around and commented on the elegance of the hotel. "This hotel reminds me of my hometown, Asheville, North Carolina. I'm fascinated with art deco, whether it is art or architecture, I love the period from which it came."

"Yes, I am an art lover, as well. Do you know the hotel's history?"

Angelica smiled. "Not much."

"Well, it was built in the late eighteen hundreds. Let's see... Construction started in 1888, if I remember correctly, and it opened in 1892. The hotel has its own artesian well."

"Interesting, I did not know that." Angelica tilted her head in curiosity.

"Yes, and the design is Italian Renaissance, crafted from Arizona sandstone. The architect created medallions depicting Rocky Mountain animals for the lobby."

Angelica enjoyed listening to the doctor. "Oh." She leaned in closer and cupped her chin.

As their dinners arrived, Dr. Goolrick was still talking. "The famous 1911 murders in the 'Marble Bar,' where a man shot and killed another man over a beautiful socialite," he announced, sounding like a tour guide. "It was quite a big deal here in Denver. She was the wife of a wealthy businessman and political candidate."

"How intriguing," Angelica said softly.

"Yes, you know, there are rumors that the hotel has been haunted ever since."

"Haunted," Angelica giggled. "That is fascinating. I hope my room is not haunted!" she said playfully. "Thank you for sharing some of the history of this beautiful hotel with me. Most of all, thank you for taking time out of your busy schedule on such short notice. As you know, I've just arrived from Elberton today, interesting trip... I spent a great deal of time with Matthew Tillman. He took me to the locations where the mutilations occurred."

"I see," Dr. Goolrick nodded blankly.

"The carcass at the Keller ranch was quite unusual, to say the least." Angelica pursed her lips and put her fork and knife down after noticing the bloody drippings on Dr. Goolrick's plate next to his half eaten steak.

"Yes, indeed, the poor animal. The stage of decomposition must have been terrible to witness. The notion that someone would perform such a heinous act is incomprehensible. Don't you agree?" The doctor took a sip of his cabernet, analyzing Angelica.

"Yes, the cuts to the animal and the removal of the organs and tissue... Who do you think is responsible, doctor?" Angelica looked intensely at him. She was anxious to hear what he would say.

In her room earlier, she had concluded that he would put some scientific explanation behind this story and give her readers something more sophisticated to contemplate.

"Angelica, I'm going to be frank..." The doctor sat up straight and his tone became deep and more authoritative. "When I started my career as a medical doctor, you would have never heard me utter the words I am about to speak. The very thought of such things did not enter my mind."

Angelica pushed her plate forward and rested her arms on the table as the doctor was speaking. "My attention was given to local research activities, attending seminars, journal clubs, and enthusiastically supporting colleagues in their scientific career... Nevertheless, a political murder of an environmental/animal activist, who just so happened to be a good friend of mine, changed the course of my interest in the field... I am convinced his murder was committed in an effort to reduce complex political issues by removing any modifier or nuance. Anyone such as my friend that challenges benign generalizations on this unique subject matter is in grave danger, my dear. Generalizations have a great effect on controlling the message to the masses – causing an agree/reject reaction before rational analysis begins. When these simple explanations are diminished by introspection and non-biased logic, only then do the true layers of truth reveal themselves. To say it in a more pedestrian manner, most people do not want to know the truth, and those that do, seldom want it to be told if it gives away any of their power or control."

"I agree," Angelica said as she nodded reflecting for a moment on her career at *The Washington Post*. Angelica shifted in her seat.

"Nonetheless," the doctor continued, "after the murder of my dear friend, I took my new mission seriously. As a facilitator in the institutions, I would teach the academic young minds to call for transparency and reject academia camouflaged as pure." Dr. Goolrick pushed his glasses back up with his index finger.

"I became a leader in the research environment. I had finished graduate school, wrote an impressive dissertation, collaborated with excellent teams, published in high-ranking journals and was finally appointed the much sought after position at the University of Colorado as the Department Head and Director of Veterinary and Biomedical Sciences." Doctor Goolrick tilted his head back, presenting an air of confidence. "Suddenly, I was in charge with formal power. I made good use of it and never exploited my leadership."

"At risk of ending up on the short list, I pursued my personal interest and started down the path of the curious subject of cattle mutilations. In the beginning, it was more of a hobby. I'd research and study the phenomena from a distance, careful not to leak the progress of my hidden hobby, for fear that once it was discovered my progress would be paralyzed by the University. I have observed the genealogy of social misbehavior and how it proliferates like an air-borne disease." Angelica nodded in agreement while taking a sip of her cabernet. Dr. Goolrick reminded her of a professor from her college days at Georgetown University. She loved the way his mind worked, and the way he spoke with such confidence. Of course, he was much younger and much handsomer than Dr. Goolrick, she thought.

Dr. Goolrick noticed Angelica's eyes were vacant, so he cleared his throat. Angelica's eyes widened. She was back in the present moment. "Please continue," she said sharply.

Dr. Goolrick nodded. "So after twenty years of research, I've concluded that the precision of the cuts and removal of skin and tissue from the muscle, even if done by one of the best surgeons in the world, would be quite difficult... and the fashion in which the organs were removed, well, impossible. My autodidactic approach to these cases has led me to a myriad of resources, and I have spent a great deal of time studying genetics. After meticulously reviewing and analyzing evidence along with the collaborative efforts of an underground research team of respected scientists from a myriad of specialties, including an astrobiology friend... our conclusion is... If it is not extraterrestrial, well, then there is no explanation."

"What is Astrobiology?" Angelica politely interjected.

"My apologies, I tend to ramble... It's the professor in me. Astrobiology is the study of the origin, distribution, evolution, and future of life in the universe... extraterrestrial life and life on Earth."

"Oh, I see," she said as she lifted her hand and firmly rubbed it across her eyebrow, wiping away the tiny dots of sweat starting to form on her face. "Is it warm in here?" Angelica asked as she frowned.

"You look as if you are deliberating, my dear."

Angelica was about to say something she never thought she'd say. Angelica leaned in. "I tend to agree with you Doctor," she whispered.

He looked at her suspiciously. "You do?"

Angelica looked around the restaurant, her voice taut with fear. "I think I may be experiencing some sort of contact... And as a serious investigative journalist, I can't believe I just spoke those words." Angelica laughed, nervously.

Dr. Goolrick leaned toward her. "And why do you think that?" he whispered.

Angelica took a deep breath. "I've experienced some strange things, such as dreams of being on a metal table, undergoing medical procedures in a room with strange beings, and waking up feeling physically as if something had really happened to me. The same thing these people in Elberton were reporting, I'm experiencing, as well." Angelica looked worried, she turned her head to glance around the room. "I don't know... I just can't shake the feeling that I am being taken somewhere after I fall asleep. I keep having the same reoccurring dream; however, it is starting to feel more and more real."

"Oh my!" Dr. Goolrick uttered in shock.

"Oh... and Matthew's friends, Ellen and Blake McKinney... What an interview that was, wow!" Angelica shook her head dramatically. "Well, he's a retired aeronautical engineer from Newton and is convinced these beings not only exist, but that they are here on Earth with us now. He says they are creating a hybrid race." Angelica scratched her forehead and laughed as she took another sip of her cabernet. "I sound like a crazy woman." She rolled her eyes and took a deep breath as she sat her glass back down.

"That's very interesting, Angelica." Dr. Goolrick peered down at his plate and then back up. "Well, since we're on the subject, I believe that is precisely what some of this is about: genetics."

Angelica tilted her head in curiosity.

The doctor continued, "The genetic code is a set of rules by which information is encoded in genetic material. DNA or RNA sequences are translated into protein, amino acids by living cells. Specifically, the code defines a mapping between codons and amino acids, as I'm certain you've learned in school. Because the vast majority of genes are encoded with exactly the same code, this particular code is often referred to as the canonical or standard genetic code, or simply the genetic code... though, in fact, there are many variations. Thus, the canonical genetic code is not universal. For example, in humans, protein synthesis in the mitochondria relies upon a genetic code that varies from the canonical code. The genome of an organism is inscribed in DNA, or in some viruses, RNA. The portion of the genome that encodes a protein or RNA is referred to as a gene. The genes that code proteins are called codons, each coding for a single amino acid, as stated in any science textbook."

Angelica interrupted the doctor. "Doctor, I'm trying to follow you but I must confess... I'm a bit confused, much like I was in science class."

The doctor laughed loudly, rolling his head back. "That's not the first time I have heard that statement." Yet, he continued. "All current life forms on Earth have twenty amino acids in their genetic code. However, most scientists believe that this was not always the case, and that organisms evolved from simpler genetic codes with fewer amino acids." Dr. Goolrick noticed Angelica was losing interest.

"Anyway, I will skip to my point." Angelica nodded and lifted her glass to sip her wine looking up to notice the server with the bottle of cabernet standing beside the table. Angelica sat her glass back down as he refilled it. The doctor placed his hand over his wine glass.

"I'd prefer a Cognac." He glanced up to the server and then looked back at Angelica. "Now stay with me here. The scientific field has discovered something very strange occurring. You see, in the human DNA there are four nucleic acids that combine in sets of three producing sixty-four different patterns of codons. We are discovering humans with twenty-four codons turned on. This is amazing and quite noteworthy... Angelica, human DNA should only have twenty codons turned on and the rest turned off. We are discovering a new race of humans with twenty-four codons activated and that, to say the least, is extraordinary. Humans are popping up everywhere with these additional codons. It is estimated that one percent of the world has this new DNA... Now, that breaks down to approximately sixty million people who are not human by the old, standard criteria. This new human race is becoming immune to disease. They are showing up with foreign DNA, and some believe this could be the future evolution of our species. The children born with this new DNA are already immune to most diseases."

Angelica took a sip of her wine, started to speak, then paused and regrouped. "So these new humans could be hybrids, genetically modified like the latest version of some exotic rose? And if I am one of those sixty million, I could be a hybrid too?"

"That is a simple yet elegant analogy. Yes, you are correct. But, what is happening with the bovine cells is entirely different. I'm sure after working with Matthew Tillman, by now you've heard the theory that the government is interested in the fact that cattle blood could be used in an emergency blood transfusion with humans. Matthew and I have spoken at great length on this, and while the science is true, I don't believe the government's interest pertains to this aspect. The bovine hemoglobin closely matches human blood-- this is correct. Hemoglobin is a protein in red blood cells that carries oxygen. The cattle chromosomes are identical to large sections of human chromosomes, meaning that cattle genes and human genes fall in the same exact sequence on some chromosomes. So the real benefit here is that cattle DNA can be used to fill in the gaps of the genetic sequence codes that do not have enough DNA on the human strand. Since bovine hemoglobin is genetically similar to humans, it could be used to cultivate the egg cells fertilized with extraterrestrial DNA to create a new life form. The bovine hemoglobin -- along with specific areas of soft tissue -- becomes the secret restorative that is critical to the success of such an undertaking."

"Really?" Angelica sat frozen with her glass in her hand.

Dr. Goolrick nodded and continued. "However, I believe this race of non-humans could be using cattle DNA as a food source, as well."

Angelica interrupted, almost choking on her sip of wine. She had a wild look in her tired light blue eyes. "So, you don't believe the cattle DNA is connected to creating hybrids?"

The doctor shifted in his seat. "I believe it is secondary. The primary purpose, however, is immediate survival in an alien world. Since they allegedly have no digestive system, these glandular substances from the cattle are absorbed through their skin, substances that come from certain mucus membranes: the tongue, genitals, rectum, and other vital organs. The DNA from these areas can be replicated over and over again, thus reducing the amount of donors needed for their food supply. One mutilated animal can produce enough food source to sustain these creatures for an extended period of time. Humans have actually used this same technology for over a decade now.

One neonatal foreskin taken from a baby that has been circumcised can be replicated into six football fields of living human dermis. This product has been FDA approved and used on patients with chronic wounds for years. Unless you had a diabetic foot ulcer that didn't heal with conventional therapy, you probably wouldn't know anything about it."

Careful not to sound condescending, Angelica questioned the doctor. "Please accept my apologies if I sound rude, but how do you know all of this?"

"Let's just say... within my underground research group there are a few in-the-know" he cocked his head to one side and ran his finger along his bottom lip.

Angelica's body instantly tensed as she observed his body language. She wondered who comprised the underground research team.

Dr. Goolrick cleared his throat. "Now that they have an abundant food supply, they are able to complete their primary objective. They are creating hybrids by combining their DNA with human DNA. It is their version of test tube babies."

Angelica interrupted him. "Dr. Goolrick, with all due respect, this underground group you spoke of... Is there someone who might possibly have inside information that, let's say... the general public would not be privy too?" The doctor looked at Angelica sincerely as he shook his head. Angelica understood he wasn't about to give her specific names and sources no matter how big his ego was. Angelica smiled respectfully and nodded.

"I would suspect this research and replication takes place in some sort of laboratory on their crafts.

At this time, I cannot make a theoretical connection, and it definitely is causing mass confusion with our underground research, but we have concluded there are two different races at work here, and whereas one race could allegedly blend in with the population, it's speculated that the other could not.

Angelica sat back in her chair. "Complicated, yet fascinating... and quite scary, Doctor!"

Her words lingered in his head. "Yes, it is rather alarming to consider what this may mean for the human race. Their ultimate agenda is still unknown. Is it benevolent or malevolent? Your guess is as good as mine."

Dr. Goolrick looked around the room and then leaned in closer to Angelica... "But if you can continue to piece this together through your investigation you may be able get this out to the general public in a manner that is palatable for them. At any rate... now you know the bovine connection."

The doctor smirked then leaned back in his chair and took a sip of his brandy. Angelica sat there for a minute examining the doctor's confident body language. She looked bewildered as she thought about the cattle sucked into the sky, and then she envisioned the non-human beings using their blood and raw organs as food. The thought gave her the jitters. Then she remembered her dream with the human fetus in the tube of fluid.

Suddenly Angelica remembered the voicemail. Why had she not been more concerned over it? That was a question she was now seriously analyzing. "You know, Doctor, I received a strange voicemail while in Elberton. It was from a man... he said I may be in danger, and that I needed to meet with him as soon as I was back in D.C. He said he would leave a note with instructions under the front door of my townhouse."

Dr. Goolrick sat straight up. "I don't know about that, Angelica! That call worries me!" The doctor's voice grew grave. "Apparently, you're in deeper than I realized. You're probably being followed as we speak, and it may be a rogue splinter of the government. Our mutual friend Matthew is convinced that they will use any means possible to quiet those who speak about this. You need to be very alert."

The doctor slowly looked around the restaurant, as if he were profiling each person. A man sitting with two women looked back at him inquisitively. "Angelica, watch everything and everyone from this point forward," he whispered, as he turned back around.

This wasn't the first time she had heard of a shadow government. First it was Blake McKinney, then Paul Colbeck, and now Dr. Goolrick. Her mind raced. It was hot in the restaurant again, she thought.

Angelica adjusted in her seat and felt the moisture in her armpits. "There were also rumors in D.C. of such a group." she paused. Dr. Goolrick sat silently, watching Angelica bite down on her thumb nail nervously with a blank stare.

"Yes, those rumors are true. Are you all right, Angelica?"

She felt as if she were coming undone. Her head had started to tingle. "If I proceed with this story, it means I could be putting myself in danger. But I've never quit a story before, and most of them involved writing about something that at least one person in a powerful position didn't want known." She took a deep breath and probed his eyes for a response. She decided, right then and there, that she'd keep going regardless of the risk involved. "My satchel with my laptop and files was stolen on the flight today."

Dr. Goolrick nodded. His face was flat. "The question is: who took it and why?"

Angelica looked at the doctor, puzzled. "Yes, I agree. This story may be more than I bargained for." Angelica hesitated for a moment. "But I can't turn back now. Well, how could I?" Her eyes shifted into a blank stare and she chewed at her bottom lip. "I have to know everything. Why the hybrids?" Angelica stared Dr.

Goolrick straight in the eyes. His eyes appraised her as she raised her hands and clenched her fingertips under her chin. "What's the connection with the government? Doctor, I don't believe in coincidences. There's a reason I'm covering this story and my gut tells me to keep moving forward."

"Do you live alone?" he asked out of the blue.

"Yes." She frowned as her face went ashen. She swallowed hard.

The doctor smiled sincerely. "You are a brave woman."

After Angelica charged their dinner to her room, they both rose from the table and walked out into the hotel lobby.

"You have my work number," he told Angelica. "Please stay in touch."

The doctor took out a business card from the inside of his jacket pocket. "Here's my cell number; if you can't reach me on it, call the university and they'll page me."

Angelica extended her hand and took the card. "Thank you, Doctor."

She watched the doctor as he walked out the lobby doors and then she walked over and stepped into the empty elevator. Leaning back against the wall, she closed her eyes, reflecting on the evening. The interview with Dr. Goolrick had zapped the last bit of energy she had and she just wanted to sleep.

Chapter Thirty-Seven

Laughter erupted in the hallway outside her door. Angelica opened her eyes to the sound. She stretched her arms out in bed feeling rested, and then pulled the sheet back as she sat up and planted her feet on the floor. She let out a horrified gasp at the sight of blood on the white sheets. She suddenly felt a sharp pain and grabbed the back of her neck. The pain ran down her shoulders and into her back causing her knees to buckle.

As she lowered her arm, she noticed a raised area of skin on her forearm. She examined it closely. Right above her wrist was a rectangular shaped object under her skin. Shocked, she gasped and raised her hands to her face, the tips of her fingers covering her open mouth.

Angelica lowered her arms and stared at it in utter disbelief. She pushed it and the object moved. She pulled her hand back in shock. Quickly, she pushed it again and it moved again before it bounced back to its original spot. "What the hell?" she blurted out.

Angelica ran into the bathroom and looked through her vanity bag. It was an impulse response and she wasn't really sure what she was looking for. She just instinctively knew that whatever was under her skin, she wanted it out. She searched her bag and produced a razor from the bottom.

Angelica held the edges of the razor carefully and bent it trying to loosen the blades inside. She looked over and saw a can of shaving cream so she placed the razor in a small white towel and began hitting it with the can. When she opened the towel, the razor was broken apart and the tiny blades were lying loosely inside. She used the towel to hold one end of the blade and began cutting into her arm. She let out a cry, gritting her teeth against the pain, but carefully and methodically continued to cut into the skin around the object. The object continued to move slightly against any pressure on it.

Crimson blood rushed down her arm, darkening as it hit the countertop in splatters and dripped into the sink and on the floor. Angelica then heard a slight metallic dinging sound as the object fell out from under her skin and was lying on the countertop in her blood. She looked stupefied, clearly trying to figure out how it got there. She pressed the towel into her arm and held it tightly, trying to stop the bleeding. She was panting fast and hard.

Angelica picked it up and observed it. "What the hell is it?" she asked out loud.

She went back out into the room and opened the curtain to let in daylight. Angelica held the object up in the light and examined it more closely. She had never seen anything like it before. *Was it some type of computer chip or tracking device?* she wondered. It seemed to have some form of artificial intelligence because it moved on its own when she pressed it. It wasn't organic matter -- that was for sure. And then, like a wave rushing onto a beach, the reality of the moment set in... Someone had somehow surgically placed it under her skin with no obvious sign of incision. She wondered how long it had been there. Like with the cattle, it was a complete mystery to her.

Angelica heard the street sounds outside of the window; it all felt surreal. She turned and walked over to the dresser where she grabbed an empty glass and dropped it inside. Frightened, alone, and desperate for comfort, she picked up her cell phone and called Michael.

"Hello," Michael answered.

"Michael, it's Angelica!" Before she could say another word, Michael interrupted...

"Angelica, Sammy just returned from town! Matthew's dead!" There was silence. Angelica looked away from the tiny metal device. Her mouth fell open.

"Angelica, did you hear what I said?"

Trying with all her will to get a sound to come out of her mouth, Angelica finally whispered with her voice cracking, "Oh... my... God! How?"

"I don't know yet, but I think it happened the night you stayed with me. Sammy said he thought he heard someone say it was a possible suicide. I just can't believe it, Matthew of all people... Angelica are you there?"

Angelica recoiled, startled by the news and the pain in Michael's voice. She stood there silently with her fingers over her mouth, shaking.

Michael continued, "I'm getting ready to head into town. I'll call you as soon as I know more."

"Okay, please let me know as soon as you find out anything. I'm speechless. I don't know what to say... please be careful, Michael."

"I will. I promise." Michael hung up. Angelica suddenly heard the street sounds from outside. She kept the phone to her ear for a few more seconds, listening in a trance-like state to the familiar sounds that now resonated ominous and frightening. The earth seemed to stop moving for those brief seconds. Every sinew of her body was now in full-on sensory overload, and she felt as if she might be going into shock. She felt the intense and sharp pain in her arm and she began to get dizzy as she sensed the pressure of her heartbeat in her throat.

Angelica stumbled back and dropped down onto the end of the bed. She sat motionless, looking into open space. She put her index finger to her mouth and chewed on the tip of her fingernail, as tears welled up in her eyes. She looked at the glass with the metal band, and then at the bloody towel wrapped around her arm. She thought about the voicemail, her satchel. There were so many disturbing events in such a short timeframe. Was Matthew's death connected? Did she possibly bring death to the quiet town of Elberton because of her investigation? She dropped her head at the thought.

After a minute, she instinctively jumped up, letting the blood-soaked towel fall to the floor. She went over to her purse and looked for Dr. Goolrick's business card. Once she found it, she stood there staring at it with her cell phone still in the palm of her hand.

Abruptly, Angelica changed her mind. She put her phone and the business card down on the dresser and went back into the bathroom. She turned on the sink and ran cold water over the open flesh, rinsing off the blood. The small piece of hanging skin fluttered under the pressure of the water and the wound started to bleed again. She quickly covered it with the towel and found the Band-Aids in her wallet. She always kept a couple in case a new pair of heels gave her a blister. After she covered the wound with the two Band-Aids, she looked into the mirror and froze. Angelica noticed dried blood along and under her earlobe. She leaned in and examined it closely. As soon as she realized she was holding her breath, she exhaled and closed her eyes. *What is going on*? she wondered.

Angelica went back into the room and started packing. All she wanted to do at that moment was to get the hell out of her room.

Angelica's flight wasn't until mid-afternoon. She needed to prioritize and concentrate or she knew she was going to turn into a basket-case. She decided logically that her first task was to go find an Apple store and purchase a new laptop.

Angelica showered and left her suitcase in the room.

Chapter Thirty-Eight

Angelica put her hand over the blood-soaked Band-Aids and forced a smile. "Where can I possibly find an Apple store in the downtown area?"

The polite and overly eager concierge quickly responded... "It's in the shopping center around the corner from here. Just take a right out the front entrance and it's a block down on the left." The concierge briskly opened the door as Angelica hurried past, outside. Even in one of the most beautiful hotels in the country, she felt as if she were walking out of prison.

"Thank you," she said, as she stepped out to the noise of traffic.

Angelica looked ahead as she walked the sidewalk, along the perimeter walls of the Brown Palace, nestled between the high-rise buildings. *How did they get into my room and in my arm? Or had it already been there?* she wondered. She took her cell phone out of her purse and found a missed text from Gail sent earlier that morning. She realized she must have been in the shower when it came through.

"How did the interview go with the doc?"

Angelica responded... "My interview with Dr. Goolrick was very interesting. Matthew Tillman is dead! I will text you again tomorrow with a time I'll be back in my office." Angelica hit the send button and put her phone back in her purse.

After a short walk, she easily found the Apple sign on the mall directory. The concierge had given perfect directions. There was a long line waiting at the counter. Apprehensive about the long wait, she almost walked back out but dropped her shoulders and stepped into the line.

People were milling around looking at devices attached to the tables around the store. There were several high-tech young men and woman with Apple t-shirts assisting customers. Angelica felt flustered at the thought of a long wait.

She started to turn and walk out just as a representative walked up. "How can I help you?"

"I need a new laptop... like that one there," Angelica pointed to the lady's laptop beside her. He took her name and said it would be a few minutes, so she found a tall stool at one of the device tables and waited patiently for her name to be called.

Out of her peripheral vision, Angelica noticed a man with tan pants and a black collared shirt walk in. She nonchalantly turned her head towards him to get a better view and immediately felt a tingling sensation on her scalp. The man looked at Angelica and she gave him an odd look before he turned and scanned the room.

Angelica was sure she had seen him before, and there was something about his body language that set off alarm bells in her head. He was trying too hard to not be noticed, she thought.

The man walked over to the case covers on the wall. After a few minutes, he left and walked back into the mall. Her heart pounded against her chest and her legs trembled as she watched him leave. Something didn't feel right about him, she thought.

Angelica was startled to see a young man standing beside her. "Miss, did you want to purchase a laptop?"

"Yes, mine was stolen. That one right there." She nervously pointed to a laptop a customer was using. Her finger was trembling.

The man looked at her curiously. "Okay, you seem to know exactly which model you want. I'll pull one from stock and meet you at the counter."

After purchasing the laptop, Angelica left the store and walked back toward the front entrance. She looked around and took inventory of the people as they walked by. There he was again, staring blankly in the window of a men's clothing store. Was he following her or was she just being paranoid? After the disturbing and macabre events of the past twenty four hours, it was a natural response, she thought.

She felt anxious and disoriented. She watched as the people rushed by with their shopping bags. She looked at the entrance and started quickly toward it, struck with a most curious thought... "Did others have the implant?"

Angelica looked at the forearm of a young woman with her daughter for any evidence of a rectangular shaped object under the skin. Maybe a strange object was under her daughter's skin or the boy walking behind them holding a skateboard, texting... the grandmother holding her grandson's hand while looking through his diaper bag. Maybe they all had the device." For a split second, she considered grabbing someone's arm.

Angelica squeezed her purse and Apple bag and pushed through the crowd. Suddenly, she found herself face-to-face with the familiar man. She ran right into him as if he were a wall suddenly erected in the middle of the mall. She gasped. Her eyes were wide. His eyes penetrated hers. They were evil and punishing, she thought. His face straight and grave.

"What do you want?" she demanded.

The man stepped aside so she could pass. Angelica ran through the crowd. At the mall entrance she grabbed the door handle and slung the door open as she rushed outside. She stood on the sidewalk panting, trying to catch her breath. The air smelled heavy of exhaust from the city bus parked at the curb. She needed to get back to the room, and quickly. Catching her breath, she picked up her pace and briskly walked down the sidewalk toward the Brown Palace.

It felt as if her feet had lifted from the ground as she rushed down the sidewalk. Her mind raced. The fearful thoughts were driving her to delirium. She looked back over her shoulder and she saw the man was now walking at the same pace as she, but about fifteen feet directly behind her. They made eye contact.

Angelica picked up her pace. As she made it to the entrance of the Brown Palace, she glanced back and he was gone. When she turned around, she ran right into a distinguished, middle-aged man in business attire, stepping out of the door. "Are you all right, Miss?"

"Yes, I'm sorry!" Angelica pushed past him and vigorously picked up her pace. Her singular focus at that moment was to get to her room as quickly as possible.

She nervously fumbled for her room card. She placed it in the slot and the tiny light above turned red. Her hands were trembling as she tried the card again, this time more slowly. She heard the familiar click of the lock as the light turned green. "Thank God," she thought aloud. The last thing she needed right now was to go back down to the lobby and get the front desk to re-key her card. She closed the door behind her and made sure it was locked securely.

Angelica walked over and sat on the edge of the bed softly dropping her purse and Apple bag to her feet. She was panting and her face was red. She put her hands to her face and cried. Silently she sat and listened for sounds. Angelica looked over at the door, wondering if he was behind it, then turned and stared at the desk until the chaos faded away and her mind cleared.

Angelica leaned down and took the laptop from the package. She stood up and went over to the desk and set the laptop down. She entered the internet access code, then checked her email. There were only a few *Liberator Magazine* employee announcements unopened in the inbox. Angelica dropped her shoulders and leaned back in the chair. The delirium had subsided. Her eyes were dry. Since she still had a little time before her flight she typed "Implants found in arm" into the Google search engine. Several links came up and she scrolled down looking for any that stood out. Down the list, she noticed a blog titled "Experiencers."

"Human abductions and animal mutilation have been reported around the world. The most commonly reported ETs are the grey beings. Experiencers of abductions usually report: Waking up in the middle of the night feeling paralyzed while hearing a humming, buzzing sound. Being taken from their bed in the middle of the night. Waking up in the middle of an examination. Odd cuts or bruises. Insertion of implants into the abductee's skin, which some believe to be tracking devices. They are most commonly reported as a small triangular shaped metal object." Angelica looked over at the glass with the rectangular object and pursed her lips.

"These advanced beings have the technology to slow down the vibrational rate of energy; thereby, moving the subject through objects such as walls, ceilings, floors, mattresses..."

Angelica's cell phone rang, causing her to jerk dramatically. She rose up from the desk and found it in her purse. "Angelica Bradley!" she answered.

"Angelica, How are you?" His tone was flat.

"Hello, Michael, I've been better. Did you find out anything?" She sighed.

"Yes, it was suicide!" He took a deep breath.

Angelica was quiet for a moment before responding as her jaw dropped… "Really?" She gasped.

"That's what Sheriff Taylor said. I overheard one of the deputies say his house was a mess, like he went crazy and ransacked it before he killed himself." He paused. "Kind of odd."

Angelica thought for a moment. "How... how did he do it, Michael?"

"He hung himself from his upstairs banister," he said softly.

The image of Matthew hanging from the banister infiltrated her mind. "No!" Angelica starting pacing back and forth as she always did whenever she was trying to process something. Angelica started to speak and then hesitated. After a few seconds, she continued. "I don't think he killed himself."

"What?" Michael sounded confused. "They found him hanging from a rope. He's gone, Angelica!"

Angelica, frustrated, interrupted him, "No, I mean I think someone else did it! Listen, I didn't want to worry you but my satchel was stolen on the plane. Dr. Goolrick thinks I'm probably being followed and I think so, as well. Actually, I'm certain of it.

And there was this strange voicemail from a man while I was still in Elberton telling me I may be in danger. And Michael, do you really think that Matthew was in any frame of mind that could have caused him to kill himself?"

Michael paused for a second then gently spoke, "I'm coming to you. When do you get back to D.C.?"

Angelica was still pacing the floor. "Not yet, I need you to do something first. I need you to go to Matthew's house and look around. Search around for files -- anything connected to the mutilations -- and bring them to me. But please... be very careful."

Michael hesitated, "Okay, I'll go there tonight. But then I'm coming to you!"

Angelica nodded to herself still anxiously pacing. She caught her reflection in the large window. "Michael, wait until tomorrow evening to come to D.C."

Michael's voice did not hide the fact that he was clearly worried. "If you're in danger, I need to be there! I'm not losing another person I care about... Do you understand?"

"Yes, you won't lose me, I promise. Just be careful, too. They probably know about you if they are watching me. I'll see you soon." Angelica waited for Michael to say good-bye, and then she hung up.

Feeling disorientated, she put her palm on the top of her head while continuing to pace back and forth in the room. "Poor Matthew!" she thought aloud.

Angelica put her cell phone back in her purse and went over to the glass containing the metal band on the dresser. She took it out and found a Brown Palace cocktail napkin with the brown mythological guardian griffins' logo. She placed it inside the napkin and tightly folded the edges around it before putting the napkin in her wallet. She gathered her laptop and suitcase and left the "Mile High City."

Chapter Thirty-Nine

He crossed over the yellow police tape and pushed the old door open. The house was dark and uninviting, and smelled faintly of moth balls. Michael turned on a small craftsman's style lamp on a side table in the foyer. He was shocked to see the house was a mess, ransacked, as the officers had said. It was much worse than he had expected. There were tables knocked over, paper's scattered about and broken glass everywhere. Matthew's body had been removed earlier that day and apparently the medical examiner had cut the rope somewhere between the banister railing and his neck since he could see the other end still hanging above him on the railing.

Michael heard a noise and flinched. He remained still, waiting for another sound. He was sure he heard the sound of something fall in the other room.

Breathing heavy, he was nervous and on edge. He didn't say a word. He stood there motionless trying to hold his breath as his chest pumped up and down, peering into the darkness, waiting to see if someone would emerge from the shadows. "Meow."

Michael finally let out a breath. "You scared the living day lights out of me, kitty." Matthew's cat, Lady, stepped out from the darkness meowing once more as she rubbed against Michael's leg, leaving long white hairs behind. Michael reached back, turned the knob and let Lady out the front door.

After shutting the door, he turned and observed the hanging rope for a moment, and then clicked on his flashlight and proceeded into the room where Lady had just come from. It was a disaster; he stepped over papers and glass, shining his flashlight down as he walked around. The furniture seemingly grew larger as he shined the light on it.

Michael leaned over and picked up a couple of irrelevant papers, quickly discounting and dropping them. Kicking things out of his way, he walked toward the dining room, leading into the kitchen. He sorted through all the clutter strewn about the floor, but found nothing pertaining to the mutilations.

In the kitchen was a plate with a half-eaten sandwich on the counter, alongside an opened Icehouse beer. The small kitchen was illuminated only by the flashlight. Although most of the drawers were pulled out, the kitchen appeared to be mostly untouched.

Michael continued through the archway leading down the hall to Matthew's study. Shining his flashlight on the floor, he saw a bronze desk lamp, so he stepped over and picked it up and placed it back on the desk.

As the light from the lamp lit the room, he caught sight of a lanky shadow beside the bookshelf. His muscles tightened as he spun around with the flashlight. Michael released the muscle tension with a quick breath. Nothing was there.

He shined the light around the study. The desk drawers were lying empty on the floor. Papers were everywhere. Michael got down on his knees and went through them. He knew Matthew had accumulated several stories through the years but nothing about the mutilations appeared to be there. Michael realized he probably wasn't going to find anything that would help Angelica. He continued to look around the study until finally giving up.

As he made his way cautiously up the stairs, Michael shined the flashlight on the old hardwood steps. Walking past the rope and to a bedroom, he turned on the light and gave it a quick look-over. It was undisturbed. It must be a guest room with a few empty drawers open, he concluded, and of no interest to whomever was here.

Michael found another guest room undisturbed, much the same as the first, so he crept over to the room directly across from it. When he turned on the light, as he had expected, it was Matthew's room. The bed was unmade and there were clothes hanging out of the open drawers. It appeared to him that someone had looked through all the drawers, leaving them open or on the floor. Clothes were thrown out of his closet and scattered about, but still there was nothing that looked important from what he could see. Michael walked across Matthew's room and into his bathroom. Stepping over his personal items as glass cracked under his shoes, he opened the medicine cabinet. Michael looked around and then went back in the bedroom. He didn't know what he was looking for, and he sure didn't see any papers or documents related to the mutilations. He also felt a bit uneasy disturbing what he now considered a crime scene. It was hopeless... There was nothing to take to Angelica, nothing that was left anyway. Was it possible that the killer was looking for and ultimately found the same documents he was now searching for in the shadows of this old, decrepit house?

He was just about to leave when he noticed a rather large hand-carved Egyptian amulet lying on the dresser. Remembering he had brought it back from his travels and given it to Matthew, without hesitation, he went over, picked it up, and put it under his arm. He turned off the light and walked back down stairs. Michael looked around one last time making sure the lights were off and then opened the door to step out.

As he pulled the door shut, Michael turned around to see Sheriff Taylor standing on the porch with both hands on his holster. "Holy shit... Sheriff!" Michael dropped his flashlight and the amulet.

"Michael, I thought that was your truck! What the heck are you doing here, son?"

Michael leaned over and picked up the flashlight and then the amulet. Michael caught the sheriff looking at it suspiciously, so he lifted the handcrafted, knot-shaped amulet. "I wanted something to remember him by. I saw it lying on the dresser and it felt right to take it since I had given it to him."

The sheriff tilted his head and nodded. "You shouldn't be removing objects from a crime scene, son. What is that thing?" The sheriff appeared curious. Michael held it up. "An Egyptian relic, a tyet-knot."

The Bovine Connection

The sheriff's eyes softened and he looked down. "I'm sure sorry about Matthew. He will be missed. I've known you boys since you were kids -- runnin' around town, drinkin' beer, and gettin' into trouble."

Michael lowered his head and looked down. "Doesn't make sense," he mumbled aloud. "What would have caused Matthew to lose control, destroy his house, and then hang himself?" Michael looked back up at the sheriff, puzzled.

Sheriff Taylor pulled at his belt and cleared his throat. "Don't know, son."

"This looks like a break in, even a bit staged. Something's off, and Matthew wasn't the type of guy to commit suicide… there's definitely more going on here, don't you think, Sheriff?"

The sheriff looked around and back at Michael, his voice low and assertive… "So, you're not convinced we've worked other angles besides just suicide. If it wasn't staged, then Matthew must have struggled with his killer. That's what you're thinking." The sheriff's eyes were suspicious.

"Did the medical examiner find any defensive wounds on Matthew during the autopsy?" Michael asked as he observed the sheriff's face.

"It's late, and you should be getting on home. I'm not gonna ask how you got in here," Sheriff Taylor patted Michael's shoulder as they walked to Michael's truck. "I know you boys were real close, Michael."

"Yes sir, we were," Michael said as he looked down at his shoes and thought for a moment, and then looked back up at the sheriff. "Hey, Sheriff, why are you out here so late?"

"Michael, you know I can't discuss the specifics of the case, but yes, Matthew had some strange defensive bruising on his body. The medical examiner is now calling it a homicide. So no, we don't believe Matthew killed himself. I knew that boy well enough to know he'd never have killed himself. And it looks to me like the killer was looking for something. But you just forget our conversation here tonight, all right. The town folk will know in the morning."

The sheriff looked firmly at Michael. "You boys were real close; you wouldn't have any idea of who might have wanted Matthew dead, would you?"

Michael looked surprised. "No, Sheriff, I sure don't, I can't imagine anyone wanting Matthew dead. Everyone that knew him... liked him. Wouldn't you agree?"

The sheriff thought for a moment and shook his head. "You go home and get some sleep, I'm gonna do another walkthrough. Goodnight, Michael. Oh, and by the way, I'm gonna want you to come by the station tomorrow and give us a statement regarding your whereabouts on the night of Matthew's death. You being here tonight kinda makes this situation a bit awkward. Understand?"

"All right, Sheriff." Michael quickly got in his truck and backed out of the loose pea gravel driveway as Sheriff Taylor stood and watched.

Michael peered out of his rearview window at the sheriff's silhouette growing smaller as he drove away.

The Bovine Connection

He reached over and picked up his cell phone on the seat and called Angelica. She didn't answer so he left her a message. "I'll be there tomorrow evening. I'll grab a cab to your place, just text me the address when you get a chance. And, please be careful until I get to you. I ran into Sheriff Taylor at Matthew's house tonight... I'll tell you everything when I get to D.C. Sheriff Taylor wants me to stop by the police station, and then I'm going spend some time tomorrow with Sammy wrapping things up. I look forward to seeing you. Did I tell you how much I enjoyed having you here? Sure have thought a lot about you since you left," Michael spoke softly. He hung up and looked ahead into the darkness.

Michael was only about a mile from his ranch when suddenly the radio turned on in the truck. The loud eruption of music startled him... "Jesus!" he shouted.

Michael impulsively pushed the button and turned the radio off. Bewildered, he took a deep breath. His face was flush. Michael tilted his head and observed the radio for a moment. He reached over and turned the radio on and then off again, completely puzzled by the strange incident. Michael checked his wristwatch, it was stuck at one thirty-three in the morning. He tapped his watch and put it to his ear. It wasn't ticking.

Michael glanced to his left and noticed an old barn and a broken down tractor in an open pasture. As he turned back around, he saw a large silver craft with bright lights hovering in the sky about fifty feet above his black Escalade, in front of him. Michael impulsively slammed on the breaks and came to an abrupt stop. His gut told him, without a doubt, it was a UFO.

Michael quickly opened the door and jumped out. He threw his shoulders back. His eyes were wide as he looked up skyward toward the hovering craft.

Michael's head started to throb. He rubbed his head, gliding his fingers down and around his face. His legs went limp and he slumped onto to his knees. The pain was sharp and infiltrated his entire skull. He slowly stood up, disoriented, squinting in the brightness of the craft. Darkness was all around him.

Suddenly, a loud humming sound penetrated the air. Michael covered his ears just as another bright light hit him like the sting of a bee, causing Michael's head to jolt back and his arms to shoot out to the side of his body. He was frozen.

Chapter Forty

Angelica awoke and noticed her room had turned chilly. As the vague remembrance of another disturbing nightmare came into focus, she pulled the covers up to her neck and shivered. The room was closing in on her.

The themes of the macabre visions were becoming more consistent and tangible. She recalled feeling again as if she were sliding or being dragged off of her bed, and she was waking to actual senses that were frightening, to say the least. She had a metallic taste in her mouth. Her abdomen was tight and painful to the touch. She recalled vaguely that the pain upon waking in the middle of the night was horrendous but she quickly passed out.

That morning, it was coming into focus. She remembered the brightness of the craft as she was being led inside it and seeing other humans there. There were men and women on metal tables undergoing what appeared to be surgical procedures. When she passed by, she tried to make eye contact, but they appeared to be unconscious or didn't notice her.

Then she remembered at one point being in a room. Her breathing was hard and dry. Drenched in sweat, she felt frightened. She looked up to see a baby as one of the beings handed it to her. She caressed the tiny body and when it looked at her, she saw it was only part human. Its black, almond shaped eyes gazed into hers, causing her to scream, right before she was hit by a blinding flash of light. The dream came back to her so vividly and felt incredibly too real. Between the sheets, she felt like a rock between two feathers. The weight of the revelation that she was being abducted as she slept was too heavy to bear; it was deeply unsettling to consider that she was being violated while she slept. She had to put it out of her mind.

Angelica rose from the bed, and absentmindedly looked around the room, thinking about the baby in her dream. She was glad to be home in D.C., where she was surrounded by familiar things and memories.

Angelica walked over to the bathroom and grabbed her robe from the back of the door, and then went down stairs into the sunny kitchen. Angelica started the coffeemaker and then opened the refrigerator. She had been too exhausted to stop by the market on her way home from the airport the night before. She grabbed the organic carrot juice and took a sip, immediately turning to the sink to spit it out. It had soured, leaving a bad taste in her mouth. She used the outside of her palm to wipe the carrot juice from her lips. Angelica turned around, opened the cabinet, grabbed a coffee mug and placed it under the pod already in the Keurig.

Fumbling through her pantry, she found a box of shortbread cookies. She took a cookie out, grabbed her coffee mug from the Keurig, and walked into her den.

Angelica held the cookie between her lips as she pulled out the drawer of her desk and located her zip drive. She slid it into the USB slot on her laptop and downloaded all of her backed up files into her new Apple laptop. Everything was there except the files on the cattle mutilation story.

Angelica suddenly remembered the man's voicemail about the note he had left her. She jumped up, ran over, and opened the front door, but there was nothing in plain sight. Even though she was exhausted last night, she would have noticed it as she walked in, she thought. Angelica bent down and lifted the mat... and there it was in a large manila envelope. She started to open it, but stopped and instinctively looked around to see if anyone was watching her. Her heart was pounding as she stood there holding the envelope against her chest. Nothing seemed out of the ordinary. There was a young woman walking a Jack Russell and a male jogger on the other side of the street. The woman looked over and smiled at Angelica. Angelica smiled back and quickly shut the door and turned the deadbolt behind her.

Angelica walked around to all the windows and shut the plantation shutters. She sat down at her desk again and twirled the envelope with a dramatic swish of her wrist onto the desk. Her instincts were telling her not to open it. She sat staring at it for a few seconds, contemplating. There were no markings or writing on the outside. No stamp, nothing giving clues. Angelica took a deep breath and started to open it, but stopped, and thought aloud... "What if it's laced with poison?" She grabbed her coffee mug and quickly put the envelope down, got up from her desk, and started pacing around the room with her coffee mug cuddled tightly between both hands. Glancing back at the envelope sitting on her desk, she finally let out a sigh and walked over and picked it back up. Taking a deep breath, she opened it.

"I have very important information for you. The story you're working on goes far beyond anything you could imagine. We need to meet." Angelica felt her heart pounding rapidly, her body instantly tensed.

"You obliviously know where the Smithsonian is - Meet me there Tuesday June 29th at noon at the Egyptian exhibit. There is something that I must show you, and Ms. Bradley, this may sound strange, but try to make sure you're not followed. And don't tell anyone where you are going."

"Why there? It was crowded with people, so there was some comfort in that, at least," she thought as she put the envelope down, unsure of what to do.

"What if he is one of them? What if he wants to kill me?" she thought aloud. Her journalistic instincts immediately took over and she decided to take the chance and meet him. She'd put off going to her office until after the meeting and although it was risky, it seemed minimal because of the location. Angelica had been to the Smithsonian many times and knew she could find her way around quickly and easily.

Angelica sent Gail a text letting her know she would be in her office some time mid-afternoon.

Chapter Forty-One

Angelica knew the Egyptian exhibition was located in the National Museum of Natural History on the corner of Constitution Avenue and 10th Street. The Smithsonian Institution was not a single entity but rather consisted of a conglomerate of nineteen museums and research facilities making it the largest of its kind in the world. Tourists could spend an entire week going from museum to museum and still only witness a small portion of its treasures. The new exhibition "Eternal Life in Ancient Egypt" had quickly become one of the most popular exhibits the Smithsonian had ever introduced. Visitors were indoctrinated into the mystical Egyptian burial rituals, and the significance of cosmology in their beliefs of the afterlife. The scientific study of mummies revealed to visitors expert burial practices, as well as the diseases that the Ancient Egyptians fought and--in most cases--lost the battle against.

Angelica made her way to the West Wing of the 2nd Floor near the entrance to the "Written in Bone" exhibition.

Pushing through the crowds, Angelica finally made her way to the entrance of the exhibition she was looking for. She was trying not to show how nervous she was to meet this mysterious man who knew where she lived, but anyone watching her closely could see she was clutching her purse a little too tightly against her chest.

Angelica stopped at a re-creation of a mummy and its tomb and began to take deep breaths as she gained her composure. She walked over to the next showcase and was mesmerized by the Egyptian hieroglyphics surrounding the ornate inner coffin of Tentkhonsu. For a few moments she was able to put the ominous meeting out of her mind. She realized there was so much she had missed during her last visit to the museum. "Beautiful, isn't it?" a male voice whispered close to her ear.

Angelica jumped. Startled, she turned to her right to see a distinguished black man with a badge hanging from his neck against an expensive blue and grey plaid button up. With pressed, khaki slacks and brown loafers, and an obvious Smithsonian badge around his neck, he appeared harmless.

"I didn't mean to startle you," he whispered sincerely. "Ms. Bradley, my name is Dr. Marc Bishop. I am the one that contacted you and left you the note."

Angelica stepped back and let out the nervous breath she had been holding. "Well, you did startle me! What is this about, Doctor?" she asked. "Why did you contact me? You said my life was in danger... Why?" "And how did you find me?"

The doctor looked sincerely at Angelica and patiently spoke, "Paul Colbeck is how I found you. Paul called me and told me you were covering the cattle mutilations in Elberton... that you were also from D.C., and appeared to be a unique journalist - You kept and open mind. I had met Paul a few years back at a UFO Conference in Phoenix. Paul was interested in my work."

Angelica nodded. "Yes, I like Paul, he is a nice guy," she said as she narrowed her eyes, analyzing him.

The doctor reached over and touched Angelica's arm, causing Angelica to step back and look down at his hand.

"Come with me. I want to show you something." He lightly tugged at her arm and led her around the corner to a door. The sign on the door read, "Authorized Personnel Only. Not an Exit." He lifted his badge and scanned it through a security device. A green light flashed and the door opened. Dr. Bishop stepped aside so Angelica could enter first, then he looked back around the exhibit suspiciously, making sure no one saw them go in. He quickly closed the door behind them, turning the knob to make sure it was securely locked.

Angelica gazed around in amazement, as he led her through what appeared to be a large warehouse--at least two stories in height--where there were enormous shelves holding crates, creating aisles.

Angelica stopped to scan for an escape route. "Wait, where are you taking me? How do I know you won't harm me?"

The doctor looked at Angelica with a genuine smile and kindness in his eyes. He chuckled slightly. "You're safe with me, I promise. I must show you something… you'll understand… just follow me."

Angelica timidly shrugged her shoulders, "Okay..." and continued in step behind him. Her heart was pounding rapidly against her chest.

The doctor opened another door and they walked into a brightly lit lab with long tables and examination lamps. He walked over to a shelf and gently pulled out a long plastic tube about four inches in circumference. "Inside this is an ancient Egyptian scroll found by the Soviet KGB in 1961," Dr. Bishop said as he put the tube on a table and picked up a pair of latex gloves and put them on. He then pulled over a large mounted magnifying glass and turned on the lamp at the table. Carefully, he opened the tube and pulled out the scroll. The doctor looked at Angelica, giving her the impression that he was nervous, cautious not to damage the valuable contents inside.

"This was found in 'The Tomb of the Visitor.' It's called 'The Zolkin Papyrus' ... named after the Scientist, Sergey Zolkin, who discovered it. Through my research, I learned that it was stolen from the Soviet government by an archeologist who defected. He brought it here in exchange for citizenship. He's now dead, however... ruthlessly killed." Dr. Bishop looked at Angelica with a rather serious expression.

Angelica felt her heart start to pound against her chest. "Okay," she murmured.

"As a journalist," the doctor continued, "I am sure you remember the Russian KGB agent-turned-journalist who was poisoned by polonium with the tip of an umbrella. Well a similar thing happened to this archeologist... never leaked to the press, so no one

The Bovine Connection

knew about it. The scroll eventually ended up here at the Smithsonian and only a select few, I suspect, have seen it. I stumbled upon it by mere accident. I was working on artifacts brought back from a recent exhibition in Egypt and while in the dry storage area, I noticed a box. This box stood out. It had red tape marked 'The Tomb of the Visitor.' So... I picked it up and carefully looked around to make sure my colleagues had not noticed. I wasn't sure what I had in my hands..."

Angelica glanced around the room to make sure they were still alone, causing Dr. Bishop to stop in mid-sentence. "I'm sorry, please continue," she whispered.

"I had researched the supposed 'Tomb of the Visitor'... and I didn't see any harm in taking a look. When I opened it, I was astonished... I couldn't believe my eyes. I wondered how many others had seen it. I realized why it was tucked away and hidden in the corner of the storage room. See for yourself..." Dr. Bishop opened the scroll as Angelica's eyes widened.

"Oh wow!" she uttered as she looked up at the doctor. "Is that what I think it is...?" Angelica pointed down to an image on the scroll, careful not to touch. Dr. Bishop just smiled and nodded.

"Oh my!" Angelica lifted her hand to her open mouth.

"This won't be in the lab for much longer," the doctor told her. "I just found out they were taking samples of the papyrus to determine the age of the scroll. It's thought to be dated around 11,000 BC. You are very lucky to be in the right place at the right time. If you want to call it luck." Dr. Bishop peered up at Angelica with a straight face.

"Now see here..." he pointed. "Depicted on the scroll are two small beings with thin bodies and irregularly large heads, the eyes large and black, and beside them... there appears to be a spacecraft."

"Yes, a spaceship!" Angelica looked at Dr. Bishop, astonished. "And those are Egyptian people on the other side of the spaceship! Amazing!" Angelica sighed.

Angelica examined the scroll. "What is that?" she pointed, carefully.

"Oh, the Tyet-knot symbol," Dr. Bishop said. "That is the symbol for the "Blood of Isis". Some believe the Tyet-knot is the vagina, the womb and the ovary. It symbolizes birth and life giving."

"Fascinating," Angelica murmured.

Angelica looked back at the scroll "Okay... So why is there a bull with large horns?"

"Well, there are several theories around the role the bull played in Egyptian history. A number of gods were worshipped in the form of bulls or cows. The domesticated bovine was the animal the Egyptian economy was based on. They were milked, sacrificed, and eaten... and used as laborers alongside the human labor force."

Angelica felt her cell phone vibrate in her purse. She reached down and pulled it out. It was Andrew. Angelica sent the call straight to voicemail, and then looked back up at Dr. Bishop. "My apologies, please continue."

The doctor smiled politely... "The Soviets started a secret mission in Egypt called 'Project Isis,' after they had learned of a legend dating back before the time of the Pharaohs. A visitor from space... Well, the legend goes... A group of visitors came from another star system, passing to the Egyptian people wisdom and technology. And some of the technology was left behind as blueprints. But I'll get to that shortly," he said calmly.

"Blueprints?" Angelica murmured.

Dr. Bishop smiled and nodded. "They called these visitors 'The Wing Gods' or 'The Sky Gods.' The Soviets were captivated by this legend and, as always, their real goal was to recover ancient technology at a low cost to win the cold war. Oh, and it gets more interesting... Many years after, in 1960, the Russians intercepted a phone conversation between two local Egyptians discussing 'The Visitor's Tomb'. Well, they eventually found the tomb in 1961."

"Fascinating!" Angelica whispered.

Encouraged, Dr. Bishop continued. "They had gone to great lengths to hide their expedition from the Egyptians, dressing their scientists in peasant and military clothing."

Dr. Bishop noticed Angelica look down at her watch and lower her brows. She shot an anxious glance at him before looking back at the scroll. She was feeling increasingly antsy to get back to her office at the *Liberator*. Wherever he was going with the history lesson on Egypt, he needed to hurry it along, she thought.

His instincts were correct. "Okay, moving along, the KGB was deeply interested in UFOs due to a rise in reported sightings of circular ships. Their goal was to obtain advanced knowledge to see if it might prove useful for military purposes."

Okay," she said testily.

"You know, many years later, a few of the scientists from the expedition founded a group called the 'Osiris Devotion Group' and returned to the secret location of the tomb in Egypt in 1985. They mysteriously disappeared that evening at a site near the tomb. Just an interesting fact."

Angelica appeared surprised. "Really, just disappeared?"

Dr. Bishop put the scroll down carefully on the table. "Yes, just disappeared. That's how it was reported in the Cairo newspapers."

Dr. Bishop took a seat on a metal stool and pulled another stool over for Angelica. "We are currently doing another excavation at a site in Egypt at what is known as 'The New Kingdom,' on the old slave route to the 'Valley of Kings.'"

"Okay." Angelica appeared puzzled, staring blankly at Dr. Bishop.

Dr. Bishop continued, "There are other ancient civilizations in the history of mankind before Christ that match the rapid advancements in knowledge and technology similar to the Egyptians. For example, Mexico and China."

Angelica put her hand on her hip and postured slightly back, "Really?"

Dr. Bishop nodded. "Yes. The Mayans also created great Pyramids, you know, but were much more barbaric. However, in spite of that, they had an incredible knowledge of astronomy, and were obsessed by it."

Without warning, Dr. Bishop stopped and stared at the door, and then gradually turned his attention back to the scroll. The air smelled ancient and musky. Angelica sneezed. "Excuse me!" She rubbed under her nose with her index finger.

Dr. Bishop glanced up at Angelica. "Bless you! My apologies... It's quite dusty back here. Where was I? Oh yes... And in China there is a legend of the first emperors of China being called the 'Sons of Heaven' and supposedly they built the first pyramids of China. Some believe there are large numbers of graves containing skeletons of strange looking beings with large heads and bodies a little over four feet tall near the site of a pyramid in China. Unfortunately, no expeditions have been permitted there after the rumored discovery." Dr. Bishop appeared disappointed.

"The Pyramid of the Sun of Teotihuacan in Mexico... Well, they have found granite stone disks with strange hieroglyphs that, according to some experts, tell of a UFO crash 12,000 years ago--roughly 10,000 BC. The translation reads 'beings with big heads came down from heaven a long, long time ago.' That makes two ancient civilizations that created the same pyramid type structures, if you were counting." Angelica nodded and shifted anxiously in her seat.

Dr. Bishop smirked. "Now here is an intriguing question... Why and how did these civilizations, completely independent and isolated from each other, create the same type of giant, triangular structures that can in some cases be seen from the moon and how did they advance so quickly compared to all other civilizations? Interesting... wouldn't you say?"

"Yes... peculiar, Doctor," Angelica said as she raised her hand and cupped her chin.

The doctor continued in almost a whisper, causing Angelica to look around to make sure no one was listening.

"You see there was a passageway discovered inside of the Egyptian 'Tomb of the Visitor,' supposedly leading to a secret chamber. I believe this chamber is what is known as 'The Chamber of Knowledge,' located under either the Sphinx or the Great Pyramid. Since 820 AD, explorers have been searching for this hidden chamber. It is unclear what the Soviets discovered when they entered it. Apparently, it was quite secretive, because they decided to delete the coordinates of it in their report and the only scientist who entered along with the military was later found dead under mysterious circumstances. Therefore, my recent discovery of this scroll proves the legend of 'The Tomb of the Visitor' is true. The tomb does exist. And I am quite certain 'The Chamber of Knowledge' does, as well. I believe that is where the ancient blueprints for highly-advanced technology were found." Dr. Bishop raised his eyebrows in confidence.

Angelica nodded. "I see."

"The pyramids were created for a purpose. Whoever constructed the pyramids could determine longitude and latitude. Longitude and latitude were not widely used until the 1600's. A Russian astronomer discovered that the Giza structures converge to one particular point. We've always speculated as to their purpose. Since it's believed all three giant pyramids are in perfect alignment with star constellations. So, we must ask ourselves *why*, Angelica. I've heard it said that the ancient aliens came to earth to build the pyramids. Some believe they were used for navigational purposes. I believe they were transmitters." Dr. Bishop's forehead wrinkled as he looked intensely at her.

Angelica lowered her chin and met his eyes. "Okay." She was definitely curious now. "Go on... wait, Dr. Bishop..."

Angelica broke her concentration and raised her hand. "It's all very fascinating, but what does this have to do with me and the cattle mutilations, Doctor?"

Dr. Bishop crinkled his chin and narrowed his eyes. "Don't you see? It's evidence that not only do aliens exist, they've been on earth all along. You started with the cattle mutilations. Now, I'm going to help you advance to the next level, Angelica. I too have been interested in the cattle mutilations. For some, it starts there, for some... leading you down a long, convoluted path of more questions than answers. I am going to speed you along. They use the tissue and blood to feed." Dr. Bishop leaned back into the chair and observed Angelica's reaction. She didn't appear shocked. He frowned and lifted his chin curiously. "You don't seem surprised."

"That's what Dr. Goolrick said." Angelica paused. "So that is what you believe, as well?"

"Yes, they soak themselves in large tanks of the concoction and absorb it into their skin. Supposedly, they don't have a digestive system."

Angelica scratched behind her ear as she held Dr. Bishop's gaze.

Angelica was lost in thought. During her investigation, she had assumed that when she finally discovered the truth behind the mutilations, it would be something more believable.

Dr. Bishop noticed Angelica was deep in thought. "Angelica?"

Angelica flinched at the sound of her name and gazed blankly at Dr. Bishop. "Yes, please continue."

"So... I have asked myself this simple question. If the Russians were heavily embroiled in this, what about our government? I have been interested in the connection between aliens and our government for quite some time, and have made some startling discoveries. Here's the biggest scoop of your entire career. There is a top-secret aerospace program being led by a private citizen... A billionaire who's connected to Elberton, Montana... no one I've spoken to seems to know who he is. He has, however, been seen at the Newton Air Force Base with the Committee Chairman of the U.S. Ways and Means, John Kaye, but no one knows his name."

Angelica looked as if someone had slapped her. "Now, that's interesting! Back to politics," she whispered.

Now get this, the mysterious billionaire purchased artifacts from the Russian Mafia... artifacts from the KGB's expedition into the 'The Tomb of the Visitor'... More interestingly, according to the defected archeologist-- before he was murdered-- the artifacts purchased actually came from 'The Chamber of Knowledge' they discovered through a hidden passageway in 'The Tomb of the Visitor' that day in 1961. The archeologist had communicated to his colleagues' right before his death that he had translated secret blueprints of highly-advanced extraterrestrial technology.

Now, the million dollar question for you is: how far you are willing to go with your story? It's going to get extremely dangerous the deeper you dig."

Angelica looked back down at the scroll. "This has taken an interesting direction," she mumbled. Angelica paused to gain her composure. "So your interest is in the blueprints for advanced technology. Okay, now it's coming together." Angelica looked inquisitively at Dr. Bishop.

Dr. Bishop nodded respectfully. "Angelica... John Kaye, the Chairman for the U.S. Ways and Means, may be helping to fund the facility with our taxpayer dollars. Peculiar, ay?"

Angelica concurred, "Peculiar, is an understatement."

Dr. Bishop observed Angelica as she sat contemplating. "It's extremely risky, you already know too much, however."

Angelica nodded her head, her eyes grave. "Yes," she said, still contemplating. Her expression indicated she might be second guessing how far she was willing to go.

Angelica met the doctor's eyes. "When you left the message at the lodge that I was in danger…"

Dr. Bishop appeared surprised by the question, interrupting her in mid-sentence. "Paul Colbeck said you were asking a lot of questions and making connections to the Newton Air Force Base, which supposedly has a hidden ET base underneath it."

Exhaling, Angelica turned her body to face Dr. Bishop directly. She gave him a dumb look. "Underneath Newton is an underground ET base?"

"You heard me correctly. Well, asking questions about Newton does not go unnoticed in a town like Elberton. We agreed on the phone, you were probably being watched, and since you were at a point of no return-- no pun intended-- well, you were exactly the person who could help us find out more about the advanced technology they are using at the aerospace facility."

"And what exactly is your interest in the facility," she asked, "just so I'm clear, Doctor?"

"My interests are the ancient alien artifacts," Dr. Bishop said. "The blueprint for the technology – perhaps hundreds of years beyond our current technology, or more. I have a strong hunch on what that might be."

Angelica thought for a moment. "Why did you leave the voicemail and the note anonymously? Why didn't you just say who you were?" Angelica held a suspicious frown.

"I probably should have," he told her, "but I was afraid my messages could have been intercepted. I was trying to show some semblance of caution. But bottom line, I genuinely want to help you." Suddenly, Dr. Bishop thought he heard a sound coming from the warehouse. He looked around the lab and then back to Angelica, raising his finger to suggest they lower their voices and whisper. "You know, in my field we are uncomfortably aware of the archaeological cover-ups. If the general public were ever allowed inside the nation's attic, as the Smithsonian has been called, they would be amazed at the skeletons they'd find. It would rock the very foundation of our society."

Angelica shook her head, "It does seem that the general public is always being kept in the dark. And here I've been, an investigative journalist in this very city, and these hidden discoveries have been right under my nose this whole time. You seem to know a great deal about this aerospace facility. How do you recommend I proceed?" she asked sincerely.

"Well, first, you should find out who the billionaire is," Dr. Bishop said.

"Do you have an idea as to who he could be?" Angelica asked with her head cocked.

"The CEO camouflages him from the public," Dr. Bishop replied.

"Can't you just follow the paper trail?" Angelica asked, as if she had concluded the best way.

"No, his name appears as F.M.G. There are no photos of him, nothing shedding light on his identity," Dr. Bishop said, as he raised his hand and scratched his forehead.

"What do you think he's doing at the facility?" she questioned.

"I may be wrong; however, judging by the artifacts found in 'The Tomb of the Visitor'... or more accurately, 'The Chamber of Knowledge'... I believe he's working on teleportation, and I think he's going to a planet where the Egyptian visitors supposedly built ancient pyramids, as well. It's a planet that is steeped in human mythology and fascination, and it's our neighbor."

Angelica laughed nervously and tilted her head as he continued. "Mars?"

Dr. Bishop smiled and nodded. "I believe he purchased the blueprints for advanced teleportation technology, perhaps thousands of years more advanced than anything we humans could discover."

"You do?" Angelica uttered, as she examined Dr. Bishop's face. "Where is the aerospace facility located?"

"Nevada." Dr. Bishop straightened his lips.

"Well, I guess I'm heading to Nevada," Angelica said, sounding uncommitted to the idea.

"Good, I'll join you."

Angelica appeared surprised. "Join me?" She chuckled.

"When do we leave?" Dr. Bishop took out a business card from his wallet and handed it to her.

"No one there is going to agree to an interview with a journalist from D.C.," Angelica said.

"We can try." Dr. Bishop smiled.

"Or an archaeologist from the Smithsonian," she said wryly. "Are you sure you want to do this, Doctor?" Angelica stared in disbelief.

"You don't want to go alone, do you?"

Angelica thought for a moment. "No, I guess that is not the best option considering I might be in danger," she answered truthfully.

"Good, so when do you want to leave?" Dr. Bishop was anxious.

"Well, let's see. I have to make some cursory preparations so... in a few days." Angelica took a deep breath. "Okay, you can make the logistical arrangements and I'll have my office line up the interview... I'll call you tomorrow." Angelica said slowly.

Dr. Bishop rolled the scroll up and placed it back in the tube. He walked over and sat it back on the shelf. "This way, I'll walk you out." He motioned and then walked over and opened the door.

"Dr. Bishop, what if they don't agree to an interview?" Angelica asked as she scrambled her feet to the floor and stood up from the stool.

"Well, I think we go anyway. We could at least get a good look at the facility, and perhaps, ask around a bit." He winked sheepishly.

Angelica stepped out and then turned around to focus on his earnest eyes. "I'll wait for your call."

Chapter Forty-Two

As Angelica stepped out of the Smithsonian's main entrance, she found herself in the middle of a group of school-aged children who had just gotten out of a nondescript, yellow school bus. Angelica stepped aside so they could pass by her, careful not to bump into any of them.

The children were speaking loudly, visibly excited to enter the museum. Angelica smiled at one of the teachers at the end of the line of children as they finally passed by her. She thought about how naïve and vulnerable they were and she felt a tinge of sadness deep in her stomach.

While at the curb, watching the last child enter the front doors of the museum, a black Lincoln Town car pulled up behind her. It couldn't have been more than five feet away and she smelled the fumes from the exhaust, pungent and thick in the heat of the summer day. She heard the car door slam and swung around to see two men in black suits stepping onto the curb as one walked briskly towards her. At first Angelica thought they were going to walk past her but then the tall, muscular man in front, who seemed to be in charge, said three words that made her blood turn cold... "Angelica Marie Bradley?" No one ever spoke her middle name. Her mother had given it to her in honor of her grandmother. Angelica stood there completely frozen and time seemed to stand still. One of the men stayed back by the car and was looking around while the man that spoke her full name stepped right up to her. "Do not publish the story, Ms. Bradley." Then he nonchalantly handed her a rolled up piece of newspaper. "Open it Ms. Bradley." Angelica slowly opened up the newspaper as her hands began to tremble. She felt moisture forming in the pit of her arm.

It was an article that she immediately recognized. An investigative journalist was found dead from a robbery gone wrong after an intruder had entered his home. Angelica stood there stunned, with her jaw dropped, holding the newspaper with the photo of the victim. The man stood very close to her and with piercing eyes, looked down at her and simply said, "Have a nice day, Ms. Bradley." She watched with her mouth open, in a daze, as the man turned and walked away. His partner opened the door for him and he quickly got into the black Lincoln. His partner then walked around and opened the passenger side door, staring directly at Angelica as he got in and slammed the door shut.

Angelica felt her body moving into a trance-like state. She stared, mesmerized by the familiar picture of the murdered journalist. Her voice taut with fear... "I covered this story several years ago," she thought aloud, as she peered at the picture of the man on the newspaper.

Angelica was familiar with all the details of the crime. Although she had never believed the police report stating it was a random crime, she was never able to gather enough information proving her suspicions that he was murdered for revealing the whereabouts of a former Nazi scientist, still wanted for war crimes. He had been living safely secluded and protected, under an alias in Virginia. The dead journalist had uncovered that the former wartime criminal was employed by Hatcher Pharmaceuticals.

A woman's voice appeared out of nowhere. Angelica jerked and turned. "The light is red, Miss. You can cross the street." An elderly lady was standing in front of her smiling, appearing concerned.

"Oh, yes, thank you." Angelica looked around and then quickly ran across the road to where her car was parked.

Chapter Forty-Three

Angelica took the elevator up to her office, passing by the cubicles in the center of the building.

She unlocked her door and turned on the light. Angelica glanced around, suddenly happy to be back. She walked over and sat down at her desk.

"Hey, you're back! How was it?"

Angelica looked up to see Andrew standing in her doorway. She was careful with her response, feeling it was safer that Andrew not know anything about what had transpired in the last forty eight hours, especially after what had happened to Matthew.

Andrew studied Angelica as he perched on the sleek white lounge chair in front of her desk with easy grace of Gene Kelly. Angelica gripped the arm of her chair and took a deep breath.

"You seem different," he announced as he narrowed his eyes suspiciously.

"Different?" Angelica appeared puzzled. "How so?" she asked, as she shot a quick glance over at him before looking at her computer screen.

"Not sure... Just different," Andrew pushed the curious thought away. "So how did it go in Montana?" he asked, his voice enthusiastic.

"It is definitely going to be a fascinating story. I can promise you that."

Andrew nodded. "Well, how about getting a drink after work?"

The Bovine Connection

Angelica appeared worried as she looked away from her laptop and met Andrew's eyes. "I'm seeing someone."

Andrew was shocked. "What? Who? When did this happen?" he said almost in a yell.

Angelica was trying to be sensitive to his feelings. She had never intended on becoming serious with Andrew and assumed he knew it. "His name is Michael Anderson. We met in Montana… It's hard to explain, it just happened. A lot has happened," she answered quickly, but softly.

"You fell in love with a cowboy while on a story in Montana. That's a little bit unexpected, wouldn't you say?" Andrew cleared his throat, noticeably shocked. His eyes were wide as he adjusted in his chair, staring blankly.

Andrew regrouped his thoughts and continued, "He shovels shit all day! And why would anyone pursue a career lassoing horses? I appreciate it… but how could you, Angelica Bradley, be content with that lifestyle?" Andrew gave a grim chuckle. "You and a cowboy from Montana… Good luck with that!" He shook his head in disbelief.

Angelica was not amused. "Let me put it to you bluntly, Andrew. He's the cowboy you read about in romance novels… and you're a Harvard Grad playboy with enough notches on your bedpost to carve a totem pole. Do I need to say more?" Angelica pushed her chair away from her desk and stood up.

"Look, Angelica, just because I don't sell myself to you, doesn't mean I'm not a deep, soulful man," he argued, his tone flat.

Angelica looked exasperated. Cleary he wasn't getting it, she thought. "If you'll excuse me, I have a meeting with Carl and Gail," she said in a breath, with a look of bewilderment.

Andrew turned his legs so she could pass by. "Well, you and I both know it won't work," he announced as he cocked his head and observed her cream colored, high-heeled shoes as she walked out, leaving him sitting alone in her office.

Chapter Forty-Four

Gail was already seated in front of Carl's desk. As Angelica entered, they both became quiet. Angelica went over and took a seat beside Gail, letting out a long breath of air while leaning back in exhaustion.

"Wow!" Angelica lifted her hand to her temple and then dropped it into her lap.

"Angelica, quite a story we've stumbled upon, according to Gail," Carl said and then looked over at Gail proudly.

Angelica nodded her head and was genuinely confused about where to start. "Guys, this cattle mutilation story has gone way beyond anything we could have imagined. First, let me mention that the reporter from Elberton, Matthew Tillman, is dead," she announced.

"Yes, I know," Carl said. "Gail told me. I'm sorry to hear the news. I understand you two became close friends while you were there. How did he die?"

Angelica took another, softer breath and looked down, shaking her head. "It was initially reported as a suicide but now it's been ruled a homicide. I suspect..."

Gail finished her sentence... "You suspect it was because of your involvement in the story."

Angelica looked vulnerable. "Yes, because of me, I suppose," she said sorrowfully as she gripped her knee.

Angelica glanced briefly at Gail who suddenly looked nervous, and then she looked at Carl. "Well then you already know you may be in danger," Carl said somberly. "Angelica, I have an obligation to inform you that what you're investigation has been linked to several mysterious deaths."

Closely examining Carl's expression, Angelica became suspicious. She instinctively sat up straight in her chair. "Did you know where this story was going? How much did you know, Carl?"

Carl looked back at Gail and she nodded, giving her approval on what he was about to say.

"Yes, I've known about Newton's connection... that there are secret projects there revolving around aliens," he answered, appearing concerned.

"Did you know about the aerospace facility and the billionaire with a fondness for ancient Egyptian artifacts?" Angelica leaned in closer to his desk, clearly pissed off. "Wait, that's why--out of all the cattle mutilations--you chose this one! I get it now!" Angelica's tone was flustered.

Carl nodded. "Yes. And it's obvious you have accomplished exactly what I expected you, as a crack journalist, to do. You are beginning to put the pieces of this deranged puzzle together."

"What the hell, Carl? We're not at the *Post* anymore - I'm your boss! The *Liberator* is my magazine! My company! I started it!" she sputtered.

"With our help!" Carl glanced over at Gail and raised his eyebrows.

The Bovine Connection

"Why didn't you tell me any of this before I left for Montana? My life is in danger! You had to know it would be! Why did I take this fucking story?" Angelica shouted, then closed her eyes and shook her head.

Gail jumped up and shut the door as a few employees were walking by trying to peep in and eavesdrop.

"Angelica, calm down!" Gail suggested sternly.

Carl looked at Angelica sympathetically. "Angelica, it's rumored that some people in very powerful positions are up to no good and that's why I felt it was an important story."

"So who were you planning on covering the story?" Angelica appeared anxiously curious.

"Steven Jacobs," he answered confidently." I never thought in a million years you'd take this story."

"Oh." Angelica leaned back and thought a moment. Well, he's building some fucking alien technology system. Hell, for all we know... he could be planning to blow us all up!" Angelica finished with tight lips.

"Listen Angelica, you must believe me... I didn't think anyone would get killed! Matthew was a small town journalist. You're a big city journalist. In the end, maybe it was a warning for you to stop... I don't know." Carl shook his head, appearing conflicted. "You can stop, Angelica, and we can edit the story and move on."

Angelica was feeling a rush of emotions... anger, fear, uncertainty. But without hesitation and with a steely resolve she had never quite felt before she looked directly into Carl's eyes. "No, Carl, I can't stop! I have to finish what you started! Come hail or high water this story will be written and published! Angelica laughed spontaneously. "Hell, no one will believe a word of it anyway!

"But seriously, this story has legs like I have never seen before and I am afraid one person has already died because of it." Angelica's eyes grew solemn.

Carl pursed his lips. "Okay... Here's the key. No one really seems to know what is going on in Nevada. That is why we had to go to Elberton. I thought we might stumble across information leading to this mysterious man that has reportedly been seen with John Kaye during the Senator's visit to Newton's Air Force Base last year. I know there is a link there, but we just don't know how deep the trench goes.

By the way, John Kaye just so happens to be the Chairman of the U.S. Ways and Means Committee."

"Yes, I found that out today," Angelica sneered.

"Oh." Carl nodded, appearing unoffended by Angelica's irritation.

"I'm going to the facility in Nevada. Can you call and set up an interview, Carl?"

"And tell them what?" Carl snarled.

"Figure something out, damn it! The *Liberator Magazine* is interested in the advancements being made in the field of aerospace, whatever..."

Gail shook her head. "Good luck. I doubt they'll buy it."

Carl glanced over at Gail and then back at Angelica. "All right, all right... I'll see what I can do." Carl stood up and walked over to a file cabinet, took a set of keys from the pocket of his khaki slacks, and unlocked the bottom drawer. He pulled out a thick expandable file folder. "Angelica, this is above top-secret. This file contains classified information that would scare the shit out of most people," Carl announced, as he dramatically held the file in the air. "This file was given to me by an anonymous source... ex CIA, that's all I'll say. We need to find out who this person is and why he built the facility – and most importantly, how and why John Kaye is involved and then we expose it."

Carl sat back down. "In this file is a document confirming that a treaty was signed with the same supposed ET race a while back, under the Eisenhower Administration."

Angelica appeared stunned, and then closed her eyes, shook her head and chuckled sarcastically.

"Yes, you heard me correctly," Carl continued. "We traded human and animal experimentation for technology... rather fucked up... wouldn't you say? We sold our souls to the Devil. And the Devil turns out to not have horns and a pitchfork... but instead eyes dark as night, and technology that could end civilization as we know it. Angelica, this information clearly implicates the government's involvement with the extraterrestrial problem for some time."

"Problem?" Angelica responded intrigued.

Angelica stared in disbelief. "Carl, you're lucky I don't fire you for not telling me this information sooner."

Carl glanced over at Gail and raised his brows. He felt a wave of relief as he looked back at Angelica.

Angelica raised her fingers to her mouth, she had an idea. "John Kaye has an office at the Capitol, correct?" Angelica reached over and took the file from Carl's desk, then scooted back in her chair.

"Yes," Gail interjected. Angelica quickly glanced over.

"Well, I'll start there," Angelica said confidently as she peered at Gail.

Carl appeared puzzled. "Are you sure that's a good idea?"

"What the hell. Why not? Let's see what the honorable Mr. Kaye has to say." Angelica smirked.

Carl leaned back and clapped his hands with a nervous laugh. "Follow the money... I'm with you." Carl's face turned solemn. "But for God's sake Angelica, please be careful. I am truly sorry I got you into a story as dangerous as this."

Angelica looked suspiciously at Carl as she rose from the chair. Gail stood up and stepped toward the door. Angelica abruptly turned away from both of them and to their surprise Angelica left without saying a word.

In the hall, Gail rushed over and took Angelica's arm softly, causing Angelica to stop and turn. Gail leaned in so no one could hear her. "Is going to the Capitol to confront John Kaye really a good idea? Isn't there another way? Can't you find a good source to do the dirty work?" Gail lifted Angelica's arm exposing a blood stained Band-Aid. "And what happened to your arm?" Gail gasped.

Angelica looked around the room and noticed a few of the other employees watching them. "Probably not, but what the hell, my life's already in danger… what do I have to lose at this point? My arm, oh, it's nothing… just an accident." Angelica quickly pulled her arm away.

Gail squinted, clearly rattled, and whispered, "I don't want to lose my dear friend," before she turned and walked off, leaving Angelica alone and suddenly feeling very vulnerable.

Angelica glanced around to see that everyone was still watching but trying to act as if they were busy at their desk. Easing her shoulders, she put the file against her chest as she walked down the hall to her office. Once inside she closed the door behind her, then went and sat down at her desk. Angelica opened the file and started to read. The first page was a classified CIA document.

"Jacque Langston, structural engineer with both military and aerospace applications with the U.S. Government was involved in the construction of twelve underground military bases. In 2005 Jacque Langston was found dead of an apparent self-inflicted gunshot wound to the head. His death initially ruled a suicide, was later reported by former Nation Security Officer, Alex Harper, to be a military-style execution. Alex Harper is now an independent journalist in San Francisco, California.

Jacque Langston was earmarked as an extremist. He was under constant surveillance for leaking classified information to the public. Langston was known to openly speak of the 1954 treaty made with the extraterrestrials which stipulated the exchange of technology for testing their implanting techniques on a select group of humans and cattle. Jacque Langston shared with the general public information regarding the extraterrestrials' decision not to abide by the agreement and the subsequent confrontations that occurred. Jacque Langston was injured during a gunfight that transpired between himself and extraterrestrials at Newton Air force Base's underground facility during its construction. During that time, other military officials and contracted mine workers were killed."

Angelica dropped the document on her desk and put her hand to her mouth. She immediately thought of Matthew and his ransacked house. "Did he know more than he told me?" she thought aloud. Was someone looking for information he had which corroborated the document that was now lying on her desk? Angelica wondered if Matthew knew about the underground ET facility. Angelica wondered how much had he kept from her to protect her?

Feeling anxious and still irritated at Carl, she stood up and put both hands behind her neck, and began to pace back and forth between her desk and the wall of windows. She wanted to continue reading through the file, but she suddenly remembered Michael was on his way to see her, and would be at her townhouse within the next two hours.

Angelica felt short of breath as if she were about to have a panic attack and she realized if she didn't calm down and focus on one task at a time she was not going to be of any help to herself or anyone around her.

People had a right to know what she was discovering whether they chose to believe it or not and she had an obligation to get it right. Angelica wondered how many people knew about the Treaty. She turned and looked back at the file lying open on her desk. Standing there, she tapped her fingers anxiously under her bottom lip as she stared at the picture of Jacque Langston. Angelica had another thought. *What about his family, did he have children... a wife? Who killed him? Are they the same people that have been threatening her, stealing her computer? Are they the same people that killed Matthew? Will they do the same to her?* She wondered anxiously. She felt a tingling and the warm wetness of her tears as they glided down to her cheeks.

Angelica looked at her purse. She impulsively felt compelled to call Dr. Goolrick and tell him about Matthew. She walked over to her desk and picked up her purse, quickly finding her cell phone. There was a missed text from Michael. "Send your address, just landed." Stunned he was already in D.C., Angelica quickly sat it back down as if it had burned her hands. She paused and nervously tapped her fingers on the desk. Angelica noticed the time was twenty-two after. She realized she needed to compose herself and get back home. Michael would be at her place soon. She picked up her cell phone and sent him the address and location of her hidden key.

Angelica decided he could let himself in if he had to... although her vanity still made her twinge at the thought that she might not have time to freshen up before he saw her. Her runny mascara notwithstanding, she decided to call Dr. Goolrick anyway.

Angelica reached down and pulled his card out from her wallet. As she did so, she accidentally pulled out the 'The Brown Palace' cocktail napkin that contained the strange metallic object that she cut from her arm the night before.

Angelica put her cell phone and his card down on her desk, unfolded the napkin and removed the device. She held it up to the light and studied it. The light bounced off its shiny, smooth surface. A tiny piece of metal... it was rectangular in shape and appeared about a half of an inch long.

Angelica laid the device down on the napkin and called Dr. Goolrick. "Dr. Walter Goolrick speaking," he answered business-like.

"Hello Doctor, Angelica Bradley. Hope I found you well."

The doctor sounded surprised. "Well hello, Angelica! Yes, yes, you did."

Angelica took a breath. "I hate to have to tell you this... but... Matthew is dead. They originally thought it was a suicide, however the medical examiner has now ruled it a homicide." Angelica went silent. And for a moment, complete silent seized both of them.

"Oh no, my God, I can't believe it... not Matthew! Do you know how?" The doctor waited with heavy breaths.

Angelica took a deep breath matching his, "He was found hanging by a rope from his upstairs banister. There were apparently signs of a struggle, however."

"I must say, I am quite shocked to hear this news... Poor dear... dear Matthew."

"I'm wondering if you could help me, Doctor. A curious thing happened the other morning while in Denver, after our dinner. I woke up to find a raised area of skin on my forearm and well, I pushed at it and it seemed to move so... I cut it out," Angelica said, barely flinching.

"You cut it out?" Dr. Goolrick blurted.

"Yes, I cut it out with a razor in the bathroom and it is sitting here on my desk. I'm looking at it now... it appears to be some sort of device made of metal or lead, I believe, but I am no expert." Angelica felt as if she were stumbling over her words as she became aware of how crazy it must have sounded and she felt suddenly very vulnerable.

"I would like to see that device. I could meet you wherever you would like. I have a friend with a lab at Georgetown and he had some very sophisticated instruments that could tell us what this thing is made of."

"That would be very helpful Doctor. Thank you. When should we meet?" Angelica sounded relieved.

"Well, let's see, I will need to free my schedule and call my friend... maybe the day after tomorrow?"

"That will work out perfectly. Just send me over the details of when and where we should meet when you have worked it out. And thank you again, Doctor. You are already becoming one of the few people I seem to be able to trust right now."

"Donec iterum conveniant fratrem!" Dr. Goolrick said in perfect Latin.

Angelica hesitated, "I'm sorry... I didn't understand what you just said."

"It's Latin... Till we meet again."

Angelica nodded to herself. "Yes, till we meet again, Doctor. Hopefully very soon."

Angelica hung up her cell phone and wrapped the device up in the napkin before she carefully put it back in her wallet. She then grabbed the top secret documents and shoved them back into the folder. She turned the light off and reluctantly walked out of her office.

Chapter Forty-Five

The building lit only by the glow of red exit signs was ominously quiet in the early evening hours. It was after six o'clock and almost everyone had gone home for the evening. Walking through, she noticed the cleaning crew moving a cart out of a storage closet. One of the maintenance men looked over at her and solemnly nodded with a cold and lonely countenance. Angelica shivered and conjured up a quick smile, then hurried down the dim hall to the elevator. She nervously pushed the button several times while impatiently waiting for the doors to open.

Angelica was startled as a bell sounded and the elevator doors opened. She exhaled a deep breath of relief and stepped into the elevator, hitting the button forcefully, hoping the doors would shut more quickly.

Once downstairs, she stepped out the front entrance and located her white, five series BMW about thirty feet away in the corner of the nearly empty parking lot.

Apprehensive, and noticing the sudden sensation of moisture in her armpits, she rushed over to her car. Angelica glanced around to her right and noticed a black Tahoe SUV parked over a few aisles from her car. Unable to make out if there was someone inside the Tahoe, she pushed the unlock button on her remote, and it made a familiar chirp as she walked briskly and confidently over to her car.

Angelica quickly opened her door and tossed her purse, laptop and the file onto the black leather passenger seat, then started the engine.

As she began to back out of the parking space, she looked in her rearview mirror and that's when she saw him. Angelica caught a glimpse of a man's face inside the Tahoe and recognized him immediately as the same man from the Apple store in Denver. Her heart sank as the sensation of fear moved through her body.

Angelica pulled out, squealing the tires, while she willed herself to not look back. All she was focused on at that moment was getting out of the parking lot as quickly as she possibly could. She turned the steering wheel fast to the right as her car began to slide towards one of the cement poles. She felt the collision of her left rear door and the pole as her BMW scraped past the narrow space. She slammed down hard on the gas as she approached the exit. Squinting, she sped towards the closed gate. There was no time to stop and use her key card to let the long barrier lift up to let her out. The BMW slammed into the barrier and it was no match for the speed and weight of the car as it broke into three splintered pieces. Sparks flew from the undercarriage as Angelica's BMW landed hard onto the asphalt and safely out of the parking lot and onto Hayes Street.

Angelica sped past *The Washington Post* right before she turned onto Jefferson Davis Highway. Angelica stepped on the gas harder, speeding down the interstate towards her townhouse, while every few seconds continuing to glance up at her rearview mirror looking for the Tahoe.

Angelica rounded the corner and onto her street. In the distance she could see her porch lights emitting an ambient golden glow. As she slowly pulled up to the curve in front of her townhouse, she glanced in her rearview mirror. His Tahoe was nowhere in sight. Did she loose him? "What did it matter?" she thought. "If these people know my middle name, they probably know where I live." That immediate thought made her blood curdle.

Angelica turned off the headlights and sat motionless as she let the car continue to idle. She looked up the walkway and surveyed the surrounding hedges. What was only a week ago her safe haven had now become a maze of potential threats and horror. She hesitated for a moment and considered going to a hotel. But she couldn't. This was her home and she would be damned if anyone would prevent her from sleeping in her own bed. She made a mental note to buy a gun. The baseball bat she had tucked away under her bed would do her no good right now. Angelica remembered she did have a small black canister of pepper spray that she kept in her glove compartment. She was supposed to attach it to her key ring but it was too bulky and looked ugly.

Angelica opened the glove compartment and pulled the canister out. Holding it in her right hand and her keys in her left, she turned off her car and gingerly opened her door. She grabbed her purse, laptop and files from the passenger seat and wedged them under her arm.

As she made her way to the front door, she turned her head from side to side anticipating at any second, someone jumping out of the shadows. Safely on her porch, she put the key in and turned the lock, pushing the door open with her left shoulder. She held the pepper spray in front of her as she walked into the foyer.

Angelica stopped breathing as she immediately noticed a light on in the kitchen. She was positive she had turned all the lights off before she left and the sudden realization that someone may be in the house was more than she could take. She felt like a small, vulnerable child whose parents had suddenly left her alone with no warning. She mustered every last ounce of courage and resolve and screamed, "Who the hell is there? I have a gun!" Suddenly she heard a rattling in the kitchen as a shadow of a male figure moved into view from in front of the refrigerator.

Michael stepped out of the kitchen with two glasses of red wine. "Well, hello there, beautiful... You can put your gun away... hope you like your wine robust." He smiled seductively.

Angelica leaned over and softly dropped her keys, file, laptop and mace to the floor. She twisted one arm around to push the door shut behind her and then turned the deadbolt. Angelica was pale and her whole body was trembling uncontrollably as she looked at Michael.

"Everything okay, Angelica?" he uttered as he turned and placed the glasses down on the counter beside him, rushed over and grabbed her, pulling her head into his chest.

Angelica started to cry. Then the cry turned into a sob. "You have no idea how happy I am to see you," she whispered as she looked up at Michael with a red face, wet with tears.

"I'm here, sweetie, you're safe... What has happened, baby?" Michael asked as he put both palms to her cheeks directing her eyes to meet his.

"I'm being followed. This man in a black hoodie... I saw him again at the mall in Denver, after Yellowstone Regional, and just now he was sitting in a black Tahoe SUV in the parking lot of the my building... My car's a wreck. I had to lose him. I'm scared Michael," she stuttered, as tears ran into her mouth. She opened her lips, trying to catch a breath between each word.

Michael examined her face with sensitive eyes. She was a woman-child. The presence of a frightened, broken little girl was still dwelling inside of her wanting to feel safe, and on occasion, when Angelica dropped her protective armor, the child emerged.

Michael softly nudged Angelica to step away as he opened the front door to the townhouse. He stepped out cautiously and looked around. There were a few cars parked along the curb, but no black Tahoe. He stepped back in the foyer and shut the door, then turned the deadbolt, pulling at the door to double check that it locked.

Taking Angelica's hand, he led her into the living room and sat her down on her white sofa. She griped her knees. Michael noticed that Angelica's mind appeared to be somewhere else. With a wet face, she sat with a blank stare.

Michael dropped his shoulders and slowly walked into the kitchen and retrieved the wine glasses from the granite countertop, then walked through the other side of the kitchen into the living room. "You need this, trust me... it will help."

Angelica looked up with red eyes and smiled. "Yes, I certainly do, thank you."

Michael handed her a wine glass and sat down beside her on the sofa.

"Do you think I should stop... walk away from the story, Michael?" she asked as she looked intensely into his eyes, examining his expression.

Michael lowered his head as he spoke... "I want you to stop... I don't want anything to happen to you. However, something tells me you aren't going to." He smiled, but she sensed his fear behind the fake smile.

"You know, it seems like I always lose those I care for... I don't want to lose you. Let me help you, Angelica."

Angelica's face softened. "You being here in D.C. helps me."

Michael couldn't hold it in any longer. He put his glass down on the coffee table. "What are you going to do when you realize no one wants to know the truth?" Michael's tone was harsh.

Stunned, Angelica moved back on the sofa, away from Michael. Her mouth dropped open. "What do you mean? Why would people not want to know the truth?"

The air in room felt stuffy. Michael stood up, walked over, and opened the patio door, before stepping out, he turned around and said, "I'm sorry."

Angelica sat on the sofa for a moment, shocked, still peering in the direction Michael was standing, confused by his outburst.

Angelica finally stood up, and with her wine in her hand, she stepped out onto the patio. The evening sky was a mixture of dark shades of grey and blue. The ripples in the cloud clusters were lit up by the moon as they moved steadily in front of it.

Angelica stopped just outside the door to admire Michael's silhouette while he peered out into the distance at the short buildings. She walked up behind him, leaning around to sit her wine glass on the ledge and then she put both arms around Michael's firm waist. "Let's not talk about the story. I've thought about the evening at your ranch, often, since I left Elberton. It's been my first thought before I fall asleep," she revealed softly.

Michael turned around, his eyes soulful and deep. "I do apologize for sounding harsh. I just don't want you to get in over your head, beautiful. I don't want anything to happen to you; missing you is the slowest possibly way I could die."

Angelica looked into his sensual hazel eyes as he spoke. His face lit up by the moon. "I'll take on the world for you if I have to," he whispered softly as he raised his hand to her cheek and rubbed it gently with his thumb.

Angelica smiled. "That is sweet," she whispered, "but it's the little things that make a woman love you." She winked and smiled sincerely.

Michael took Angelica's small, trembling hand. "I won't pretend to know what you're going through. I know you feel you have to do this, I get that... just know that I am here for you, okay?"

Michael lifted Angelica's hand and placed it over his heart. "You have it, baby," his tone sensual and gentle. She felt aroused.

Angelica felt her chest flutter as she lost sense of her surroundings and leaned into Michael. Michael met Angelica's swollen lips and they kissed passionately, pressing hard into each other. As their lips released, they both stepped back and smiled flirtatiously. Angelica glanced down and away shyly.

Michael laughed. "Aren't you cute... How about another?" Angelica watched Michael's hand as he lifted her glass.

"Why not?" she said as she laughed, feeling more relaxed. "Are you hungry?" Angelica asked, following Michael inside. "We could order something to be delivered," she announced, feeling refreshed and energetic. "There is this delivery service that will swing in and pick up your carry out order from the restaurant of your choice. There's Chinese, Italian, Thai, Indian... you name it. Oh, I forgot... you're a cowboy. You're probably not used to such things." Angelica giggled, teasingly.

Michael peered up intensely from the bar in the kitchen while he finished pouring their merlot. Suddenly, he grinned suspiciously, as he came running around the bar toward Angelica, causing her to scream out, "No you don't, oh my God... You're not..." Before she could finish her sentence, he had lifted her in the air and was tickling her. Angelica laughed. "Please stop... Please stop! I hate being tickled," she screamed as he continued. "Seriously, oh my God, you're a handful," she managed to utter as he eased his fingers from her waist.

Michael was smiling as he slowly put Angelica down. Angelica was struck by the look in his eyes as her feet touched the floor.

Michael's eyes were intense. "I'm just being myself... just a cowboy in D.C., like a duck out of water," Michael rubbed his fingers alongside his head, pushing back the silky black waves of hair. "Now, how in the world could we get bored?" he asked.

Angelica smiled while composing herself. "You're right, how could you get bored?" she said, as she smiled mischievously. Angelica stepped back. "Okay, what's your choice?"

Michael reached over and straitened her blouse. "How about Thai... Sound good to you, beautiful?"

"Perfect!" Angelica spun around feeling lighter and went into the kitchen to find the "Food TO-GO" menu.

Michael announced, as he stepped into the living room, he'd have the green curry with chicken, extra spicy. He walked over to the fireplace and lit the candles decoratively placed inside, in lieu of firewood. "Nice! A real fireplace! And you have candles in it!

"Yes, it is D.C.," she told him. We appreciate character. Who wants a gas fireplace... how unromantic. Angelica mused. "Anyway, this was the home of the famous poet Jonathan Marsh's lover, Isabella. When the real estate agent shared that little tidbit... it was a done deal. I'm a bit of a hopeless romantic, besides the fact I loved the location." She tilted her head and smiled. "The idea of living in a place where such passion and love inspired some of the most remarkable poetry of all time, well..." Angelica glanced away...'My noble heart burned a fire, naive your intent to dull. When your immortal love returns, it will love you once more. Ye, temptation...' or something like that," Angelica laughed self-consciously. Michael squinted at her. He was amused and intrigued.

Angelica dialed the number and began ordering their dinner while watching Michael as he took the lighter from the mantle and lit the candles by the sofa. Angelica hung up the phone as Michael was finished adjusting the lighting. "Much better," he said softly as he glanced up to see Angelica watching him. Caught off guard, he laughed. "Sorry, I don't care for bright lights."

"Oh, I'm the same way... dim lighting is so much cozier," she said and smiled approvingly.

Angelica stepped over to her liquor cabinet at the wet bar in a hallway between the kitchen and dining room. "So, would you like another glass of wine? I have white Pinot, red Pinot, red Cab... or shall I pour you a single malt?" Angelica looked over her shoulder and winked, playfully."

Michael let out a belly laugh. "You sexy, beautiful, smart, sassy woman... I'll have the Scotch, of course."

Angelica opened the cabinet and found two Riedel wide-bowl whiskey glasses. She leaned down opened the stainless steel ice freezer next to the wine cooler and put one small cube in each glass. Michael stood studying her. "Are you starting to feel better?" he asked, as he came into the kitchen to meet her.

Angelica met his eyes, appearing fragile. "There's that look again," she said softly, feeling her stomach flutter. "I'm not sure how I feel. I'm kind of numb, actually. Right now, I'm trying to focus on us and enjoy our time together. When you think about poor Matthew, it makes you appreciate the time you have here. He was so young. It breaks my heart he's gone, and the weirdest thing is I only spent a couple of days with him and I feel as if I had known him for years," she said, glaring at Michael with a look of betrayal.

"Matthew was a great guy. I still can't believe he's gone. To think he was murdered. It hasn't sunk in for me, either." Michael dropped his chin and shoulders in sync.

"Michael, I have to show you something." Angelica frowned as she set their glasses down at the bar in front of Michael. She pushed her sleeve up, as Michael watched, to reveal the large Band-Aid soaked with blood. "I wish it would stop bleeding," Angelica whispered. Michael's eyes grew wide, but he didn't say a word. Angelica peeled the Band-Aid off exposing a small wound of open flesh.

Michael clenched his jaw, genuinely shocked. "What the heck happened?" he demanded.

Angelica looked up, her eyes narrow and lost. "I cut it out. It was a metal object of some sort. It moved on its own. I didn't know what to do. My first thought was to get it out, so I grabbed a razor." Angelica analyzed Michael's face. "Do you think I'm crazy?"

Michael stepped over and took Angelica's arm, lifting it up and looking closely at the wound. "When did this happen? You need stitches!"

"Yesterday morning in Denver. I woke up and noticed blood on the sheets. It had come from my ear, I think. While examining the sheets, I noticed an area of my arm with something under it. I pushed at it and it moved. I couldn't believe it... I have it in my wallet if you want to see it." Angelica's voice was weak and as Michael studied her, she appeared delicate. "I'm meeting Dr. Goolrick here in D.C., at a lab, to examine it."

"Of course I want to see it!" Michael demanded.

Angelica walked over to her purse and pulled the cocktail napkin out of her wallet. She unfolded the napkin and extended her hand so Michael could examine it more closely.

"You took that out of your forearm?" Michael gasped, horrified. "What do you think it is? How did it get there?"

Angelica looked down at it while chewing on her bottom lip. "I don't know, but I would like to find out! What do you think?" Angelica handed it to Michael.

"I don't know... it looks like... You said it moved on its own, huh?"

"Yes, it's obviously some sort of device. I don't know why I've kept it with me. It's probably tracking my every move. I just didn't know what to do with it. You can examine it all you want. I don't want to look at it anymore! I just want to forget about all of this alien stuff tonight, here – I need to freshen up for dinner." Angelica turned dramatically as she handed him the device. "Do you mind grabbing the door when the food shows up? I've already paid... thanks, be right back."

Michael didn't respond, he was too busy examining the strange object. He held it up toward the recessed lighting in the ceiling and noticed the edges were transparent. He thought he could make out something inside, and considered finding something in the kitchen to break it open. He changed his mind, recalling Angelica's meeting with the doctor the next day.

After a minute, he sat the device down on the granite countertop in the kitchen, then grabbed his Scotch, walked over and opened the patio door. Leaving it open behind him, he went out and sat in one of the cushioned chairs to wait. Michael watched the ripples of clouds rushing past the moon as he thought about Angelica. He thought back on the way her body moved in perfect rhythm with his when they made love. The image of her firmly caressing him, causing him to harden between her fingers as she looked up at his eyes and then closed hers before lowering her head. The memory caused him to feel immediate desire for her.

Michael walked into the living room right as the doorbell rang. Rushing through the foyer across the camel-colored, woven sisal rug, he opened the door to a youthful, dark-haired delivery man. He quickly handed Michael the brown bag and left.

Michael shut the door and turned the deadbolt, then went into the kitchen and located the plates and silverware. After setting the table in the dining room, he distributed the food, then lit the candle on the table.

Angelica came down the stairs and into the dining room as he was placing the two glasses of Scotch down on the table beside the plates.

"Smells so good," she announced as she stepped into the dining room.

"Yes, it does... come eat, beautiful!" Michael said as he looked up. "Wow, you look amazing!" Michael pulled her chair out and motioned for her to sit.

Angelica had changed into her light pink Victoria's Secret sweat suit. The jacket was unzipped just enough to reveal her cleavage. And the sweatpants hung off the curve of her hips, exposing her belly button.

Angelica walked over and sat down at the table. "I just wanted to get comfortable," she said as she pushed her hair back off of her neck and twisted it.

"Wow!" Michael chuckled and shook his head. "Well, I obviously find your figure amazing, but it's your almost shy sexiness that kills me." He smiled seductively.

"Almost shy sexiness, huh?" she laughed softly. Angelica thought for a moment as she observed Michael as he sat down at the table.

"So, do you like country music?" she asked playfully.

"Yes. Is that a problem? I heard in town, you do too," Michael said teasing with a sneaky grin.

Angelica narrowed her eyes and smirked, "I suppose you are talking about that night at Buffalo Billiards. Right? I had a little too much tequila. Let's change the subject and talk about you, shall we?" She continued to hold eye contact while taking a bite of her red curry.

Michael shook his head and laughed. "What am I going to do with you?"

Angelica took a sip of her Scotch, smiling seductively, "I can think of a few things."

Michael smiled playfully. "Did I tell you my butterfly analogy?"

Angelica gleamed at Michael. It was so entrancing watching Michael's lips move as he spoke. "No, I'm sure this will be interesting," she thought.

"Well, women are butterflies and men are butterfly catchers. If a butterfly catcher wants to catch a butterfly, he has a couple of options, you see. He can catch one with a big net, but that usually just scares the butterfly away. On the other hand, he could catch the butterfly with his fingers, holding tightly onto its wings while it flutters to be free, and most likely injure it... and the butterfly is never able to fly again... Or, he can just be still and patiently wait, and if the butterfly likes the butterfly catcher it will fly to him and land gently on his hand."

Angelica was amused, although she had heard a similar analogy before, she acted as if she was hearing it for the first time, and let out a girlish laugh. "You make me smile."

Angelica put her fork down, placed her palm to her chin as her elbow rested on the table… "I like you, cowboy."

"I know you do, and I like you," he replied.

Angelica looked down toward her plate, appearing worried. Michael raised his elbows to the table and leaned in. "What is it, Angelica?"

Angelica looked into his eyes. "It feels like we are moving perhaps too fast…" Angelica lowered her chin as she held his gaze. "I'm scared, scared of us… I can't believe I just told you that, but it just feels we're moving really fast." She frowned and bite her bottom lip. "We've just met and…" Angelica took a breath. "You sound sincere…"

Michael appeared deflated. "Angelica, I'm serious about you." He pushed his chair out and stood up. Getting down on one knee, he looked genuinely into her eyes. "I'm the same man that held you, looked deep into your eyes and made you feel safe. When you doubt my character, remember what you feel when I'm with you. I'm not going to hurt you, baby."

Angelica looked at Michael and took a deep breath. It was too late, she was in love.

Chapter Forty-Six

Angelica struggled to open her eyes. The room was blurry. She felt dizzy as she tried to move her head and rise from the bed. Angelica sighed as she managed to slightly open her eyes. She sat up on one elbow and continued to push herself upright. The room began to spin and she wondered if she'd been drugged. Angelica felt her heart race as panic seized her entire body. She slowly lifted her legs from her bed while making out just enough of her surroundings and recognizing her cream duvet. Angelica, slightly wobbling back and forth as she planted her feet firmly on the floor. She looked up and saw a figure standing in front of her. Her head was heavy, trying to drop forward. Angelica managed to hold it up just enough to see a man with a black crew cut and a black suit glaring blankly at her. Reluctantly, she extended her hand out toward him, causing her to sway back and forth, and then collapse back onto the bed into a sedated sleep.

"Angelica, wake up! Can you hear me? Angelica, wake up!" Angelica opened her eyes to see Michael leaning over her. Her head felt as heavy as the kettlebell she used at the gym. "Michael, yes, I'm awake," she whispered. "How long have I been asleep?" Angelica glanced over and saw the time was twelve twenty-two.

Her bedroom was lit up by the morning sun. "I can't believe how tired I was... felt as if I had been drugged."

Angelica peered up at Michael, "Did you just wake?"

"No, I have been awake for a while. I decided to let you sleep in, so I headed out to the corner café for coffee and a newspaper. I brought you a few things back. Hope you like éclairs. The lady in line behind me said they were the best in town." Michael gazed tenderly into Angelica's eyes as he stroked her pink cheek.

"You had me worried... wasn't sure if you were breathing for a minute there."

Angelica slowly got up from the bed to reveal the curves of her nude body. She gracefully raised her hand to her head to sooth a slight headache thumping at her temporal lobe.

Angelica noticed her clothes from the night before scattered about the floor. "Maybe it was the wine and Scotch," she thought aloud, applying more pressure to her temple.

"You should eat something. I'll go start your coffee," Michael announced, as he bent over and picked up her bright pink lace panties and pink sweat pants. "And you really shouldn't wear these around me." He winked, teasingly, as he tossed them onto the bed. Angelica smiled and nodded as she walked to the bathroom. "I better shower. I have a meeting this afternoon. Oh, I almost forgot... when is your flight to New York?"

"It's at four o'clock." Michael appeared disappointed.

"Michael, I don't want you to leave." Angelica pursed her lips as she pouted.

"Do you have time to grab lunch?" Michael asked.

"Yes, perfect... we'll have lunch before you leave... I know a great place!" Angelica smiled before she turned to step into the bathroom.

"You're like a little girl sometimes... It's cute. Who would have guessed you were such a softy?"

Angelica looked back to meet Michael's eyes and grinned sheepishly, forgetting her headache for a moment. "Last night was nice," she mused, before disappearing into the bathroom.

"Nice? Just nice?" Michael murmured as he tilted his head and scratched it.

Chapter Forty-Seven

Michael opened the restaurant door and allowed Angelica to step in first. With the lunchtime rush well underway at La Bistro in D.C., the trendy hotspot was busy with professionals.

Still fighting a slight headache, the clinking of glass was annoying her... Determined to enjoy her time with Michael, she tried to ignore the subtle thump in her head and smiled graciously.

La Bistro was known for its sophisticated cuisine, with black tablecloths, brown and terracotta brick walls, and an open ceiling exposing the beams and piping, painted black. The atmosphere provided a perfect setting to bring Angelica back into the swing of things.

Michael handed his small duffle bag to the woman at the hostess stand. "Do you mind holding this for me?" he asked. The woman smiled and took the bag, placing it out of sight behind the stand.

Angelica watched as a curious thought occurred to her. "Is that all you're taking to New York?" Angelica asked, as they were being lead to a table close to the bar.

"Heavens no, I have clothes at my loft in Midtown." Michael chuckled just as the server approached in a white apron to announce the specials for the day.

"Manhattan?" Angelica uttered, surprised.

"Hello, my name is Winton and I will be serving you today. Have you dined with us before?" he asked matter-of-factly.

Michael looked up at the server and smiled politely, oblivious to Angelica staring at him curiously. "Winston?" he asked inquisitively. "No, I have not."

"It's Winton," the server said politely.

Michael nodded. "Interesting name." He smiled and then looked at Angelica.

Angelica managed a smile as she peeled her eyes from the side of Michael's head and glared up at the server, still digesting Michael's revelation.

"Yes, quite frequently," she replied business-like.

"Well, I'm sure you will not be disappointed sir... Our specials today are duck burger with thyme aioli and Boursin cheese. I would personally recommend the herb and Dijon roasted chicken with lemon chicken stock reduction, garlic spinach and potato puree. And last... but not least, if you are in the mood for fish, we have a delicious pan-roasted lemon sole with champagne citrus puree and roasted fingerling potatoes... my favorite."

As soon as they made their decision, Michael looked at Angelica with a sneaky smile. "Should we have a glass of wine?"

Angelica grinned, thinking about her ambush on Chairman John Kaye. "With the day I have ahead of me... I probably should. Yes, I'll have your house Pinot Grigio."

"I'll have the same," Michael said, as he handed the server the menu.

"So you have a place in New York? That's certainly more convenient to D.C. than Montana," Angelica stated, her mouth pressed tight.

"Yes, you should come to New York." Michael said over the muffled conversations in the background.

"Yes, maybe I should. Of course it will depend on the story as to when." Angelica's face softened as she raised her brow.

"When is the deadline?" Michael asked, half-jokingly.

"Oh, there's no deadline for this story... it's quite unique," Angelica said, as the server sat down the thin wine glasses of Pinot Grigio.

Michael stared at Angelica and thought how exquisitely beautiful she looked in spite of everything she had been through.

"What? You have that look again," she laughed nervously.

"You take my breath away, Angelica." His eyes were intense. Angelica glanced down shyly.

"Breathe Angelica," Michael said playfully. Angelica looked up and smiled sincerely. He had a way of making her feel pouty.

"Last night before dinner I mentioned that people don't want to know the truth," Michael set his glass down. "Well, at dinner you made a valid argument." He looked her straight in the eyes.

"Yes, however, some of that was the alcohol talking. I tend to ramble after a few glasses." Angelica grinned.

"Well, I think people should voice their opinion - even if that opinion differs from everyone else's." Michael lifted his glass and took a sip of his wine.

"Yes, I agree." She thought for a moment. "I will admit however that my opinion has gotten me into a bit of trouble at a few dinner parties."

"You're a paradox!" Michael mused, while taking a bite of his Sole. "I understand how stubborn and closed-minded people can be, but it's just ignorance and fear. Don't let them take your spark and your desire to find out the truth -- no matter how unpalatable it might be for this insecure world we live in."

Angelica lowered her chin as her eyes rose to his. "I'd felt lost for a long time, you know, wondering why my father left. Once I got to D.C., I shed all that baggage… Know what I mean? I focused on college and my career."

"Yeah, I do," Michael whispered, his eyes sincere.

"Now I feel like I don't know who I am anymore – it feels as if I'm lost again… I dread the late hours of night… I don't know where that came from, sorry… too deep." Angelica rolled her eyes and glanced away, embarrassed. Michael frowned sympathetically.

Angelica took a breath and leaned back.

Michael glanced down and then back up to meet Angelica's eyes. "So why did you become a journalist?"

Angelica thought for a moment. "Investigative journalism is like surfing. You rush in and catch the wave, and while riding it… you let go of your inhibitions to experience the excitement… and then you glide into the shallow waters. That is, if you're lucky and get ahead of the wave. Then you rise up from the sand as the tide attempts to pull you back. You then sit patiently on the shore, and look for another wave to ride." Angelica laughed. "One of my many dumb analogies. I guess the simple answer is – It's exciting, never boring." She gleamed.

Angelica noted Michael's smile was different, his eyes indicated his desire for her. He looked as if he wanted to ravish her, and she felt that if no one were around, he wouldn't have hesitated.

Michael took the black napkin from his lap and dabbed at the corners of his month. "So the implant – how are you feeling about that? That has to be one of the main reasons you have been questioning whether to continue with the story. I don't know but if it were me, I'd seriously consider walking away after removing a thing like that from my arm." Michael appeared worried. His forehead crinkled.

Angelica knew he was not so subtly trying to convince her to give the story up. "The implant only validates why I have to continue," she said confidently.

Michael shook his head as Angelica moved forward and raised her elbows up to the table, while cupping her hands under her chin. "I've been contemplating how I am going to write this story. First, the cattle mutilations, and then some type of hybridization program... and now different groups of ETs and implant devices... the KGB and 'The Tomb of the Visitor'... a whole group of crazies disappearing off a tour bus in the desert... and let's not forget there's some billionaire lunatic running around,... seriously... what the hell? Where does one even begin?" With a look of bewilderment, Angelica laughed and rubbed her fingers across her eyebrows before lowering her hands feeling a rush of anxiety.

"Do you want my observation?" Michael said dryly, rubbing his chin.

"Yes," Angelica raised her eyebrows in surprise as if he were going to bring it all together, all at once.

"You shouldn't do the story... It's affecting you, maybe in an unhealthy way," Michael's lips closed into a flat line. He raised his eyes and observed her reaction.

Angelica felt disappointed. Her shoulders dropped. That was not what she wanted to hear. Angelica gave up and changed the subject. "So, what type of business do you have in New York?"

"I thought I had told you. I'm a private equity investor."

"Oh! I thought you were a photographer, for some reason. I thought that was why you traveled." Angelica tilted her head. "You're not the billionaire I am looking for, are you?" she asked jokingly, appearing slightly startled.

Michael responded quickly, through a laugh, "Hell no, no billionaire... wish I were one! Photography is a hobby," he replied.

"Oh, I assumed with all the photos," Angelica sensed the conversation had taken an awkward turn. "I jumped to that conclusion and underestimated you. Not that photography isn't a great career. I should have asked. Well, that explains your house..." Angelica felt she was stumbling over her words, conscious of how rude and materialistic her comment must have sounded. "It's just so lovely and…"

"Yes, thank you," Michael said. "I've been quite fortunate in my career - to have made connections with some significant intellectual capital over the years. Okay, enough about business, let's make the most of the time we have together," Michael said as he grinned.

Angelica noticed his perfect white teeth and sexy smile, her favorite features of his. She shifted anxiously in her seat as she took a bite. She continued to watch his mouth as he took a sip of his wine. He was amazing… the perfect man, at least, in her eyes. There would never be a loss of desire for him. The sex was amazing… and great conversation, she thought. But she questioned how she had become so close to him while never asking what he did for a living. She wondered if she was losing her head too quickly with Michael. As she stared blankly at her wine glass, Michael noticed her worried expression, he sensed she was starting to pull back and interrupted her thought. "I know this must be difficult for you… It is for me, as well. We live very different lives. I have been known to take things for granted in the past; however, not this time."

Angelica still appeared concerned so Michael moved his arms across the table and took Angelica's hand. He rubbed softly at the creases in her wrist. "We just have to be careful not to ruin this amazing connection."

Angelica leaned back hard in the chair and took her napkin from her lap to dab her lip. *"What did he mean by that?"* she wondered, inwardly irritated.

"Just enjoy the moments as they come. You know what I mean." he sat back confidently. Angelica wasn't sure what he meant, but she nodded anyway.

Michael continued softly... "Journalists are skeptical by nature, which is smart... While no one should just dive in head first, there are a lot of different variables here. If we open our hearts and move forward as if this is a very special, deep connection... that is evolving, we'll stay in a healthy place. I see a future with us, Angelica." Michael's eyes were soft and sincere.

"Yes, I agree," Angelica released the breath she was holding. She understood what Michael was trying to say, and she was getting a strong feeling that she had finally found her perfect man. He was handsome, intelligent, driven, and probably just a little bit crazy, she concluded.

"I'm going to miss you, Michael Anderson," she said, straight-faced, with deep soulful eyes.

"I'm going to miss you, too, Angelica Bradley," he said in a deep breath.

Angelica was relaxed after finishing her Pinot Grigio and taking the last bite of her lunch. Their presence together at the familiar bistro was utterly romantic, a sensation she had been without for far too long. There was no lack of passion between them, and a continual flow of deep conversation, but she knew from experience that too much passion could also cause big problems.

Outside La Bistro, Angelica stood with Michael at the valet stand while he waited for the cab to take him to the airport. Michael put his hand on the back of Angelica's neck and pulled her in closer to him. She leaned in meekly and absorbed the intense desire exchanged between them as he softly kissed her forehead.

"I feel like the luckiest man in the world right at this moment." Michael grinned and pressed his palm firmly around the back of her neck.

"Well, you are," Angelica whispered.

Michael laughed and squeezed her tightly. "Just stay safe, baby," he whispered as the cab pulled up to the curb.

The valet walked over and opened the passenger door, "Your cab, sir," Michael tossed his duffle bag in first, then stepped in, and before closing the door said, "How could we ever get bored? Bistro's, bovine blood, billionaires... and the next time we meet... breakfast in bed. Talk to you soon, beautiful."

Angelica raised her hand and nodded before he shut the door. She was watching his cab drive off when her cell phone rang. Angelica saw Gail's name on the caller ID. "Hey Gail?" Angelica was still watching Michael's cab round the corner.

"You owe me big time, girlfriend. I got some information for you that is going to rock your world! I got a name for you! The billionaire's name is Francis Giano. Apparently, the government is cutting back on space exploration... budget cuts... NASA's shutting down space programs right and left. Strange, huh?"

"Yes, that is odd, considering the fact that the Ways and Means Committee would have a significant hand in these cutbacks," Angelica interjected, listening intently as she walked on the sidewalk toward her townhouse.

"Now here's where it gets interesting... The International Traffic and Arms Regulation prevents companies from exploiting in space. That is, everyone except for the billionaire, Francis Giano."

"How did you find out who he was?" Angelica appeared perplexed.

"I did some digging. You and Carl aren't the only ones with sources."

"Great job, Gail!" Angelica mused.

"Oh, and you are spot on, Angelica. The House Ways and Means Committee is responsible for all legislation that has to do with taxes, trade... that includes international trade... social or entitlement programs, and God knows what else - meaning the Committee controls most of the issues affecting the finances of our country.... Interesting, wouldn't you say? Follow the money!"

"That is very interesting! So you think this aerospace facility is funded by our tax dollars?" Angelica probed.

"Not sure what to make of it just yet, but supposedly Francis has unseen bankers-investors. My source also said, there is a 'no weapons in space' treaty, and guess what... Francis Giano is exempt."

"Sounds like John Kaye was bought! And does Giano own his ass? I suspect he does," Angelica thought aloud and shook her head.

"Sounds as if he might." Gail sighed.

"Maybe an alien invasion?" Angelica laughed nervously.

Gail was silent for a moment. "God, save us if that were the case! Carl was right, Angelica, people have been killed over this – are you still going over to the White House to barge in on John Kaye?" Gail's disembodied voice echoed... Before Angelica could answer... "Well as your best editor I recommend you..."

"What the fuck? What the hell was that?" Angelica yelled.

Gail suddenly pulled the phone away, looked at it, and then put it back up to her ear. "Angelica, what's wrong? Angelica, tell me what's happened? Are you there?"

Angelica stood dazed as she watched in slow motion as a black Tahoe pulled up beside her BMW parked along the curb in front of her townhouse. A man in a black mask got out with a baseball bat and slammed the hood and then walked casually all the way around the front of the car, before assaulting the windshield. He flipped the bat over his shoulders, and sauntered back to the Tahoe. As he got in the SUV, he glared back at Angelica before he drove away. Angelica ran over to her car as other observers rushed over to the scene. She stood there, wide-eyed, with her jaw dropped.

"Is that your car?" a middle-aged man asked her.

"Yes, and that asshole just hit it with a freaking baseball bat!" Angelica said as she threw her hands up in the air.

A young man still panting after running over leaned down and nonchalantly stated… "Wow, now that was crazy…"

Still stunned, Angelica just looked at him blankly. The middle-age man leaned in to take a closer look and remarked, "At least it was just the hood and windshield. It's still drivable. Looks like you already had some damage. Your left front light is broken and the bumper is all shot to hell. I'll wait for the police and give a statement if you'd like for me to," he said kindly.

Angelica managed a smile. "Thank you!"

Angelica suddenly realized her cell phone was still clutched tightly in her hand. "Gail?" she bellowed out anxiously.

"Angelica, what the hell just happened? I heard your voice… I was too afraid to hang up!" Gail blurted.

"My car… those motherfuckers beat the crap out of my car – the man in the black Tahoe. The one I saw in the parking lot last night when I left the office. I'm being followed and fucking harassed!"

Gail let out a deep breath. "Oh shit! First, how's your car?"

Angelica rubbed her head. "Drivable - but it looks bad! He took a freaking baseball bat to it! Fucking seriously?" Angelica closed her eyes in disbelief.

"Okay… well, good news you can still drive it! Second, what are you thinking? Let's drop the story woman before you look worse than your car on a table in the morgue!"

Angelica stood frozen as the image of her pale stiff body, laid beaten on a cold metal table, formed in her mind. Then she looked down at the wound on her forearm. "No, they aren't going to scare me! I'm going to the Capitol!"

Gail laughed spontaneously, out of shock. "You are a mad woman! You know they have places for people like you – they're called institutions!"

"Bye, Gail... I'll touch base later!" Angelica hung up and walked over to her car as she heard the police sirens coming around the corner onto her street.

The police car pulled up and the officer immediately got out of his car. Angelica watched as he walked toward her and the small crowd of observers.

"Hello Officer!" she said without even taking a breath... "A man just pulled up in a black Tahoe and got out with a baseball bat and started hitting my car." Angelica looked bewildered.

The officer was looking over at the hood, curiously. "I see that... Any idea who this man was? Why he would want to hit your car with a baseball bat, ma'am?" The officer glared suspiciously at Angelica.

She innocently shifted her eyes to her left and thought for a moment and said, "No."

"Okay, ma'am, I'll write a report. Are there any other witnesses?"

"Yes... that gentleman over there," Angelica pointed to the man standing on the curb talking to people as they were walking over to see what had happened. After talking to all the witnesses, the police officer left Angelica alone with half-a-dozen strangers still milling about. Angelica got into her car and drove off to hopefully find John Kaye at his office.

Chapter Forty-Eight

Angelica kept looking around anxiously for the Tahoe, worried that she was going to be blindsided by it. She noticed a few odd glances at her damaged white BMW as people passed by in vehicles.

Trying to prepare herself for the ambush, Angelica hoped she would catch him in his office. She wondered what John Kaye looked like. She assumed he probably wasn't meek. Angelica abruptly stopped as a yellow light had just turned red - almost hitting a pedestrian walking across the street. The man looked at her and angrily threw his hands up. "What's wrong with you?" he yelled as he hit her hood with his open hand.

Angelica could still see through the windshield although it was splintered like a giant spider web. She sunk down into her seat and raised her hand almost in front of her face. "I'm so sorry!" she murmured.

As the light turned green, she accelerated past a handful of curious onlookers.

Angelica could see the round dome of the Capitol in the distance. As many times as she had visited it or driven by, it's majestic beauty and historic significance was always awe inspiring. She pulled up to the security gate. An armed officer stepped out and looked suspiciously at her damaged BMW. "Can I see your identification? What is the purpose of your visit, ma'am?" the officer peered at her BMW suspiciously.

Angelica smiled kindly as she pulled out her press badge and driver's license. "I'm here to see House Ways and Means Committee Chairman, John Kaye."

"Is he expecting you, ma'am?"

"Angelica responded confidently. "Yes, he is... I'm Angelica Bradley with the *Liberator Magazine*."

"Just one moment, please." The officer took her identification and stepped into the booth. Angelica watched as heavily armed security officers with dogs and mirrors inspected her car.

After a few moments, the officer stepped out and handed her license and press badge back to her. "Okay, that way. Have a nice day!" The security officer pointed her in the direction of the administrative offices. Angelica hadn't been worried about getting through security. She was in their system – as a member of the White House Correspondents' Association, she frequently attended meetings and the annual dinners. The trick would be getting past Kaye's secretary.

Inside, Angelica followed the directory to John Kaye's office, passing congressmen, lobbyists, and other officials along the way. Finally finding his office, she opened the door and was immediately face-to-face with his secretary, sitting at an ornate mahogany desk facing the door. The woman looked up, "Ms. Bradley?"

Angelica nodded. "Yes."

"He'll see you," the secretary said. "Go on in."

Angelica took a subtle breath, walked over, and opened the door. "This was too easy," she thought.

The Bovine Connection

"Well, hello, Ms. Bradley! How may I help you?" John Kaye stood up from his desk. "Please have a seat." He pointed to the brown leather, wingback chair in front of his desk. John Kaye was younger than she had expected. She had only seen him briefly, from a distance, once before. He appeared to be in his mid-forties, dark-brown hair, an average build with somewhat of a normal square face. His thick neck bulged out around his white, pressed shirt, tucked neatly under a navy blue suit that looked like it was perfectly hand-tailored for him. His voice was deep and assertive, giving Angelica the impression that he wanted to appear older.

Angelica looked him straight in the eyes. "Chairman Kaye, I have a few questions regarding your connection to the billionaire, Francis Giano," Angelica stated confidently, awaiting his response.

John Kaye shifted in his chair and eyed Angelica speculatively. "Francis Giano, huh... Now what sort of questions would you have for me in regards to him?" He smirked while maintaining eye contact.

Angelica felt a lump in her throat. She immediately thought, "Another asshole to deal with... great." She knew it wasn't going to be easy, just walking in on him like this, it never was. John Kaye had a forceful and downright dominating persona, and he was trying to intimidate her. Remembering what got her where she was in her career, thus far, she continued. "Let's not pretend, sir. You've been seen with Mr. Giano at the Newton Air Force Base. I'll just cut to the chase because I have had a long two days – What is going on at the aerospace facility?"

The chairman paused and then spoke very calmly. "Oh yes," he said, "the aerospace facility. I've heard mention of it but, dear – I know nothing about it. As for the Newton Air Force Base, I met him there briefly through some colleagues a while back... Afraid I can't help you, Ms. Bradley. You're barking up the wrong tree." John Kaye smirked.

Angelica slid up closer in her chair. "I see how this is going to be. With all due respect, Chairman Kaye, I've dealt with your kind throughout my entire career here in D.C. and you don't intimidate me. You can pretend all you like, but I will get to the bottom of what you men are up to, and when I do people will read about it, and..."

The Chairman cut her off, "Look here, Ms. Bradley, you come barging into my office unannounced, and I give you the courtesy of an impromptu meeting because I respect your magazine, but you aren't being very polite. No small talk, no questions about the First Lady's outlandish dress last night at the dinner with the Iranian ambassador... You are obviously tougher than I gave your pretty face credit for, but I suggest you get back to chasing Senator's with a taste for the exotic because you are in way over your head on this one, honey."

Angelica relentlessly continued... "Can I quote you on that?" she asked sarcastically. "As I understand it, you have a great deal of power. The power to influence tax laws and generate revenue for the federal government as you see fit, within Constitutional parameters, of course. Is that correct, sir?"

John Kaye tilted his head. "Yes, that is correct. Where is this going, Ms. Bradley?"

"Are you using tax payer's money on the aerospace facility, Mr. Chairman? You know -- the one that Mr. Giano is involved with?"

"That facility is privately funded." John Kaye's lips tightened after his response.

Angelica noticed his face was turning a shade of scarlet. He appeared flustered.

"Ms. Bradley, I will not be answering anymore questions today."

Angelica didn't let up, and kept at him. "What is your involvement with Francis Giano?" Angelica sat sturdy, staring at him, wishing she could smack the condescending grin off his face.

"Do I need to escort you out?" he asked, appearing irritated.

Angelica ignored his question. "Are there ETs involved?" John Kaye laughed. "I find this incredibly entertaining to watch you come at me from all angles – ETs, now that is funny! Is Jesse Ventura waiting outside to tackle me?"

Angelica knew who she was dealing with. John Kaye held one of the most powerful positions in government. The Chairman of the House Ways and Means Committee was considered by many to be the most powerful and influential position by the people in Congress. John Kaye controlled the finances in regards to how much of the country operated. He was in a respected and sought after position with a great deal of power. Angelica had done her research, and wasn't naïve. She knew she couldn't overpower him, but perhaps she could cause him to slip up. "Please answer my question, Chairman. What is your involvement with the billionaire, Francis Giano?"

"Ms. Bradley, you can either leave peacefully or I will have you escorted out," John Kay said as he sat back in his chair like a cat hiding a canary.

Angelica reluctantly stood up and smirked. She turned and walked toward the door, and right before opening it, she looked back around. "I don't believe you were what our founding fathers had in mind," she spoke softly, sarcastically.

John Kaye's eyes were piercing. "Ms. Bradley, the United States Constitution arose from the necessity to create a new government, rather than fix an inadequate existing one. We are in a new era and times are changing in ways... well, Ms. Bradley this conversation is over. Good day." he said as he stood up from his chair.

Angelica turned around. "Really... how so?"

John Kaye chuckled sarcastically. "Ms. Bradley, you just be careful now about turning over too many rocks -- never know what you'll find underneath one of them. Things that like damp, dark spaces can be dangerous when..." His words were unsettling and they were clearly threatening.

Angelica's scalp prickled as the hair on her arms stood on end. "Can I quote you on that, sir?"

John Kaye narrowed his eyes and smirked. Angelica smiled. "I suggest you do the same. Sometimes things that like damp, dark spaces have great difficulty surviving when they are forced into the light." Angelica smirked. John Kaye stiffened.

"Look, Mr. Chairman, a friend of mine was murdered in Elberton, Montana, right in the shadow of Newton's Air Force Base. My laptop was stolen. In the last few days I have been followed all the way from Denver to the parking lot of my magazine. If any of this can be traced back to even a semblance of what you are embroiled in, I promise you I will make it my life's mission to see that you personally hand deliver your resignation to the President. I won't be intimidated. Not by you... Not by anyone! Good day, sir," Angelica stated, her muscles tight, before disappearing, leaving the door open behind her.

John Kaye instinctually yelled out... "You just be careful, Ms. Bradley," before he sat down, leaned back in his overstuffed leather chair and rubbed his thumb and index finger across his top lip.

Chapter Forty-Nine

Angelica shut her car door and slumped back, raising her hand to her forehead and letting out a sigh. "Asshole!" she shouted. She opened her purse and found her cell phone. There was a missed text from Gail, along with two new voicemails.

Gail was short and to-the-point. "How'd it go with Kaye? You should stay the night at my place to be safe!"

Angelica responded to her text, "Good idea, thanks! I'll fill you in tonight. Need to stop at my place and grab a bag first."

Angelica started the engine and pulled out while listening to her voicemail. The first was from Dr. Goolrick... "Hello Angelica, this is Walter Goolrick. My flight lands at nine in the morning. My colleague is expecting us. Meet me inside the Regents Hall building at the Georgetown University Campus at eleven o'clock in the morning. Hope this message finds you well my dear." Angelica nodded to the security guard at the gate as she drove past.

The next message was from Dr. Marc Bishop. "Hi Angelica, Marc Bishop... Have everything arranged. Can you leave tomorrow afternoon? Just let me know. Thanks."

Angelica called Dr. Bishop back immediately and got him on the second ring, "Hi Marc, Just got your message. There's a slight problem, I have a meeting in the morning... I won't be able to make an afternoon flight unless it's late in the afternoon."

"I see, well, I suspected it might be inconvenient. There is another flight out. Could you leave around six o'clock tomorrow evening?"

Angelica was glancing around while driving back toward her townhouse. "That would be better. What time do I need to be at the airport?"

"Meet outside of United at five tomorrow evening. I'll make the reservations now. I'll try to upgrade us to first class. If not, I'll buy you a Scotch in coach," his tone playful.

"Okay, perfect!" Angelica said as she nervously looked out of her rearview mirror.

"The aerospace facility is right outside of Vegas. Is there somewhere you prefer to stay?" he asked.

"Oh, let's see. You know, I'm not that picky," Angelica said sarcastically, "but I do like the newer, more modern hotels when I stay in Vegas... How about the Cosmopolitan? I've never stayed there, and I'm sure it will be crowded with people," Angelica finished, feeling that would make her feel safer.

"Works for me!" he said enthusiastically.

"And Marc, The magazine will take care of the cost for my room and flight, just keep the receipt. Thank you for doing this – going with me and making the flight arrangements!"

"Angelica, no, thank you for letting me tag along! See you tomorrow!"

Angelica passed the Bistro a block from her townhouse. She looked over at the very spot where she had stood with Michael earlier in the day while they were waiting for his cab. Angelica remembered the firmness of his hand behind her neck as it caressed her. It felt protective and strong. She wondered where he was at that moment. God only knew how much she needed him, she thought. Angelica suspected he was already at his loft in Midtown, Manhattan, getting ready for dinner, and she felt a tingling pinch in her chest.

Angelica pulled up to the curb outside her townhouse and hurried up the steps, as she glanced around nervously at her surroundings. After opening the front door, she immediately went through the kitchen, and into the butler pantry to pour a small glass of single malt Scotch. Taking a single ice cube from the freezer, she dropped it in, hearing the familiar crackling sound as the cold cube met the warm golden brown liquid. Angelica took a couple sips. "Wow, what a day!" she blurted. She set the glass down and went upstairs to pack, in case she had to head straight to the airport after finishing with Dr. Goolrick.

Angelica noticed Michael's white undershirt, left behind on the upholstered ivory chair in the corner. She recalled the details of their sensual love-making the night before. How it had started in the chair as he sat down to slip off his shoes. Angelica had slipped off her clothes, then walked over and gently ran her hand through his thick black hair, sliding her hand down and gliding her fingers along the curve of his broad shoulder, watching him shiver slightly. Michael caressed her thigh and pulled her to his lips, kissing her with soft pressure by pushing his lips firmly on her skin along her thigh.

The image of Michael's warm tongue as it slid up her thigh to meet her moist petals of flesh played through her mind. Angelica put her fingers to her slightly open mouth and felt her warm breath, as she felt another sudden flutter in her stomach. She missed him. Her body began to heat up. Angelica pressed at her lips with her fingers as she remembered Michael's lips release from the wetness between her thighs as he lifted her up onto the bed.

Suddenly, there was the sound of a car horn outside her window. Angelica hurried over and peered out. Startled back into the present moment by the abrupt noise, she turned her attention to her bag in the corner, letting the image of the evening with Michael fade away.

Chapter Fifty

Well over her price range by several million, but Angelica still loved Georgetown. She enjoyed visiting with Gail over lunch and shopping on an occasional Sunday afternoon at the upscale restaurants and boutiques along the cobblestone streets. Gail was like an older sister or even at times like a mother to Angelica. Since Angelica lived far from her mother in Asheville, and had no siblings or immediate family, she considered Gail an ideal substitute.

Gail lived in a two hundred year-old restored white house with black shutters, close to the Potomac River and the O & C Canal. With a passion for gardening, Gail spent most of her free time planting flowers and creating beautiful English inspired landscapes. Gail had created a garden with rows of boxwood's along mossy cobblestone pathways leading to the fountain in the middle of her backyard, bordered by dark, crisp green hostas... where she and Angelica spent many evenings.

Angelica enjoyed spending time with Gail at her home in Georgetown, especially in the spring and summer when they could relax in the café style furniture with overstuffed cream cushions, under the veranda trellis covered with delicate soft pink roses.

Gail was the perfect host, lighting candles and sitting out tapas as snacks. An elegant and sophisticated woman in her late forties. Gail had undergone a few facelifts and although she looked flawless, it was evident she was slightly older than she would like you to believe.

They had relaxed many evenings into the late hours of the night talking about politics, men, and design... and even on a rare occasion, after too many glasses of wine, Gail would nostalgically speak of her husband who had passed away of a heart attack eleven years prior. However, those conversations about the love of her life were short. Gail was never able to hold the tears back long enough from the deep emotions still lingering under the surface. Angelica remembered how Gail wiped her eyes with the back of her hand, choked up, and abruptly stopped the conversation.

Gail had never remarried and Angelica suspected she never would. After all, she said she was committed to her career, and that was consuming enough to fill the void left by the loss of her best friend and lover.

Angelica pulled up, grabbing her bags she stepped out of her banged up BMW. Gail's golden retriever was lounging on the perfectly manicured lawn. Theo saw Angelica and wagged his tail in excitement.

"Well, hello there Theo!" Angelica announced.

"Hey you! Look at your car! Whoa!" Gail was wearing gardening gloves, standing beside the flowerbed along the front walkway. She appeared shocked.

"Hey! Yeah, I know... lovely isn't it? Aw, hey Theo!" Angelica leaned down and patted his head after he had slowly made his way over to her. "How are you, buddy?"

Angelica glanced up. "Theo's happy to see me!"

"Come on in... I'll open up some wine!" Gail said, as she took off her gloves and tossed then on her tan and hunter green garden wagon.

Angelica stepped in and passed by Gail smelling the lilac scent of her perfume. Gail looked around outside suspiciously before closing the front door.

Angelica stepped into the foyer between the grand entertaining rooms, with arched openings. The house was enormous. A historical home, it had thirteen-foot ceilings and each room had a wood burning fireplace, maintaining its original architectural details. Extravagant crystal chandeliers hung from the ceiling in every room, making the home comfortable as well as elegantly decorated. Gail certainly wasn't cheap and spared no expense overstocking it with furnishing. She had a preference for alabaster lamps – and she had several.

Gail looked over at Angelica and smiled. "You can sleep in your usual room. I just put fresh sheets on the bed for you."

"How sweet! You didn't have to go to the trouble, Gail."

"Don't be a silly girl! Come, let's have some wine!" Gail turned and walked down the hall toward the kitchen.

Angelica left her travel bag by the staircase and followed Gail down the long hall.

Gail's kitchen was bright and airy with several tall narrow windows to take in the reconstructed replica of the gardens at Colonial Williamsburg's Governor's

Palace. The house was surrounded with old concrete ornaments, shrubbery and flowers in soft shades of light pink and white.

Gail's decorating style was no doubt extravagant; she had even installed a large crystal chandelier above the island in the kitchen. Like the rest of the rooms, the kitchen also had a wood burning fireplace.

Fresh flowers were placed throughout, a tradition Gail continued after her husband had died. He was a hopeless romantic. Gail had shared the sweet details with Angelica on many occasions, over wine, telling her once of how he would get up in the mornings and cut fresh bouquets from the rose bushes surrounding the house. When she would come down in the mornings for coffee, the house was filled with the lovely fragrance of roses. He would glance up from his paper and smile at her.

Gail's husband had been a successful real estate developer and left her everything. Gail clearly didn't have to work for a living, but she loved being an editor, and proved successful at it over the years. Angelica knew Gail's career was her way of surviving after her husband's death.

As Theo slept comfortably on his plush doggy bed in the corner of the kitchen, Gail poured the Syrah.

"Do you think they followed you here? Whoever 'they' are."

"Probably! I don't want to get you involved, Gail. I shouldn't have come," Angelica's eyes were sincere.

"No worries, it's too late anyway," Gail shrugged.

"Well, what are you going to do next?" Gail asked solemnly.

Angelica leaned in over the white marble countertop, lowering her voice. "I'm going to see the aerospace facility in Nevada with Dr. Bishop, an archeologist from the Smithsonian."

"Why him... How do you know him?" Gail sounded surprised, yet curious.

"He's the strange voicemail from Elberton – remember?"

Gail stepped back as her mouth fell open. "Is he trustworthy? Is it safe?"

"I hope..." Angelica laughed nervously. "Yes, he appears harmless. Paul Colbeck, the ufology investigator, put him in touch with me."

Gail stepped back and leaned against her Sub-Zero stainless steel refrigerator, clutching her wine glass. "Well, I'm worried... Damn that Carl for bringing this story to the magazine!" Gail sounded frustrated as she put her wine down and stepped over to the sink.

"I'm questioning why we should even care if aliens exist. Why don't they just show themselves so we can all just get on with our lives?" Gail sneered.

Angelica laughed. "Am I hearing you correctly? You think it is that simple, huh? People like you and I would adjust... we'd find a way to adapt. However, Gail, you are not considering the weaker of the human race. A shift in their paradigm of this magnitude could be too much to bear, I'm afraid. The cognitive dissonance of the human species is bad enough as it is."

Gail nodded and took a small sip of her wine, then put the glass on the countertop. "So, Dr. Marc Bishop's going with you to Vegas?"

"Yes, as an archeologist, he is very intrigued with ancient artifacts and is convinced there's some connection pertaining to ancient aliens and the aerospace facility, and get this – he alluded to Mars. He wouldn't come right out and say it, but it was obvious. He believes whoever helped build the pyramids on earth also built them on Mars."

"Aliens... Mars? What do you think about all that?" Gail tilted her head curiously.

"I don't know, maybe it's true... Regardless, I want to know what John Kaye and Frank Giano are up to – Something doesn't feel right about that, and I don't like secrets, especially the ones kept from the public of this magnitude."

Gail appeared confused. "What do you think they are up to? You must have some idea by now. And something tells me this has become quite personal."

"Ya' think?" Angelica asked playfully -- more as a statement, distressed. "Someone beat in my car today, and a friend of mine was hung by a rope." Angelica took a sip of her wine and thought for a moment. "I guess I'm also searching now for more proof that aliens do exist. I believe my involvement cost Matthew his life. So yes, this is no longer about little grey or green men. This has definitely become personal." Angelica appeared angry.

"And then what?" Gail asked, as she tightened her lips and tilted her head curiously.

"And then, well, let's see..." Angelica took a strand of her hair along her neck and twirled it as she considered Gail's question. "I don't know." Angelica frowned and appeared to be contemplating.

"I can't believe we are having this conversation. This is all very crazy!" Gail chuckled in disbelief.

"Hey, grab your wine! It's a beautiful evening, let's go outside and eat on the veranda. I made a delicious Italian salad with parmesan cheese, pepperoncini, chickpeas, olives, and red onion... your favorite! I'll bring it out – go relax!"

"That sounds perfect! I am so hungry!" Angelica grabbed the bottle of Syrah and their two glasses.

"Well, you could use the food. Doesn't look like you've been eating much." Gail examined Angelica's petite frame as she walked away.

There was a soft breeze early that evening. The sound of the fountain was flowing harmoniously in the background. Angelica heard the chirp of a bird and she saw a red cardinal launching from a bird feeder. As she glanced away, she caught a hummingbird sipping from the bleeding heart bush along the pathway under the hundred-year-old, white-blossomed crape myrtle trees.

"Do you see hummingbirds out here often?" Angelica asked as Gail was stepping outside from the glass atrium leading from the kitchen to the veranda.

"No. Why, did you see one?" she asked surprised.

"Yes, just now over there sipping from your pink, heart-shaped flower bush."

"The bleeding heart bush? I love hummingbirds -- peaceful little creatures," Gail said, as she put the salad bowl and plates down on the table. "Lovely out here this time of day. Just look at that sunset," Gail announced.

"Yes, I love it here, Gail. You should let me move in," Angelica said, as she leaned back and smiled innocently. They both laughed.

"Sweetie, I've lived alone for eleven years. I could not imagine what I'd be like to live with now. I've become a bit set in my ways."

Angelica lifted her glass. "A toast to my dearest friend who I couldn't even begin to imagine living my life without!" Gail lifted her glass and smiled sincerely.

After Gail set her glass down, she lifted the large bamboo salad hands and filled Angelica's plate with Italian salad. "So, tell me about this cowboy."

Angelica looked inquisitively at Gail. "Cowboy? Oh, Michael Anderson?"

"Yes, you know exactly who I'm referring to." Gail giggled.

"How did you know?" Angelica's eyes were wide.

"Angelica, you told Andrew – how else? You know he's quite heartbroken."

Angelica shrugged her shoulders. "I like Andrew, Gail, but let's be honest, he's a playboy. He'll be fine in no time, trust me, in no time." Angelica smirked.

Gail nodded. She knew Angelica was right. "Well, Andrew came into my office, hoping I'd plead his case to you. I sincerely listened, but I too have known his type, and he's not good enough for you, Angelica. And you are his boss... Never a good idea." Gail shook her head.

Angelica looked down at her watch and bit down on her bottom lips. "Yes, it was a mistake." Angelica clearer her throat sounding uneasy.

Gail understood his persistent sexual innuendos that gradually turned into happy hour drinks and late night casual sex was just that – casual sex. She knew, although Angelica was young, she was wise, and a relationship with Andrew would lead to heartbreak, no doubt. "Well, enough about Andrew," Gail stated and flung her hand into the air as if to clear the space for her next question. "Tell me about Michael!"

"I don't know what to say other than he is the most handsome, sexy, interesting man I've ever met!" Angelica smiled sheepishly.

"That's all? Anything else?" Gail laughed. "You are blushing! Okay, details – do share." Gail smirked as she raised her palm to her chin.

"Well, I certainly wasn't in Montana looking for the love of my life, but I think he may have shown up. Michael's father, Hugh Anderson, experienced the first cattle mutilation on his ranch in Elberton back in 2000."

Gail interrupted Angelica. "Really? Michael's part of your story?"

Angelica nodded and continued. "Michael wasn't living there at the time. He didn't officially move back until after his father had passed away of cancer. He came back to sell the ranch but decided to keep it, and rebuilt the house into an amazing log home, like the homes you see in Aspen and Vail. It's truly stunning, Gail," Angelica said in a deep breath.

"I gathered he's only there a small percentage of the time – it's more of a retreat, I think, to get away from the city."

"Really, what does he do for a living, if he's not a rancher?"

"He's a private equity investor and has a loft in Midtown, Manhattan."

"Who takes care of the ranch?" Gail appeared confused.

"There's this sweet old man, Sam -- he calls him Sammy -- who lives on the property. He runs the ranch for Michael."

"Manhattan, fascinating! Have you guys... well, you know?"

Angelica finished Gail's sentence. "Had sex? Yes, and it was nice." Angelica smiled shyly.

Gail lowered her chin... "Nice?"

"Yes, nice," Angelica grinned. "Okay, intense may be a better word." Angelica grabbed a stand of her hair and twirled it. "He was here last night, left for New York this morning." Angelica looked down and then laughed. "We're a lot alike."

"Oh Lord, now that's trouble." Amused, Gail chuckled spontaneously.

"When will you see him again?"

"He wants me to come to New York soon. This story has my life on hold... I don't know when that will be." Angelica sighed. "And what if I don't survive this story, Gail? What if they kill me?" Angelica's eyes grew grave.

Gail appeared worried. She knew she couldn't convince Angelica to give up the story.

Gail laid her palm over the top of Angelica's hand. "No one is going to kill you! Don't you worry; everything has its perfect timing. You'll be with your cowboy," she said softly.

"So I hear," Angelica murmured as she rolled her eyes, snatched her wine and took a sip, appearing to pout.

Gail leaned in lowering her voice. "You are certainly not the average woman... I think you're gonna come out of this just fine."

Gail frowned. "That poor journalist, Matthew... Well we have no idea who or what he was involved with. His death may have had nothing to do with this story."

Angelica's tone was intense. "You may be right. But my intuition tells me his death had everything to do with this story. Who do you think is really behind all of this? Is it the billionaire, the government, aliens?" Angelica eyed her salad as she pushed around a caper with her fork. She looked up at Gail. "Nothing is connecting with me yet. This story has layers and the deeper I peel them back the more confused I get... and the more dangerous it becomes."

"I don't know, Angelica... Carl believes it's the industrial military complex."

"You know, I think he may be on to something – Carl's a strategic guy, highly intelligent. But I still think we are circling around the real truth here."

"Did Carl show you the secret file before he gave it to me?" Angelica asked curiously.

The Bovine Connection

"No, honey, he didn't... However, Carl has said enough... I've connected the dots. Why don't you tell me what else is in that file so I don't keep guessing?"

"I hesitate to say. Well, it's..." Angelica's eyes grew grave and she paused. "It's probably better that you don't know too many details, Gail. You know, now that I think about it... why would Carl take such a risk anyway? A story like this could get him into serious trouble and the file would probably be traced back to him... He obviously wanted to get to the truth no matter what. He knew when I grabbed the story that I'd see it to the end – the perfect little patriot journalist that I am. He had to be thrilled, or was that his plan all along? He threw the bone, and I took it, and ran with it." Angelica thought for a moment and then continued, "Do you trust him?"

"I trust Carl, I guess, but obviously not as much as I trust you. I know he has ties to the CIA... Hell that's not all that uncommon in this industry, since you could practically throw a stone over at them in Arlington, Virginia. How else would he have gotten that file full of CIA documents? There was a rumor at one time that he was a 'CIA Journalist Asset' while at the *Post*... however I don't think he'd want to publish a story of this nature if he were working for them now."

Gail took a deep breath. "So tell me about the dinner with Dr. Goolrick."

"Well, to sum it up... it is his opinion that the cattle are used for food for the ET's, kind of like a delicacy." Angelica raised her eyebrows.

"Really, like truffles or caviar... to humans, huh?" Gail pursed her lips and appeared worried.

"I guess... nothing shocks me anymore, Gail." Angelica looked down at her salad and pushed the plate forward. "I've lost my appetite, I'm afraid. It was very good though, thank you."

Gail leaned back. "Just be careful, Angelica, you never know who the real players are in games of this nature." Gail's eyes were wide as she took a sip of her wine and then sat the glass down.

"While I believe in telling the truth – is it worth risking your life? If it were me, I'd tell Carl to find another patsy, no offense." Gail laughed sarcastically.

Angelica was ready to change the subject. Gail worried enough about her and if she kept talking, she might accidentally mention the device.

"So I've asked you this before, but I'll ask again... why won't you date? I hate to see you here alone. You're a gorgeous lady, smart, a great cook, an incredible gardener..." Angelica gestured at the potted white flowers beside her in the stone pot showcasing years of moss growth, and laughed playfully.

"I guess I'd rather be alone than with someone that doesn't understand me the way my husband did. I'm a conversationalist and need to talk, communicate, you know what I mean?"

"Yeah, I do, actually." Angelica smiled and glanced over at the sunset almost hidden behind the fence.

Gail placed her hand on her cheek, appearing relaxed and introspective. She looked out at the sunset's golden rays shining between the cracks in the fence and spoke softly. "Well, when I was young like you, lust was important, but you grow out of that. Priorities change. I would imagine it to be much lonelier with someone who is not compatible with one's idiosyncrasies. Some of my friends are in some very toxic relationships. But they would rather not be alone, I gather... very sad."

Angelica sipped her wine and considered the truth of Gail's life experience.

"Anyway, too much trouble... men." Gail laughed. "Besides, I have Theo." They both looked over at Theo as he raised his eyes in response to hearing his name, while lazily lying on the lawn close by.

"Sweet Theo!" Angelica agreed.

Gail poured more wine into their glasses. "What's on your agenda tomorrow?"

"Busy day to say the least. I meet with Dr. Walter Goolrick and a colleague of his at the Georgetown campus at eleven o'clock in the morning. Then I'm off on an evening flight to Vegas."

"Science and gambling... That should be interesting," Gail said, as she chuckled and lifted her glass in the air toward Angelica.

"You'd like Dr. Goolrick; he's an intriguing man... Not sure if he is married, though."

Gail laughed spontaneously... "Oh, no you don't!"

"Well, he's certainly not of your typical western medicine mindset; although, he still retains a rather large ego." Angelica rolled her eyes with straight lips.

Gail leaned over deliberately towards Angelica, "Honey, I believe that comes with the territory."

"True," Angelica agreed, as she finished the last sip of wine. "I have a busy morning. We should probably get to bed."

"Yes, we need our beauty rest." Gail said, as she stood up from the table. I'll grab the salad and plates if you'll get the wine bottle and glasses."

Angelica blew out the candles and called to Theo to follow her inside.

In the kitchen, Gail was placing the dishes in the sink.

"I have everything, even Theo, here," Angelica said. "And I locked the back door," she added, as the dog sauntered past to lie down on his bed.

"Thank you, sweetie! You can get on to bed; I'm almost finished in here."

Angelica started down the hall but then turned around and looked back at Gail. Gail sensed that Angelica had stopped and she turned around. "What is it, honey?"

"If I don't see you in the morning before I leave... thank you for that amazing salad and another wonderful evening!"

Gail smiled. "Go get your beauty rest! Oh, and Angelica, you'll be with your cowboy soon enough! However, you are not moving to New York or Montana and leaving your dearest friend!"

"You needn't worry... Goodnight, Gail. And thank you again, my sweet friend."

Chapter Fifty-One

Angelica awoke the next morning to the sound of her iPhone ringing. She had set the alarm for seven thirty, but the alarm was the same as her ring tone and it always confused her. She reached over and pressed the red snooze icon in the middle of the screen, and fell back in the soft bed and buried her head in the pillow. Nine minutes later it sounded again so she got up from the bed, walked over and opened the guest bedroom door.

Gail's door was already open and her bed was made. There was a lingering scent of lilac perfume in the hall. Angelica clambered out of the room in her white silk panties and Michael's white undershirt, cautiously peering down the hallway as she started down the staircase. She ran her hand along the banister as she went downstairs. Angelica walked over and looked out the glass door in the foyer, before proceeding down the hall to the kitchen.

The smell of fresh roses fumigated the air. Gail had left the coffee maker on with a half a pot of coffee for her. Angelica found a clean white coffee mug with the words "I love Rome" printed in black beside the coffee maker. She poured her coffee, leaving off the cream and sugar. The house was quiet. Theo was lying in the corner peering up at her with his chin propped up on the edge of his bed.

Angelica stepped into the glass atrium. She watched as the birds flew around the feeders, listening to their morning song.

After a moment, she looked down at the wound on her forearm. Everything was surreal. At that moment everything that happened last week felt like a dream – Elberton, Montana... the cattle mutilations... Matthew's death... the man in the black Tahoe... the secret file detailing what appeared to be a CIA cover-up... She was beginning to feel major sensory overload again. Angelica caught herself in the trail of deep thought and blurted aloud, "Fuck! What am I doing?" She put her hand to her chest and looked up at the sky blankly. "Who are you? What are you?" Angelica thought aloud, looking at the sky, before she lowered her head, catching a glimpse of her reflection in the glass. "Who am I? I don't know anymore," she whispered.

As Angelica turned and walked out of the sunny atrium and back into the kitchen, she noticed a new magnet on Gail's refrigerator, so she went over and took it in her hand.

"We are all on the same pathway to understanding... That is the art of existence." Angelica put the magnet back on the refrigerator and considered that humans were just a tiny microcosm in the vast universe. So how could we be so naïve to believe that the human race is the only intelligent life form in existence? In the end, we might turn out to be not-so-smart after all, she thought.

Chapter Fifty-Two

Angelica pulled through the Georgetown University campus. The historic landmark in Romanesque revival style stood predominately along the O&C Canal, reminding her of an old castle. Driving along the road between rows of trees and well-maintained landscaping, she found Regents Hall, the University's newest and most innovative research facility.

Angelica parked her badly dented white BMW, then stepped out and looked around for Dr. Goolrick.

College students and faculty were rushing to get to their next classes. The campus was like a beehive; humming with activity.

Angelica took the paved walkway toward the front entrance of the new sustainable facility. It was a drastic contract from the main buildings on campus, most built in 1789. Regents Hall was a juxtaposed paradox, constructed of mostly glass and steel, completely unlike its stately counterparts.

Inside, Dr. Goolrick was nowhere in sight, so Angelica found a seat on the bench near the entrance nestled by the staircase.

Angelica looked down at her fingers intertwined together in a tight grasp that had caused her knuckles to turn white. The anxiety had returned. Her mind drifted back to Matthew. She thought about the day he picked her up at the lodge and shared the details of his childhood. Angelica realized she had never personally known anyone that had been murdered before. She and Matthew had become good friends in such a short period of time. The thought sent a chill up her spine. She contemplated the risk she was facing if she went to Nevada. She considered Dr. Marc Bishop's safety and her own. Angelica sat on the bench preoccupied with thoughts as she considered giving up the story. She paid no attention to the students and faculty as they passed hurriedly by.

"Angelica!" Dr. Goolrick's loud, assertive voice startled her, and she looked up to see the doctor and his colleague standing there.

"I'm afraid she is quite far away," Dr. Goolrick stated, looking to his colleague.

"My apologies," Angelica jumped to her feet.

"No apologies necessary. This is my colleague, Hamilton Howell. He is the Professor of Physics and Interdisciplinary Chair of Science here at the University, and this, as you know is Angelica Bradley with the *Liberator Magazine*."

Dr. Howell extended his hand and smiled. "Walter said you used to work for *The Washington Post*."

Angelica eagerly took his hand and shook it. "Yes, that is correct. It is very nice to meet you."

"Nice to meet you, as well." Dr. Howell smiled.

"Hello, Dr. Goolrick, thank you so much for arranging this meeting." Angelica turned and met the doctor's eyes; her voice weaker than he remembered. He noticed she looked different from their last meeting… frailer, he concluded.

The Bovine Connection

Dr. Goolrick was visibly eager to see the device. "Should we go take a look at the object?"

"Oh, yes, this way to the lab." Dr. Howell turned and started toward a hallway. Dr. Goolrick stepped aside so Angelica could catch up to Hamilton and keep pace with him.

"I understand you discovered something quite unusual in your arm." Dr. Howell glanced back.

"Yes, unusual is a good word to describe it," Angelica responded and then exhaled, still trying to process it all.

The three of them walked into the broad doors of Regents Hall and took the elevator to the third floor. As the elevator opened, Dr. Howell walked with a purpose, turning immediately left as Dr. Goolrick and Angelica followed close behind. He took out a key from his pocket and opened a door marked 'Room 33.' He let them pass by as he shut the door and relocked it. Angelica looked around. It reminded her of Dr. Marc Bishop's laboratory at the Smithsonian. However, this lab was considerably newer and adorned with bamboo furniture. Large windows stretched across the back of the room letting in the sunlight. Regents Hall was an eco-friendly building making use of all natural lighting available.

Dr. Howell sat down on a stool and extended his hand with his palm facing up.

Angelica curiously looked down at his hand. "Oh yes... I have it right here," Angelica stated as she opened her purse, pulled out her wallet, and took out the Brown Palace cocktail napkin. Angelica looked up and met Dr. Goolrick's eyes as she opened the napkin and then she reached her hand out for them to see it. Both doctors leaned down to observe the device, obviously questioning whether to touch it. Dr. Howell looked over to Angelica's forearm and at the Band-Aid.

"May I see the area where you removed the object?" he asked, business-like.

Angelica nodded and extended her hand out to Dr. Goolrick so that he could take the napkin with the device on it. She squinted and gritted her teeth as she pulled the Band-Aid back until it released from her skin and came completely off.

Dr. Howell raised his chin while lowering his eyes to observe the wound. "Interesting," he said. "It appears to be healing; however, you could have used stitches to lessen the appearance of the scar." Dr. Howell put his hand on her wrist. "May I?" Angelica nodded as he pulled her arm closer and stepped in to examine her wound. "It is roughly less than a centimeter in length, and slightly less than half a centimeter depth." He turned around and flipped the switch on the lamp and then looked over at Dr. Goolrick.

Understanding the gesture, Dr. Goolrick handed him the napkin. Dr. Howell put on a pair of latex gloves and then handed Dr. Goolrick a pair.

After he lifted it from the napkin, he carefully put the object on a petri dish and studied it through a stereo light microscope. "There is a brownish red material I believe to be Ms. Bradley's blood."

After a few moments of examination, he carefully fixed it onto double-sided sellotape, mounted it on an

The Bovine Connection

SEM holder, and put it into the scanning electron microscope. As Dr. Howell was doing so, he raised his eyes to look at Angelica. "I have a PhD in physics, not chemistry; nonetheless, I am familiar with extraterrestrial and military implant devices. Dr. Goolrick and I have been fascinated with the subject of the visitors for some time, and I have been fortunate enough to examine a few implants over the past twenty years."

Dr. Howell looked down again and watched the electron microscope as it scanned the object. Angelica now suspected Dr. Howell was a member of the Doctor's covert research team.

Pictures started to appear on the monitor in various surface magnifications. Dr. Howell was particularly interested in the metallic appearing fibers, alongside copper-colored fibers. "There are metallic fibers curling away from one edge and about forty microns long, as well as some fibrous looking surface structures about five microns, roughly. Appear to be miniature technology or mechanical components – similar to a tiny electronic circuit used to perform a specific electronic function. It is unusual... I am not seeing the common wafer, with hundreds of integrated circuits. These results are indicating military implications... Alien technology tends to be unrecognizable to human eyes so I am especially enthusiastic when I find unidentifiable structures. Unfortunately, even without the wafer, I recognize similarities to a military implant... although it is too early to form a definitive conclusion."

Angelica looked over at Dr. Goolrick as he raised his eyebrows inquisitively. Dr. Howell continued, "We must go through one final step for confirmation of analysis. Therefore, the final step will be to use Energy Dispersive X-ray Microanalysis, or what we call EDX, to determine the object's composition. Possibly, to reveal a combination of elements found on earth, if my assumption is correct.

"I am using an "EDAX PV9100" system. This machine will show a series of peaks and troughs at different wavelengths, and the set of lines to be predictable from any element known. We will be able to look along the spectrum and identify each major peak."

Dr. Howell continued his analysis with an intense and meticulous approach. After a few minutes, he announced with high confidence that the elements in the top layer of the device were some type of non-metallic composite compound, and the other ingredients underneath the layer were non-ferris metals consisting of forty percent titanium, thirty percent copper and sixteen percent silver. Ignoring all the other unidentifiable elements in varying proportions, he had completed his analysis.

"The mystery is solved. The implant appears to be more similar to the military devices," Dr. Howell stated confidently. Dr. Goolrick was initially disappointed... but quickly his demeanor turned to one of concern.

"Well, Angelica, it appears you are quite the intriguing creature. The military has implanted you

The Bovine Connection

with some new form of tracking device." Dr. Goolrick clenched his teeth.

Dr. Howell interjected, "We assume it is military. It certainly does not appear to be extraterrestrial in nature." Dr. Howell raised his eyebrows. Angelica's face was pale; she didn't flinch.

Dr. Howell appeared concerned. "Are you all right, Ms. Bradley? Would you like some water?" Angelica looked at him and she could feel her blood pulsing in her neck. His mouth was moving; however, she didn't hear a word.

"Angelica, dear, are you all right? Dr. Howell asked if you would care for some water," Dr. Goolrick repeated.

Angelica's tense body instantly became alert. She looked at Dr. Howell. "How accurate are those tests?" she snapped loudly. "There was no incision! How did it get in my arm?"

"Precise," he stated confidently.

Angelica turned to Dr. Goolrick appearing lost.

"What does this mean? How would they have implanted it in my arm without my knowledge? I'm confused. Angelica felt as if her head was spinning again. "I need to sit down!" She felt dizzy.

Dr. Howell found a stool and slid it over. Angelica took the seat and with a quick gesture, raised her hand to her forehead. "I don't know what is worse," she exclaimed, "an extraterrestrial implant or military implant!" She looked up at Dr. Goolrick as if she needed him to say something.

"My dear, take a deep breath." Dr. Goolrick rested his hand on her shoulder.

"I don't understand why it's just now sinking in. I feel as if I am having an anxiety attack. I suppose I wanted to deny it had really happened. Or maybe, in the back of my mind, I thought there would be some reasonable explanation." Angelica broke into spontaneous laugher.

"After the test and confirmation from Dr. Howell, reality has now sunk in... Well, I don't know what to say," Angelica appeared bewildered as she looked out the windows. "I can't believe this is really happening to me. One moment my life feels so normal and the next, it's like a surreal dream that I can't wake up from."

Dr. Goolrick stepped closer to Angelica and tightened his grip on her shoulder. "We can arrange a place for you to go... out of the country. It would be safer for you to get away from here -- at least, for a while." Dr. Goolrick peered over at Dr. Howell as he nodded, appearing concerned.

Angelica glared at Dr. Goolrick. "And leave my magazine, my mother, my friends, Michael... and hide? I can't do that. Besides, something tells me they'd find me," she said, her face had turned pink and her eyes were vacant.

Dr. Howell let out a one-syllable chuckle. "You are truly unique. Most would run... and yet, you forge ahead... Such courage."

Angelica took a deep breath, mollified. "The aerospace facility in Nevada... What do you know about it? I'm leaving this afternoon to go there. Look, no offense but, I'm done playing games. You two are obviously experts on the subject of aliens and their connection to the government... it's time you two started talking." Angelica's face had now felt hot as she stared dramatically at both of them.

Dr. Howell glanced over to Dr. Goolrick, as Dr. Goolrick's face softened. Dr. Goolrick exhaled, "Hamilton, be my guest" Dr. Goolrick glided his open palm gently towards Dr. Howell's midsection.

"Are you talking about the privately owned aerospace facility with the underground base off 'The Great Basin Highway' with the launch pad for Cygnus that is designed to shuttle personnel and cargo to Mars?" Dr. Howell asked, a bit mischievously.

Angelica tilted her head. "Cygnus? Is this a space craft?"

"More like a stealth space shuttle," Dr. Howell said.

"Really?" Angelica announced, surprised.

"Yes, and Francis Giano is currently working on going further, if he hasn't done so already."

Angelica looked over at Dr. Goolrick. "He's correct," Dr. Goolrick said. "Francis Giano has technology to travel further... Time travel from an interplanetary spacecraft, launched from the Mars base."

"Seriously? Is he working with ETs?" Angelica shot a look of curiosity over at Dr. Goolrick.

"Depends on who you ask," Dr. Howell responded vaguely.

Angelica peered back at Dr. Howell. "Do you believe he is working alongside ETs?"

"Yes, I believe he is," Dr. Howell answered.

"Why doesn't the public know about it? I can't believe they are able to keep information as extraordinary as this secret - pisses me off!"

"I agree with you, Angelica... I feel the same way. However, some hold to the belief that no one would believe it anyway." Dr. Goolrick spoke softly.

Angelica stood up from the stool and scooted it back with her heel. "I spoke with an aeronautical engineer in Elberton who says the grey race is colonizing on an earth-like planet. He heard from colleagues the grey beings were creating hybrids by cross-breeding with specific humans to create a new race to occupy that planet. Do you know anything about that? Would it have anything to do with the billionaire, Francis Giano?" Hamilton smiled at Dr. Goolrick.

Dr. Goolrick prompted. "Yes, this has been a main topic of discussion among our research team. In the Ufology community, individuals have claimed to have been taken there by the grey beings, and are reporting that they are creating a new race using hybrids on this planet. Apparently, they have been for some time. We were skeptical in the beginning, however too many witnesses have come forward with the same claim." Dr. Goolrick said, turning his voice deeper.

"Last year, a team of researchers at NASA discovered an earth-like planet and named it Eplar. They are calling it a super-earth," Dr. Howell said as he glanced at Dr. Goolrick.

As a physicist, I was quite excited about the discovery. It is clearly in the 'Goldilocks Zone' and is habitable for humans. Moreover, after much research, I found it coincidental that NASA named the planet Eplar, the same name reported by alleged abductees. More confirmation we are in close contact with the grey beings," Dr. Howell said.

"Eplar?" Angelica asked. "Very interesting." She nodded, remembering her conversation with Blake McKinney.

Dr. Howell continued. "Yes, indeed, and it continues to get more interesting. You see, the planet is orbiting in the habitable zone of a star similar to our sun and has liquid water. However, the star has a mass and radius a third the size of our sun. As a result, it is slightly less luminous, furthermore, creating a temperature in the seventy-degree range... comparable to a calm spring day on earth."

"How far it is from Earth?" Angelica asked.

"It's reported to be four hundred light years away," Dr. Howell said excitedly.

Angelica caught Dr. Goolrick's eye and laughed, "That's all?"

Dr. Goolrick interjected, "The stealth spacecraft is said to only take sixty-two hours to get there from Earth, and a third of that time if launched from Mars."

Angelica crinkled her brow. "What is on Mars? Are we talking about an operational space station? Seriously, this sounds so insane! Is this really true?"

Dr. Howell grinned and nodded confidently. "Oh yes, most certainly true, Angelica."

"I see," Angelica said.

Dr. Howell responded without hesitation, "We are doing the extraordinary – Space-time travel."

Angelica thought for a moment. "So I am on the right track, heading to Nevada," she thought aloud.

Dr. Goolrick appeared concerned. "Do you think that is a good idea?"

Angelica looked innocently into his eyes. "Probably not."

"You aren't going alone are you?"

"No, I will be accompanied by a colleague of mine," Angelica said quickly.

As a good investigative journalist her antenna had gone up. She had definitely underestimated these two. "How are you so well informed?" she asked, looking inquisitively at Dr. Goolrick.

"My dear, I don't believe in coincidence; you are not here by accident."

"I've heard that before." Angelica chuckled sarcastically.

"It was just a matter of time before some smart, ambitious journalist grabbed ahold of this story."

Angelica appeared wounded as she glared at Dr. Goolrick. He noticed her were eyes soft, her face delicate. "How will my life ever be the same?" she mumbled.

Dr. Howell smiled and spoke kindly. "I heard this quote once: 'the pain of hell never heals. A smoldering burn'. Emotions are natural and not always out of line."

Dr. Goolrick stepped over to the implant and picked it up. "Will you be taking this with you?"

The Bovine Connection

Angelica picked up the napkin and placed the device back inside and folded it up. "I suppose... I should... evidence," she stated, and raised her eyebrows.

Dr. Howell smiled. "You know, there is someone in Nevada you need to meet with. She lives in Henderson, a suburb close to the Vegas strip. She's a scientist who worked at the facility. She would be a good source.

In addition, she has information regarding the facility on Mars. Of course I will need to contact her and put her in touch with you. I can't promise anything."

"Would you ask if she would meet us tomorrow?" Angelica asked. "Maybe somewhere near Vegas. Better yet, ask her if she could meet us at the Cosmopolitan on the Strip, in the front lobby around eleven o'clock. It's busy, you know," she murmured.

Dr. Howell nodded. "I'll give her a call when I get back to my office. Like I said, I can't promise anything. She may not agree to meet you."

Dr. Goolrick took Angelica's hand. "Do you mind if I take a hair sample before you leave? I would like to check for something."

Angelica stepped back and looked the doctor curiously in the eyes. "Only if you tell me what you are checking for."

"Nuclear DNA indicating possible viral resistance," he said matter-of-factly.

Angelica tilted her head back; her expression indicated she wasn't satisfied with his response so Dr. Goolrick quickly continued. "Well, if the hair sample contains two deleted genes for CCR5 protein and no intact gene for normal undeleted CCR5 – then that indicates disease resistance... a commonality between the new hybrids we are seeing."

"Well, I suppose." Angelica tilted her head down. "Be my guest..."

Dr. Goolrick plucked a few strands from the top of Angelica's head. "Perfect, tissue's still intact."

Dr. Howell handed him a small plastic bag. Dr. Goolrick placed them in the bag and handed it back to Dr. Howell and then looked at Angelica. "I will walk you out."

"So," Angelica said, "you believe I could be one of these new hybrids?"

Dr. Goolrick glanced confidently over at Dr. Howell and then back at Angelica. "You did remove a military implanted device from your arm."

Angelica sighed. "Why would I not be surprised?" she murmured. Angelica turned to Dr. Howell. "Thank you."

Dr. Howell smiled sincerely. "It was a pleasure, Ms. Bradley."

On the way through the main hall, as they passed the staircase, Angelica recalled Dr. Howell mentioning the lady scientist. "Will you make sure he contacts the scientist in Nevada?"

"Yes. That should be an interesting conversation. I've heard Olivia speak at one of the Exopolitics Conventions. I found her quite creditable, as will you."

Dr. Goolrick opened the door as Angelica stepped past him. "Beautiful day!"

"Yes, Doctor, it is. And thank you again!" Angelica smiled.

"Stay safe, Angelica," he whispered.

Angelica started down the path toward her car and then turned around. "Donec iterum conveniant fratrem!" she announced.

Dr. Goolrick smiled and raised his hand, holding it steady as if to salute.

Chapter Fifty-Three

Angelica was quiet and introspective, reflecting on her meeting with Dr. Goolrick and Dr. Hamilton Howell. Dr. Goolrick's request to take a hair sample from her was certainly unexpected. She was also completely stunned by the amount of corroborating information they gave to her investigation. Suddenly, she heard a loud noise as her car was hit from behind. Angelica was jolted forward.

Angelica looked up in her rearview mirror and saw the black Tahoe as it bumped her car from behind once more. Impulsively, she leaned forward and looked out her cracked windshield and accelerated the gas.

She shouted at herself, rationalizing the situation, "Angelica, calm down, breathe!"

As she continued toward her office, she watched, as the Tahoe continued to speed up behind her, so she accelerated again, and then weaved into the left lane. The Tahoe weaved in the left lane behind her, coming close to her bumper before she quickly weaved back into the right lane and immediately onto the highway exit ramp. Angelica floored it as she went onto the highway. The Tahoe was gone.

Angelica's jaw relaxed and she released the breath she was holding. She looked down at her purse in the passenger seat, thinking about the military implant device. She wanted to get rid of it somehow, but she couldn't just throw it out the window of her car. It was evidence... valuable evidence proving she was not crazy. She would give it to Carl to keep safe. Even though Angelica trusted Gail more than Carl, she did not want to risk involving Gail any further.

Angelica pulled into the *Liberator* parking lot and parked her wrecked BMW. Once out of her car, she looked around suspiciously, and then ran toward her office building. The black Tahoe had disappeared when she entered the highway and was nowhere in sight.

Inside, Angelica went through the lobby and rushed past the reception desk, never saying a word. Angelica always greeted Hannah, the young intern, but today she had no time for small talk. She wanted to see Carl immediately.

After what felt like an eternity, the elevator door opened and there stood Andrew in the elevator. "Shit," she thought aloud as she stepped in and turned to face the doors as they closed. Angelica stared up at the number display, eagerly waiting for the door to open.

"Are you not going to acknowledge me? All I get is a 'shit'... wow!" Andrew whispered. His eyes appeared surprised.

Angelica took a deep breath. "Yes, I'm sorry. I just don't have time to argue with you," she whispered. Her pulse sped up.

"I'm not arguing," he said softly.

"Yes. I see that. How are you today, Andrew?" Angelica was still looking at the number display panel as it blinked to the number two. Angelica let out another deep breath, dropping her shoulders, relieved as the door started to open.

"I'm doing well. I would appreciate a moment of your time, if you could spare one... Just a moment," he said while trying to look at her face.

Angelica clenched her jaw, still facing forward. "I really have to take care of a few things before my flight. I need to meet with Carl." She turned and looked at him sincerely. "Can it not wait?"

"Just a moment," he pled. Angelica raised her hands to her temples and shook her head as she sighed, "Okay," she conceded.

Angelica stepped around the corner and Andrew followed. There was a small dark hallway with a supply closet to the left of the elevators. Angelica pointed at the door. "Let's go in there." Andrew stepped ahead and opened the door. Angelica stepped in and cracked the door behind them. Andrew took Angelica's hands. Angelica started to pull them back, but relented. "Andrew, please. What is this about? I told you... I am seeing someone. I think I'm in love with him," she stated softly as she held eye contact, hoping he'd let go of her hands.

"Angelica, yes, exactly, you think you are... you are infatuated with him because he is a cowboy - It's not real! You and I... we're real!"

"What?" Angelica pulled her hands away. "Andrew you and I were having sex, and having a good time, that's all! Look, I don't have time for this! You have no idea what..."

Andrew's face reddened as he interrupted her, "Another fucking slinging dick to deal with, fuck!" he shouted as he jerked his head.

Angelica quickly turned around and pushed the door shut. "Someone is going to hear us! This conversation is over!" Angelica swung around and grabbed the door knob to walk out.

"Wait! I'm sorry." Andrew leaned in and looked her deep in the eyes, hoping to reignite a connection.

Angelica sarcastically chuckled, "I swear, men like you; you only want what you can't have! Grow up!" Angelica started to open the door.

"That's not true, Angelica. Listen, please don't turn from me, just hear me out. I know that's what you think, but I've always had deep feelings for you. I just wasn't sure that was what you wanted. At times, you acted as if it were a game."

"Game?" Angelica blurted out in almost a yell, "Really?" Angelica cocked her head sideways. "You have to be kidding? Are we in high school?" Angelica was looking intensely into Andrew's eyes, "No, you're not kidding." She let out a laugh. "Wow!"

Andrew grabbed Angelica's wrist. "Not game, game was the wrong word. Just wait, please wait! I thought maybe over time you'd fall for me and see who I really was."

Angelica's eyes softened. "Well instead of assuming... you should have asked what I wanted."

"What did you want?" Andrew leaned in close and held eye contact as she tried to look away.

"I don't know, Andrew; I guess at one time I may have wanted more... but looking back now... just the way it was."

Angelica stood tall with her shoulders back. "It doesn't matter..." Angelica's voice got firmer as she began to use her hands to speak. She didn't believe Andrew, and she was certain she was falling in love with Michael. "Besides, nice try, but if you wanted more from me, hum, let's just say, a relationship, then why didn't you just ask for it?"

Andrew knew Angelica was speaking out of anger, maybe even trying to punish him, he thought. "Angelica, I know what you want, the kind of man you need." Andrew tilted his head and gazed into her eyes." I can be that man if you'll give me another chance."

Angelica held up her hand and continued, "You think you have me all figured out, Andrew... you don't. You don't have any idea what I want. I'm sorry, but I'm just going to be blunt... I've found what I want, and I am happy. No games! No bullshit! Uncomplicated! Please respect that." Angelica pulled away, opened the door.

Andrew ran his hand through the front of his copper tinted straight brown hair in frustration. "That's fine! Hey, I know how you think!" Andrew lifted his shoulders and postured forward. "You know, you doubt my depth sometimes – you always have. I understand you, Angelica, yep, understand you quite well. You wanted me to become vulnerable, expose myself. I was just a challenge for you to conquer. Well, he doesn't understand you like I do and I feel sorry for him. Once you're done with him – God help him!"

Angelica broke eye contact and looked down at the floor. "Are you done?" she asked before she turned and walked off, praying none of her employees overheard them.

"You'll get bored with the cowboy!" he announced, unconcerned if anyone heard him. Angelica never turned around, although she heard every word.

Andrew leaned onto the doorframe hoping she'd turn and walk back with a change of heart, but Angelica was already to the other end of the hall.

Shea looked up. "Ms. Bradley, hi, I didn't see you there. Carl is gone for the day."

"Oh, okay. Have you seen Gail? I just walked by her office and she wasn't at her desk."

"Nope, I haven't seen her since she left for lunch. She is usually back by now. Shea looked at her watch. "It's after three o'clock. Yes, three thirty-three to be exact. She may have left early today."

"I suppose she has," Angelica said. "I going to leave a note on Carl's desk?"

"Absolutely, Ms. Bradley, go right in. There should be a pad and pen in there somewhere... under that mess." Shea giggled.

"Thanks, Shea, you're a dear." Angelica managed a sincere smile although she was weary.

Angelica went in and looked around for a manila envelope. After a moment of useless searching, she called out to Shea, "Do you have an envelope? Small manila one will do."

"Yes, here, will this work?" Shea stepped in with a small manila envelope in her hand.

"Perfect, thanks," Angelica said and then waited for Shea to leave and tucked the device still wrapped in 'The Brown Palace' cocktail napkin into the envelope. Then she took a black sharpie from Carl's drawer and wrote, "Please keep safe for me! Angelica." She impulsively looked out of the window up to the sky before sealing it with her tongue.

Angelica stepped out and pulled the door shut. "Thanks Shea!" Shea shot Angelica a curious look as she rushed by and headed straight for her office, hoping to avoid Andrew while passing her employees working at their desks and managing a slight smile to everyone who looked up at her. The suspicious glares didn't go unnoticed. Angelica was working an unusual story and she couldn't hide the stress it was causing her - a story that had turned personal.

Inside, she shut her door and called Carl's cellphone, getting his voicemail as she walked over to the large window and surveyed the parking lot and then the sky. "Hi Carl, this is Angelica. I left a package on your desk. Please put it away and keep it safe. I'll explain later. I'm at the office getting ready to fly out to Nevada tonight. I'll fill you in soon." Angelica hung up.

She turned on her desk lamp, then sat down at her desk, leaned back and stared blankly at the white-painted brick wall. Nestled in a corner on the second floor, hidden by a maze of cubicles, her office had become the only place she felt safe.

Angelica knew investigative journalism could be a dangerous career. She was well aware of that fact from the beginning. Journalists could be sent overseas to report in war zones or find themselves sitting in a secret meeting with a dangerous source in a seedy area of town... it was just another day on the job. Therefore, it wasn't uncommon for her to find herself in harm's way. However, blowing the cover on a government cover-up involving ETs was never in the job description and completely new territory.

Angelica scooted up in her chair and grabbed her cell phone. She needed to hear Michael's voice. Hesitating, she put the phone back on her desk fearing he might be in a meeting and she didn't want to come across as a needy girlfriend and possibly scare him away. But Angelica needed desperately to hear his voice so she relented, picked up her cell phone and dialed his number. After three rings Michael answered. "Well, hello, beautiful... sexy lady! What a nice surprise!" Michael sounded excited.

Angelica swallowed the lump in her throat and her chest fluttered as she heard his voice again. "Hello, Michael! I hope I didn't interrupt you while you were working." Her blood heated.

Michael responded softly, "You could never interrupt me. I miss your pretty voice."

Angelica blushed. She wanted to feel his strong arms around her making her feel safe. She imagined his lush full lips as he spoke on the other end of the phone.

Angelica pictured him sitting at his desk in a fine dark custom tailored suit with his black wavy hair tamed down by grooming gel, like a Brioni suit model in a Robb Report magazine. She felt an exhilarating shiver. "I just wanted to say hi," Angelica said softly and then was quiet. She rolled her eyes and leaned back conscious of the shy little girl emerging again. Angelica immediately shook her head -- feeling embarrassed -- and wondered why he had such an effect on her. This was definitely a first, she thought. Her heart was wide open. She felt vulnerable. Angelica took a deep breath. Michael was obviously amused and she heard a slight chuckle on the other end.

"You are an interesting woman, Angelica." His tone was sensual. "I've been thinking a lot about you… Your sweet smile is always my first thought, and then…" he chuckled. "I want you here with me. I should get on a plane, grab you up and bring you here." He laughed, but she sensed he was half-serious.

She let out a breath, feeling unusually pouty. "I so want to be there with you. I leave for Nevada this evening. I need to spend a couple days there to wrap up the story." Angelica rubbed her forehead, feeling the tension move through her.

"Nevada, huh? … What's going on in Nevada?" Michael's tone changed; he sounded shocked.

"Oh… just following a lead. I don't want to bother you with it. All we talk about is the story."

Michael interrupted, "I want to hear about it. You haven't shared much with me, and out of respect, I've refrained from asking. I figured as we grew to know each other better, you'd start to trust me. I worry about you, Angelica. We both know this isn't just about covering a story for you – it's become personal. I haven't forgotten Matthew or what happened to my father." Michael's voice changed again… his tone was

The Bovine Connection

even lower and stern. "I know what you're going to say, but hear me out... I think you should walk away... Don't go to Nevada... I have a bad feeling. Like I've said, I just found you, Angelica, and I can't lose you. Please consider giving it up. Think about the device you cut from your arm. This is only going to go from bad to worse, baby," he finished in a whisper.

Angelica closed her eyes, wanting to change the subject. However she knew he was right. Down somewhere deep inside of her, she was very much afraid. Unfortunately, she was already too far in to turn back. After the discovery of the military tracking device, she couldn't see how it would be possible to walk away. She didn't want Michael to know the details of the meeting with Dr. Goolrick and Dr. Howell. He'd be on a plane to get her, no doubt about it, she thought.

"It's hard to picture you without a cowboy hat." Angelica giggled.

"I see -- we're changing the subject. You are a stubborn woman."

"Look, Michael, I understand, and I've thought about it. I've been a journalist long enough to know when I'm in danger. I also know if they wanted me dead, they would have already done it. The guy in the SUV was meant to scare me, but I think the military needs me for some reason. I don't know why yet, but I just have this feeling."

"You think the military is watching you?" Michael asked quietly.

Angelica frowned and bit down on her bottom lip. "Well, some form of military group or covert agency. I'm still putting the pieces together – I am getting closer though. I can't quit, Michael, you know it and I know it. This is my job. This is who I am." Angelica didn't mean to mention the military. *Shit!* she thought.

"Angelica..." Angelica heard Michael sigh. "I, well, I'm falling in love with you. I'll say it. I'm falling in love with you. You had my heart from that first day at my ranch." Michael's disembodied voice echoed in Angelica's head. Her eyes grew wide. *"Did he just say he was falling in love with me? Oh my,"* she thought.

"I'm trying to be sensitive to your feelings... your career... you, Angelica. I don't want to lose you. Please consider walking away from this damn story. If you're looking for proof of ETs, haven't you found it by now? After what I've told you about my father... Jack Keller, Paul, Matthew... Matthew! Angelica isn't what happened to Matthew enough to wake you up? Forgive me... but I'm going to say it again... You are one stubborn woman!"

For a moment Angelica felt confused. Maybe he was right. She contemplated giving up the story for a moment, and then quickly made up her mind. "I understand, and I'm trying to be sensitive to your feelings, as well." Angelica sighed. "I want to be happy... and being with you makes me happier than I've ever been. The last thing I would ever want to do is upset you, but you have to trust me. I can't explain it... I have to see this to the end or you won't get all of me – there will always be a piece missing. I'm not the same person I was before this story – it's changed me." Angelica took a deep breath and waited for Michael's response.

Angelica heard Michael sigh, releasing a deep breath indicating his frustration. The long moment felt like eternity... It was obvious he was unhappy. "Please understand, sweetie, I'm expressing my feelings for what I see in us – our future. I have never felt this way for any woman before. It saddens me you won't listen."

Angelica shook her head and tightened her lips. This was a new side of Michael. She was starting to see how he worked all angles in an attempt to get his way. And he was determined.

"So, change your mind. Don't go to Nevada! Leave the story where it is – walk away and be done with it," he whispered.

Angelica looked up and raised her fist in the air. Why couldn't he understand? She marveled as she shook her arm in irritation. "I can't," she whispered.

There was silence on the other end, and after another long moment, Michael replied. "Okay, Angelica... Have it your way."

Angelica looked down. His tone was odd. Her head was starting to ache and she felt charged with emotion. The conversation had turned so quickly. "Are we having an argument?" she asked half-jokingly.

"No... sweetheart, of course not," he murmured.

"Okay, I'll call when I can. Good-bye." Angelica said softly.

Michael leaned back in his chair, looked out the window at the skyscrapers of the New York skyline, lifted his index knuckle to his chin, and clinched his lips. "Good-bye beautiful," he whispered.

Angelica glanced at her cell phone before hanging up and saw a missed call and voicemail from an unknown number. She pushed the button and listened to the voicemail.

"Hello, Angelica, this is Dr. Hamilton Howell. My friend has agreed to meet with you at the Cosmopolitan Hotel at nine o'clock tomorrow morning. Her name is Dr. Olivia Wallace. She will be alone in the front lobby wearing a brown blouse. She has black hair."

Angelica put her cell phone in her purse and then glanced at the clock to notice the time was four twenty-two. It struck her as odd that the time was either twenty-two or thirty-three after each time it was brought to her attention. And even more odd was that it was usually twenty-two after when she was either with Michael or thinking of him. *What was going on?* she wondered. She considered it too strange to be a coincidence.

Angelica wondered if Michael was right. Should she quit now before going to Nevada. She knew she was under their surveillance. However, she was a good journalist... it seemed the only logical next step. She gathered her things and left her office.

Chapter Fifty-Four

Angelia pulled into the long-term parking lot at the airport. Grabbing her bags, she wondered if she was being tailed and glanced around. After glaring around suspiciously for anyone out of the ordinary, she quickly shut her car door. Angelica hit the lock button on her remote causing her car to chirp as she hurried toward the United Airlines terminal to find Dr. Bishop.

As Angelica approached the entrance she saw Dr. Bishop standing outside the automatic glass doors, facing in the other direction. He was wearing blue jeans and a light-blue dress shirt. As he turned and noticed Angelica, his face softened into a sincere smile.

Angelica picked up her pace and extended her hand to wave as she passed over to the taxi curb to where he was standing by the outside check-in stand.

"Hey! You're here! Great, let's get checked in." Dr. Bishop didn't hesitate; he grabbed her duffle bag and turned towards the man in a United uniform.

"Have you been waiting long?" Angelica attempted to make conversation and be polite. Dr. Bishop looked back at Angelica as he handed the man his boarding pass and a two-dollar tip. "No, not too long... I was early. We can grab a bite to eat closer to our gate after we check our bags here. The line is too long inside. This will save us enough time for an extra drink before we board."

"Perfect," Angelica whispered.

After they checked their bags and made their way through security, they found a crowded sports bar and were able to grab a table just as a young family was getting up to leave.

Dr. Bishop appeared more relaxed and ordered a Bloody Mary. Angelica ordered a Sierra Nevada Pale Ale. Dr. Bishop smiled, amused at Angelica. "Nice one!"

Angelica smiled playfully. "Why not... I like beer every once in a while. I also like symbolisms, even silly ones." She laughed softly and shook her head. "The truth is I'm not much of a beer connoisseur; it just happened to be the first one that came to mind," she quipped. "So, are you ready?" Angelica asked.

Dr. Bishop looked as if he were confused. "Ready for what?" he asked. "Oh yes -- our adventure into the unknown. I don't know... but I have a funny feeling this will be an interesting trip." Dr. Bishop put his glass down after taking a sip and removed the celery, placing it on the cocktail napkin.

"I agree. I'm actually a little nervous, if you couldn't tell?" Angelica glanced around before taking a sip of her beer.

"Do we have a plan?" Dr. Bishop asked as he narrowed his eyes and leaned in.

Angelica contemplated for a moment, "I thought *you* did, Marc." She laughed.

Dr. Bishop was obviously surprised. "Oh, no, I..." He stumbled over his words. Angelica watched him closely as he shifted in his seat. He was your typical intellectual, she thought. His expressions indicated it took him a moment to register her jokes.

Angelica relaxed her hands into her lap and leaned back. She was becoming comfortable with Dr. Bishop and could tease him playfully a little but decided not to go any further. She knew it would be more comfortable for him to unwind at his own pace.

"Well, we are meeting Dr. Olivia Wallace in our hotel lobby at nine o'clock in the morning," Angelica stated confidently. "She should be a good source since she claims to have worked at the aerospace facility. I thought the hotel would be perfect since it will be crowded with tourists and gamblers. I guess we could be included in both categories." Angelica continued enjoying the fact that she was taking charge. "Staying in crowded places just feels safer."

"Yes, I agree. Wow! That is great. How did you find Dr. Wallace?" he asked, astonished.

Angelica had taken a bite of her club sandwich and then a sip of her beer. She raised her palm to cover her mouth as she swallowed. "The scientist... Dr. Walter Goolrick. He was the expert on the Elberton mutilations," she answered with her hand in front of her mouth, trying to hide the food she was chewing, and then lifted her napkin and wiped her mouth.

"So, Dr. Bishop... I know we spoke at great length about your interest in Mr. Giano; however, going to the facility could be dangerous. It's not too late to turn back, you know. Are you sure you want go forward with this?"

"First, you called me Marc earlier, please continue. I believe we are certainly on a first name basis by now. Second... yes, without a doubt. I'm not letting you go alone. And, I live for this Indiana Jones stuff!" He chuckled.

Angelica laughed. "That's funny. Well, here's to Indiana Jones and his sidekick. Am I the cute girl with freckles in the first movie or that blonde bitch in the 'Temple of Doom?'" Angelica winked playfully as she lifted her beer and Marc met her toast.

"You are neither. You are Angelica Bradley, journalist extraordinaire. Here's to you and our safe return back to D.C.," he announced.

Just as Angelica was lowering her beer, she caught a glimpse of the large flat-screen television hanging on the wall behind Dr. Bishop. A national news medium was reporting a woman's body had just been found floating in the Potomac River.

Angelica looked down from the screen and met Dr. Bishop's eyes with a worried expression on her face.

"What is it Angelica?" Dr. Bishop turned and looked at the screen as a woman's photo appeared. He turned slowly and looked back at Angelica to see her mouth wide open and her face in shock.

"What is it? Did you know her?"

Angelica looked at Dr. Bishop, and then around the bar, blankly. "Can someone turn this up, please?" Angelica shouted, her face ashen.

Dr. Bishop quickly jumped up and adjusted the volume so that it was much louder than the background noise in the bar.

The Bovine Connection

Everything became still and frozen in that unspeakable moment. Angelica couldn't move. "Oh my God...," she stammered as she looked down at Dr. Bishop, bewildered and then back up to the screen. "Oh, my God! It's Gail! They've killed Gail!"

Dr. Bishop tried to keep Angelica calm by reaching over and patting her hand. Angelica pulled it away and placed it over her mouth, her eyes wide, dazed.

"Angelica, are you okay?" Angelica started to shake her head continuously, almost involuntarily. "No, no... no."

Dr. Bishop turned around and looked back at the monitor. "Holy hell!" he whispered in a deep breath and listened.

"All right, they are saying there doesn't appear to be foul play. The police said either accidental drowning or suicide," he restated, after the newscaster finished each sentence.

"No! Not possible!" Angelica snapped.

Angelica's cell phone rang. Dr. Bishop looked at it on the table. Angelica was mute watching the T.V. and hadn't noticed it. His gaze suddenly was drawn to the faces around the bar staring at them.

He turned back around. "Angelica, okay, calm down!" He glanced around the bar and noticed everyone was still staring. The two bartenders were leaning in and whispering to each other, peering in their direction.

Angelica glared absently into Dr. Bishop's eyes. "No!"

Dr. Bishop lowered his head. "Okay, okay... breathe."

Angelica snapped her hand up quickly, "Shush, what did they just say? I missed it." She looked up and then back at Dr. Bishop with tears streaming down her cheeks.

"They said her golden retriever was found at the bank of the river, and that is apparently how they discovered her body. Okay, wait, they just said... someone saw the dog and thought he was lost. They tried to get him to go with them so they could locate the owner, but he wouldn't move. He kept looking out into the water."

Angelica appeared fragile, about to break at any moment. Her eyes were red and watery. Her face was pale and vacant.

As the commercial came across the screen Angelica grabbed her cell phone from her purse and dialed Carl. "Carl, Carl... Gail... They found Gail... they found her body in the river!"

Carl's disembodied voice answered calmly and firmly. "Angelica, I've been trying to call you! We don't really know anything yet. I'm on my way to the station now."

Dr. Bishop was sympathetically observing Angelica's face as she met his eyes while she was on the phone with Carl.

"I can't believe it! No, that is just not possible, Carl! We both know Theo wouldn't do that. It's a lie! You know it!" Angelica was silent for a moment, listening to Carl, as Dr. Bishop continued to try to listen in on their conversation.

"No, I'm at the airport. Yes. Okay, I'll call you when I get there. Yes, please find out what you can. Thank you!" Angelica hung up the phone, looked at Dr. Bishop, and then took a large gulp of her beer before getting up and walking over to the bar. Dr. Bishop watched her as she said something to the bartender. Then the bartender returned with a glass half full of brown liquid and a single ice cube.

Angelica with the glass in her hand walked back over to the table and sat down. She lifted the glass and started taking several slow sips. Dr. Bishop was concerned that after the news of Gail's death, Angelica may not be stable enough to make the trip.

"Should we cancel the flight?"

Angelica looked at him with a blank stare and after a moment shook her head. "No, we go! We fucking go! They are not going to stop me! They killed Matthew and now my best friend!"

Dr. Bishop nodded his head. "I'm so sorry about your friends, Angelica," he said softly and then tightened his lips.

Angelica managed a slight smile. "Thank you. I'm sorry about the language... I just don't know what I'm going to do without her. I can't even think about that right now." Angelica's eye watered and tears once again slid down the sides of her cheeks.

They sat quietly for a few minutes, finished their drinks, and paid their tabs. Angelica appeared to still be in a daze, and Dr. Bishop wasn't sure what to say to her.

As they got up to leave, Angelica noticed several people staring at her. She realized she must have caused a scene, but at that moment, she was oblivious to the world and to what anyone thought of her. Her only thoughts were of Gail.

Chapter Fifty-Five

It was a little after ten o'clock. The desert air was warm and dry, a perfect evening. In the cab, Dr. Bishop observed her flawless, milky complexion and the smooth, light blonde hair that surrounded her face. She looked like an angel – delicate, yet strong.

Dr. Bishop re-folded his newspaper and placed it in the side pocket of his briefcase. He relaxed his head back and took a deep breath. He wondered about Angelica's life. How did she live and where did she grow up? How did she end up here with him, traveling to Nevada, and did she really comprehend the risk involved with pursuing Giano? Dr. Bishop found it deeply unsettling to think he may have put her life in greater danger by contacting her.

Angelica glanced over and smiled, then she lifted her arms into a slight stretch. "I'm so tired," she said as she yawned.

"You slept the entire flight." Dr. Bishop smiled sincerely. "And you needed it... How do you feel?" He observed her curiously.

"I still feel tired," she replied. "I could have just dozed off in this cab," she added with a frown.

"You looked very peaceful, in spite of everything," he murmured.

Angelica rubbed her hand across her forehead, struggling to push her hair away from her face. "Well,

I feel as good I can feel under the circumstances. You know, I had a dream about Gail on the plane."

Dr. Bishop lowered his eyes. "You did?" He appeared curious.

"She was in her garden. Her hair was shining in the sunlight and she had this beautiful soft golden glow around her. She was so radiant... just glowing. She said, 'Angelica, aren't they lovely?' I said, 'What Gail, what is lovely?' She said, 'The flowers' and pointed down to a gorgeous pink peony. I said, 'Yes, Gail, they are lovely.' Then she smiled... strangely." Angelica frowned, her eyes appeared worried as she tilted her head back and rested it on the seat. "Then she said... 'I'm happy.' That was it... she disappeared holding the pink peony."

"I'm so sorry, Angelica." Dr. Bishop glanced down.

"You know, when I first woke up," Angelica continued, "for just a moment, I had forgotten she was gone. I wanted to call her and tell her how beautiful and youthful she was in my dream. I wanted to hear her voice, and then I remembered." Angelica stopped then turned and looked out the window at the lit-up Vegas strip. "I remembered," she whispered to herself as a tear drop fell from her cheek and hit her lap. Angelica shivered.

Dr. Bishop watched as the tear fell, and then placed his hand on top of Angelica's. "I'm not afraid of death because I don't believe in it. It's just getting out of one car and into another... John Lennon." Dr. Bishop suddenly appeared concerned. He wished he had not spoken his mind; however, it just came out, unexpected. "I don't know where that came from."

Angelica lifted her head and looked at Dr. Bishop. "Gail adored John Lennon. That was strange."

"I'm sorry," he dropped his chin.

"No, don't be! Thank you, Marc. Thank you!"

As they passed by the swarms of tourists walking the sidewalks underneath the flashy neon signs, Angelica looked over at Dr. Bishop; he appeared mesmerized by the fountains of the Bellagio's water show as they were passing by it.

The water gracefully glided up toward the dark blue and onyx sky, and against the beautiful backdrop of the brightly lit cream Bellagio Hotel. Sitting in traffic, and only a block from their turn into the Cosmopolitan... Angelica broke the silence. "Do you come to Vegas often?"

Dr. Bishop looked ahead toward the driver and then briefly at Angelica. "Not too often. Let's see, the last time I was here, was, three years ago... Yes, three years ago. I came here to attend the 'Science of Consciousness Convention.'"

Angelica moved to face him. "Really? What is that? ...sounds interesting."

Dr. Bishop adjusted in his seat to face Angelica. "Well, it's essentially the study of the non-material world."

Angelica sat up straight. "Fascinating... Do you believe in ghosts?"

Dr. Bishop laughed, clearly tickled at Angelica's question. "I believe anything is possible." He chuckled.

"There is very little talk of ghosts, if any, at the convention. We are more interested in metaphysics as a systematic approach to developing skills in our everyday lives. It's interesting; you would appreciate it. We focus on how to shift into a new and better paradigm; right up your ally."

"I think you may be right." Angelica smiled.

"It's the key to survival, in a sense... Basically the point is... we must learn to use our intuition. We have found ourselves at a benchmark, a time when change must occur on a large scale or it will be catastrophic for our planet. The old systems can no longer support the new paradigm. There are humans starving daily in spite of overwhelming quantities of food. And, as you well know, our resources are controlled by less than -- I'd say less than ten percent of our global population." Dr. Bishop noticed Angelica shift in her seat and then look out the window.

"Well, this is not in the best interest of the other ninety percent. I'll finish with that."

Angelica looked back at Dr. Bishop. "I was sincerely interested. I find this conversation quite stimulating, sounds like a perfect article for the *Liberator*," she said softly. "It's just that I am a little distracted, over, you know."

Dr. Bishop lowered his eyes. "Well, there is plenty of time for conversations like these."

Angelica nodded in agreement. "Yes, very true, and I look forward to them, Marc."

Dr. Bishop smiled and glanced away to notice they were in front of the Cosmopolitan Hotel. "We have arrived," he announced.

The cab driver looked up with a sneaky grin. "You guys make a nice couple…"

Dr. Bishop's eyes grew wide and he appeared uncomfortable. Angelica abruptly blurted out. "No… We are just colleagues. We're here on business." Angelica looked at Dr. Bishop, lowered her eyes, visibly embarrassed.

Dr. Bishop smiled noncommittally, and nodded in approval of Angelica's response. "Yes, we're business colleagues!"

Angelica instinctively reached into her purse and grabbed her compact to freshen up her face. Dr. Bishop looked up in the rearview mirror to catch the driver peering at him with a look of pity. Dr. Bishop had only thought of Angelica professionally until that moment. He was a distinguished man. He had always put work before romance. He had not considered the idea of a romantic situation with Angelica… suddenly amused with himself for letting the thought enter his mind, he chuckled aloud.

Angelica glanced up curiously and half smiled before looking back down and applying a pink tinted gloss to her lips. Watching Angelica out the corner of his eye, she certainly wasn't his ideal, all-natural type. However, she was intelligent… he thought.

Angelica caught Dr. Bishop observing her. She held the tube up before putting the cap back on… "A necessity, especially in the dry desert."

Dr. Bishop managed a nervous smile and quickly glanced away.

Chapter Fifty-Six

After a small line, the cab was finally in front of the valet at the Cosmopolitan Hotel. The hotel was situated between the Bellagio Hotel and the City Center. The gleaming structure of glass and steel was modern sophistication.

"Just my style," Dr. Bishop announced, self-assuredly, as he stepped out onto the curb and looked around.

"Yes, mine too!" Angelica murmured.

Dr. Bishop straightened his belt and looked over at Angelica. "Do you want to meet in the lobby for a quick drink? We are in Vegas, you know... maybe just to sleep better? Say around eleven fifteen or eleven twenty?"

Angelica was grabbing her bags from the curb and placing the strap around her shoulder. "Yes, that would be nice -- I never sleep well -- actually dreading it lately," she mumbled... "And it looks like everything is just getting started here in Vegas." Angelica gestured for Dr. Bishop to look behind him. When he turned around, there was a group of twenty something's walking out of the hotel. Two of the women were riding piggyback on two of the men's backs. They were shouting and laughing, drawing attention from the other guests.

Dr. Bishop shook his head. "The good ol' days!"

"Looks fun!" Angelica giggled.

Dr. Bishop pressed his shoulders back. "Okay. See you in the lobby around eleven twenty. Oh, and Angelica, I'm very sorry about the loss of your friend... I sincerely mean that."

Angelica had forgotten about Gail for a few moments. Her stomach dropped as she remembered. "Thank you. I've lost two amazing people since I began this story." Angelica looked down. "Let's just meet in The Chandelier Bar," she said as she walked into the lobby.

Dr. Bishop lowered his face as he followed behind, regretting bringing up the subject again.

Both Angelica and Dr. Bishop were immediately taken with the stunning modern décor of the Cosmopolitan - A visual treat of quirky modern artist details. It was over-the-top dramatic, Angelica thought, as she glanced around. The atmosphere was cool, sleek, and creatively different from what she had expected.

Angelica was in awe at the lobby's columns, embedded with high-definition video screens playing images of brightly lit bubbles floating against dark blue. The hotel lobby was dark with soft white neon lighting.

Angelica usually stayed at the Bellagio. However, something about the Cosmopolitan felt perfect for the occasion. Angelica felt camouflaged like a chameleon, hidden between the eye-distracting modern décor of the hotel.

Dr. Bishop was in the line a few aisles over. He glanced at Angelica, accidently making eye contact with her as she was peering around before stepping up to check in at one of the many large, red, ornate front desks. Angelica noted his inquisitive expression before he quickly glanced away.

As Angelica removed the electronic key and entered her room, she was immediately drawn to the dramatic view from the floor-to-ceiling windows. She walked over and opened the large curtains to see the lights of the Vegas strip and the Bellagio fountains. The exciting nightlife was in full swing... signs with flashy advertisements for shows and dance clubs lit up the desert sky, enticing everyone who saw it to come out and play. Leaning against the window, her thoughts turned to Matthew and Gail. She desperately tried to push the recent and horrible news of Gail's death from her mind. She needed to freshen up before going downstairs and didn't want to become an emotional mess. Angelica bit down on her bottom lip as she fought the tears trying to well up in her eyes.

As Angelica blankly stared out past the Vegas lights into the dark, vast desert, her thoughts drifted to the underground facility somewhere out there, well hidden. Her heart suddenly became heavy and she felt an enormous sense of loneliness, as if the desert were pressing down on her very soul.

Angelica opened her duffle bag and pulled out the only evening wear she had packed: a sleeveless, black, cotton-wrap dress. She slid off her skirt and blouse, and slipped the dress over her dark grey, nude, lace lingerie, tying it around the waist. She then found her tan sandals with straps. She just wanted to be comfortable. Her feet were still swollen and red from the air travel.

After she finished wrapping the straps to her sandal up her ankles, she brushed her hair and dabbed a red lip color on her full peach lips. She grabbed her small black Chanel purse and headed downstairs in hopes of beating Dr. Bishop to the bar so that she could enjoy a quick single malt Scotch alone for a few minutes.

Angelica left her room and took the elevator back down to the lobby, where she found The Chandelier Bar. It was an enormously sophisticated architectural wonder consisting of beaded curtains of light hanging from the ceiling. It had three levels and she had overheard someone checking in say that level 1.5 was the most laid back and had great bartenders, so she made her way there.

She walked up to the bar and found an empty chair, while glancing around to notice there were several people in the chic lounge as she placed her small black purse up on the bar. When she looked up, the bartender was coming her way. He had shoulder length dark hair pulled back into a ponytail and appeared to be in his early thirties. "What's your poison?" he asked. Angelica smiled and then looked back down at the bar as if to think about it, although she already knew what she wanted. "Macallen 18, neat, thank you," she stated confidently, without blinking.

Angelica quickly turned and searched around the room for Dr. Bishop, never making eye contact with the bartender. Surprised by her choice, the bartender stood there for a moment peering at her with an amused smile on his face. "I was expecting you to say a martini or wine," he laughed flirtatiously. "The young lady is a Scotch drinker," he said softy, almost in a whisper.

Angelica was distracted and continued scanning the room for Dr. Bishop or anyone who may be tailing her. Most of the crowd was somewhere between their early twenties and late forties. Everyone appeared to be engaged in conversation and her intuition told her there was nothing going on that was out of the ordinary. Everything appeared copasetic, at least for now, she thought.

Angelica turned back around to the bartender as he was setting the cocktail napkin down. "I apologize... Did you say something?" Angelica's thoughts were a million miles away.

The bartender smiled sincerely. "Rough week?"

Angelica took a deep breath. "You don't even know."

The bartender topped off the high-end Scotch with a little extra pour. "Well, you're in the right place... By tomorrow you'll be a new woman! That's what Vegas does... if you let it. It's the perfect distraction."

Angelica widened her eyes in agreement as she took a slow sip of her golden colored sleep aid.

"Angelica!" Angelica heard Dr. Bishop's voice and shot around. "Hi there! Scotch?" he asked inquisitively as he quickly glanced down to her hand hugging the elixir. Angelica smiled. Dr. Bishop's face lightened as he looked at the bartender. "I'll have the same."

Angelica moved her purse out of his way, "Good choice. I ordered Macallen 18."

Dr. Bishop nodded. "Wow, I see you changed... You look great!" he mused.

Angelica feigned an agreeable smile but couldn't hide her emotions over Gail's death, which was finally starting to sink in. Her face was tired and her eyes heavy and red.

"How are you holding up?" Dr. Bishop asked patiently but his question brought on a confusing array of emotions to Angelica.

"In shock... Numb... I suppose." Angelica lifted her fingers over her mouth and appeared to drift away for a moment.

Dr. Bishop observed her tenderly and decided to change the subject. "So, our game-plan for tomorrow... I'm eager to meet this scientist. I feel a bit like 007." He smirked. "Although, I'm sure I don't resemble him." He pushed his chest out amused at himself.

The bartender brought over two glasses of ice for the Scotch while looking at Dr. Bishop, entertained by his body language. Angelica took a single ice cube and dropped it into her glass.

"After we meet with the scientist, as we discussed... we go take a look at the facility."

Dr. Bishop nodded with a flat expression. "We'll get as close as we can," he stated confidently.

"Maybe we could just show up and ask for a tour," Angelica said as she looked him directly in the eyes with a seemly serious expression, and then laughed sarcastically.

Dr. Bishop inhaled and then laughed nervously as his muscles clinched. "No, you're serious," he mumbled as he did a double take.

"Yes, I want to go inside," Angelica said. "I'm waiting for Carl to let me know if they have agreed to an interview. If not, well, new game plan." Angelica looked up to contemplate.

It took a second before it fully registered for Dr. Bishop. "Now that is 007 dangerous." He leaned back hard in his chair and took a deep gulp of Scotch. "Well, fingers crossed."

"They know I'm here, Marc, and they aren't going to let me just walk in. Think about it... They are letting me get this far because they know I will show up only to realize I can't go any further. They think I'll hit a dead end, and then I'll go back to D.C. with my tail between my legs and write my story... with no conclusive evidence to back it up. Then -- and I'm sure I am not telling you anything you don't already know -- they will put out disinformation to contradict my claims and make me look like just another crazy conspiracy theorist. Welcome to reality," she said sarcastically as she took a small sip of her Scotch.

Dr. Bishop sat his glass down and turned toward Angelica, shocked at her blunt pessimism. "Then why did you come?" Dr. Bishop asked, frowning.

Angelica glanced down and shook her head. "Because despite what I think will happen, I'm cautiously optimistic... and maybe a fool." She laughed nervously. "I only hope that Dr. Howell's scientist friend isn't a waste of our time." Angelica raised her brows.

"So tell me more about what you know about the aliens and Egypt." Angelica leaned back.

"What I know... huh... Well, there have been sightings of UFOs through the ages. You know, it was around the time the Russians first opened 'The Chamber of the Visitor' that abduction reports were starting to surface... in the 1960's. Claims of examinations and artificial inseminations were being reported. Women came forward believing they had been impregnated to give birth to alien hybrids.

It seemed to me that the Egyptians' stories of genetic colonization programs had resumed. I wondered if perhaps they were cloning themselves by combining their DNA with ours. Are they changing humans into a genetically engineered species? The ancient Egyptians always believed that our DNA came from the heavens and our creators would someday return."

The bartender returned. "Another?"

"Yes, thank you," Dr. Bishop said before he smiled playfully at Angelica.

Angelica had her jaws clenched. "Crazy," she murmured as she tilted her head and closed her eyes for a split second.

"So... not married?" Dr. Bishop asked.

Angelica was at a loss for words. She looked down at the bar, and then looked back up "Husband? ... No." She shook her head while looking to her side in a distracted stare. "A boyfriend... sort of," she said, as she looked up to meet Dr. Bishop's eye.

"Oh..." Dr. Bishop seemed a little taken aback. "What does he think of all this?"

Angelica wasn't prepared to talk about Michael. Hearing herself say he was her boyfriend was strange. It had been a while since she used that word.

"He didn't want me to come to Vegas," she replied. "He has been encouraging me to give up the story."

"I see." Dr. Bishop's eyes narrowed. "What does he do?

"He's a venture capitalist. He lives in Manhattan. He also has a home in Montana. That's where we met... Montana," she answered quick and flat.

"Oh, interesting... So you met him just recently in Montana while you were covering the story?" Dr. Bishop had lifted his chin, observing Angelica's expression curiously.

With straight lips, Angelica raised her eyebrows and nodded. "Yes, while I was there covering the mutilations. His father's ranch was the location of the first reported incident in Elberton. That one happened about ten years ago. Well, anyway, we became quite close rather fast."

Aware of how it must have sounded, moving so quickly from just meeting a few days prior to calling him her boyfriend, Angelica shifted uncomfortably. "That is unusual for me... I mean I don't usually move that quickly with someone. However... I can't explain it – we just knew."

Dr. Bishop was watching the movement of Angelica's eyes as she spoke. "No need to explain. That is wonderful. Will you be leaving D.C. and relocating to the Big Apple?"

Angelica put her glass down once she noticed she had been tightly clutching it. Self-conscious, she looked away, appearing concerned as she thought for a moment.

"No. I don't plan to leave the D.C. I have the magazine."

Dr. Bishop nodded approvingly. "Well, he is very fortunate to have met you."

Dr. Bishop's words caused Angelica to purse her lips. "Thank you. How about you... No wife or kids?"

"Not yet. So, how about we get some rest? I'm exhausted."

"Sounds good," Angelica didn't hesitate, "I'm with you." She smiled in agreement.

They were silent as they walked to the elevator. Once the door opened, they both stepped inside and remained quiet, reflective of the day and thinking about the day to follow. Dr. Bishop was also on the thirty-third floor; however his room was closer to the elevator. "Well, this is me! See you in the lobby at nine o'clock?"

"Yes. Goodnight, Marc."

Angelica continued past him and to her room. Dr. Bishop watched her as she walked down the hallway and stopped in front of her door. Angelica turned and with a quick wave of her hand, she mouthed the word "goodnight" before going in her room. Dr. Bishop pressed his lips tight and gave her a slight nod, signifying he was watching out for her safety.

Chapter Fifty-Seven

Angelica had forgotten to close the curtains before going to bed and woke before the alarm went off. She glanced over at the clock and saw that it was seven thirty-three. Now she was feeling irritated at the coincidence. Angelica rose from the bed and walked over to the large windows. Standing in front of the window, she noticed her reflection. Her eyes were puffy and tired, she looked different to herself as she glared vacantly at her more slender reflection eerily staring back at her. This new persona was entirely unfamiliar.

The sun was rising over the desert hills, creating a blood-orange glow as the light pushed through the darkness. As if it were painted with watercolours in shades of orange, red and brown between shadows of dark grey, and illuminated with yellow streaks of sunlight.

Angelica raised her arm to cover her eyes. The sun had shone over the horizon. Wearing only her dark grey bra and panties with nude lace, she sat in one of the two upholstered chairs in front of the window and lifted both legs up under her chin, wrapping her arms around them. Angelica sat peacefully, and somewhat lost, watching the bright yellow ball of heat rise up over the desert turning the sky bright red.

Angelica though about Gail and her stomach sank again, causing her to feel nauseous. She felt pressure on the back of her shoulders as the painful emotions moved down her spine. "It shouldn't have happened... Gail shouldn't have died that way," she thought aloud, shaking her head and pressing her chin into her knees. It all felt so surreal. If only she could pinch herself and wake up to realize it was just a nightmare.

The image of Gail walking Theo along the Potomac riverbank came into her mind. She then saw the image of a large man in dark clothes grabbing Gail, hitting her over the head with something in his hands and throwing her body into the river... knowing it would immediately surface and float... lifeless in the water for everyone to witness. There was no garden of flowers surrounding her as she violently left the world to join her lover -- only cold, dark waters.

Angelica once again looked out past the skyline, along the desert hills, and thought about the aerospace facility. This story was consuming her. It had invaded her life like an intruder, stealing her sense of security in the long and lonely hours of the night. And, with Gail and Matthew gone because of her involvement, her life had now forever changed. She wondered what life was going to be like without Gail. Angelica's eyes watered and a tear softly glided down her cheek.

Angelica's cell phone rang. She closed her eyes, forcing the remaining tear to drop against her body, running down the slope of her smooth, firm breast as she rose up and answered it. Carl's voice was low and thick. Carl and Gail had worked together for over twenty years and had become close friends.

"Angelica, I have news. First... they declined an interview. I was told to make a request and someone would be in touch. I asked how long would that take and got the old faithful response... it could be months."

Angelica exhaled. "Why am I not surprised?"

"Now, let me say this... just listen... okay... before you say anything in response to what I am about to tell you..."

Angelica managed the word, "Okay," through her clenched jaw, even though her throat felt closed.

"They are calling it an accidental drowning. The report says a witness claimed to see her dog pulling at the leash. He said she was struggling to keep him calm while they were walking. Apparently, Theo must have caused her to fall into the water and hit the back of her head on a sharp rock or something at some point.

Angelica blurted out, "Bullshit, Carl... Fucking bullshit! They killed her! And you know it!" Angelica's hand flew up, and she walked back over and stood in front of the window, peering out into the desert.

"Angelica, calm down," Carl admonished her. "We can't prove anything... we don't know that for sure!"

Angelica squeezed her cell phone causing the space between her knuckles to turn white. "Really? That's what you think, Carl? After what happened to Matthew Tillman? No, someone is sending me a clear message, Carl. You know in your heart Gail's dog, Theo, would never cause her to drown! Gentle Theo? Carl... Come on!"

Carl took a deep breath. "What do you want to do, Angelica?" Carl went silent.

Angelica thought for a moment. "Did you get the envelope I left on your desk?"

"Yes, what is that thing? Looks like some sort of device. I couldn't resist, I opened it."

"Carl, lock it away and keep it safe for me. I'm meeting this morning with a scientist who worked for Frances Giano, and I think she'll turn out to be a very good source. I'll be back as soon as I can."

Angelica hung up, turned around, walked over and tossed her cell phone onto the bed. She was fired up and needed to cool down. She stood there staring at her cell phone on the white sheet, contemplating. "I'll find out who killed you, Gail," she whispered.

Chapter Fifty-Eight

Downstairs, Angelica saw Dr. Bishop standing in the middle of the lobby anxiously looking around. The eight large digital columns with twelve individual screens had rotated and were now displaying shadowy silhouettes of human bodies. It was eerie, Angelica thought. It appeared as if people were trying to escape from behind the screen. Dr. Bishop had walked over and was standing beside the screen with the image of a dark hand pressed flat. As she approached, it unnerved her.

Angelica walked over behind him, leaned in toward the back of his neck and softly said, "Good morning."

Dr. Bishop swung around, visibly surprised. "Good morning!"

Dr. Bishop noticed Angelica staring at the hand... "Creepy isn't it."

Angelica gave a quick nod and then looked around the lobby noticing a woman sitting alone in a secluded area. Angelica nudged Dr. Bishop softly and pointed. Dr. Bishop turned around to see the woman in a brown silk blouse with long black hair pulled loosely into a bun. "Think that's her?" he asked.

"Probably... Let's find out." Angelica walked over to the woman sitting alone with her head lowered scanning a sheet of paper. "Hello. I'm Angelica Bradley. Are you a friend of Dr. Hamilton Howell?"

The woman looked up and stared suspiciously at Angelica before her eyes moved over to Dr. Bishop. Angelica felt slightly uncomfortable under her penetrating gaze. "Yes. I am Dr. Olivia Wallace," the woman said, as she stood up and extended her frail hand.

Dr. Bishop stepped around Angelica and took charge by shaking her hand first. "Hello, Dr. Wallace... I am Dr. Marc Bishop."

Dr. Wallace nodded. Angelica sat down in the chair across from the woman, and Dr. Bishop quickly took a seat beside Angelica.

Angelica waited for Dr. Wallace to sit down again before starting the interview. Dr. Wallace slowly looked around as if she had lost something before taking a seat. She glanced around the hotel apprehensively. It was obvious she was nervous and somewhat disoriented.

"Thank you for meeting with us, Dr. Wallace," Angelica said. "As I'm sure Hamilton mentioned... I am an investigative journalist, I have a magazine, the *Liberator*, and my friend here is an archaeologist for the Smithsonian. We are interested in Francis Giano and the aerospace facility." Angelica was patiently speaking in a soft tone which was hard to hear over the noise of the hotel guests.

Dr. Wallace's eyed gleamed. "An archaeologist with the Smithsonian... fascinating! Yes, Hamilton briefed me yesterday over the phone. Where would you like for me to start?"

Angelica pulled out her recorder, notepad and pen. "First of all, if you will, please tell me your area of expertise."

Dr. Wallace looked around the hotel again and then back to Angelica. "I am a Physicist. I earned my Ph.D in experimental nuclear physics."

Angelica was making notes on her pad, and glanced up curiously. "Can I ask why you keep looking around the hotel? Are you concerned that you are under surveillance?"

Dr. Wallace shifted in her seat. "Ms. Bradley, I speak openly in regards to my work at ASTIC."

Angelica glanced up for a moment, and then continued writing on her pad. "That is Giano's facility?"

"Yes, Aerospace Sciences and Technology International Corporation: A-S-T-I-C. They are well aware of my actions. I tend to look around out of habit more than concern. But there is no doubt we are being watched as we speak," Dr. Wallace stated confidently.

Dr. Bishop felt a chill run through him as he slowly looked around the lobby. No one looked out-of-the-ordinary, so he turned back around to catch Angelica peering at him. Dr. Bishop shrugged his shoulders.

Angelica continued. "Dr. Hamilton Howell said you worked at the base on Mars. Is that correct?"

Dr. Wallace didn't flinch. "Yes." Her face went flat.

"Okay, first -- what can you tell me about Francis Giano?"

"I've met Frances once," Dr. Wallace said. "He is a brilliant man. Very reclusive, however. I worked in the laboratory at his facility here in Nevada mainly on antigravity technology. We worked on reverse engineering ET crafts during the first few years of my tenure there."

Dr. Bishop was clearly fascinated and quickly asked the next question. "What other projects were you involved in?"

Dr. Wallace smiled devilishly. "Are you referring to the blueprints?"

Dr. Bishop nodded. He wasn't entirely sure what she meant from her sarcastic tone, but he was going to play along and hope she was referring to the ancient blueprints from 'The Chamber of Knowledge'. "Yes, the blueprints." Dr. Bishop examined Dr. Wallace's face.

Dr. Wallace continued. "Well, how else would we have figured out how to teleport to Mars? They don't just hand over knowledge of that magnitude without expecting something in return, you know." Dr. Wallace's eyes grew grave. "However, we've become weary of their barters. They don't exactly hold up to their end of the bargain, you see."

Angelica was confused. "Who are... they?"

"The ETs... the ones interested in our resources, and that isn't limited to non-organic minerals and elements, if you know what I mean."

Angelica thought for a moment. "Humans?"

"Yes." Dr. Wallace frowned as she nodded.

Angelica made a quick note in her pad and then sat up straight in her chair. "Okay, Mars... Tell me what you did there."

Dr. Bishop leaned in closer. The noise in the casino was distracting, he thought.

Dr. Wallace was silent for a moment. She appeared to be in deep though. Angelica and Dr. Bishop stared in unison at Dr. Wallace. Dr. Wallace continued. "I worked on a top clearance project at the base called, 'Project Cetus'. There were only a few of us working on it. No one else knew about this particular project... All the other scientists were there to work on much more benign projects and less secretive... Well, a little less secretive," Dr. Wallace laughed. "Anyway, it was an unpleasant experience, and that is why I left. They've labeled me a whistleblower now. I've been called crazy and unstable. They have tried to discredit me and have essentially destroyed my career. I think the only reason I am still alive is they have managed to ruin my reputation and now I appear to be just an old disgruntled ex-employee. And if they killed me, well, then maybe some might conclude that I was in fact telling the truth. You see?"

Angelica nodded. "How did you travel to Mars?"

"Unwillingly! I was taken by force! I was blindfolded."

Angelica arched her neck in surprise. "Blindfolded?"

"Yes," Dr. Wallace said with a straight face.

"Can you give me more details around how all that happened?" Angelica asked.

"Well, I was taken to a room and I sat there for several hours. Then after what felt like an eternity, I finally heard people coming, and then I heard the door open. I remember feeling an injection in the side of my neck. I was out for an unknown amount of time and when I finally awoke I raised my head, and boy did my head hurt like hell. I realized that I was sitting at a table with the blindfold still over my eyes. A deep, almost metallic male voice began asking strange questions like: what color is a lemon? Who is the President? Felt like it was some type of mind control procedure. And obviously, it was. Then, I remember another injection that gave me the same sensation. I now believe the injection induced memory loss."

Dr. Bishop interrupted. "They were distorting your memory. How long did it take you to remember these details? Do you feel you have recovered all of the memories from that experience?"

Dr. Wallace glanced down and thought for a moment. "It took a year for it to start to come together... Only time will tell if anything else surfaces."

Angelica looked sympathetically at Dr. Wallace who appeared deeply wounded from the emotional scars. "Please continue with how you were taken to Mars," she whispered as she glanced at Dr. Bishop to notice his mouth was slightly open as if he were going to speak. Angelica took a deep breath and shifted in her seat.

Dr. Wallace glanced around anxiously. "Well, after the mind control receptivity testing, I remember being in the back of a vehicle of some sort, maybe a bus or van. I could hear voices and feel the motion of traveling. I'm not certain how long I traveled, but it didn't feel like it was for very long. When the vehicle stopped, the door opened and I felt someone grab my arm and lift me. They escorted me out of the vehicle. At this time, my blindfold had loosened and slid slightly down. I tried to look around. It was dark... however I saw there were others blindfolded, as well. I had sensed the others while in the vehicle. Then we were escorted into a facility. I was taken into another room and they sat me down on a metal bench. I recall looking around through the opening of my blindfold and seeing an armed security guard. We were all told to keep quiet and not ask questions."

"Oh my!" Dr. Bishop blurted. Angelica looked over at him curiously before gazing back at Dr. Wallace.

"Suddenly," Dr. Wallace continued, "I felt a sharp pinch on the back of my neck and I was out. I'm not sure how long I was unconscious." Dr. Wallace went silent and looked up in the air. "Had to be a while... When I came to, I was drowsy. Those shots have a strong effect on you. My blindfold was gone and I looked around and realized I was in a small room, wearing a white hospital gown."

"That had to be terrifying!" Angelica said as she raised her hand to her mouth.

"There was a round window in the room," Dr. Wallace continued, "about thirty or so inches in diameter. As I walked over to look out the window... well, at first, it looked like the Nevada desert. I realized it was not any desert on earth - it was different."

"How was it different?" Angelica asked.

"The sky was baby blue and the geography was similar, however it obviously wasn't Earth. I had seen pictures of Mars, and after seeing a strange tan, red, and brown camouflaged four wheeler Polaris style jeep driving towards what looked like large eco-structures within glass domes... I knew I was there. *Stunned* -- that would be a good word to describe my emotions at the time."

Angelica interrupted her. "Did you say the sky was baby blue?" Angelica then looked over at Dr. Bishop with her brow furrowed.

"Yes," Dr. Wallace said flatly and confidently. Dr. Wallace then stopped and looked down to her lap.

"And..." Dr. Bishop said. His voice cut sharply through the air. He was anxious for Dr. Wallace to continue.

Dr. Wallace looked back up and directly at Dr. Bishop. Her eyes were grim. "It all was happening so fast. Well, as I looked around I saw there were several facilities enclosed in glass domes and a massive pyramid structure, much as you see in Egypt. I soon learned there were underground facilities running throughout the planet – we have now renovated and inhabited much of them. I was told these facilities are where the ancient Martian culture eventually had to live. They had moved underground. Fascinating isn't it?"

Always a skeptic, Angelica was struggling to believe Dr. Wallace. "Who lived there?"

"The civilization that once inhabited the planet," Dr. Wallace said, as if it sounded completely normal.

Angelica wrinkled her forehead and observed Dr. Wallace's face.

Angelica glanced over at Dr. Bishop. He was smiling as if he had suspected it.

"We've been going to Mars for several decades, Ms. Bradley."

Angelica tapped her pen against her cheek. "Okay. Go on."

"Well, I later learned you could breathe the air after you had undergone a slight adjustment period. The atmosphere on Mars is similar to Earth. The sky is blue, quite extraordinary. You see, the photos you have seen of Mars are altered," Dr. Wallace raised her eyebrows. "You just have to adjust to the atmosphere slowly, I learned."

"That's interesting," Angelica said. "Please continue." She lowered her shoulders and relaxed back into the chair.

"I soon found out the room with the round window was to be my bunker," Dr. Wallace told her. "There was a door with a control panel. On the panel was a large button labeled "CALL"... so I pushed it, obviously. After a few minutes, a man in a black uniform appeared with a holstered gun; once again... all the security personnel are armed. He entered the room and said 'Come with me, Dr. Wallace.'"

"Wow!" Angelica exclaimed. "What happened next?"

"I didn't appreciate being told what to do," Dr. Wallace continued. "However I didn't want to get shot, so I complied. I was taken to yet another room where I was pushed and instructed to put on a silver and white laboratory suit and over it -- a white lab coat. I was then taken into a brightly lit room and seated at a table."

"What was their purpose," Angelica asked. "Did they want to interrogate you?"

"A few minutes later," Dr. Wallace said, "a very serious looking gray-haired older man in a white lab coat and with a German accent came in with a very polished man in a black suit. I was told that I was brought there by a space craft to work on an important mission and everything that I saw and experienced there was above top secret. "This is the most important thing you will ever do in your life," he said. I was chosen because of my expertise. He went on to tell me in an arrogant tone, 'It is a great responsibility to be a part of such a mission and an honor.'" Dr. Wallace lowered her voice in attempt to mimic the man.

"He informed me that I would be well compensated. I sat staring at the German scientist across the table in disbelief. I was in shock, as you can imagine. The man in the black suit just stood in the corner and watched us. He was creepy -- almost robotic. Well anyway, after that little welcoming speech, I realized I was contracted against my will to work on a top secret project to continue the construction of a teleportation chamber."

"How did you feel about living and working under those conditions?" Angelica asked. Her voice sounded anxious. Angelica rolled her eyes. The thought of being taken against her will and treated like a prisoner unnerved her.

"The facilities were quite comfortable and modern," Dr. Wallace responded, "so I made the best of it and did my job without argument."

Angelica stopped Dr. Wallace. "Interesting. Did you see any other individuals while there -- outside of ASTIC personnel or the man in the black suit, such as top government officials?"

"Maybe," Dr. Wallace told her. "It was hard to distinguish who wasn't working for ASTIC."

"Did other scientist know why they were there? Meaning, did others appear to be under mind control, as well?" Angelica probed.

Dr. Wallace frowned, then squinted and quickly shook her head. Before answering Angelica's question she looked around the hotel again.

Angelica was beginning to wonder if Dr. Wallace was unstable. "Are you okay, Dr. Wallace?"

"Yes, mind control," Dr. Wallace answered. "Yes, all of the scientists were probably under mind control. I recall one of the scientists stating that we were saving the world." Dr. Wallace went silent and looked confused.

"Okay, please continue," Angelica suggested.

"Frankly, I just wanted to go home... get back to Earth, and safely. Toward the end, I was exhausted, they worked you to death. I was sleep deprived, and thinking back, I believe I was under mind control most if not the entire time. I'll never get those neck injections out of my mind." Dr. Wallace held eye contact with Angelica. Angelica looked down at Dr.

Wallace's frail hands, tightly squeezed together in her lap.

Dr. Bishop was impatiently waiting for an opportunity to ask Dr. Wallace a question. Angelica looked over and noticed Dr. Bishop was thumping his fingers on his leg. "Do you have a question, Dr. Bishop?"

Without hesitation, Dr. Bishop glanced at Angelica and then immediately to Dr. Wallace. "What exactly are we doing there, Doctor?"

Dr. Wallace turned fractionally toward him. "Exploring... Mining... Researching... Building. We live in a duality... Welcome to reality, Doctor Bishop."

"The more advanced a race becomes in our galaxy," Dr. Wallace said, "the further they move out."

Angelica looked up from her pad at Dr. Wallace as she continued.

"While there, I heard about ship activity all over our little celestial neighborhood."

Dr. Wallace hesitated, searching for words. "You know, there are supposedly more ET races out there than we can count. The government will never give full disclosure. I heard one scientist with ASTIC say the general public would continue to stay in the dark... they'll never know the truth. That makes anyone that attempts to enlighten society extremely dangerous to them. And that makes the three of us marked individuals in extreme danger. They will use every means possible to discredit you, Angelica. Then they will kill those around you that are on the periphery of

The Bovine Connection

the research to slow you down and send you a message. And if that doesn't work, they will kill you."

Angelica's eyes grew wide. She thought about Matthew and Gail as she looked over at Dr. Bishop, before asking Dr. Wallace another question. "Do you believe the government is involved with the Mars project?"

"A branch of it, I've gathered... It's very complicated, you see."

"How so?" Angelica asked.

"Well," Dr. Wallace said, "there is a group that deals with the ET's... a very secret and covert group. They supposedly operate under a hidden power structure, above the constraints of the law and above the White House. I don't believe the President even knows."

Angelica leaned back and thought for a minute. "Have you heard of John Kaye?"

Dr. Wallace looked up for a moment. "No, I don't recall hearing that name before. Who is John Kaye?"

"He is the Chairman of the Ways and Means Committee. Has an office at the White House, powerful man. He's connected to Giano somehow. I'd like to find out what his connection is."

Dr. Wallace smirked. "Well, obviously: money."

Angelica leaned back and held her breath for a second. She knew in her heart, this had nothing to do with John Kaye, she was after something bigger.

Then Angelica reflected back on her conversation with Dr. Goolrick and Dr. Hamilton Howell. Dr. Wallace was fidgeting and glanced around. Dr. Bishop sat back while watching Angelica curiously.

Angelica looked at her watch. "How are you on time?"

"Oh, I'm fine, dear," Dr. Wallace smiled.

"Good. You have an amazing story. In my entire career, I have never met anyone who's claimed to have gone to Mars." Angelica shook her head. "You are fascinating, Dr. Wallace. Thank you for meeting with us and telling your story. Fascinating... Wouldn't you say, Dr. Bishop?"

"Yes, oh yes, extraordinary," he agreed.

Angelica looked back over at Dr. Wallace. "What do you know about the hybrids?" Angelica asked coolly.

"The hybridization programs... hum." Dr. Wallace appeared restless, repositioning in her seat.

Dr. Wallace took a deep breath. "The greyish beings are creating a hybrid race to occupy an earth-like planet. You know, humans are considered genetic royalty, from what I hear, so I speculate... they just want our DNA."

She is obviously a member of Goolrick's secret research team, she thought. Angelica peered up from her pad. "That seems to be a popular theory. Okay. What about implant devices, say from a human group. Would you happen to know anything about that?"

After reading Angelica's body language, Dr. Wallace narrowed her eyes suspiciously. "Were you implanted with a device, dear?"

Angelica looked uncomfortable.

Dr. Wallace nodded her head and puckered her mouth. "I see, well, if one were implanted with a device by... let's say a non-alien group, then you are more than likely an abductee and that would make you a hybrid, so I've heard."

Dr. Wallace glanced over at Dr. Bishop. He appeared puzzled, and was staring at Angelica. "Yes, you heard me correctly Dr. Bishop."

Dr. Bishop shook his head and looked at Dr. Wallace, bewildered.

Dr. Wallace continued. "The secretive group I just spoke of is a branch of the military, however, they go way beyond the military as we know it. They report directly to the top, and are funded by a black budget, embedded within the air force. Do not quote me on this," Dr. Wallace said firmly, before she continued. Angelica nodded.

"It's an implanted tracking device," Dr. Wallace explained. "It's used to extract information from those who are being taken and monitored so we can better understand the alien's agenda. The aliens have clearly gone off the grid and are going way beyond what was agreed to. The military is losing control."

Angelica had gathered that much from her meeting with Dr. Goolrick and Dr. Hamilton Howell. "Well, that is interesting." Angelica stated, for lack of a better word.

Dr. Bishop appeared concerned as he observed Angelica. Her voice cracked as she spoke. "So, back to the project... If I understand you correctly... while you were working on Project Cetus, you worked on a teleportation chamber - to go where, exactly?"

"Yes, you heard correctly," Dr. Wallace chuckled.

"It is used to travel between Earth and Mars, but only for a select few. There are special crafts that take passengers and cargo."

Dr. Wallace smiled sarcastically. "The teleportation chamber or -- if you will -- 'The Jumper,' is top secret." The casino's noise had picked up. The sound of the slot machines rang out in the background just before the sound of quarters pounded the metal baskets.

Angelica raised her voice over the background noise. "This all just sounds so unbelievable." Angelica put her pen down. Dr. Bishop watched anxiously as Dr. Wallace glanced around the hotel.

Dr. Bishop straightened his back. "Dr. Wallace, there was a scroll found that told of portals opening... I'll call them doorways, opening for travel between time and space. It was from 'The Tomb of The Visitor', or rather "The Chamber of Knowledge'. I believe Giano purchased it to build the teleportation chamber."

Angelica looked at Dr. Wallace. "Okay, what is Giano's objective, I wonder?"

"I do not know. Maybe it's about Eplar." Dr. Bishop scoffed.

"Yes, Dr. Bishop, you are on to something there. 'The scroll or blueprint,' as we called it, is for teleportation technology... After it was deciphered... we built 'The Jumper' just as we were told." Dr. Wallace's shoulders dropped revealing her frailty. As she repositioned in her seat, her bun rubbed against the back of the upholstered chair and several strands of black and gray hair fell loose.

The Bovine Connection

Dr. Bishop had an idea. "What about the teleportation chamber at the facility here? If we could get inside... you know how to operate it. We go to Mars," he announced. Angelica laughed spontaneously.

Dr. Wallace frowned... "Yes, if we could get inside and to the chamber without being seen."

Angelica's face straightened and she bit down on the edge of her thumb nail. "Dr. Bishop, I'm trying to follow you. Say we get to Mars. Once there... what's next?" She laughed sarcastically.

Dr. Bishop sat back, appearing to give up on the idea. "Well, you wanted to go inside the facility so why not go to Mars, once inside?"

Angelica chuckled as she shot a look of bewilderment at Dr. Wallace. "I wanted to go inside upon approval of an interview. I never said I wanted to break in, Dr. Bishop."

Angelica then appeared to contemplate. She looked around the room and then back to Dr. Wallace. "Teleportation chamber... and you know where it is. Could you get us in the facility, Dr. Wallace... if we went tonight? Perhaps, just for a few photos." Angelica asked.

Dr. Bishop perked up, his eyes grew wide. Dr. Wallace jerked... "Oh, no," she said. "Not a good idea." Dr. Wallace shook her head back and forth. "We will be killed! There are armed guards in SUVs everywhere on the property; they'll spot you a mile away. I thought you were speaking hypothetically." Dr. Wallace laughed nervously. "You two are nuts!"

Both Angelica and Dr. Bishop appeared disappointed. Dr. Wallace pursed her lips and tapped her foot on the floor.

"Well then, where is the facility located?" Angelica looked sharply at Dr. Wallace. "I want to see it."

Dr. Wallace took a deep breath and thought for another moment. She looked around the hotel, squeezing her hands tighter. "Perhaps... I could show you. What the hell. I'll contact my friend at the base and see what I can do."

Angelica smiled at Dr. Bishop but Dr. Wallace wasn't smiling. Dr. Bishop suddenly appeared to be deep in thought. He sat back confidently. "Say we were to get in and see the chamber, you know how to use it..."

Dr. Wallace bellowed out, "You two are brave -- but nuts!"

Chapter Fifty-Nine

After working on the story back in her room for several hours, Angelica closed her laptop. She raised her fingers to her temple. She was anxious and second guessing whether they should try to enter the base, she knew she needed to rest to clear her mind. She slipped off her clothes, pulled the sheets back, and lay down onto the bed. She quickly drifted into REM sleep.

Suddenly she found herself standing at the edge of a sapphire blue lake, shimmering with sparkles of sunlight. The grass under her feet was short, green, and lush.

Angelica looked around, unsure of where she was. The landscape was unfamiliar. She had never seen a place as exquisite. Angelica took a step back and looked up in awe of the calm, perfect blue sky... the landscape was vibrant and mesmerizing. She decided she must be dreaming.

Angelica looked across the lake to the buildings on the other side. They were unusually shaped modern white structures of mostly glass. The material in between the glass was shiny and sleek.

The air was pleasant and fresh, no smog... no pollutants... pure. It felt like spring. Angelica filled her lungs and then allowed it to flow back up through her chest. It was intoxicating, leaving her feeling high.

Angelica suddenly sensed someone standing behind her, and quickly turned around and gasped. A young boy around the age of six or seven with large black eyes was smiling endearingly at her. Oddly, she could recognize some of her own unique features... the shape of his mouth and the high cheekbones that were a distinct genetic trait of her lineage. But the boy was clearly non-human and a bit frightening. His skin was translucent grey. His frame was thin but with well-defined muscles and bluish veins visible just under the dermis. The child's head was proportionately bigger to his body but he exuded a majestic and confident aura.

"Hello," she said as she smiled apprehensively. The boy stepped forward, appearing nervous. Angelica stepped back startled.

"Hello," he said while tilting his head wondering why she was acting strangely.

Angelica stood statuesque, examining him. She smiled and extended her hand as she took a step cautiously toward him. He appeared to be harmless. "Don't be afraid. I won't harm you. Can you tell me where I am? I think I am lost."

The boy walked methodically over to Angelica. "You don't remember? He tiled his head once more, curiously. You are on Eplar."

Angelica flinched as her heartbeat accelerated. "Where did you say?" She was frozen with shock. "No, you are mistaken. That is far away from..." Angelica shook her head and lifted her fingers to her lips. "Eplar?"

The boy appeared confused. "Yes."

Angelica took a deep breath and looked back towards the buildings. "What city is that?" She pointed.

The boy smiled and tilted his head. "You don't remember?" Angelica shook her head with a blank expression. "Where is your family?"

The boy smiled warmly with patience, appearing to take pity on Angelica. "You are my family, you are my mother."

Angelica started to shake her head and took another step back. "No, you are mistaken. I am not your mother," Angelica quickly confirmed while noting his unusual eyes; they were so large and black, but felt sincere. She looked at his smooth head, his features... he was definitely not human, well, not entirely, she thought.

"You do look familiar. Do I know you?" Her shoulders dropped.

The boy moved closer. "You are my mother, Angelica. Do you not remember me?" the boy asked, as he lowered his head.

"Wait, yes I do," Angelica quickly replied. She didn't want to upset the boy. "Do you mind helping me? I seem to have lost some of my memory. I do remember you, I just don't remember myself. I think I just need to rest and I will feel better." Angelica raised her hand to her temple. "Will you help me remember things?" she asked carefully, in almost a whisper.

The boy's face lifted. "I was worried about you. You left me on the transporter vessel and said you would be back soon. You didn't come back soon... as you said. I couldn't find you. I waited..." His voice sounded wounded.

Angelica lowered her chin and knelt down onto her knee. Her eyes were wide. She opened her arms and extended them. "It is all right. I am here now."

The boy rushed over and hugged her tightly. Angelica smelled his neck and observed his flawless grey hairless skin. "You are so perfect," she whispered, as she ran her hand softly down his cheek.

Angelica felt warmth in her chest. She was mystified by the revelation that she felt love for the boy.

The boy stepped back, away from Angelica and pointed up to the sky. "We are all connected and we are made of light. Don't you remember, Mother?" Angelica peered up at the sky.

Angelica took a deep breath. The sound of the word mother was strange to her, and it was impossible, she thought.

The boy took her hand and squeezed it. Angelica looked down and observed his long sinewy fingers in hers. He had no thumbs. She pulled him back and observed his face. Angelica was beginning to remember him.

Angelica leaned back and placed both of her hands on the top of the boy's arms, just below his shoulders. She looked into his large oval shaped black eyes, so dark that she could barely discern where his pupils began, and she could see her reflection. "How long have I been away from you?" she asked softly.

The boy suddenly appeared sad. He lowered his chin before looking back up and glaring deep into her eyes. "A long time."

Angelica frowned. "I'm sorry I left you."

The Bovine Connection

The alarm sounded. Angelica shot up startled. She needed to hurry and get ready and meet Dr. Bishop and Dr. Wallace out in front of the hotel, so she tried her best to shake her dream that was the most vivid and real of her life.

Chapter Sixty

Angelica stared out of the passenger window into the darkness at the baron Nevada terrain, preoccupied with thoughts about the boy from her dream. Angelica was deeply conflicted over her emotions. She couldn't stop thinking about him. She felt incomplete.

Dr. Wallace glanced over at Angelica. Angelica was quietly peering through the glass with her knuckles folded under her chin. "Having second thoughts?" Dr. Wallace asked.

Angelica looked over at her. "No," she responded, her expression sullen.

They pulled off the paved highway after about a forty minute drive and onto a dirt road with a noticeably large white metal sign shining in the headlights of Dr. Wallace's red Ford Explorer. The sign simply read, "No Trespassing."

Dr. Wallace turned off the headlights and drove slowly, relying only on the light of the full moon to guide them.

Dr. Bishop's stomach was upset and feeling queasy, and he instinctively rubbed at it. It had been a quiet drive. No one said anything... And there was no doubt that they were all second guessing their decision to go to the facility.

Angelica thought about her mother in Asheville. She wondered if she'd ever see her again. If her mother knew she was preparing to break into a facility in the middle of the desert with armed security ready to shoot to kill, she'd probably fall over of a heart attack, she thought. Then there was Michael. What a fool she was. She could be safe with him in Manhattan, in his arms... making love. Angelica reflected back on their evening together in Elberton when he whispered in her ear, "The true strength of one's character is their resilience." She still wondered if he was referring to her.

Angelica felt apprehensive and the tension in the SUV was palpable. It was clear to her that she had lost her mind. Angelica looked over at Dr. Wallace to speak, but no words came out. Dr. Wallace stopped and turned off the engine. "We'll leave the Explorer here behind this ridge."

Angelica glanced back at Dr. Bishop in the backseat. He didn't look so well, she thought. "Everything okay, Dr. Bishop?"

Dr. Bishop looked nervous. "Yep," he said, but obviously he was not. He appeared extremely anxious.

They sat in silence for a moment, and then stepped out onto the dry desert soil. Dr. Wallace opened the rear hatch as Dr. Bishop stepped around to assist her. Angelica walked towards the other side of the ridge where the lights of the ASTIC Aerospace Facility glowed down in the valley.

Dr. Wallace took a gun from a dark blue back pack in the trunk and handed it to Dr. Bishop. It was a black military issue Colt M45. "Best handgun for close quarter combat," Dr. Wallace said with confidence and an air of authority.

Dr. Bishop looked at it as if it were made of radioactive material, and then stuck it in the back of his jeans. Dr. Wallace put the back pack on and then closed the hatch. They both walked over to Angelica, where she was standing at the edge, peering out at the brightly lit white metal buildings.

Angelica's hands were trembling. "How far is it... do you think?" Her voice shook. She was visibly nervous.

Dr. Bishop diverted his eyes and said dryly, "Maybe a half mile or less."

A long runway extended out from an aircraft hangar. Angelica's eyes widened as she observed the metal gate with barbed wire around the perimeter of the facility. She dropped her shoulders, and took a deep breath. "We're really doing this aren't we?"

Angelica looked Dr. Bishop in the eyes, he was clearly as nervous as she was. "Where would the teleportation chamber be located in the facility?" Angelica asked bluntly.

Dr. Wallace pointed to an area of the building. "There... under that section... There is also an underground facility so you're only seeing a small percentage of it."

Dr. Bishop appeared concerned. "I forgot to ask... How long will it take us to teleport, if we get in the facility and to the chamber alive?" He exhaled. "Can we travel together?"

Angelica looked over at Dr. Bishop from the corner of her eyes. "Good question!"

Dr. Wallace tilted her head. "If we make it to the chamber alive, once we start the teleportation, you'll feel as if you've jumped through a tunnel. The teleportation process will occur within a spit second, one second there, the next on Mars. And, it fits four, Dr. Bishop."

"Oh," Dr. Bishop put his hand over his stomach. Dr. Wallace looked over and smiled at Angelica, amused by his sudden onset of nerves.

"Theoretically, we are traveling between the extra dimensions, hyperspace. We will essentially be moving between time and space, between dimensions... On the macro-level, Dr. Bishop. The chamber creates a wormhole and we will be pulled through it."

"That is extraordinary, Dr. Wallace!" Angelica blurted, appearing shocked.

"Yes, indeed... think of yourself gliding down the highest water slide if you want a real world comparison."

Angelica sighed. "Look there!" She pointed. "Security!"

Angelica looked over at Dr. Bishop. His eyes were grave. He said in a dry whisper, "Maybe we should turn back... I'm not feeling it."

She shot him an irritated look, "Are you serious?"

Dr. Bishop shrugged his shoulders, wide eyed as he watched the guards get into a white SUV.

As the SUV drove off, Dr. Wallace stepped forward. "We should go now! Stay right with me." Dr. Wallace led the way down the hill toward the valley. "We are going to that door right there." She pointed to a door in the middle of the building. "An old colleague of mine has left the security gate unlocked for us and is waiting behind that door. He's agreed to let us in. Of course, I think he is less than thrilled about it."

"I have three of my old white lab coats rolled up in my back pack. We'll put those on and then I will lead the way through the facility. I have an old badge. As long as I have it on, no one should stop and look too closely at it. Just stay behind me and talk quietly to each other, paying no attention to anyone. Remember, you are scientists and you are supposed to be there."

Angelica stepped over the desert brush, right behind Dr. Wallace. "Got it," she stated sternly. Dr. Bishop nodded his head anxiously and stayed in step with Angelica.

Angelica was impressed that Dr. Wallace had done what she said... and worked out the details after she left the hotel before coming to pick them up. Angelica glanced over at Dr. Wallace. Dr. Wallace didn't appear as frightened as her and Marc, she thought.

As they moved into the valley, Angelica stumbled over something. Dr. Bishop quickly grabbed her arm to keep her from falling.

Angelica looked up and smiled. "Thank you, Marc!"

"You're welcome!" he whispered politely.

Dr. Wallace was worried the SUV would make its way back around before they could get to the gate. "We need to move faster." They picked up their pace. Angelica's heart was pounding from exertion and adrenalin. "Look, there's the SUV; it backed up. Stop!" Dr. Wallace extended her hand out behind her. "Down!" They all stopped and obeyed her command.

"What are we going to do?" Angelica looked at Dr. Wallace, worried.

"Wait to see if they get out or drive off." They stayed as still as statues until the SUV finally pulled away. Dr. Wallace reached into her pocket and grabbed her cell phone. Angelica glanced down to notice, and shot Dr. Wallace an incredulous look, clearly shocked at the timing of a phone call.

"I almost forget to text my friend that we're here," she whispered. Angelica pursed her lips and glanced away.

Dr. Bishop reached his hand out in an effort to steady himself as he sat down. When doing so, he placed it on something firm and rubbery. Dr. Bishop jerked his hand up. "Holy hell…?"

Dr. Wallace looked back at Dr. Bishop as he was looking down to get a better look. "Quiet!" she whispered darkly. Angelica quickly turned around. "Everything okay, Dr. Bishop?"

Dr. Bishop didn't respond. Then suddenly, they all heard something move beside them. Dr. Bishop leaped into the air, and yelled. "Snake!" Angelica jumped, pushing into Dr. Wallace causing her to fall forward.

"Holy shit!" Angelica squealed. Dr. Bishop grabbed Angelica's arm and pulled her as he leapt up and started to run. Dr. Wallace ran as quickly as she could behind them. "Right there… the gate door!" Dr. Wallace said in a heavy breath, while panting.

They stopped at the cyclone style chain link fence. The door was unlocked and slightly open. Dr. Wallace pushed slowly through as Angelica and Dr. Bishop followed behind her. "Look to your left. There is the main door we need to get through! Stay with me and run... Now!" Dr. Wallace snapped. Angelica was feeling increasingly worried as she hurried behind her.

The door was approximately a hundred feet from the security fence. At the door, Dr. Wallace knocked two firm times and the door opened. "Dr. Wallace..." a voice whispered.

"Hello, Dr. Sayre, thank you!"

Dr. Sayre looked at Angelica and Dr. Bishop and then back to Dr. Wallace. "Be careful!"

Dr. Sayre turned and walked away.

"Well, he was friendly," Angelica commented sarcastically as she wiped the sweat from her brow.

Dr. Wallace whispered. "He put his life in danger to help us. He also manipulated all of the security cameras. The guards are viewing footage of this time last night. Let's hope, for his sake, it never gets traced back to him."

Angelica looked around, noting a new thumping sensation in her chest. "How did you get him to agree?" Angelica looked amazed.

Dr. Bishop's eyes were wide. He was watching Dr. Wallace as she took the white lab coats out of the backpack and unrolled them. She handed one to Angelica and then one to him before putting hers on. Dr. Wallace took a deep breath and turned. "Let's just say he's disgruntled... This way... Remember what I said: you are supposed to be here, you are scientists."

They stepped out from the small hall where they had come in through the emergency exit door. Dr. Wallace led the way down a long hallway past several doors. They entered a hallway of interior windows to view inside what appeared to be small laboratories. Every so often someone would turn to look their way and see Angelica and Dr. Bishop closely following behind Dr. Wallace, engaged in conversation as if they were discussing something important.

"Here we are." Dr. Wallace stepped up in front of the sign that read in bold letters... '*Private. Authorized Personnel Only.*' When Dr. Wallace put her hand on the knob, Angelica looked up at the security card scanner and then down at Dr. Wallace's hand. The door was cracked slightly open. Dr. Wallace smirked. "Dr. Sayre."

Dr. Bishop looked around and behind them to make sure no one was watching as he followed them inside.

Dr. Wallace stepped back and made sure the door closed and locked behind them. They were standing inside a large warehouse with metal walls. Metal cage style walkways crossed above their heads.

"Follow me this way." Dr. Wallace started toward a large titanium round dome in the middle of the warehouse about twenty feet in diameter and twelve feet high.

The dome looked familiar to Dr. Bishop. "That almost looks like a flying saucer."

"Yes, it was designed according to the blueprints. There are four seats inside and a control panel. Come, let's get inside." Dr. Wallace pushed a button and the side hatch opened. It raised up above their heads and stairs smoothly glided down for them to step up into the chamber.

Once inside, Angelica looked at Dr. Bishop. They were both in awe. The interior walls were shiny and black, and there were no windows. The lighting was dim with a pulsating florescent neon blue light circling the interior. There were four black chairs with gold lights pulsating on and off. The chairs were in two rows positioned in the middle of the chamber.

Dr. Bishop stepped over and leaned down to observe the control panel. "Quite complicated."

Dr. Wallace nodded. "All constructed from the alien blueprints," she announced.

Dr. Bishop rubbed his hand across the headrest of the black chair. "Alien's don't use seatbelts, I see."

"The craft would not be leaving the ground, only the passengers, Dr. Bishop," Dr. Wallace cracked a smile at Angelica.

Dr. Bishop stepped over to the control panel on the left side of the armrest of the first seat and looked at Dr. Wallace. "Your seat?"

"Yes," Dr. Wallace appeared anxious. She looked around. "Just as I remember... Everyone take a seat.

"How does that work, Dr. Wallace?" Angelica was curious.

"Much like a navigation system in your car... You key in the coordinates," she replied.

Angelica and Dr. Bishop leaned over to watch. "You take this dial and turn it to the location you are attempting to reach. See how a map of the solar system appears on the screen? As you turn this dial, it highlights the area as it moves across it. You stop on your destination... you see?

We have stopped on Mars. It has been engineered to communicate with the other teleportation chamber there. Once you position it on Mars, you will see the words 'Cydonia Chamber' appear on the screen here. We will then confirm that this is the correct destination. I will push this button to accept. Then we wait for the five-to-one countdown. This is how it calibrates and configures the chamber. When it gets to one, the walls will become invisible and it will say that we are ready for teleportation. At that moment, you will see sparks of light, like stars appearing all around you... So, everyone sit back and relax and prepare for travel." Dr. Wallace appeared a bit excited.

Dr. Bishop instantly cringed. Angelica bit down on her thumbnail, a nervous habit she was doing a lot lately. She glanced back at Dr. Bishop, sitting directly behind Dr. Wallace. He was leaning all the way back in his chair squeezing the armrest with his eyes tightly closed, as if he were preparing for some type of turbulence.

Angelica took a deep breath. "Will we be in the same seats when we get to the other side?"

"Yes. These seats are designed to read your individual DNA and communicate it to the other chamber. Highly advanced technology, Ms. Bradley," Dr. Wallace said. Angelica glanced down and noticed the gold lights had sped up and appeared to be scanning her body.

"Oh!" Angelica uttered.

Dr. Wallace looked over at Angelica. "It's compiling your DNA data."

"What are we to expect once we get to the other chamber?" Angelica's voice shook.

"Or who?" Dr. Bishop asked, his face taut with fear.

Dr. Wallace looked over to Angelica. "If we are lucky... no one. The areas where the chambers are held are usually unoccupied unless someone is preparing for teleportation. Let's hope the flight isn't overbooked."

Suddenly they heard a whooshing sound. Dr. Wallace looked around at Angelica and smiled sheepishly. A computerized female voice appeared in a slow methodical tone. "Ready for teleportation... Five, four, three, two, one..."

Dr. Bishop squeezed down harder onto the armrest as the room filled with static electricity. Angelica glanced down at her hands as they were starting to disappear. The matter of her physical body appeared to be separating and she felt a strong vibration that shook her bones. Everything around her, including herself, seemed to separate and turn into what appeared to be tiny dots. Just as Dr. Wallace described, she saw a bright flash of light, and then immediately began spiraling through a shimmering tunnel. Angelica couldn't see the others but she felt their presences with her.

Angelica heard a popping sound as she felt the sensation of every molecule of her body connect back together in solid form. She looked around to see Dr. Wallace rubbing her head and Dr. Bishop in the chair behind her, sitting in awe, holding his hands up and observing them.

"You all right, Dr. Bishop?" Angelica asked sincerely. He nodded in agreement.

"How about you and Dr. Wallace?" Dr. Bishop asked while rubbing his fingers together. "That was the most incredible feeling I have ever experienced in my entire life. I can't believe…,"

Dr. Wallace interrupted him… "We are on Mars, ladies and gentlemen. Now let's see if we have anyone out there prepared for our arrival. Let's hope not." Dr. Wallace mumbled as she stood up slowly and pushed at her bun to straighten it. "Oh, and I recommend you take your time getting up; it's a bit disorienting."

Dr. Wallace pushed the button on the hatch and it lifted. As she stepped down the stairs and out into the room, she was relieved to see the large warehouse area housing the chamber was empty.

She looked back to Angelica and Dr. Bishop who were peeping out of the chamber from behind Angelica. They both appeared disoriented.

"Coast is clear," Dr. Wallace announced.

Dr. Bishop appeared troubled as he looked at Angelica. "We shouldn't have done this."

Angelica dropped her shoulders. "It's too late Marc, it's done… we're on Mars! You want to just teleport back to Earth right now?"

Angelica was growing more and more frustrated with Dr. Bishop constantly second guessing… She narrowed her eyes and looked over at him clearly irritated. "Dr. Bishop, how are you holding up?" she asked aloud to remind him to compose himself in front of Dr. Wallace.

Dr. Wallace glanced back around at Dr. Bishop, concerned, anticipating his answer.

Dr. Bishop stood up straight and nodded at Dr. Wallace and then met Angelica's eyes. "I'm good. No, I'm good, Ms. Bradley. This is um... amazing, never would have imagined being on Mars," he stated, business-like.

Dr. Wallace smiled. "Well, you're here... Welcome! Now, let's go. Remember, follow close behind me, and do not make eye contact at least for more than a second. Stay engaged in conversation amongst each other. I am going to lead you through the facility so you, Ms. Bradley, can get some photos for your story, but very discreetly, and you, Dr. Bishop, can see the pyramid while on our little field trip. Sound like a plan?"

Angelica did a double take. When did Dr. Wallace become GI Jane? Maybe Dr. Wallace was tougher than she had given her credit for. She certainly wasn't normal -- "but what person capable of building a teleportation chamber to go to Mars was?" she wondered.

They followed closely behind as Dr. Wallace cautiously led them through the door and down a hallway. The facility was brightly lit with shiny white structural features and round windows. It was very much like Angelica had imagined it would be.

After turning down two corridors, they found themselves in an area that was heavily occupied with personnel. "Stay close, don't make eye contact and remember, you're supposed to be here," Dr. Wallace whispered back to them.

Angelica nervously shook her head and smiled apprehensively. Dr. Bishop started the conversation. "It will be resolved shortly. These system failures are certainly a nuisance, however…" He went on into some high-tech tangent. Angelica continued to nod her head in agreement although she had tuned him out. "I certainly agree, Dr. Coble."

They were almost down to the end of another corridor when they passed a small group of people in white lab coats, huddled together speaking in front of a large glass window. Behind the glass, in the room, with his back turned, stood a tall man with long white hair. He was standing beside a table covered in what appeared to be graphs and maps of some sort, from what Angelica could make out.

Unexpectedly, the man turned and looked directly at Angelica, as if he knew they were behind him in the hallway.

Angelica suddenly forgot her thoughts and her mind went blank. He looked like the biblical descriptions of an angel, she thought, as she looked back at him. She knew immediately that the being in front of her was not human. His hair was long and pure white. She estimated his height to be over eight feet. He was wearing a bright white, tight-fitting body suit that emphasized his well-defined muscular frame. His facial features appeared youthful and human. She immediately thought of the famous marble statue of

Michelangelo's David, and then she recalled depictions of Archangel Michael.

Dr. Bishop almost bumped into Angelica, catching himself before the collision. Angelica had stopped and was completely paralyzed. The unexpected encounter brought attention from the group.

Dr. Wallace noticed the strange methodical tilt of the being's head as he observed them. Just as the group in the lab coats looked over curiously. "Dr. Coble and Dr. Estes... This way please. The system's central control was not communicating properly with the track switches this morning. I am certain you will have it fixed in no time," Dr. Wallace said abruptly after breaking out into a sweat. She felt the moist drops as they ran down her back.

Dr. Wallace nodded curtly at the group and extended her hand out to lead the way. Dr. Bishop -- aware of the fact that they may have just blown their cover -- played along exceptionally well. "Oh yes, should be back up in no time."

Angelica reluctantly turned around and followed, while still glancing back at the being. "He is magnificent," she thought aloud.

Angelica's heart was racing. Holding it together and maintaining her composure was nothing short of a miracle. Dr. Bishop was biting his bottom lip. He had planned for the possibility of a strange encounter while at the Mars facility, however, he was unprepared and bore the classic "deer in the heads light" expression on his face as he glanced over to Angelica. "That was not human," he whispered.

The Bovine Connection

Finally, they rounded a corner and stopped. Dr. Wallace released the breath she had been holding as she peeped back around to the hall. "Compose yourselves," she said angrily.

"Good job, you two... we'll be dead in no time if you don't keep it together," she whispered hastily. "Hurry along. We're going through that door there," Dr. Wallace waved her hand frustrated.

Dr. Wallace opened a door to large greenhouse where there were rows of vegetation on long tables. The room was encased in a clear, hard dome, and was about the size of a football field. Dr. Wallace led the way. "These greenhouses are spread out everywhere," she announced as they continued toward a door leading outside.

Angelica looked up to see a beautiful baby blue sky outside of the dome. "I can't believe it... It's true, Dr. Bishop."

Dr. Bishop smiled and looked up in amazement. "I can't believe my own eyes, Ms. Bradley... astonishing... truly astonishing! Who would have thought the sky would be so blue?"

Finally, they came to a door. Dr. Wallace's face was impassive as she stopped right before opening it and turned toward them. "Welcome to Mars!" she mused, as she opened the door, and they heard a vacuum sound from the shiny metal box over head as the gust of pure air rushed in. Angelica wasn't sure what she had expected to happen. She had closed her eyes for a moment. "Can this be possible?" she thought and then she was hit with an odd feeling, a feeling of dread. Angelica frowned as Dr. Bishop was speaking.

"It's just like the atmosphere on Earth," he proclaimed as he took a deep breath.

As they were following Dr. Wallace outside, Angelica couldn't shake the feeling that something was very wrong. "Something doesn't feel right," she stammered.

Dr. Bishop stopped and turned around. "What is it, Angelica?"

"I'm not sure... I just have a bad feeling. Different than just a feeling though. I think..." She took a breath and shook her head as she noticed Dr. Wallace peering at her inquisitively. "It's nothing," she murmured, as she raised her hand and scratched the top of her head, worried.

As Dr. Wallace and Dr. Bishop turned back around, Angelica lowered her hand and rubbed her eyebrow.

"Oddly, it is as if we just stepped back onto the Nevada desert, however it was now daylight when we left and the terrain is somewhat different," Dr. Bishop said as he glared around curiously and immediately noticed the giant pyramid in the distance as they came around the greenhouse.

"The Cydonia Pyramid!" he said, as he gasped. It stood predominately in the middle of the dome structures. Dr. Bishop was bewildered, in comparison to the pyramids in Egypt... It was three times as big as the great pyramid. "It's true," he chuckled.

Angelica looked around to notice people walking about. "Are they settlers?" she mumbled her thought aloud. "There appears to be some type of commerce and structured community underway. Who are these people?"

Dr. Wallace remembered what it felt like when she had first arrived on Mars. "Not what you expected, I know. Even for me... Coming here again... it all hits me as if I were seeing it for the first time. How quickly my mind wanted to compartmentalize it when I returned home." Dr. Wallace shook her head in awe.

"We, the human race tend to take for granted that we are not as evolved as we'd like to believe; we are all but a small microcosm in this grand universe, and beyond... would you not agree?"

Dr. Bishop quickly nodded his head as he observed the people. "I completely agree, Dr. Wallace. Are they not worried about alien bacteria?" he asked, lowering his brow.

Dr. Wallace's eyes looked earnest. "We are uncertain of the antibodies here. In the beginning they wore suits but have gradually become more confident. So far, they have not experienced any problems, to my knowledge."

"You remember when Columbus came to America, what happened to the Native Americans..." Dr. Bishop murmured.

Angelica noticed a man look oddly at them, riding on the passenger side of what looked like a Polaris jeep as it passed by them.

Dr. Bishop and Angelica followed Dr. Wallace as she started for the pyramid. Dr. Bishop looked down at his feet while walking across the brownish red sand.

"What are they doing – right there... with those machines?" Angelica asked.

Dr. Wallace lifted her chin and peered out. "They are mining. Those men are mostly geologists, and some other scientists, I suppose."

Dr. Bishop looked at Dr. Wallace. "What about water? You have to have water to sustain life."

Dr. Wallace smirked. "There is water here, Dr. Bishop. We discovered a frozen sea that was liquid once... maybe five thousand years ago. According to a colleague on Project Cetus, we were able to build an underground canal to run the melting ice. We created an underground water filtration system, as the ancient Romans taught us. Much like our ancestors, the Mars water system provides a constant supply to centrally located areas." Dr. Bishop looked at Angelica as he widened his eyes and raised his upper lip indicating he was impressed.

"These smaller round structures running on each side of this manmade roadway here, what are they?" he asked.

"Bunkers... living facilities."

"They are unusual. I've never seen anything like them," Angelica stated, as she took a picture.

Dr. Wallace looked over at Angelica. "Be careful. Don't let anyone see you take photos. There is a very strict policy around photography. And I imagine they don't make allowances for investigative journalists," she whispered.

They stopped while Angelica took a few more photos of the white bunker pods and the pyramid. As she put her cell phone back in her pocket she sighed, catching a glance of four armed men getting out of one of the Polaris jeeps. They had just pulled up and were stepping out of the vehicle and coming toward them.

"Oh shit!" she said, causing Dr. Bishop and Dr. Wallace to take notice.

Dr. Bishop mumbled, "This is not good!" he quickly raised his palm to the top of his head and turned his body as if he were going to make a run for it, quickly giving up on the idea. Angelica's legs went weak as fear seized her.

"Dr. Olivia Wallace, we need you and your guests to come with us," one of the men said as he approached them. There was a red, camouflaged van pulling up beside the camouflaged Polaris jeep, and another armed man was opening the back doors.

Angelica's hands started to tremble. She looked at Dr. Bishop, who appeared frightened, as well.

"What is this about, gentlemen?" Dr. Wallace demanded.

"Dr. Wallace, you know what this is about. Please come with us." The security guard grabbed her arm and pulled her toward the van.

"Excuse me, but you are hurting my arm!" Dr. Wallace proclaimed.

One of the other guards had gotten behind Angelica and Dr. Bishop and had his gun extended. "Move along... into the van!"

As Dr. Wallace stepped up into the back of the van, Angelica glanced up to see her get an injection in the back of the neck. She watched, terrified, as Dr. Wallace went limp... and was caught in the arms of another guard and placed on the floor. Angelica screamed and went hysterical. "Marc! Help!"

Marc's eyes were wide, he was frozen. His mouth fell open but he couldn't speak as he watched Angelica receive an injection in her neck. He knew he was next.

Chapter Sixty-One

Angelica rubbed her eyes as she lifted her head, and felt a sharp burning sensation in her neck. She reached back and pressed her hand against it as she rose from the metal bench. Angelica was shivering uncontrollably. The room was small, bright, and cold, and there were no windows -- just a camera in the corner of the ceiling pointing down at her. She instantly tensed.

Angelica began to panic, realizing she was locked inside. "Please! Let me out of here!" she shouted at the camera and then waited for a sound.

"Please, let me go!" she screamed out. "Someone please help me," Angelica whispered as she fell to her knees and wept uncontrollably. She lay on the cold floor and trembled until she finally stood up and crawled onto the bench, curling up into a fetal position. Tears ran down her cheeks, pooling beside her on the metal bench, as she peered up at the camera until she fell asleep.

Angelica awoke to a sound at the door. She jerked her head up from the fetal position she had formed to keep warm.

Angelica sat up and scooted back against the wall, away from the door. She rubbed her face with the inside of her arm. She looked at her arm as she lowered it, and noticed there were dark red flakes of dried blood. Angelica flinched and started shaking as she noticed her white lab coat was soaked with blood.

Angelica watched anxiously as the door opened and a tall, thin man with jet black hair stepped in. He appeared Italian. He had olive skin and a beak shaped nose. His eyes were dark and cold, and his face pronounced and triumphant.

"Ms. Bradley... How nice to make your acquaintance. I've heard so much about you," he stated sarcastically in a slight Italian accent. Angelica scooted back, as close as she could get to the wall... trembling. Her lip felt swollen and she put her hand to her mouth to check it and felt a large gash. When she lowered her hand, she noticed more flakes of dried blood. She jerked her hand up to get a better look. Angelica tasted iron when she licked across the gash in her lip. Her lip had started to bleed again.

"Yes, appears your lip is bleeding." He let out a deep breath as if he were genuinely disappointed.

"We had to extract some information from you. Seems the injection took a little longer to take effect. You are quite a fighter, Ms. Bradley, I must say, given your size. Angelica started to shake uncontrollably as if she were standing inside of a freezer. "Please, do not kill me," she stuttered through her bloody split open lip.

He stepped closer. Angelica tried to open her eyes wider, but the room was too bright, causing her to squint. "Ms. Bradley, did you think you were going to just step into the chamber and jump unnoticed?" He laughed an unusual laugh... a frightening chuckle as he shook his head.

"Where are Dr. Wallace and Dr. Bishop?" Angelica asked as blood ran down her chin. He looked down and then back up to meet Angelica's eyes. "Well, why don't I just show you?" He reached out his hand toward the door for Angelica to get up and walk out. She shook her head, terrified. "No, you are going to kill me, aren't you?" she stuttered. Her lips were blue and shaking.

"Now Angelica, come on, get up. Let's go see your friends. Come now... come with me."

Angelica slowly stood up, trembling almost out of control, and still weak from the neck injection. She walked reluctantly slouched over and out of the room into a hallway, slowly turning to look at him and noticing the security guard behind him.

"Go on, that way." He pointed. She walked slightly sideways, trying to keep an eye on him and the guard that followed behind.

"I heard you've been asking a lot of questions about me," he murmured. Angelica realized at that moment he was Francis Giano.

"Through that door, there..." Francis pointed. Angelica looked back and into his cold eyes one more time before she turned the knob and opened the door.

Slouched over from pain in her shoulder, soreness in her neck and trembling out of control, she looked up into the lab and screamed. "No!"

Floating in a large cylinder tank of light green liquid was Dr. Wallace's frail, nude body. Her eyes were still open and her long black hair had come completely loose from the bun and was steadily swaying toward the top of the tank. Angelica dropped to her knees, with her hands over her face, crying and shaking her head. She was afraid to look around for fear she'd see Dr. Bishop had suffered the same fate.

All of a sudden, the guard grabbed her arm and yanked her up. Her body was too limp to walk on her own so he dragged her and sat her down in a chair. Angelica was sobbing. "Why did you kill her? Where is Dr. Marc Bishop?"

Francis looked Angelica directly in the eyes... "She took an oath and broke it. We retrieved that cylinder tank from a crashed craft here on Mars, still works, you know. Oh and Dr. Bishop is safe, for now." Francis smirked as he tossed his hand in the air. His condescending smile sent chills down Angelica's spine.

Francis stepped closer to Angelica. "So, how do you like the Red Planet?" Angelica shook her head, unwilling to speak.

"Quite impressive, isn't it!" His voice was assertive, quiet, and deep. Angelica dropped her head. "Angelica, dear, I need your full attention, please." Francis walked around her chair, reached down, and lifted Angelica's chin. She tilted her head and watched him out of the corner of her eye.

"How rude of me... It's like going to third base without even getting to know one another." Francis stroked the back of Angelica light blonde hair. "You are a beautiful woman, I'm sure you know that. Shall we get to know each other, Ms. Bradley?" Angelica eyes watered and tears streamed down her cheeks.

"I am Michelangelo Francis Giano," he announced proudly with an Italian accent. "I built this facility." Francis gestured his hand about the room. So, how did you like your tour of Cydonia?"

Angelica looked up, and then scanned the room. There was no way to escape. The guard was in front of the only door.

"Now Angelica, you've seen a lot. Taken a few photos… now, now, you should know we don't allow photography here."

Smeared with blood, Angelica's face was red. The tissue on her lip was swollen and split wide open. She could taste the metallic blood in the salty tears as they ran into her mouth.

"Why did you build the teleportation chamber, the aerospace facility? What are you doing here, Francis?" Her voice shock.

Francis laughed. "Good, we are on a first name basis, makes for candid dialogue, don't you agree?"

The door to the chamber swung open and Angelica watched, stunned, as a man confidently walked towards her. She recognized him immediately.

"Why is he here?" Angelica shouted.

Francis looked over at John Kaye. "He is a friend." John smugly smiled. He appeared to enjoy watching their interaction.

Angelica kept her eyes on John Kaye as he walked over and sat down in a chair to her left. His expression didn't change. He was peering right through her. "He's your money man," she mumbled.

Francis laughed. "Very good! And that was a hard one to figure out," he said sarcastically.

"You are as smart as you are pretty," he said, condescendingly. "I am a wealthy man; however, a lot of people have invested in this project, and Mr. Kaye is their go-to guy. I'm not much on socializing... I have people for that. I'd rather use my spare time to enjoy my ranch in Montana."

The door opened again and Dr. Bishop was brought in. He was hunched over with a blood-soaked gag tied around his mouth. He had a swollen black eye and bloody nose... he was badly roughed up.

Angelica gasped. "Marc! What have they done to you?"

The guard dropped Dr. Bishop, with his hands tied behind his back, into a chair in the right corner, facing Angelica.

Francis looked over at the second guard and gestured him out. Dr. Bishop's fearful eyes were staring at Angelica.

"Now, where was I? Oh, that's right... you've just recently visited there – what did you think?" Angelica lowered her head and ignored his question. The sight of Dr. Bishop unnerved her.

"Elberton... my hometown! My family settled there from Italy. My great-grandfather, Michelangelo Giano was intrigued by the stories of gold in Elberton so he went there in search of it... a miner... damn good at it too. He made his fortune mining gold and silver.

The Bovine Connection

The men in our family followed in his footsteps and we were living the American dream... my sister and I... my lovely sister Giuliana. Ana as we called her. She's passed on... to the other side years ago. She was a special woman. She married a local rancher by the name of Anderson. I believe you met his son," he said nonchalantly.

Angelica lifted her head and sighed. Her heart was pounding in her chest so hard she felt it in her throat. She closed her eyes for a moment and started to tremble. "Did you say Anderson married your sister?" she mumbled.

"Yes, I did. Nice couple they were -- at least, until those damned grey ETs destroyed their lives."

Angelica started trembling uncontrollably again. She was astute enough to know where he was heading. She felt trapped in a nightmare.

"They took a liking to my little sister and started taking her from her bed in the middle of the night. They were especially interested in her reproductive system; yes, they messed her up. She eventually went crazy and..." Francis looked down. "She killed herself. We covered it up and called it an accident... didn't want to bring shame to her or the family. That husband of hers, Hugh... a weak man. Couldn't protect my sister." Francis laughed. A laugh that penetrated Angelica's bones.

"The military came to Elberton and wanted to build a base, and not just any base, an underground base." Francis said.

Dr. Bishop looked to his hard left and saw Dr. Wallace floating in the tank. Becoming distraught, he jerked around and dropped his head in frustration.

Francis continued. "And that is when my father started working with the military to build the Newton Air Force underground base. They knew my father was an expert miner and understood which explosives to use with certain types of rocks, so he worked alongside their geologists. Since he knew the lay of the land, he advised the military. He led a crew of miners during the construction. That was until the day he stumbled onto the well-hidden underground ET base and story short – he was killed in the crossfire. That day everything changed for me. I would get my revenge on the grey race."

Angelica soaked in sweat, nervously moved her eyes back and forth from John Kaye to Francis.

Francis turned to the guard and said... "He can come in now."

Angelica looked up anxiously at the door in anticipation of the only missing piece to Francis's story, Michael. The door opened and he stepped in. He looked strange. His eyes were sympathetic, yet different. He was wearing the fine, dark suit she had imagined he wore while on the phone with him.

His hair was perfectly groomed, slicked down, and he was even more incredibly handsome than she had remembered. Images of their lovemaking ran through her mind as the tears started to flow again. She remembered how he caressed her face and pulled her to his lips... kissed down her neck while his tongue glided down her skin as he moved toward her breast. Could it have been all a lie? The thoughts were too much to bear and she quickly snapped back to reality.

Now the pain was overwhelming, so unfamiliar, she felt as if she were coming apart at the seams and going to explode. Angelica opened her mouth to speak and suddenly choked as streams of tears rushed down her face into her mouth. "Why, Michael?"

Dr. Bishop had his head lowered, depleted of every last ounce of energy, but he jerked his head up. He recognized the name and heard the stress in Angelica's voice as she screamed it through a heavy, panted breath. Dr. Bishop's eyes grew wide as he shook his head in anger and mumbled under the bloody cloth tied around his mouth. He stated to get up but the guard grabbed his shoulder and pushed him back down.

Michael dropped his head for a moment and then looked Angelica in the eyes as he moved closer to her.

"I told you to walk away! I begged you to walk away, you stubborn woman!" Michael looked down at his feet and appeared to be debating a thought. When he looked up, his soulful hazel blue-green eyes peered deep into her eyes again. "You know you are the reason Matthew is dead, Angelica. And your friend, the lady..." He spoke softly as he stepped up to her and kneeled down. Angelica's eyes grew wide.

Francis rolled his eyes and stepped away, turned his back to them, facing John Kaye. Tears were rapidly streaming down Angelica's face and running into her open mouth. She was in shock. She started shaking her head. "No, no, no... I trusted you!"

"Angelica, I want to propose something to you. I want you to think about it for a moment before you respond. We can still be together. You would just have to change, my love. Do you follow me? Do you understand?" Michael touched Angelica's cheek softly as she jerked away and made eye contact with John Kaye. "I love you and want you with me." Angelica's face flattened - she was pale and her expression blank. All life had drained out of it. Trying to avoid eye contact with Michael, she looked over at Dr. Bishop, who was shaking his head, wide eyed, and mumbling through the mouth gag.

"How?" Angelica asked, for lack of a better response, as she turned her head to face Michael directly. Angelica felt as if her body was burning from the inside out. It dawned on her that she was staring at a complete stranger, not the man she had fallen in love with.

"You can come back with me... we can be with each other. Francis has agreed."

Angelica was confused. What is going to happen? What is this about, Michael? Why are you doing this? I'm confused... no, I don't know..." She felt as if she couldn't breathe, as she forced the words out.

Michael stood up and paced the floor in front of her. "It's about Eplar. It will be destroyed."

"Why... Why, would you do that?" Angelica shouted, sounding alarmed.

The Bovine Connection

Michael rubbed his palm across his forehead, clearly agitated. "They are seeding that planet with alien-human hybrids. Don't you understand? It is wrong... against God's will! And those fuckers caused my mother's death after they took her eggs and destroyed her!" Michael yelled... showing an entirely new persona, causing Angelica to flinch. "I'm sorry, baby... I didn't mean to frighten you," he said quickly and softly.

Angelica turned around and looked at the tank with Dr. Wallace's pale, nude body exposing the thick purple veins protruding from her skin. "Why?" Angelica made eye contact with Dr. Bishop as she turned back around. "I don't... I don't..." Angelica stuttered and dropped her head. "... Understand," she mumbled.

Michael looked at Francis and Francis nodded his head. "My uncle will let you live. And you won't remember any of this, I promise. Baby, I am not the bad man you think I am." He spoke softly.

Angelica straightened up in the chair and looked at Michael. "If the ETs destroyed your family's lives, why are you working with them?"

Michael pursed his lips and tilted his head to rub his eyebrow. "I don't know what you are talking about. We are not working with the greys."

"What about the hybrid race they are creating? Are you just going to kill all of those innocent beings?"

Michael nodded with tight lips. "You know, Angelica, you have a child there," his eyes were cold.

Angelica went numb. "My son!" she gasped. "It's true," she moaned. Angelica felt sick. "What have they done? They are innocent! They didn't have a choice in the matter," she shouted.

"Yes, you make a good argument, however they have ET DNA and over time will become like the others. They will believe they are superior to us and there is no telling what they will do down the road." Michael smirked. Angelica covered her face with her hands.

"All right, enough of the sweet talk; you need to decide what you want to do, Ms. Bradley. Go back with my nephew and leave everything you've seen behind you, or..." Francis had stepped back over to the two of them. Angelica glanced over at John Kaye, who appeared uninterested and restless.

Angelica sighed. "You can't destroy Eplar." Angelica thought for a second and looked at Francis. Francis chuckled. "Michael you're going to have your hands full with this one."

Michael looked sypathetically at Angelica. Angelica looked over to Dr. Bishop, observing his eyes. He had an odd look.

"You can't destroy that planet and the people. It's not right!" Her voice shook.

Michael raised both hands to the top of his head and grabbed two hands full of his black hair. "Hybrids! You stubborn woman! They are fucking hybrids! Not people!"

Francis looked at John Kaye while shaking his head back and forth. Francis couldn't resist, in frustration he yelled out... "Make a decision!"

The Bovine Connection

Angelica looked up directly into Michael's eyes and said, "No!" she lowered her head and waited for the repercussions she expected to follow.

Michael reached into his pocket and pulled out a syringe. "You are a fucking stubborn woman. Well, I'll make it for you. You will never remember any of this, baby. You will have a new life with me."

Angelica looked back up and her eyes widened when she saw the needle; she started trembling. "You're sick," she moaned.

Dr. Bishop was struggling to get up and out of the grip of the guard holding him down. He was mumbling loudly through the blood-soaked cloth gagging his mouth.

"I don't want to lose you, baby, and I don't plan to," Michael said as he stepped toward her.

Angelica's eyes watered. The tears started to drop rapidly down her cheeks again.

"Now baby, please don't do that, don't cry. You know you carved a way into my heart. I didn't intentionally set out to fall in love with you, but you know we're meant to be together."

Angelica couldn't believe what he was saying. "Don't call me baby. You are crazy." she whispered.

Her eyes heavy with pain turned fierce. Angelica had stopped crying. She had become mad. "No!"

Michael dropped his head. "The last thing I wanted to do is hurt you. I asked you to walk away from all of this, but you're so fucking stubborn." He laughed sarcastically. "You broke into my uncle's facility and used the chamber. I never thought you'd go that far. What were you thinking? Damn!" he yelled.

"Please don't hurt me... My mother, my life... You can't just strip that from me!"

Michael narrowed his eyes as he moved closer and held up the syringe.

"Michael, please don't! Think about my mother and your mother. My mother is alive and she needs me." Angelica lowered her head to notice the tears had soaked into her clothing.

Michael looked away. He was clearly struggling emotionally. He shook his head and yelled. "Fuck! Fuck! Fuck! His voice softened. "Don't you see, Angelica, Francis will not let you live otherwise. This is your only option."

Francis walked over and jerked the syringe from Michael's hand. "I'll do it for you!"

Michael flung around and launched at Francis, knocking him down, bumping into Angelica forcefully, and causing her chair to flip backward, and knocking her unconscious.

When Michael rose up, he felt an odd sensation in his chest. Looking down slowly, he saw the needle stuck below his collarbone. Michael yelled out at Francis. "What have you done?" Michael glanced up and made eye contact with Francis. Francis's mouth fell open, his face turned ashen as he stepped back. At that moment, Michael knew Francis had changed the solution in the syringe. "What have you done?" Michael looked at Francis, bewildered.

The Bovine Connection

Francis's shook his head. "You didn't think I'd really let her live, did you? You had to go and fall in love." Francis turned to walk away.

The guard had started toward Francis and Michael, allowing Dr. Bishop a split second opportunity to leap forcefully up from the chair and pull his hands free. He ran over tackling Francis from behind, knocking him to the ground. Michael was dizzy and going in and out of consciousness, swaying back and forth.

John Kaye jumped up and shouted at the guard, who had already rushed at Dr. Bishop and began hitting him in the back of the head with his fist. Francis managed to stand up. Dr. Bishop swung around and grabbed the guard's gun from his holster. As he did, Francis was knocked backward landing against the tank containing Dr. Wallace's nude body, knocking it back against the wall, causing the glass to crack, and green liquid to explode everywhere. Dr. Wallace's body slid out and landed on top of Francis, pinning him down.

As the men were struggling with the gun, Francis managed to get up from under Dr. Wallace by sliding her limp body off of him.

There was a gunshot. Dr. Bishop and the guard suddenly stopped and stepped away from each other, both looking down, examining their own bodies. Dr. Bishop took another step back as the guard dropped dead. Wild-eyed with the gun in his hand, Dr. Bishop turned to Francis who had flung his hands into the air. "Wait a minute, now... you don't want to do that!"

Dr. Bishop surveyed him with a look of primordial rage. Dr. Bishop had gone mad. He had become an untamed animal in the wild. "Yes, I do," he pulled the trigger shooting Francis in his Adams apple. Francis's eyes widened as he grabbed his neck with both hands. The dark crimson blood flowed between his fingers as he slowly dropped to the floor.

Dr. Bishop gazed around wild-eyed and continued to survey the room. He was in a zone from the rush of adrenalin pumping through his blood.

John Kaye was hiding behind a cabinet. Dr. Bishop caught a glimpse of his shoe. He walked toward him with rage in his eyes. John was shaking and lifted his hand. Dr. Bishop closed his eyes and shot the gun through John's hand and into his head.

Soaked in blood, wild-eyed, he turned to see Michael lying beside Angelica's body with one hand against her cheek, his eyes wide open as if he were still staring at her.

"Angelica!" he mumbled as he slowly stammered toward them.

Dr. Bishop glanced over to Angelica's lifeless body and blood splattered blonde hair. His heart was racing. He knelt down onto one knee and pushed her blonde hair from her face. As he looked down at her peaceful expression, he slowly began to come down off of his adrenaline rage.

The door opened behind him and he flung around. The tall, majestic human-like being they had passed in the hallway was standing at the doorway. Dr. Bishop slowly lifted the gun and pointed it at him. The being raised his large hand with his palm flat, and the trigger jammed as Dr. Bishop pulled it. He clicked it over and over as the being walked toward him, and then he was paralyzed, unable to move.

As the angelic looking being stepped up beside Dr. Bishop, he leaned down over Angelica, causing Dr. Bishop to flinch and drop back onto his hands. In his head he heard the words, "I will not harm you. I am Tyruk. I will take you home." Dr. Bishop watched curiously as the being put his hand on Angelica's chest. Dr. Bishop heard the words, "She will live."

Dr. Bishop peered at him, mesmerized as he watched the being stand up and walk away.

Angelica slowly opened her eyes. Dr. Bishop was leaning over her, covered in blood, but smiling in amazement.

"Marc!" she said in disbelief. Tears began to stream down the corners of her eyes. She could feel their coolness running along her ears. "I have a son," Angelica whispered.

Dr. Bishop leaned in closer. "It's time to go home."

He reached his arms under Angelica's back and helped her off of the floor. Her hair was stiff with dried blood. She looked down and saw Michael lying with the syringe protruding from his upper chest. Dr. Bishop squeezed her tightly as she lowered her chin. Physical and emotional pain seized her body.

Dr. Bishop tugged at Angelica. She looked away and stepped with his help around the dead bodies and heavy pools of blood mixed with the liquid from the tank. Angelica looked up at Dr. Bishop's face as he glanced down at her. They didn't have to say a word. She knew he had saved her life.

While still holding on to Angelica, Dr. Bishop managed to push the door open. He cautiously peered out into the hall. "This way."

Angelica looked concerned, but she trusted him, so she leaned into him as they walked toward a door cracked open, allowing natural light into the hallway.

Dr. Bishop pushed the door open as they stepped outside and onto a paved landing area where there was a strange, saucer-shaped craft, silver and narrow, about thirty-six feet in diameter. The craft had a round center and a circular, tube-like structure extended out and around it.

Angelica looked at Dr. Bishop, surprised. He was looking intently at the craft. When Angelica looked back, the human-like being with long white hair was stoically standing beside it.

Dr. Bishop took Angelica's hand tightly. He then looked at her and smiled sincerely before leading her to the craft. Angelica felt clumsy. The drugs still lingered in her blood, and she had a lump the size of a golf ball on the back of her head.

When Dr. Bishop and Angelica stepped up to the craft... the being came over to Angelica. She glared into his pale blue eyes, appearing childlike and frail, but she was not afraid of him. She felt peaceful and safe in his presence.

Dr. Bishop said nonchalantly, "Angelica, this is Tyruk. He will be taking us home."

The Bovine Connection

Angelica looked down, then up and into Tyruk's eyes. "Where is my son?" Angelica felt a pinch of pain in her heart.

Tyruk's mouth never moved but his voice was stern, yet soft in her head -- his majestic blue eyes, sincere as they penetrated her eyes. "He is with his own kind."

Angelica dropped her head feeling lost. "Why did they create him?" she managed to utter through the tears.

Tyruk's eyes met Dr. Bishop's eyes before gazing at Angelica. Dr. Bishop appeared curious. "To teach him about love. The grey race no longer has the capacity to feel emotions, such as that of a mother and child. These children are their attempt to breed it back into their DNA. He is well taken care of there. Your DNA is changing, Angelica. A new race of humans are evolving and will play a role in Earth's future. And after Earth has cleansed itself, your kind will lead the others. You will see your son again." Angelica smiled and nodded as she began to weep.

The being stepped up through the opening in the middle underneath the craft.

Dr. Bishop slid his hand across Angelica's back and slightly pushed for her to go next. She turned to Dr. Bishop, apprehensive, and then walked over. As Angelica entered the craft, she lifted her hand and felt the large lump on the back of her head. Dr. Bishop looked back at the pyramid in the distance and then turned around and followed Angelica into the craft.

Suddenly, there was a whooshing sound and the craft disappeared into the blue sky.

Chapter Sixty-Two

Angelica turned onto her back and stretched her arms while opening her eyes to see she was in her bedroom. Her eyes popped wide open as she shot straight up, scrambling to gather her thoughts.

Angelica happened to glance down and notice a large, powdery, light pink peony on the bed beside her. She frowned, confused for a moment, but then remembered the dream she had on the plane of Gail in her garden. She lifted the flower and smelled its pleasant fragrance before placing it on her bedside table and rising up. Angelica noticed a few of the soft pink petals scattered on her white linen sheets as she turned and planted her feet on the floor.

Standing nude by her bed, she closed her eyes and welcomed the fresh familiar scent of her room. She walked into the bathroom and straight to the mirror to look at her face. It was clean; no blood and the wound on her lip had vanished. She quickly ran her hand across the back of her head. The lump was gone. *"Was it a dream?"* she wondered.

The penny round tile floor was cool under her feet. Feeling a chill, she shivered. She grabbed her white terrycloth robe on the back of the door and wrapped it around herself. Stepping out of the bathroom she noted the calm silence. Her cell phone rang. Her eyes focused and she looked around the room to see it on the bedside table. Angelica slowly walked over and picked up her cell phone to see she had no missed calls. She frowned, drawing in her breath. She placed the cell phone back down and lowered her brows. Angelica felt confused as she stood perfectly immobile, with lost eyes as she stared out the window, her heart pounding hard against her chest. Her cell phone rang again and startled her. Dazed, she turned her head, and she heard the name "Marc," in her mind.

She peered down and then slowly lifted her cell phone without looking at the caller ID and put it to her ear. "Hello... Marc?" she asked curiously.

"Angelica, are you all right?"

"Yes, Marc... I'm fine," she answered softly. There was silence.

"Good," he murmured.

Angelica looked at the peony on the bedside table, turned and walked out of her room.

"Marc," Angelica whispered. "Michael... It wasn't a dream was it?"

"No," he answered delicately.

Angelica's knees buckled. She closed her eyes and nodded as she grabbed the railing of the staircase to steady herself. Angelica took a deep breath. "Marc, something weird just happened."

"What happened, Angelica?"

"I could hear the phone ring before it actually rang... and I somehow knew it was you." He was silent.

"Marc... are you there?"

"Yes, yes, I'm here."

"Marc, are you standing in your kitchen in front of a window over the sink?"

Dr. Bishop glanced out the window. "Yes, Angelica, I am."

Dr. Bishop was quiet. "Marc, are you there?" Angelica blurted.

"Yes," he whispered.

Downstairs, Angelica held the phone between her chin and shoulder as she started the Keurig and grabbed a coffee mug from the cabinet.

"Marc? Something has happened to me. I feel different." Angelica bit down on her bottom lip. "I think I can hear your thoughts." Angelica frowned.

Dr. Bishop stood straight up. He looked out the window at a large Crape Myrtle tree with white blossoms swaying in the wind and took a deep breath. "Oh," his disembodied voice whispered. "Angelica, how about we go to my beach house at Chesapeake Bay for a few days? I feel it's too early for us to return to work."

Standing at her counter, watching the coffee as it finished dripping into the mug, Angelica considered his suggestion for a moment. "No."

Angelica picked up the coffee mug and turned toward her den. "I have a story to write."

"Yes, I suppose you do. Are you going to write everything?" he asked, lowering his shoulders.

Angelica thought for a moment... "Hey, how about we grab lunch soon?"

Dr. Bishop smiled. "Perfect."

"Good," she whispered. "I'll call you in a day or so. Oh, and Marc... Thank you for saving my life!"

"You're welcome, Ms. Angelica Bradley."

The Bovine Connection

Angelica started to hang up... "Angelica wait... Are you sure you are okay?" he asked, as he looked up at the sky and saw a bright flicker of light. Exhaling slowly, he felt a deep sense of peace.

Angelica glanced down and noticed a pink peony petal stuck in her hair. "Yes," Angelica said softly as she lifted the pedal to her nose and smelled it.

Kimberly Thomas

Epilogue

It was very quiet in the lab. A storm had been brewing all afternoon. The evening sky lit up with flashes of lightning. He could hear the sound of rain drops harshly hitting the windows. With each loud roar of thunder, the lights flickered.

Everyone had left the University of Colorado for the day. The room was brightly lit with overhead lighting and table lamps. Trays of small empty tubes covered open spaces on the lab tables. The thermal cycler device holding a block of tubes containing PCR (polymerase chain reaction) mixture had finally stopped, after raising and lowering the temperature of the block in pre-programmed steps. It had separated and then amplified the DNA, creating many copies of the strand.

Dr. Goolrick looked away from the computer screen as the lights flickered off and on. "Oh dear," he murmured as he stood up, rushed over, and sat down at his old dulled down desk. Lifting his fingers slowly to his chin, he considered who to call first.

Dr. Goolrick picked up his cell phone. After several rings, Dr. Hamilton Howell answered. "Hello Walter!"

"Hamilton, the results from Ms. Bradley's hair sample are conclusive. The nuclear DNA indicates viral resistance, as I suspected. Ms. Bradley's hair strand contains two deleted genes for CCR5 protein and no intact gene for normal undeleted CCR5. As you may recall, the CCR5 deletion factor has been implicated in AIDS resistance."

"Yes, yes... go on," Hamilton urged.

"Ms. Bradley has the advanced DNA... showing up around the world. Are you sitting down?"

Hamilton glanced around curiously for a place to sit in the men's locker room at the gym. He had just showered and wrapped a towel around his waist. Hamilton stepped over to a teak wood bench. "Yes."

"The profile indicates biological material matching some of the individuals in the abduction cases, confirming Ms. Bradley is also most probably an abductee.

My analysis confirmed the strand came from someone biologically close to normal human genetics; however, this particular strand was..." Dr. Goolrick was silent.

"Well go on," Hamilton said hastily.

"A rare Chinese Mongoloid type."

"Really?" Hamilton gasped.

A man dressing beside him looked over. Hamilton smiled at him, indicating everything was fine and then turned his head, lowering it into the phone. "A rare Chinese Mongoloid? Are you certain?"

Dr. Goolrick rolled his tongue across his top teeth. "Without a doubt."

"Walter... that is one of the rarest human lineages known!"

Dr. Goolrick nodded. "Yes, and considering that Ms. Bradley's hair is light and not black, that is most curious. Hamilton, Ms. Bradley's white blonde hair shaft appeared translucent, revealing an optical transparency and pronounced mosaic structure... Showing reflections to light. This is not what you would expect from an Asian type mitochondrial DNA."

"Could there be a mistake in the results?"

"No, I am certain. I preformed the test and viewed it with my own eyes."

"Exciting news, Walter!"

"Indeed! The root section confirmed the rare Chinese type DNA in the hair shaft so I focused my analysis on the root of the hair strand and it revealed Ms. Bradley is a hybrid according to the DNA profile. The donor had the rare Chinese mongoloid DNA and the "unknown," I would presume to be alien DNA. Therefore, along with the biological normal human DNA, Ms. Bradley had the other two, as well.

As we have concluded through our research over the years, the CCR5 deletion factor has been determined to be the utility in fighting disease. This would allow for the grey beings to create their hybrids and show up with this advanced DNA, eliminating the concern for human diseases while crossbreeding."

"The donor DNA is a match to the strand retrieved from the abduction case in North Carolina, correct?" Hamilton asked.

"Yes, the strand obtained by the woman who claimed angelic humanoid beings visited her in the middle of the night. When she woke, she had a long white hair stuck to her wedding ring. She put it in a baggy and that was our first of the many showing up," Goolrick replied.

The Bovine Connection

"Do you think they are trying to tell us something by leaving hair samples?" Hamilton asked.

"They very well could be." Dr. Goolrick pursed his lips and raised his index finger to his chin.

"Well, I have to say the argument of Darwinian selection pressure is not holding up for the human species. Sooner or later mainstream is going to have to contemplate alternatives," Hamilton said.

"Indeed." Dr. Goolrick leaned back in his chair and was silent for a moment. "Yes, panspermia and non-Darwinian intelligent intervention," he said flatly.

"So have you called Ms. Bradley?" Hamilton asked.

"She's my next call."

Made in the USA
San Bernardino, CA
19 April 2015